Riders Up
Book Two

Heat Wave

by

Adriana Kraft

This book is a work of fiction. The names, characters, places, and incidents are products of the writer's imagination or have been fictitiously and are not to be construed as real. Any resemblance to persons, living or dead, actual events, locale or organizations is entirely coincidental.

Riders Up: Book Two
Heat Wave

By
Adriana Kraft

ISBN: 978-0-9907476-2-8

B&B Publishing
1970 N. Leslie St. #560
Pahrump, NV 89060

Cover by
Rebecca Poole
Dreams2Media.com

Riders Up

Book One: Cassie's Hope
Chicago, 1996
Available now

Book Two: Heat Wave
Iowa, 2000
Available now

Book Three: Willow Smoke
Chicago, 2002
Available now

Book Four: Detour Ahead
California, 2004
Release Date: January, 2015

2000

Scorching hot. It shouldn't be this hot in February. Dreamily, she reached out her hand into the hazy air, then heard someone banging on the door and shouting. Strong arms pulled her out of the bed and urged her down the stairs. Horses whinnied frantically in the distance.

The scene shifted. A tall man staggered towards her, carrying the limp form of another man. Flames shot high from some building in the background. She strained her eyes trying to see better but failed to identify either man. Was he dead?

The shock woke her. Safe in her own bed, at a perfectly normal temperature, she tried to make sense of what had just happened. Maggie Magee Anderson *never* had nightmares. Should she be frightened? Somehow, she didn't think so. In the dream, she'd been rescued. She'd trusted those strong arms—whose arms? Would she ever find out? Maybe, maybe not, but in her bones, she could feel the dream's message: She'd be safe, even if she had to walk through fire.

CHAPTER ONE

From its outside appearance, Maggie Anderson decided the two-story Resting Arms Hotel should have been declared unfit for human habitation ages ago. Its sign hung at a rakish angle. Layers of old paint peeled off the once brown door. She'd never thought such places existed in Des Moines, Iowa.

Yellowed newspapers fluttered on the sidewalk in the unusually warm March breeze. She stepped out of her car and her nostrils immediately flared at the stench; she didn't want to try to name what she might be smelling. She gulped deeply in a vain attempt to hold her breath.

Maggie pulled her jeans jacket tighter, as if it could protect her, and moved away from the security of her car. Carefully, she picked her way around the trash that littered the sidewalk.

Two shaggy, unkempt men soaked up the early spring sunshine, their wooden chairs tilted back against the brick wall. They hadn't been in a shower for far too long. She couldn't keep from wrinkling her nose as she passed them by. Neither man acknowledged her presence.

Trying to ignore them, Maggie approached the entrance and turned the doorknob. It twisted freely in her hand. She put a shoulder to the door and shoved hard; it reluctantly gave way.

From the dark entryway, Maggie could see a smallish man behind a paint-chipped counter scowling at her suspiciously. Maybe he thought she was with social services. Thankfully, she was dressed well enough not to be mistaken for a bag lady.

She clutched her purse to her waist and approached the clerk, trying to appear confident and in control. Clearing her throat, she said, perhaps too loudly, "I'm looking for a Mr. Ed Harrington. I'm told he's a resident here. Can you tell me where I might find him?"

"A resident! What kinda business you got with him?"

Maggie tried not to recoil. "I don't think that's any of your business." She reached into her purse, pulled out a ten-dollar bill and placed it on the desk. "I do, however, realize that you are a businessman. And I'm willing to pay for information."

The clerk gave her a slanted grin and pressed his hand on the bill. "Well, in that case, lady, you're in luck. Harrington is in his outer office holding up the wall—he's the tall one. You just walked right by him." He stuffed the money in his shirt pocket. "Appreciate your business."

Haltingly, Maggie retraced her steps to the sidewalk. Sure enough, the tall, sandy-haired man was still there, leaning against the wall as if he was responsible for bracing the entire building. His friend was nowhere to be seen.

Should she just keep on walking? She'd pushed

her longtime friend and insurance agent Ben Templeton until he finally came up with this lead, referred to him by sources he trusted. She sighed and tried to remember what Ben had said — *this guy may be too much for you to handle.* She knew he hadn't wanted her to go this route. But desperate or cocky, it didn't matter which, she'd pressed him until he came up with this trainer — banned from racetracks because of some kind of trouble in Chicago, but still respected and highly regarded by Iowa trainers who did business with Templeton. Not only was the man good; Ben had told her that because of the scandal, he'd work for cheap.

Now, she shivered against the chill of Ben's prophecy. Maybe he was right. Ed Harrington didn't look like any horse trainer she'd ever imagined. Could this ghost of a man really help her? Could he walk, let alone ride a horse? Should she just keep right on walking? She owed him nothing, and he didn't even know she existed.

- o -

He knew.

Ed Harrington had watched the neatly dressed woman pussy-footing around the junk on her way to the flophouse entrance. He spied her when she wanted to grab her nose and blot out the offending odors. Hell, he couldn't blame her for that; it took some getting used to, even for him. He might still be hung over, but he knew damn well

5

the woman didn't belong anywhere near the Resting Arms. And he'd heard her asking for him.

He'd almost run off when Sonny did, but he wasn't going to let any woman chase him away, no matter how sassy she might be. She dressed sharp, at least for this part of town. Filled out a denim jacket real nice.

Clearly, he wasn't what she expected.

Through narrowed eyes he watched her trying to decide what to do. Would she flee? Or would she stay? He'd bet on her running like a spooked filly.

He was wrong.

"I'm told you're Ed Harrington," he heard the tiny blonde say. Her voice held more power than her size suggested.

"That's right." He scowled. "What's it to you?" Harrington kept his eyelids nearly closed and his back pressed against the wall. It was requiring a lot of work just to stay focused on her words. He saw her bite her lower lip and stand as tall as her small frame would allow.

"My name is Maggie Anderson." Her voice did not crack. "I'm told you're an expert with racehorses. I need your services. And I'm willing to pay modestly for them."

Lurching up from his chair, Ed stood unsteadily. He towered over her, taking her measure. Sunshine bounced off her short-cropped straw colored hair, nearly blinding him. He brought a hand to his brow. Why did she want him? Why did she have to reach into the bottom of the barrel for a horse trainer? He liked the way her name, Maggie Anderson, rolled off her lips.

His head pounded as if a dozen wild horses were galloping around inside his brain looking for an escape route. He closed his eyes trying not to remember earlier times, better times. Times with fast racehorses and faster women. All that was gone now. He wished it wasn't even a memory. He reopened his eyes and glared at the woman causing him to remember.

At last, Harrington replied, "You come right to the point, don't you, lady?"

"You asked."

"What makes you think I want a job? The sun is nice and warm right here." He slurred his speech, unable to keep dinner and breakfast from clouding his voice. He could see well enough to know the woman was damn pretty. He'd seen many a jockey bigger than her, but none more attractive. He smiled crookedly at his wit, not knowing quite what to say next. She didn't appear very intimidated. Maybe she was a fool.

"If you don't want a job, Mr. Harrington, you are more stupid than I was led to believe."

Ed shoved his shaking hands deep into his pockets. Why should it bother him if she saw him quaking like a drunk? He could almost hear the woman's brain ticking off the pros and cons. Why would she risk coming down to this place to find him? What the hell did she really want?

She could walk away, for all he cared. He hadn't invited her to his palatial surroundings.

He watched her stretch to the top of her toes and let out a deep breath. "Do you have transportation, Mr. Harrington?"

"Yeah, Mabel's sitting around the corner." He jerked his head toward a junk-filled parking lot just visible beyond the hotel and grinned broadly. "She's more than transportation, lady. She's a first class workhorse."

"Okay, if you're interested in learning more about a paying job—after you sober up—" she reached into her purse, "follow these directions. I run a farm about forty miles north of here. Here's thirty bucks for gas, a decent meal, and a shave."

She eyed him directly. "I have two kids, Mr. Harrington. If you work for me, you'll have to leave the bottle behind."

He hesitated. Stupid do-gooder. Why did she have to come and disrupt his world? It was too damn hard to concentrate. He scraped a hand through his hair. Her voice was so tempting. He wondered if she sang country western love songs.

Reaching for the slip of paper and the money, his hand trembled. "This will keep me in good supply for quite a spell." Harrington stuffed both paper and money into his shirt pocket. "What makes you think I won't just go out and buy more booze?"

Harrington glanced away from Maggie Anderson's penetrating blue eyes. They reminded him of robin's eggs. He grimaced. He hadn't seen a robin's egg since he was a kid. But that wasn't the reason he'd looked away. The woman was carrying too much pain; he already had more than enough pain for any one human being. He sure didn't need to borrow any of hers.

- o -

Maggie scrutinized the man without flinching. She'd witnessed something that gave her reason to believe in him. Oh, he'd tried to hide behind toughness and bravado. He'd even tried to intimidate her. But he certainly didn't belong in a flophouse. Harrington still had pride in simple things — like his truck.

Had she imagined a flicker of hope in his clouded features? Maggie recognized grief when she saw it, and Ed Harrington was wallowing in grief and self-loathing. Maybe she and he had some things in common. Her offer of a job could help both of them. Did he have enough courage to move beyond grief, or would he continue self-medicating his pain with booze?

"I don't know what you're likely to do," she finally said, folding her arms and squaring her shoulders, her voice strained. "It's your choice, Mr. Harrington. I can't make it for you. This is your lucky day. You've been thrown a lifeline. Use it, or drown yourself in gallons of cheap booze. Either way, it's your lucky day."

Disgusted with herself for needing his help, Maggie spun around and quickly retraced her steps to her car. When she opened the car door, she heard him holler from down the block.

"It's my choice!"

Her heart leapt. Maybe it wasn't too late.

In a matter of minutes, as she pulled out of the parking space and witnessed him wobbling unsteadily down the sidewalk, her heart sank again. He was probably heading for the nearest watering hole with her money clutched in his fist.

"Oh well, I can't save the world," she muttered, spinning her car tires. She was back to square one, but she would never give up.

She'd trusted the wisdom of her bones telling her to seek him out, and he'd turned out to be a bust. Maybe her friends had been right after all. Maybe all that *bones* stuff was just her imagination.

Yet, she usually could discern changes in the weather. She'd known her husband was dying before the doctor diagnosed him with pancreatic cancer. Her dad had said she carried that important Scottish Magee *bone* gene, capable of peering into the future.

She grimaced. The story of the bone gene was simply that—a story told by a loving father to a very impressionable child.

Still, she'd relied on that bone gene before. And it had seldom let her down.

Three weeks later, the singsong warbling of the auctioneer numbed Maggie's senses. She jerked herself alert; even though the day was nearly over, she had a job to do. Maggie pulled the bill of the soiled John Deere cap down lower over her eyes.

Still, she could see the steady fingering and assessing of objects on the flat wagon by strangers and neighbors. They were like turkey vultures searching for the best road kill. The items on display were those of a working farm: skill saws, hammers, socket sets, de-horners, ropes. Some were old; all were well used.

Men and a few women huddled under heavy coats to keep the sharp wind from penetrating as they searched for bargains. She didn't see much concern for the Ames family, even though they'd been longtime members of the Beaverhill community.

Maggie turned her head slightly and watched Sara Ames scurry between sale items, avoiding eye contact with her neighbors while whispering words to the auctioneer. The woman was determined to make the best out of a bad situation. Her husband, Ted, hadn't come back for the auction. He'd already taken a job working on an assembly line producing generators in Cincinnati. Sara would take the children and join him as soon as she could finish disposing of the farm machinery and their other non-essential possessions.

Maggie chewed on her lower lip. Ted had probably used his job as an excuse for not witnessing the end of their dream. An old Allis-Chalmers tractor, a couple John Deeres, an International combine, plows, planters, hay rakes and mowers, and an assortment of covered and uncovered wagons stood like tombstones between

11

the barn and the house. Sara had drawn the short straw on this day.

The bidding on a skill saw had stalled at a ridiculous five dollars. Maggie nodded at the auctioneer, who had sought her out of the crowd. She raised the bid, as she had done throughout the afternoon in an attempt to boost the price. So far she'd only bought a corn planter she didn't need, but she could use it for trade with the local implement dealer.

She pulled her coat collar tighter around her neck. The corn planter notwithstanding, she was satisfied. She'd been able to increase the prices on a lot of items for the Ames family. They deserved that; they'd been good neighbors.

Maggie shivered against the chill, never wanting to find herself in the position of Sara Ames. She'd sacrifice everything but her children to avoid having her neighbors come and grimly pick over her things. Auctions had the feel of funerals, and she didn't like going to either.

She let the skill saw go for fifteen dollars and moved toward the canteen tent sponsored by the community church Women's Society. She badly needed a cup of coffee to warm up her insides. Maggie hadn't taken a half dozen steps before Ben Templeton fell in step beside her.

"You locate Harrington yet?"

Without breaking stride, Maggie nodded.

"Was he sober?"

"He could still talk. Thanks for giving me a bead on him." Maggie stuffed her gloved hands inside the large pockets of her coat. "Don't know if he'll dry out enough to help or not. It'll take some time, I guess. It's already been three weeks."

Ben nodded, smiling benevolently. "And you don't like to wait any more than your dad did. Colt Magee was often in a rush. Reckless, some would say."

Maggie didn't see any need to respond to the obvious. Many folks thought she was too much like her father. That was their problem, not hers.

As they neared the canteen, Ben reached out and pulled her to a halt. Maggie saw that mixture of admiration, love and concern she often recognized in the old man's eyes. She told herself to be patient. Ben meant well, and he could still help her in a lot of ways.

"Maggie, I know you loved your folks dearly and all those who came before them, but do you really think they'd want you to risk losing everything with this hair-brained horse racing scheme? If you sell now, Con-Ex Farms will pay you handsomely. If you force them to squeeze you out, you'll be lucky to keep yourself and the kids in clothes."

Maggie's eyes narrowed. "I'm not a Sara Ames, Ben. She and Ted may have made the best decision for their family. It's not the best decision for my family. I won't be squeezed. My great, great grandparents were the first to plow that land. It won't be taken over by some hog corporation executives who couldn't tell a boar from a sow."

Ben chuckled as he held the tent flap open for Maggie. "They may be able to figure that out, given enough time."

Ignoring Ben's attempt at humor, Maggie stepped to the counter and ordered black coffee and a doughnut. She handed Flo Zimmerman the money and returned the gangly woman's soft grin. She and Flo had been good friends since grade school. Flo had been timid then and still was. She'd been married and divorced and had no children. Maggie couldn't imagine her own life without kids. "When are you going to come out and see me, Flo? It's been too long."

"Oh, I'd love to come out," the tall woman responded, brushing back mousy brown hair. "You just seem so busy of late. I thought I'd be in the way."

"That's nonsense, Flo. Stop by any Sunday after church — it'll be so good to catch up with you."

Maggie turned and walked toward a card table covered in blue and white plastic. Ben followed and pulled out a chair.

After sipping his coffee, Ben said, "I'm glad you bought that extra crop insurance, Maggie. This winter's been so dry we'd better get a lot of rain pretty soon, or farmers are gonna be in a lot of trouble."

Maggie nodded. "There's no snow left in the fields, frost is almost out, and flies are already hatching. It's an early spring, all right, though you can't tell it today with that raw wind out of the northwest."

14

"So with Harrington out of the picture, what will you do now?"

"I didn't say he was out of the picture. He just hasn't gotten back to me yet."

Ben shook his head. "Why don't you try something else? You're as stubborn as your father ever was. I seldom could talk sense to him either."

"Thanks for the compliment." Maggie took a bite of her doughnut. "I know there are a lot of risks. But whatever I do involves risks. The stock market has risks. Moving to the city is not without danger. I can learn about horse racing, and I'm willing to work hard."

"There's no doubt about that. You're a bright young woman. Always thought you should have done college." Ben stroked his chin. "You know, it's not too late for college. Lots of folks are going back."

The combined smells of canvas, grilled onions, and human sweat made Maggie's stomach roll. And if that wasn't enough, Ben Templeton was becoming more than a little irritating. "I've got two kids to raise — I'm not going to college. I need someone to teach me about raising race horses. I always loved working with horses when I was a kid."

"But this is different," Ben countered. "Thoroughbreds are finicky. Trainers are often at work by five in the morning, and who knows when their day is done. Where do your children fit into that schedule?

Maggie glanced away from Ben's piercing stare.

"I don't know. I don't have many of the details worked out, but I can't afford to wait much longer." She paused and looked back at her friend. "It's been two years since Mason's death. I've got to get on with my life. And I have to find a way for the farm to pay for itself. I won't risk everything I have, but I am going to find out if horseracing is do-able. With or without your help."

"Now there's no need to get huffy, young lady. I could still take you over my knee."

"I'm sorry." Maggie's cheeks burned. "I do appreciate everything you've done for me."

He laughed and nodded. "What about your brother? Have you asked him for help?"

"Brad? You've got to be kidding. Last I heard he was still in San Francisco chasing skirts and partying on a nightly basis. If he got wind of the Con-Ex Farms interest in the farm, he'd be doing everything in his power to get me to sell out."

Ben dropped his gaze to his plate before looking up and continuing, "Hoped maybe he'd straightened out by now."

Maggie closed her eyes and shook her head.

Ben coughed. "Maybe I can come up with a couple more trainer possibilities for you. They'll be much more expensive than Harrington, though."

"I'm not impoverished, but I can't behave like a big spender, either." Maggie rubbed her shoulders. "I need an expert for cheap. That's where Harrington filled the bill quite nicely. But he may be more down and out than I had hoped." Maggie shuddered, remembering the lanky man with trembling hands. The man's pain still gnawed at her heart.

Ben glanced up at her, then back down at his plate. "Your folks were good people, Maggie. My best friends. It's been five years, and their death is still one of the biggest tragedies of my life. They didn't deserve to die because some guy got himself loaded up on booze and headed down the highway on the wrong side of the road."

"I know, Ben. But nothing can be done about that now." Maggie tried to keep at bay a twinge of guilt. What was she doing trying to sober up a drunk to work for her?

"You don't want a drunk around the kids."

Maggie shook her head. "Of course not. But I know about grief. It took me two years of pain and tears to get to this point. And Ed Harrington is grieving. Maybe he needs some honest work and a decent place to live."

At that moment, Maggie noticed Flo Zimmerman cocking her head toward the CD player. It was an old cue between the two of them. Maggie winked in response. Flo was always listening to country western classics and looking for hidden messages in the old songs. Some people would let the Bible fall randomly open in search of inspiration—Flo tuned randomly to country western. She heard the familiar deep baritone of Johnny Cash singing *Ring of Fire*. Maybe Flo was onto something this time. Maggie knew she was stepping into an adventure. Her veins were running hot like a radiator in danger of boiling over.

She turned toward the hand tugging on her coat. Maggie looked up into the dead-fish eyes of Sara Ames and flinched.

"Don't get up," Sara said. "I just want to tell you how much I appreciate what you did today."

Maggie narrowed her eyes.

Sara shook her head. "Don't try to deny it. You pushed the bidding on just about everything we had up for sale. I don't know how much more we earned because of your efforts." The older woman squeezed Maggie's arm. "Thanks. I just hope you never have to hold your own auction."

Nodding her head, Maggie watched her former neighbor hurry out from the canteen tent holding back sobs. Ben patted her hand. Through a haze Maggie heard his words: "You're so much like your dad; you just might make it, yet."

Maggie set the thermos back down in the shade of the oak and walked toward the tractor. It had been nearly a month and she still hadn't heard a thing from that Harrington guy. She shuddered at the memory of him. The man reminded her of her childhood image of Ichabod Crane: all arms and legs, baggy eyes, thin lips and bony fingers.

Sitting on the tractor, Maggie admired the neatly plowed furrows of the forty acre field. An unspeakable pride filled her lungs. The land had always done that for her—it filled her in ways nothing else could.

Oh, there were times when she wondered what lay beyond these familiar surroundings. The land had given her a rare kind of freedom, yet it also held her captive.

So why was she holding out for him? She knew a little about drinking problems from watching her brother fight back from binge drinking. Not hearing from him yet meant little. Probably it would take the man several weeks to pull himself together. She just hoped he would — but why?

She mulled that thought for a moment. Maybe it was that she hoped he was as good at working with horses as Templeton had told her.

Who was she kidding? It was his eyes — she could see them clearly even now, the pain and anguish and the fleeting spark of life that had reached though his haze and tugged at her. A remnant of who he used to be? How had such a successful horse trainer wound up at the Resting Arms? She shook her head. Maybe she didn't want to know.

If he wasn't sober, he wouldn't last long on her farm. She wasn't about to take on a charity case. If he stayed, he'd have to earn his keep.

She'd give him two months and not a day longer. Four more weeks. She engaged the clutch and began to turn over more ground. She groaned. Waiting was not a skill that Maggie Anderson had come close to perfecting.

CHAPTER TWO

Ed Harrington glanced down at the truck seat again to read the tattered slip of paper he'd carried in his pocket for six weeks. North for twenty more miles, and then left on a gravel country road another eight, and he should be there. Another half hour, at least. Still plenty of time to turn around. Maybe he should have called. But then he might lose his nerve.

He glanced in the rearview mirror. Not much other traffic out for the middle of a warm April Sunday.

She'd thrown him a lifeline, all right. He still couldn't decide exactly why the spunky blonde with blue eyes had shaken him up so much. He'd like to think he could have quit drinking at any point; he'd always told himself he would someday. It just always seemed like tomorrow would be a better day to start.

Why had he needed her? Once he made up his mind, it was all up to him anyway. He hadn't had a drop since he stumbled down the sidewalk with her thirty dollars in his fist.

Thirty dollars. He hadn't spent it on a shave or on dinner—he didn't have to. Wouldn't that shake her up, to know he still had some savings stashed away, that he wasn't totally destitute?

Nope, he'd probably never tell her what he did

with it: every day since he met her, he'd found a twelve-step meeting, and when they passed around the hat at the end of the meeting to pay for their meeting space and support the organization, each day for thirty days he'd put in one of her dollars. He smiled to himself—he liked that. He'd given her money away.

His hand drifted to his pocket where he felt the thirty day chip he'd carried for two weeks now. Sort of silly, that a tiny piece of plastic could mean so much. And be so hard to get.

So if he didn't need this job, why was he driving to her farm like a lemming to the sea? He could get other work. Hell, if he stayed at the Resting Arms, his savings alone would see him through for a long time, without a job. If he didn't start drinking again.

But she'd seen him staggering away from her. Somehow he just didn't want that to be her last picture of him. Ed the drunk. He had to set her straight.

Why in hell did that matter? Maybe he wasn't Ed the drunk anymore, but he was still Ed the washed up trainer, Ed the disaster, Ed the failure. She'd probably see right through him. He should just keep on driving.

Who was he kidding? What he really needed, more than money, more than odd jobs, was to be training horses again. To do the one thing he knew how to do really well. And that was what this Maggie Anderson was holding out to him—a way back to working with horses.

Sunday on the farm was different from any other day of the week. Maggie slept late, getting up in time to take the kids to the community church two miles down the road. Then it was lunch at Sarah's Diner, or occasionally she would take her family into Des Moines and splurge at a fancy restaurant. They would usually be back home by mid-afternoon to finish reading the paper, to curl up with a book, or to work on homework.

The same routine was followed this Sunday: church, Sarah's Diner, and now reading the comics. Sitting in an old but comfortable couch on the screened-in porch, Maggie thought back to a piece she'd finished reading earlier about preparations for the coming summer racing season at Prairie Meadows. The track didn't operate year around. In the off season, trainers typically vanned their horses from track to track in places like Minnesota, Illinois, Oklahoma or Arkansas. She hadn't thought about that—how much more money would it take to really be in the horseracing business?

"Mom?"

"Yes, dear." Maggie glanced over at Carolyn, who was working the crossword puzzle. She was turning into a beautiful young woman right before Maggie's eyes. Fifteen in September. Where did the time go?

"What's another word for ebullient? Six letters.

With a v as the third letter."

"Try...lively."

"That's it! How do you do it, Mom?"

Maggie smiled. Her daughter never could quite overcome the shock of discovering that her mom was smart. She'd go to college and study to be a veterinarian. Carolyn had often talked about building a large animal clinic near the barn and helping her mother keep the farm.

Maggie watched her teenager brush a wave of long blond hair from her face. It had become such a habit she imagined Carolyn never even knew when she lifted her hand.

She stared out the screen porch toward the nearly empty barn. Would it ever be the home for mares and foals, for horses with a burning desire to win races?

Her brow furrowed. So much change had already occurred. The place didn't seem as alive as it had when she was a kid. Then, hogs and beef cattle overflowed from outlying sheds as well as from the barn. And, of course, the riding horses. Her brother had never liked to ride. She had, though. And she did well showing the horses in 4-H.

But her husband, Mason, had thought the horses were merely a waste of money and time. They got rid of them shortly after their marriage. She'd always regretted that decision. Now she wished she'd battled harder to keep them, but with a baby coming, it hadn't seemed like she'd have much time for them then.

And Mason wasn't about to help out. He was a good man. She'd loved him very much, but he never wanted to be a farmer. Though Mason enjoyed tinkering with machines, he was always timid around animals of any kind. Looking back, Maggie suspected he'd often been frustrated that the land was her heritage and her wealth, not his.

Now there were hardly any animals on the farm: just a few beef cattle and several cats. The bulk of the corn and hay she raised was sold as cash crops. She missed the activity of that earlier time when so much of her life had been centered on the needs of animals.

Maggie blinked as if to close off the past. Glancing back at her comics, she couldn't focus. Her thoughts continued to tumble. She hadn't thought about the shaggy man leaning against the Resting Arms Hotel for some time. How long had it been since she'd talked to him? Close to six weeks. No doubt he'd drunk up all her money by now. She chastised herself for having waited so long to make contact with other possible trainers, though she nearly broke out in a sweat imagining their fees. Maybe she was getting cold feet.

With one foot tucked under her, she tried again to concentrate on the comics, but she couldn't shake her melancholy mood. She wasn't desperate, yet."

"Mom. Mom!" shouted the smallish tow-headed boy dashing up the porch steps.

"What is it, Johnny? You'd think the devil was chasing you." She'd never understand why boys always rushed around so.

Johnny skidded to a halt before her while the screen door banged loudly behind him.

"Somebody's coming, Mom."

"Who?"

"Don't know. The truck ain't familiar," the boy drawled.

"Isn't," both mother and sister corrected.

Johnny rolled his eyes. "There he comes now."

Everyone on the porch looked toward the driveway as an old faded green pick-up lumbered toward the gravel patch where Maggie's car and truck were parked. She didn't recognize the man getting out of the truck.

The man stood tall in western boots, clean Levis, and a white dress shirt with an ancient feed mill cap dipped low over his eyes. Unable to make out his features clearly, Maggie rose to welcome the stranger.

As he rapped on the screen door, he said dryly, "Afternoon, Mrs. Anderson. It took a while for me and Mabel to figure out your directions."

With those few words, Ed Harrington doffed his cap. A hint of a smile tugged at his mouth. His gray eyes remained cool and guarded.

Maggie's mouth fell wide open and her heart skipped a beat or two. He was standing there like an apparition. Was this really the malnourished man she'd last seen stumbling down a Des Moines sidewalk?

"Who is he?" Johnny demanded, tugging at his mom's elbow.

26

"Yeah, Mom, introduce us," Carolyn said.

"Well, of course." Maggie heard her disembodied voice sound more in control than any other part of her body. Where had the shaking drunk gone? This man looked much more alive — earthy, and dangerous. "This is Mr. Harrington, children. Mr. Harrington, this is Johnny and Carolyn.

Harrington pursed his lips and nodded at them. "Hi. How are you? You can call me Ed."

Carolyn looked stunned.

Johnny crossed his arms and widened his stance. "The land's not for sale, mister. No matter how much money you got."

"Johnny," Maggie scolded. "Mr. Harrington isn't here to buy the farm. He's here because I wanted to talk to him about working for us." Glancing awkwardly at Harrington, she said, "But that seems like a long time ago."

Why did she have to sound so accusing? She flexed her fingers and continued evenly, "Mr. Harrington, would you like something to drink? We have tea, coffee and pop. I don't have anything stronger."

He smiled. "Coffee will do. Black will be fine. Haven't touched a drop of that other stuff in a long time now. Not since some do-gooder woman confronted me on the sidewalk. By the way, call me Ed."

Relieved, Maggie felt her pulse quicken. Her vision cleared. He might be her man after all. "Carolyn, would you run and get Mr.

Harrington…" He cocked his head at her. "Ed," she corrected herself, "a cup of coffee. Bring me one, too. Then you and Johnny can pick out a drink and go upstairs to finish your homework while Ed and I discuss some business."

"Aw, Mom," Johnny grumbled. "We don't have to do that until after supper."

Smiling, Maggie said, "Today's a little different than usual, young man. Now run along and do what I say."

"Nice kids," Harrington commented, watching them leave the porch. "Well behaved."

"Yeah, well, most of the time."

"Here you go, Ed," Carolyn said, returning with coffee.

"Thank you, young lady."

"Mom."

Maggie reached for the drink. "Thanks, dear. I'll let you know when we're finished."

Maggie stared thoughtfully at the curious man while her daughter climbed the stairs to her room. Her stomach muscles tightened. She needed his help desperately. But she hadn't counted on her body acting like that of some giddy teenager.

She feared her heart was doing more whispering than her bones. Ed Harrington was still thin, but there was a blurring of pain and challenge and mystery in his face that pulled and scared her at the same time. His hair was still shaggy, but it had been washed. His face, with its distinctive roman nose, reminded her of a shattered mirror. Was *haggard handsome* a decent way to describe a man? And his hands. He had long fingers. And they were steady.

- o -

"Well, I'm here. What about the job you wanted me to do? Didn't see any horses when I drove in," Ed said gruffly.

"You get right to the point, don't you?"

"That's why I'm here." Ed tried not to be too obvious, but the woman looked even better than the one he vaguely remembered from their first encounter. He'd recalled that she was a tiny thing, hardly five feet. And as he remembered, she filled out a blouse nicely. But how could he forget her face?

Her straw-yellow hair was styled in a functional short pixie that would not get in the way of doing farm work. Short, stubby fingernails also attested that she was no stranger to manual labor. Most stunning, though, were her round eyes. He'd remembered they were the blue of robin's eggs, but he had forgotten how round and expressive they were. An impish nose and small naturally puckered lips looked perfect in her heart-shaped face.

She projected an air of innocence. Counterbalancing that chaste look was the toughness apparent in the pinpoints of those round eyes. He expected she could be as smooth as rye whisky and as harsh as straight tequila. She exuded a kind of class that came from confidence and roots.

Although she was fetching and could easily become bewitching, he quickly decided he had no designs on getting to know her body better. As far as he was concerned, Maggie Anderson might as well wear an *off limits* sign around her neck. All he wanted was an opportunity to work with horses, get his career back, and build up his reserves some.

He owed this sassy looking blonde for getting his attention back on living. They might be able to help each other out for a while, but that was all. He wasn't about to sit around the Iowa countryside with third string horses. Damn, he missed Chicago.

Right now, though, Ed didn't like Ms. Anderson's perplexed look. Surprisingly, she seemed unsure of herself. "Well, what is it? Do I have a job or don't I?"

"Yes," Maggie responded haltingly. "We'll have to work out arrangements. I can't offer you much, but it should be better than the Resting Arms."

"I don't doubt that."

She raised her eyebrows slightly. "I'm having a loft efficiency apartment built in one end of the haymow. It should be ready within a couple weeks."

"I was hoping to get out of the Arms sooner than that."

"I've got a spare room in the house. I'd need a day to clean it up."

"I'd prefer the loft." Ed glanced furtively toward the kitchen door.

"I know. But it can't be helped. The room will be ready by tomorrow night. Two weeks at the most, and you'll have more privacy. I'm prepared to offer the loft, three meals a day except Sunday — you'll be on your own that day — and a thousand dollars a month." She took in a quick breath and rushed on. "I know it's not much for a top trainer, but that's all I can afford for now. Maybe later…"

Ed grimaced. "No need to apologize, ma'am. That's darn generous. I'm not a top trainer anymore."

"But you have the same skills, if you can stay away from booze."

"Yeah, about that." Ed glanced around the porch to assure himself of their privacy. "I've been dry for more than thirty days. They say that's the toughest. Not that any day is a cakewalk. Even got my thirty day chip." He reached into his pocket and produced the chip.

"I'm pleased."

"Not looking for sympathy, lady. I'm looking for a job. And I'd kind of like to keep the drinking problem private, between you and me."

"I don't have a need to broadcast anything about your private life, Mr. Harrington."

He arched his eyebrows.

"Ed."

"Good. Now tell me about this job. Where do you keep your horses?"

"I don't have any."

"What? You got me to dry out, to come out here for nothing—"

"Not at all. You're going to help me build a racehorse stable from scratch. You can look at it this way: I haven't made any mistakes yet."

"That's certainly open to debate." Ed studied her again. She sure had guts. He wasn't sure she had much common sense, though, trying to hook up with a dried out drunk to start a racing stable.

"Do you have any ideas about how we might begin?" he asked, running his fingers through his hair. "And how much it will cost? This is not a pauper's game."

Ed watched her pause and look wistfully toward the barn. What did she see there—the past, present or future?

Maggie looked directly at him. "I may not be rich, but I'm not a pauper." She looked away.

"Other than my children," she began, "this land is the most precious treasure to me. It's been a part of my family for generations. It's my children's legacy. I have to make this farm pay for itself. The cash crops aren't enough." She glanced back at him.

He waited.

"My husband died over two years ago," she continued. "He left a sizable insurance policy. It may be enough to make the farm profitable. If not, Con-Ex Farms or some other conglomerate will swallow up this land and my family's heritage like it's just so much dust."

"Ah, so now I at least know something about the larger game you're in." He nodded grimly. "So that's why you had to resort to digging a broken-down trainer out of his hiding hole. You have to play some ace cards or fold. It's ante up time, and I'm part of the ante."

"I hadn't thought of it that way." Maggie frowned. "This is no game to me. But I see your point. Anyway, I want you to teach me how to train horses."

"What?" Ed jumped to his feet. "I thought you wanted me to train them and then turn them over to someone else at the track. You're hardly big enough to swat a fly!" Uh oh, his mouth had gotten him into trouble again. When would he ever learn to engage brain before mouth? But the sparks firing out of those large round blue eyes might have been worth the gaffe.

Scrambling to a stand, Maggie gestured toward door. "If you are incapable of working with and teaching a woman—even a short one—to work with horses, Mr. Harrington, you can leave right now. I don't need you. You can crawl back from wherever you came from."

"Now, don't jump to conclusions," Ed backpedaled. "My mouth often gets me into trouble. I didn't mean you were incapable of learning. It's just...you're so pretty, and we're talking long hours and a lot of hard work. And no promises of getting rich quick, if ever."

"No matter," Maggie said, blowing bangs off her forehead, "this is what I intend to do. It's what

I must do. I've worked hard all my life. These small hands you're looking at have calluses just like those of any other farmer. Don't mistake me for some sniveling female who has to be pampered. If you do, you'll be in for loads of trouble. And I don't see this as some get rich quick scheme either, Mr. Harrington."

"The question is, is this something you want to do? Can we work together? And believe me, if you take this job, we will be working as a team. I'm not hiring you to do all the work or make all the decisions. I wish I didn't need your help, but the fact is I do."

"It's clear you wouldn't accept any pampering, ma'am, even if you needed it."

Her eyebrows shot up.

"Not that that's any of my business one way or the other. As far as working together — guess we won't know till we try. But there is a lot to what you're asking. Lots of planning. A lot of dollars to buy horses and refurbish the barn area so it will be safe for horses."

Ed stopped and looked out toward the barn. What was he getting himself into? He had to have a screw loose somewhere to even be thinking about helping the woman. She was so green about racehorses she hadn't even earned the label greenhorn. Yet he admired her spunk. And it might just work. She had the land and the desire. He had the skill and the know-how. With a half smile creeping across his face, he wondered what kind of a student Maggie Anderson would be. He expected she did her homework thoroughly.

"Doesn't have to be top of the line horse farm right off," he resumed, "but it must be safe for horses. You're gonna have some expensive investments running around out there on four long spindly legs. Race horses are finicky and prone to injury. We've got to protect them the best we can. And that'll cost some money. If we don't buy quality horses, we won't have the potential for making large enough purses for them to pay their way.

"Most horses don't win, you know," he said, watching her intently. "Many don't even make it to the track. And just when you think you've got one in good form and who can run, something goes wrong. Are you really prepared for the disappointments that go along with horseracing?"

For a moment, he wished he hadn't asked that question. The fire quickly drained from those sapphire orbs and was replaced with familiar hollow pain. "Yeah, I guess you know about disappointment and loss," he acknowledged, slouching back down onto a chair.

- o -

"I expect that's one thing we have in common," Maggie murmured, taking her seat. "Mr. Harrington, have you decided to take the job?"

"Well, it's not like I have a lot of other offers." He grinned faintly, like a child returning from a runaway attempt.

That smile tore at Maggie's heart. Did he really think she was pretty?

"You may be getting in way over your head," he cautioned. "Hell, maybe me, too. But I'm willing to try. Of course, I don't have much to lose. If you're going to be in this business, it's important to know something about all elements of the game. In the long run, you may not want to take on the track responsibilities of a trainer. There are a lot ways to play the game.

"We do need to clear up one matter." Harrington sighed and dropped his gaze. "You know I can't take your horses to the track. Can't help you out there."

Maggie nodded. "I know about the ban, Ed. That doesn't have anything to do with me. You've been vouched for. That's enough. There are likely a lot of bridges yet to cross. Let's take them one at a time."

"I'm all for that, Maggie." Harrington lifted his cup in salute.

That was the first time he'd called her Maggie. It sounded too familiar, yet they had to be on a first name basis if they were going to work together as a team. She took a short breath, excited about actually beginning to put in place her plan to save the farm. Her nerves tingled at the prospect.

Or, perhaps they were responding to the man who pronounced Maggie in a gravelly voice that oozed intimacy.

"I had no idea this room had so much junk in it," Maggie complained, wiping her brow with the back of her hand. She glanced over at Flo Zimmerman, who was filling a box with odds and ends Maggie had set out for her. "I so much appreciate you coming out to help on such short notice. I can't believe Harrington is starting work tomorrow. It's going to happen."

"It all sounds so scary." Flo wrapped a tarnished softball trophy in newspaper and tucked it into a large cardboard box. "I know you've done a lot research on this horse business and you've set aside CDs for the kids' college, but what about yourself? You could lose everything."

"They claim horseracing is one of Iowa's fastest growing agribusinesses. Racing purses have been growing steadily, ever since they opened that casino at the track to support them. People are making it. And some aren't. That's the nature of business. Hell, that's the nature of living off the land." Maggie took the quilt off the bed and started removing the blankets and sheets.

"I imagine you're right. Maggie, if anyone can do it, you can. You've always had more determination and grit than any two people."

Maggie stuffed the quilt in a chest of drawers. Would determination and grit be enough? Although the half million life insurance settlement sounded like a lot of money, it wasn't. And it was all she had. She'd have to be extremely prudent.

"It'll work. Once all the pieces are in place. It's got to be more realistic than dairy. I can't make enough money at hogs. And there's not enough land to survive only with cash crops. Besides," she said, grinning at her friend, "this is an adventure of sorts."

"Adventure? We had enough of those when we were kids."

Maggie shook her head. "I loved Mason, but sometimes he was so conservative. We should've tried other things with the farm years ago."

"I was always so jealous of you and Mason." Flo stared at her and then looked away. "It seemed like you were the ideal couple. You had each other. You had kids. What else would anyone want?"

Maggie folded her arms across her chest and leaned against the dresser. "Maybe spark. Maybe challenge. Maybe adventure. I can't explain it, Flo, but lately I keep remembering that young girl on top of a horse racing across the pasture."

"I remember." Flo nodded. "You and Betsy Cunningham used to be best of friends, and you'd ride your horses like you were glued to them. I'd come by now and then and watch. I miss Betsy."

"Yeah, I get a Christmas card each year. She and her husband seem to enjoy Seattle."

"You're lucky Carolyn and Johnny are so excited about your horse ideas."

"Neither of them wants to leave Beaverhill." Maggie picked up a broom and started sweeping the wood floor. "Carolyn doesn't want to have to make new friends, and Johnny can hardly wait until we have horses."

"I just hope this Harrington fellow will work out okay," Flo said, taping a box. "Aren't you afraid of having a man living under your roof? He could be a molester or something."

"I've checked him out. He has good references." No need to say anything about the scandal Harrington was still embroiled in. "He's had some bad luck. He'll only be in the house a short time. I'd prefer to have the loft finished, but it's not. We'll get by. We have to."

Maggie worked the broom rapidly across the stained floorboards. Having him in the spare bedroom did make her nervous. She wasn't afraid of him — it wasn't that. She didn't like the fluttering in her tummy when he'd called her Maggie. She was the boss and he was the hired hand. That was the way it would stay.

The next day Maggie stopped by the Beaverhill Bank to withdraw some cash. After completing her transaction, she turned to leave the lobby only to be summoned by the banker, Josh Prater.

"Step into my office for a minute, would you Maggie? I've got some exciting news for you." Without waiting for a response, the bank president guided her toward his door.

Maggie cringed as she allowed herself to be escorted into the man's office. His oversized rosewood desk formed the centerpiece of an ornate office. Prater's desk was excruciatingly neat. How could any normal human be so organized?

"Sit down. Sit down." He gestured towards a chair. "Would you like some coffee?"

His mouth was smiling, but his eyes weren't. Maggie shook her head and remained standing. "No, I really need to be going, Mr. Prater. I have a lot of errands to run before getting back. Please be quick."

She pulled her jacket tighter around her torso. She had never trusted Prater—his dark, narrow features and fixed smile always reminded her of a mortician. Her dad hadn't liked him either. The two of them had grown up together. Apparently they were never great buddies.

Prater folded his arms and leaned back against the corner of his desk. "You know Con-Ex Farms continues to be interested in your dad's farm."

"It's *my* farm, Mr. Prater. Has been for the past five years, since Dad and Mom died." She scowled. "And it's still not for sale. How many times do I have to tell you that?"

"Everything is for sale one way or another. Your brother would sing a different tune if he were here."

"He's not here, and he doesn't own enough of the land to make any difference. How we manage things is our business."

The banker moved away from the desk and towered over her with a smile stilled glued to his face. "Maggie, I just meant that there comes a point when wisdom should prevail over loyalty. I know all about your love for your heritage and that particular piece of ground of yours. Times change. In addition to Con-Ex Farms, there's another party interested in your farm."

Maggie took a step back.

"You, young lady, can be very rich, very quick. There will be a bidding war between two giants if you but give the word."

"And how much commission do you stand to make from this bidding war?" Maggie's mouth turned up a little as the banker paled, reached for his glasses and began polishing them. "My answer is simple, Mr. Prater. Let me spell it out for you. N, O! What part of that two letter word don't you understand?"

Maggie hurried toward the door and grabbed the doorknob before turning to face Prater. "Please don't bother me with any more offers. I'm not in the least bit interested."

Prater's voice rose. "You must be out of your mind, young woman. You just turned down over a million dollars. You're not acting in the best interests of your children. Do your in-laws know how arrogantly stupid you're being?"

Maggie rushed out of the bank. How dare he bring her children's interests into this as if she didn't consider them! And her in-laws shared no commitment to the land. Mason's mother had always believed it was beneath her son's station in life to live on a farm.

Out on the sidewalk, she breathed deeply and wished there was another bank in town. It was very tempting to move all of her accounts to Walker. But that small community was an eight mile drive out of her way. She grinned. Did Prater have any idea she'd stashed the bulk of the life insurance money in the Walker bank?

She could hear her dad's voice: "It's often wise to divide your assets among several banks." Had he distrusted bankers in general, or Prater in particular?

Glancing over her shoulder, she saw Prater staring at her from his office window. She hastened her steps. Why did that man seem so eager to get her to sell? Was it just the commission?

And why did she mistrust him? He was a well respected member of the community. He supported local charities, funded a high school scholarship, sat on the board of the small, local hospital, and was a church trustee. The only knock against his reputation was that he seemed harsher with area farmers in financial trouble than with small businessmen. Whatever his motives, she was tired of him leaning on her.

CHAPTER THREE

Maggie couldn't get away from him. He was too close; too much a man. They'd worked side by side for two weeks refurbishing the barn, making plans for purchasing horses, and developing a vision for the long term growth of Anderson Stables. Harrington had proven to be a good teacher.

Though he could be gruff and sparse with words, he exhibited much more patience with her than she had imagined possible. His knowledge of thoroughbreds and what was required to turn them into competitive race horses was expansive. And her pulse quickened when his eyes caught fire with the awe and thrill he clearly felt for the challenge of horseracing. There was no question she'd hired the right man for the job.

But she couldn't get away from him. Snap! "Shit," Maggie blurted, examining the spatula she used for scraping dishes. She avoided glancing at Harrington, who was sitting at the table finishing his last cup of coffee, oblivious to her turmoil.

As was part of the original agreement, he ate his meals with her family. But he also slept in the same house and used the same bathroom. Hers was a farmhouse, not some expensive home in the woods built by people trying to escape the city for fresh country air.

His scent invaded her space; it was as simple as that. Not that they were unpleasant smells, but they were man smells, and they were undeniably Harrington smells.

Occasionally, she would peek across the table or over a newspaper to find him staring at her. Seldom would he turn away. Her privacy was compromised. He bothered her. Not on purpose, she was sure. He probably never even noticed her discomfort.

- o -

Ed sighed heavily watching temptation scraping dishes as if her life depended upon getting them spotlessly clean before stacking them in the dishwasher. Thank God, the loft would be ready to move into in another week. He hoped he could last that long. He hoped *they* could last that long. He tried his best to ignore her, but the damn woman was getting under his skin like a boil that wouldn't go away.

She was quick learner and a hard worker; he'd give her that much. But she cooked too good. And she was a fine, creative mom. It had been comical, at first, to see how she out maneuvered her children, and then his heart wrenched as she patiently meted out wisdom along with kindness and discipline. Too bad she hadn't been around to teach his folks about parenting.

But she could be cantankerous, stubborn, pesky, annoying and downright pushy at times.

She was the boss, but that didn't give her the right to praise him for just doing his job. And he didn't need her encouragement in his fight against the booze. He didn't want her thinking he was some damn emotional cripple.

And then there were all those women things about. Was there any place else to hang robes and nightgowns than in the bathroom? And why did she always have to look so damn innocently sexy? It didn't matter if she wore a sweatshirt and baggy pants or a thin blouse and shorts—she was as tempting as the devil herself.

And he had to stop noticing. He needed blinkers like some horses to avoid distractions.

Did she know her upturned smile and peppy personality served only to tease him? Her hair could stand on end and she would still look like a woman who needed to be touched and caressed and yes, dammit, pampered.

Pushing away from the supper table he frowned at Maggie's back one last time before muttering, "Thanks for the meal. I've got to be going."

Hurriedly, he exited and climbed into his truck. For once it started without protest. Ed was grateful for that as he eased the pickup toward the dirt road that would lead him back to civilization...and to some measure of sanity.

- o -

Maggie watched the faded pickup lurch along the rutted road. He was headed to a twelve step meeting. He wouldn't discuss what went on at those meetings, but she was pleased he went. It was good for him, and it was good for her to have some distance from the man.

When she'd first met him outside the Resting Arms, she wouldn't have bet a bent penny that he'd straighten out enough to come work for her. She'd hoped. She'd even put up thirty bucks as a challenge, but she would never have bet on it.

But he'd gotten himself together. And he was working out better than she'd imagined. Watching the pickup tail lights disappear in the darkness, Maggie hugged herself tightly as waves of heat coursed through her body only to be followed by a riptide of chills. He was gone, but his scent filled her nostrils.

- o -

Ed used the end of a shovel to tamp dirt tightly around the fencepost while Maggie held it in place. They'd been building fencing for the paddocks for days; this was the last post. It was the post they'd both been looking forward to.

"Done," Ed said. "There are still a lot of rails to attach, but that's it for digging post holes." He cast his gaze over the half dozen acres they'd been dividing into pastures with an eye for how it would change over the next few weeks. "It's looking good. Won't be long now and you'll see

46

some horses out there."

"It can't happen too soon," said Maggie, stretching her arms high above her head and scrunching her shoulders. "I just hope this works."

"You having second thoughts?"

"Third and fourth, probably. Don't worry. I'm not going to back away from our plans." Maggie squinted against the morning sun. "I just wish we could get on with it. Waiting is the hardest."

"It's not like we've been sitting around watching the grass grow these past weeks," said Ed, bending to pick up his tools.

"I know. I know. But it still seems…so unreal. Having horses running around these paddocks is going to make it much more real."

"Yeah, I can think of something else that will make it real enough."

"What's that?"

"Bills."

"Right. That part of reality is already happening. I don't really want to think about that now," Maggie said, removing her cap. "It's time to sample Carolyn's lemonade. She put it in the shade of the maple tree. How does that suit you, Mr. Carpenter?"

"Just fine," Ed responded, dusting off his pants. "We've earned it this morning. It's as hot as blazes and it's not even noon yet."

Slowly, he drank his fill of Carolyn's lemonade. With pride, he admired the corral fencing he and Maggie had nearly completed. It was new vinyl. Hardly cheap, but barbed wire fencing was too dangerous for race horses — or any other horse, for that matter.

Out of the corner of his eye, he considered the woman sitting on the grass beside him. Maggie Anderson did not shy away from work. She probably didn't shy away from much, if anything. They sat in the shade of a maple tree. Even though it was only mid-morning, the heat of the day was intensifying. It would be a scorcher, and it was still only early May. He looked up at the cloudless blue sky. They could sure use some rain.

At least he could get away from her now — well, some of the time. The loft had quickly become his own personal cave for retreat, and he welcomed that a lot. For the first time in a long time he was beginning to feel like a human being. His chest filled with air as he contemplated working with horses. Soon. A couple more weeks, a month at the outside and they would be ready. He wondered how Ms. Anderson and her kids would take to caring for thoroughbreds.

Had they been too adventurous? Had he?

"The call of the mourning dove sounds so wistful this morning," Maggie said quietly.

"Huh." Her voice startled him. He listened and heard the bird cooing. Sounded like any other morning, to him.

Maggie lay back on the grassy incline. "I wonder if she's lost her mate. There's no response. Usually there's a response."

Ed couldn't avoid hearing the sadness in her voice. But they were only birds. "Maybe," he said, shrugging noncommittally. Light laughter greeted his ears.

Maggie sat up abruptly, watching him closely. "You think I'm crazy, don't you?"

Ignoring her question, he tried to keep his features passive. He might think her crazy, but he didn't want her knowing that.

"Do horses have feelings?"

"Of course they do."

"Well then, why not birds?"

"Don't know. Hadn't thought about it, I guess."

"Well, I have, and I'm certain they have feelings. Losing a mate is hard for any creature."

"You still miss your husband," Ed said, not quite believing he wanted to further this particular conversation. He knew the woman had her troubles. But then so did he, and it was best if they dealt with their own, privately.

Maggie tipped her head to the side as if considering his statement. "Of course I miss Mason. We loved each other very much. I see him in my children, particularly Johnny." She paused.

"I don't know," she added wistfully, "I expect there'll always be a hole in my heart somewhere. It'll get smaller—it already has, but there will always be a hole."

"Expect you're right about that."

"What would it say about what Mason and I shared if I just completely forgot him? That wouldn't be right."

"No, it wouldn't."

"So, how was your meeting last night?" Maggie

asked softly.

"Fine," Ed grunted. He stood and pulled on his gloves, eyeing what yet needed to be done to finish the fencing.

"I dunno, Maggie. He seems so, so masculine," Flo Zimmerman stuttered. "How can you work side by side so much of the time and not be attracted to him. He might not be the best catch..."

"Humph. Ed Harrington is a means toward an end. That's it. No romantic interest on my part, or his. No way." Maggie heard her voice and confidence waver a trifle. It must be the lemonade.

"I'm not so sure—Dolly and Kenny were singing *Islands in the Stream* when I left the church for your place. It must be a sign of something."

Maggie snickered. "Girl, you're going to drive me batty with all that stuff."

Maggie leaned back in her chair and closed her eyes. It was Sunday afternoon and she had invited Flo home for dinner after church and had also asked Harrington to join them if he liked. Putting shy Flo and cryptic Ed at the same dinner table had not made for scintillating conversation, but at least it should have satisfied her friend's curiosity about the new hired hand. Flo had been so afraid Maggie was putting herself and her family at risk by hiring an unknown man. Ed had gone back to his loft as soon as dessert was finished, leaving the women to talk about whatever they wanted.

"He's awfully quiet, but he does seem like a nice enough man," Flo said, sipping coffee, gazing from the porch to the barn. "And the kids seem to be taking to him nicely."

Opening her eyes, Maggie gazed at her friend, whose long fingers were playing idly with strands of dark hair escaping her tight bun. Maggie thought the gangly woman actually looked like she'd been smitten by Harrington. "If you think he's nice enough, maybe you ought to try and get him to ask you out." Maggie winced at her own words.

"Oh, my, I wouldn't think of doing that," squeaked Flo. "He's...he's your hired man."

Tucking a leg under her torso, Maggie nodded. "Yeah, he is that. A hired man. Not a hired lover or anything like that."

She sat back again and closed her eyes. It seemed so important to keep the man in his place, yet it was dangerous to even have him around. She was a woman. He was a man. He could definitely be a problem; she could feel it in her bones.

"Do you think we're going to get any rain soon?"

Maggie smiled at Flo's attempt to find a safer topic for discussion. "I sure hope so. We need to get some pretty soon or there'll be trouble for everyone in Beaverhill."

"I remember the last bad drought." Flo stretched her long legs out in front of her, crossing them at the ankles. "Sarah kept me on, but had to lay off two of the other girls. And the tips dried up just like the ground."

"Maybe it will rain soon." Rocking back and forth, Maggie prayed that the rain gods were kind this summer. They had to be. They just had to be. What would she do if she couldn't get a decent cash crop?

- o -

Two weeks later, Ed stood beside his boss at the end of the barn driveway overlooking the paddocks. Removing his work gloves, he said, "Nothing fancy, but it will be functional and safe."

With reconstructed stalls and paddocks, the barn and corrals could handle a combination of eight racing age horses, along with four broodmares and ten yearlings and weanlings. Not bad. And it hadn't cost an arm and a leg either. It had required a lot of hard work, but now they were ready for some horses. At last.

"It looks great," Maggie chirped, grinning broadly. "It'll be something to see these paddocks filled with horses."

"As I've said before," Ed said, trying not to share his own excitement, "I think you should do that in stages. Pick up a half dozen racing stock now. Maybe a couple yearlings. In the fall, we might want to see about buying three or four broodmares who are already in foal. That's a good, efficient way to get started. Afraid you can't expect much return on your investment this year."

He headed into the barn. Maggie followed. Stopping in the tack room, Ed reached for an old

English saddle and began checking its leathers for wear. He'd been collecting and repairing tack since the day he started working for Maggie.

Maggie stood in the doorway and watched. "We need a financial cushion to see us through this year," she said. "All the corn should be planted by the end of the week. Mr. Jacobs and his son will put up the hay. He gets half and I get half. I'll hold some money back in reserve, but the cash crops are critical for our plans. So, are we ready to make that trip to Chicago you've been talking about?"

"Got to either buy, borrow, or rent a six horse trailer first. I've been talking with some contacts up there who raise some decent stock and know of plenty more. We should be able to do all right."

Pulling down hard to test the irons, Ed looked across the saddle at the profile of his boss, who had busied herself sorting through a stack of halters and bridles he'd picked up at a saddle shop the day before. Things had sort of settled out between them. He liked that. No longer was he intimidated by her confidence or frustrated by her sensuality. He could take in her subtle beauty without fear of grabbing her. He liked being near her. She always smelled of lavender.

He appreciated, too, the freshness she brought to the business of horseracing. Things he took for granted were eye opening surprises for Maggie. It had been so long since he'd broken into the business he'd forgotten how stimulating it could be. And they hadn't even worked with a horse yet.

His nostrils narrowed. Maggie Anderson had to have the most expressive, kissable lips he'd ever seen. Quickly, he ducked his head back to the saddle he'd been working on. That line of thinking could only lead to trouble — big trouble.

- o -

Without turning, Maggie could feel the warmth of his appraising gray eyes. Surprisingly, she'd become quite comfortable with the man hovering around. He looked at her like a man looked at a woman, although he tried not to let on that he did. His disguised interest flattered and chilled her. She knew he'd never touch her in a romantic way unless she asked.

Maggie Anderson wasn't about to get involved with a man no matter how appealing he might be, she promised to no one in particular.

She was pleased to see that her hired man was putting some weight on. At least three evenings a week he disappeared to attend his meetings. His commitment to staying off booze, so far, was genuine and strong.

As Maggie reached up to place a yearling halter on a hook, a shadow of a smile formed on her lips. She hadn't expected Ed Harrington to change so. He cleaned up real well, she supposed. But that wasn't her business. When would he start dating again? Certainly, a man as good looking as Harrington must have plenty of women to choose from.

Her right cheek twitched.

"Now what are you upset about?" Harrington asked. "Did you know your cheek vibrates when you're angry?"

"What?" Maggie's hand flew to her cheek. "Oh. You must be mistaken," she stammered. "I was wondering if the kids would be okay with Mrs. Murphy checking in on them, or whether she should take them on home with her. Carolyn will have a fit if I make her stay with the Murphys. Do you really think we'll be gone an entire week?"

Harrington nodded. "It'll take a day to van each way. We'll need time to look over some horses. And depending on what's happening at the track, Cassie may want to take you to the races to claim a horse. Can't do all of that in less than a week."

"Are your friends going to want us to stay with them the whole time?"

Harrington dipped his chin but failed to hide a trace of a smile. "Don't worry about it. You'll like them, and they'll like you. We go back through some tough times together. There was a time they didn't like me much, and I didn't like them either. I was a cocky bastard to be around." He stiffened.

"But Clint and Cassie Travers were among the very few folks who stood by me during the scandal. Clint still has a guy looking into the whole affair from time to time to see if some piece of evidence was overlooked or if anybody is ready to change a story. Odd, how it turned out. I owe them a lot. The least we can do is give them some business."

Maggie thinned her lips but did not speak her mind.

"You'll get some of the best bred horses in the Midwest. I don't just do business with friends. I do business with friends who raise very fine horses."

Ducking away briefly from his intense stare, Maggie replied, "I imagine you do. It's hard to picture you as cocky, though." Embarrassed by her own words, Maggie gulped, but couldn't look away quickly enough to avoid seeing his frown.

"Guess I've been humbled over the years."

"No playing hooky," Maggie said again.

Ed watched her push her scrambled eggs back and forth across her plate.

"Mrs. Murphy will call you at seven to see if you are up, again at eight to be sure you made the bus, and stop by in the evening. You are welcome to stay overnight at her home any time. And on the weekend, Carolyn, you will be with Barbara and her family. And Johnny, you'll go home with David. Do you have all of this down?" Maggie rubbed the tips of her fingers across her temples. "Emergency numbers are on the fridge. The number where we will be staying—Travers—is at the top of the list."

Both children rolled their eyes toward the ceiling.

Ed sat mesmerized by Maggie's incessant chatter. He'd not witnessed this side of her before.

She caught him staring at her. "Oh," she

stuttered. "I guess we've been over this a few times already. Was I rattling on?" She reached over to ruffle her son's hair. "Why didn't you stop me?"

"A tornado couldn't stop you when you get nervous and fidgety, Mom," Carolyn chastised.

"Yeah," Johnny teased, "sometimes you talk so fast my ears can't keep up with you."

Ed laughed aloud. It was a comfortable family. Each individual had foibles, but was remarkably tolerated by the others. Had it always been that way, or did part of the camaraderie come because of having to deal with the death of a husband and father?

"Well, I hope you've had some fun over of my concern," Maggie protested easily. "It's just that I've not been away this long since..." Her eyes widened and became misty. "I know, Carolyn, you're a teenager. And neither one of you wants a babysitter. I wish I could take you with us. But you can't miss that much school this close to the end of the school year."

"Mom, we'll be okay," Carolyn insisted. "We'll have to send Mrs. Murphy home to get rid of her. And you know Hank isn't going to come and go without checking in on us. He's almost family."

"You're right, dear. I forgot to mention I've instructed Hank whenever he is planting or mowing to take a moment and see how you're doing. Okay," she said with a lopsided grin. "No more lecturing. You know I love you. You're just growing up too fast. I'll try not to worry again until we're driving out of the driveway."

Ed sat back and relaxed as tension dissipated around the table.

"Can't wait till you get back," Johnny yelped. "I still can hardly believe it. Racehorses!"

Maggie looked hurt. "You sound more eager to see the horses than me and Ed." She smiled at her son. "But it will be great fun to see them in our paddocks."

"Don't think anyone knows how much work these animals are going to require," Ed grumbled, draining his cup of coffee. "There will be plenty of jobs for everyone."

"Fantastic!" Johnny shouted.

Carolyn remained quiet.

CHAPTER FOUR

"Well, now that the guys are in the city, Eddie's down for his nap and Lester and Sammy won't get home for another three hours, we have the place to ourselves," Cassie Travers said, smiling broadly at Maggie, who sat at the kitchen table finishing her lunch coffee. "What would you like to do?

"Oh, you've been so helpful already," Maggie said, looking over at the redhead putting leftovers away. "It's just nice being here. I've been away from my kids for as much as two weeks, but that's when they go to camp. I've never gone off and left them like this. That's different."

Cassie nodding knowingly. "Yeah, it is." She filled a cup with black coffee and sat down across from Maggie. "Sometimes I'll travel with Clint. And you know what? The kids seem to survive quite well. I suspect yours are doing fine, too."

"Yes, I'm sure they are. Carolyn is quite capable and Mrs. Murphy will likely be a nuisance checking on them. And of course Hank — he works part-time for me planting and harvesting — he'll always find a reason to stop and ask how things are going. No, I'm sure they're doing fine…I'm less certain about me."

Maggie frowned. Where had those words come from? She'd liked Cassie instantly, but she didn't need to bare her soul, either. The Travers kitchen did remind her of home, though — light, airy, filled with smells of cooking, a good gathering place for family.

"I can see that we need to keep you busy," Cassie said. "Tomorrow we'll go to the track. There are a couple claiming possibilities, one in race three and another in race five. Has Ed explained claiming races to you?"

Maggie nodded. "That's where an owner puts his horse in a race for a price tag. If someone else wants to buy or claim the horse they put their money in some kind of box just before the race. And the horse is hers."

Laughing, Cassie said, "That's about it, except there might be several other owners who want the horse. I've attempted many claims that I never got because I didn't win the roll of the dice to decide who would actually get the horse."

"Oh. There's so much to learn."

"You're picking up on things quickly, that's clear. And you have a natural nose for horses. That was evident yesterday when we drove over to Broken Wheel Stable to evaluate their yearlings. And from what I can tell, you have a realistic head on your shoulders. I'm sure Ed has told you that in this business it's okay, even necessary, to dream, but you still have to be prepared to make hardheaded decisions about horses and about people."

Maggie winced. "Ed has tried to make us all understand that we shouldn't get too attached to any one animal. Not all horses are meant to be racehorses, he says. If you just want to own a horse, don't bother to buy a racehorse."

Chuckling, Cassie agreed. "That sounds like Ed, all right." Sobering, she continued, "The best decision you made regarding your horse business was hiring Ed Harrington. You can't find a sharper mind or a harder worker. He has a touch with horses that is rare, particularly for a man."

Maggie paused, chewed on her lower lip, and listened to the ticking of the kitchen clock. "Tell me about him."

"Ah." Cassie laughed softly. "I believe there's more behind that question than horses."

Maggie felt herself blush, but she remained silent.

"Okay...Ed Harrington." Rubbing her hands vigorously, Cassie obviously warmed to the topic of discussion. "When I first met him, I thought he was an arrogant bastard who knew more about horses than he had a right to know. He was attracted to me, I guess, but I wasn't interested in him. The word on shedrow was that Harrington not only was a hard worker, he also drank hard and went through women like they were disposable containers."

"Oh."

"I'm not saying he's like that now." Cassie shrugged. "You said you wanted to know, and I started at the beginning.

Maggie nodded.

"It wasn't long after Clint and I were married that Ed seemed to go through some big changes. I think there were some health problems. Anyway, he cut way back on his drinking. And he found a steady woman."

Maggie brushed her fingers across her twitching cheek.

"At the same time, his career was skyrocketing," Cassie added. "Within a year or two there was no question that he would be working with Triple Crown candidate horses."

Cassie rose to pour more coffee. Returning to her seat, she shuddered slightly before continuing with her story.

"I always respected Ed as a horseman, but it was only through personal crisis that I came to respect him as a man. There is no other way to put it, Maggie — Ed saved my life, as well as that of our baby."

Involuntarily, Maggie gasped and her stomach clenched.

"I was six weeks early with Eddie. No one expected that. Clint was away on a trip. The labor started when I was at the track. There was bleeding." Cassie sighed. "Ed rushed me to the hospital and stayed with me throughout the whole ordeal. The doctor said if we had been another hour later we would most certainly have lost the baby and maybe, possibly even me."

"I didn't...know," Maggie murmured, forcing back tears.

"Of course you didn't. It would be the last thing Ed Harrington would want to talk about. That might hurt his image as some kind of tough guy."

Thoughtfully, Maggie ran an index finger around the rim of her coffee cup. Seldom would the man allow a glimpse of his heart, yet she'd known all along that it was a good heart.

"We named our son after Ed," Cassie continued, "and he is the boy's godfather."

"Really!"

"Uh huh—I'm not sure how keen he is about that, but he agreed. Until he really got deep into alcohol, he remembered birthdays and special holidays."

Those words warmed Maggie's insides. "Why did he run? From the scandal. He had friends who stood by him. He had you and Clint."

Shrugging, Cassie drummed her fingers on the table. "You'll have to ask him. I can only guess. Fear of failure. Fear of rejection. Fear of himself. Who knows? We tried to help him. But once he got heavily involved with booze, he wouldn't let us help. That was difficult for everybody."

Maggie watched Cassie search for words, for an answer to a question she'd obviously struggled with many times before.

"I imagine shame drove him away," Cassie said at last. "Sadly, shame for something he didn't even do."

"You're convinced of that," Maggie probed cautiously.

"Absolutely! He and I have had our differences, but Ed Harrington would no more throw a race than I would."

"And then he just disappeared."

"After awhile, he did. He couldn't get work around here. And he wouldn't accept a job from us. The man has too much pride for his own damn good. Anyway, Clint stayed aware of his whereabouts through a private investigator. We'd had no direct word from him for months—not until you came along." Cassie's eyes sparkled as if she was about to disclose a secret. "You're good for him, you know."

Again, Maggie felt her cheeks warm. "I just gave him a job."

"Right. You gave him a hell of a lot more than that. Respect. Even some hope. I don't know how you did it, but somehow you penetrated that alcohol haze in a way no one else had. You must have found him at the right moment. Or maybe he saw something in you that was worth changing for. He likely doesn't even know."

"He probably saw brazen stupidity," Maggie confessed. "I was pretty hard on him when we first met."

"No doubt that's what was needed. And maybe he was tired of running. I suspect you scare the hell out of him."

"Me?" Maggie frowned.

"When I was a practicing social worker, I had plenty of opportunity to work with alcoholics. I imagine Ed's afraid of the bottle and its potential power over him. You likely scare him in less clear ways. He owes you; he knows that. Yet he's probably afraid he won't live up to your expectations. And mostly he's afraid of himself.

Can he trust himself to make the right decisions? What will he do in the future when things don't go well? Will he run? Or will he stick?"

Maggie nodded. Those questions lay at the back of her mind whenever she worried about Ed Harrington and her future. Those questions underscored her vulnerability.

Would he stick when — not if — things blew up around them? They wouldn't always agree on how best to establish or manage the stables. He would advise, but she had to make the final choices. How would he handle her overruling him?

"What about the woman?" Maggie inquired hesitantly. Cassie's return stare was blank. "The steady woman you talked about earlier."

"Oh, her. She dumped him as soon as the scandal hit. I don't think Ed's ever had a family. He's comfortable with you and you with him." Cassie paused. With a provocative look she added, "And he is handsome in a rough sort of way, isn't he?"

Maggie's eyes rounded. "I wouldn't know about that."

"No matter," breezed Cassie, getting up to clear away their empty cups, "whatever woman is able to lasso Ed Harrington someday will be a damn lucky woman."

"Thanks," Maggie mumbled. Suddenly, she couldn't find a place to put her hands.

Cassie shot her an inquisitive look.

"For telling me about Ed. I've got a lot riding on

him."

"Can we use it?" Maggie inquired, watching Harrington examine the six horse trailer as if it might be booby trapped. Clint Travers had referred them to Tom Basswood, the son of a trainer who had recently died. The son had no use for the racehorse business and was dispersing all his father's horses and equipment.

"Can't find any sharp edges," Harrington grunted. "It should do. Old man Basswood always took good care of his horses. And the price is right."

Harrington stepped out of the trailer and nodded at Maggie. She turned to the waiting Tom Basswood and said, "We'll take it."

The middle aged man gave her a quick smile. "That's great. Don't know why a pretty thing like you would want to get into the horse business, but as long as you do, I'm more than willing to take your money. Dad had more horses than he knew what to do with."

Tom Basswood folded his arms across his massive stomach. "As long as you're here and own a horse trailer, why don't you look at our horses? I can guarantee you won't find better prices for what you're getting."

Maggie glanced at Harrington.

"Why not?" he muttered. "Doesn't cost anything to look."

As the three of them walked toward the paddocks west of the sprawling barn, Maggie asked, "So why are you so determined to get out of the horse business, Mr. Basswood?"

The man grunted. "It was my dad's dream, never mine. I had to bust my ass as a kid grooming his horses, treating them for colic, getting my teeth jarred loose whenever I was thrown. Long hours. No time for family. Owners treat you like you're cheating them. You have to have a lot of money to make money. Traveling from track to track." He stopped and looked at Maggie. "Have I left anything out?"

Maggie shook her head. He was a distasteful man. Thankfully, for the sake of the horses, the overweight man didn't try to ride them. But some of what he said had a familiar ring to it. Templeton had warned her about the long hours, the pressures on family, and the fact that many stables netted little profit.

She caught Harrington staring at her with his quizzical look. Was he wondering if she would have the courage for the long haul?

As they continued walking toward the paddock, Maggie remembered Cassie's praise for Harrington. A top notch trainer ready to move to the big time by taking on Triple Crown contenders.

Maggie shivered. If Harrington was cleared of wrongdoing, which Cassie fully expected, how long would he stay in Iowa helping a widow get started in a business where failures outnumbered successes? Wouldn't he dash back to Chicago and pick up where he left off? Any sensible person would do that.

And where would that leave Anderson Stables? Maggie shook her head. She didn't want to think about it.

They came to a stop before a large paddock. Six horses were eating hay from a large round bale sitting in the center of the area. Maggie thought none of the horses seemed very alert. One had an obvious sway back. She was curious what Harrington would have to say about them.

"Each of these was competitive at Hawthorne and Arlington. The two bays on the left were running in allowance races. The others are claimers." Basswood scratched his chin. "I think they were high end claimers, but I'd have to check to be sure. Dad could tell you every race a horse ever entered. In any case, I'm sure you'll find them quite competitive in Iowa."

The man's disdain for racing, for her, and for Iowa was becoming too much. Maggie felt her cheek twitch. She opened her mouth to speak.

"We'll look them over," Ed said, winking at Maggie. "Maggie's got quite an eye for horseflesh. If they're what we want we'll get back to you. Why don't you give us some time?"

"Sure, no problem. You know more about horses than I do," Basswood grumbled. "I just want them out of my life."

Maggie sighed. She knew Harrington had jumped in so she wouldn't chop off Basswood's head. She watched Harrington's eyes narrow as he assessed the horses from a distance.

"Is there anything there that we want?" Maggie asked.

Grinning at her, Harrington replied, "Do you think so?"

"Don't know. Just because I don't like the seller doesn't mean he doesn't have some good horses. But I don't see them. One of the bays is more sway backed than my davenport. The other one has a right front knee that's at least three times its normal size. As for the others, I'd be shocked if they're high priced claimers."

"Very nice," drawled Harrington. "You're a quick learner. I don't see anything here that will be competitive, in Iowa or any place else. These have to be the dregs that Basswood's son couldn't palm off. Let's take the trailer and be happy."

As they pulled out of Basswood's driveway, Maggie said, "Trailer seems to be pulling okay."

Harrington nodded. "This trailer will last for many years. No need to buy a new one if you can get something like this used. I'm just as happy I couldn't find anything we liked around Des Moines—plus, we didn't have to pay for extra gas to pull it all the way up here."

Maggie couldn't help but wonder if the trailer would outlast Harrington. The corner of her mouth turned up. She had enough worries. Why did she want to worry about him? He'd stay as long as he wanted, and that would be that. "So do you really think we'll be competitive by later this summer?"

"If we continue to play our cards right. We've seen some good horses these last couple days. That little chestnut you bought yesterday should be competitive right away. And I know Cassie has a bead on a couple claimers. Still have to check out Clint's broodmares." Once he got the trailer on the main road, Harrington glanced over at Maggie. "You having doubts?"

Maggie thinned her lips and sighed deeply. "This is huge. I'm not sure I realized just how huge until coming to Chicago. Clint and Cassie are talking about some horses that are way too pricey for my bank account. And then that Basswood fellow. He sure doesn't like horseracing."

"Doubt that guy has worked hard a day in the last three decades. So do you want out? It's not too late."

Leaning back on the seat, Maggie looked over at Harrington. His features were firmly set and his stare was fixed on the road. He had as much riding on her decision as she did. She admired his guts. It would have been so easy for him to stay with the comfort of the bottle. Instead, he straightened himself out and came to her.

And he had heart. She'd heard it when he talked of horses. And Cassie had confirmed it with the story of little Eddie's birth. If she had to trust someone to help her save her farm, she could do a lot worse than trusting a man like Ed Harrington.

"No, I'm not going to change my mind," she said. Her voice was an octave lower than normal. She sounded like a stranger to herself.

"Good. I figured you'd stay the course." He glanced quickly at her and grinned lazily. "It's going to be a fairly bouncy course, you know."

"I know, but I don't want to back out. A Magee always finishes what she starts."

Harrington nodded and smiled.

Maggie leaned her head back on the seat and let her eyelids fall close. Her nose wrinkled. She smiled. She was becoming accustomed to his scent. Maybe too accustomed. What had Cassie said? Any woman who lassoed Ed Harrington would be a lucky woman. Well, she'd lassoed him. Not in that way. But she still counted herself lucky.

Her nipples tightened and her eyelids flew open. She stared at Harrington, who paid no attention to her. Again, Maggie shuttered her eyes. No. She was his boss. *You're good for him and he's good for you.* Those were Cassie's words. How good? Maggie drifted off to sleep before she could form a response.

- o -

"So do you think your new boss has the guts to stick with racing?" Clint asked, placing two leaves of hay in a hay net. A bay mare stepped forward from the back of the stall to sample this new food offering.

Ed chuckled. "Oh, she's got the guts all right. I don't know if she'll have the sense to duck."

As the two men walked from stall to stall,

71

several broodmares greeted them. Ed's attention was caught by a regal black head with luminous dark eyes poking out over the end stall door. The mare arched her neck and raised her head high. Her haughtiness drew a breath from Ed as he appraised the animal. He knew he was looking at something special. Real special. Good legs. Deep chest. Strong lines. And a pride bespeaking champions. "Well," he muttered, "you're a classy thing aren't you? Bet all the guys think you're as sexy as sin."

The mare rapidly raised and lowered her head as if in agreement.

This one could be the foundation mare they were looking for. "I'll want to know more about this one come fall," he said noncommittally.

"Not sure Midnight Dancer will still be here by then," countered Travers, a sly frown working across his face.

"Okay, hotshot horse trader," Ed retorted, shooting Clint a knowing look. The man was in the business of selling horses; he couldn't just hold onto a horse until the time was right for a potential buyer, even for a friend. "So tell me about her."

Grabbing the halter hanging on the box stall door latch, Clint began to lay out the mare's racing history. "We didn't start her as a two year old. Wanted her to mature more before getting out on the track. Between her three year old and five year old seasons she ran twenty-eight races and was in the money all but four. She has twelve allowance and stakes wins, including one Grade Two victory. We matched her with a sire out of Seattle Slew's lineage."

Ed whistled softly.

"Why not take her out to a paddock so you can see her in action?" Clint suggested, moving to halter the eager animal.

A few minutes later, the mare was prancing as if she was leading a parade.

"Yeah, she's all you said she would be." Ed folded his arms, knowing that he could not let this one get away. She was a thousand pounds of thoroughbred promise. One couldn't expect to find much better, unless there was an unlimited bankroll. "So, what will it take to hold the mare until we make a final decision in October?"

Clint scratched his chin thoughtfully. "Considering feed, care and risk — five thousand, ten percent, would guarantee that no one comes along and buys her out from under you."

"And if we take her the money goes toward the purchase price?"

"Of course."

"And if we decide not to buy, you pocket the money?"

"Naturally." Clint folded his arms and smiled broadly.

Ed nodded. "I'll talk to Maggie about it, but expect you've got a deal." Turing to the ebony mare, he added, "You, young woman, take care of yourself and that baby you're carrying. That's all you have to do. No racing. No showing off. Just take care not to hurt yourself or the little one."

As they retraced their steps back to the barn, Ed said, "Appreciate all you're doing to help us find some good horses."

"That's what I do for a living." Clint shuddered. "Besides, I owe you a few."

"Don't even go there again!" Ed's voice rose. "If I hadn't been there, someone else would have taken Cass to the hospital. Let's forget it, okay?"

Clint shrugged and looked away.

"I think it will be pretty easy to decide on buying your Midnight Dancer," Ed said, turning the conversation back to a subject he preferred. "Maggie will be thrilled with the mare."

"You sound quite committed to Anderson Stables," Clint observed, turning off the lights before leaving the stable area.

"Why shouldn't I be? That's how I get paid."

"Uh huh. You have a damn sexy looking boss, too."

"So."

"No need to get huffy about it. It's just that I expect you're rather vulnerable at this point. And Maggie has done a lot to help you turn some personal things around. Just don't want you feeling overly obligated to her, that's all."

"Travers, you have always been in my face about something," Ed snapped, picking up their pace heading toward the house. "No, I take that back, partially. You've been a good friend these last few years and that's appreciated, but no advice is needed in this corner about women.

Maybe I've drunk a hell of a lot of booze, but I'm not blind. It's no revelation to me that she's damn attractive. It would be better if she were ugly, but she's not. In any case, I simply work for Maggie Anderson. That's all there is to it. That's all there ever will be."

"Okay, Ed," Clint replied, placing his arm around Ed's shoulder and squeezing him roughly. "No doubt you're quite capable of handling the woman. I just thought you wouldn't want to get too tied down in Des Moines, Iowa. I'm still confident that we can beat this betting scandal rap. And when we do, you can come back and pick up where you left off. There'll be plenty of owners who'll jump through hoops to be first in line to get their horses in your stable."

"I'm not so sure about that," Ed responded, shrugging off the compliment. "Hope there'll be a chance for you to prove me wrong, though. In the meantime, I'm going to help Maggie build the best damn racing stable she can afford."

CHAPTER FIVE

Warm June sunlight spilled through window panes into the upstairs guest room at the Travers' McHenry home. Lazily, Maggie awoke, stretching, basking in her surroundings. Tiny rainbows danced on the nearby wall as light played through prisms hanging in the window.

Light blue lace curtains billowed before the morning breeze, casting a spell of fantasy and romance. The antique four poster bed on which she lay dated back to the colonial period and had been crafted in Ireland. And the lush feather pillows augmented a luxurious setting that Maggie had not anticipated. Cassie Travers had a lot of taste.

Maggie mumbled incoherently. She needed to get up and start the day but didn't want to leave her delicious surroundings. Sinking back into the fluffy pillows, she succumbed to their sensuous comfort.

She'd liked her plucky auburn-haired hostess right off. Cassie managed with aplomb being a wife, mother and horse trainer. Yet, the woman seemed very true to her own core. Maggie envied her sense of being okay with herself. Someday. Maybe someday.

Not once had Cassie tried to dissuade her from the goal of forming a racing stable. Her hostess, as well as her husband, had been very helpful in identifying horses in the area that might fit into Maggie's plans.

Clint had agreed to keep Maggie's needs in mind when he went to the summer Keeneland Sales in July. He and Cassie concurred with Harrington that to build for the long run, Anderson Stables would want to purchase mares in foal later in the fall.

Clutching a pillow tight to her chest, Maggie reflected on the news Cassie had shared about Harrington's background. Maggie sighed softly. She'd chosen well.

Cassie had said he'd once had a reputation as a fairly heavy drinker and a lady's man. Maggie hadn't seen evidence of either since he'd shown up on her porch that Sunday afternoon in a dusty feed mill cap ready for work. She grinned.

He'd better not try to bring any floozy to her haymow loft. Maggie jutted her chin forward. She'd send him packing so quick he wouldn't know what hit him. There were the children to protect.

"Right," Maggie groused, sensing old stirrings in her loins. Rolling over, squeezing a pillow tightly between her thighs, she wondered how long it had been. She missed the feel of a man holding her, caressing her neck, grazing her nipples, kissing her lips. She missed running her fingers lightly across a man's back, feeling straining muscles, knowing she was the reason for the hardness pressing against her hip.

There were these haunting moments when she missed Mason so terribly. He would never again touch her in those intimate ways. There hadn't been desire or time for men since his death. She hadn't looked at another man in that way.

Not until Ed Harrington. He'd been in her dreams more than she wanted to confess.

What would he be like in bed?

She'd only made love to one man. Maggie chewed on her lower lip. Would it be the same with her hired man? Different? Could it be even better?

Absently, she brushed her fingers over her aching breasts through the thin, worn nightgown. She'd been a teenager when she first made love with Mason. Now she was a mature woman...So what was she doing thinking and behaving like a teenager?

Slipping the sleepwear down her torso, Maggie pulled gently on first one rising nipple and then the other.

"Oh my," she moaned. *It's okay. It's okay to feel, to be aroused, to want.*

Maggie's head lolled back and forth, swaying with the erotic electric charges radiating from her breasts upward to her nape and downward through her inner thighs to her toes.

A litany reverberated from one tiny brain cell to another: *It's okay to seek satisfaction.*

As if of the same mind, her fingers moved leisurely over her belly, first sketching invisible circles clockwise and then counterclockwise around her navel. In that balance of concentric movement, awareness of time was lost. No reality existed beyond those bubbling internal sensations straining for more tactile encouragement, demanding release.

Descending lower, her hand sought the warmth of her loins. Her palm paused, resting as if waiting further instructions.

Maggie's breath came haphazardly. Cupping her mound, she pressed tentatively inward. Her lower torso jerked upward. A finger slowly penetrated. Without further hesitation, her thumb skimmed her clit. A second finger slid easily into her wetness.

Maggie thrust urgently against the slickness. A tiny red-orange ball pulsed somewhere within. It grew, spreading in ever larger circles. Perspiration beaded across her upper lip. Her breath stopped. The ball exploded, dissolving muscles and bones into nothingness.

Curling into a fetal position, trapping her fingers deep within, Maggie screamed into a pillow.

Minutes later, still quaking, she reclaimed her fingers. How long had it been since giving herself the chance to feel that exquisite touch? Months. Nearly a year. This was only the third time since Mason's death.

Keeping remnants of shame at bay, Maggie reveled in the warm toasty afterglow. How she had missed that simple, elemental act. By denying herself all these months of such exquisite gratification, had she been punishing herself, trying to atone for her husband's death? This gift of life, she decided firmly, should not be sacrificed to the past.

What would it be like to make love to a man again? A real man. She hugged herself. What would it be like making love to him?

"Did you sleep well?" Harrington inquired, when Maggie pulled out a chair at the breakfast table.

"Very. I'm afraid I overslept. Don't know how long it's been since that happened." Maggie focused on breakfast options, hoping no one could fathom what she had been doing not so long before.

A squabble erupted between Sammy and Lester over the last warm pancake, diverting everyone's attention from Maggie's flushing cheeks. And Eddie began screaming so as not to be left out.

Thankful for the diversion, Maggie smiled at the children's mom scolding the older ones and rescuing the cup that had dropped to the floor. Clint reached for the Eddie, picked him up and soothed him. While a single parent could manage such escapades quite well, these were moments, Maggie acknowledged, when another pair of hands could be decisive.

Once the commotion was settled and Cassie plunked down another round of hot pancakes, the woman opted for peace and quiet. "Lester, Sammy, I've had about enough closeness for this early in the morning. Both of you are done. I want you to take your dishes to the sink and then go out and do your chores." Softening her stern look, she said, "Love you, but be gone."

"Okay, Cass," replied the twelve-year-old boy, rising from his chair.

His younger sister, Sammy, followed on the run and then dashed back to give Cassie a hug. "Sorry, Mommy. Didn't mean to get you mad."

"It's okay. I'm not mad. Just a little grumpy. Eddie was up most of the night with an earache. Run along now," she whispered, kissing the girl's forehead.

After the screen door clattered shut, Clint said, "Cass and I have been talking about your plans, Maggie. We'd like to make a suggestion or two, if you don't mind."

Maggie loved the drawl of the copper skinned man with hair as dark as night. She met his eyes easily. "Not at all. What do you have in mind?"

"Well, it's a lot to expect of anyone to learn the ins and outs of training race horses all at once. People work for years as apprentices to learn what you need to know." Glancing at his wife, he continued, "We thought you might want to leave the horses that are still racing with us so Cass can continue their training and entering them in races on the Chicago circuit. When they're ready for a couple months rest to freshen up, we can ship them down to you."

"That way," Cassie said, breaking in, "Ed can teach you how to prepare some of the younger horses for racing without the pressure of immediately tackling track management."

Whoa, Maggie wanted to shout. Things were moving too quickly all of a sudden. Dollar signs nagged at her brain. She couldn't afford racing on the Chicago circuit. Not in the beginning. But neither did she want to offend her new friends.

Biting her lower lip, she mumbled, "I don't know." Instinctively, she looked to Harrington for his advice.

Harrington raised an eyebrow. "It's probably a good idea, Maggie. You'll need time to develop along with the horses. We could work with two or three yearlings and two-year-olds and with those on R and R from the track. This way we might not even have to race at Prairie Meadows until the fall or even the next season."

"You'll want to watch your horses race," Cassie said, turning to adjust Eddie in his highchair. "I'll bet you could catch most of the races via satellite at Prairie Meadows. We'll keep our eye on the stakes races they'll be offering down there. It may pay to ship a horse or two, and that would give you more hands on experience at the track. And, of course, you could always come up here and work with me for however long you can get away. There is no better substitute for learning the ways of the backside than being there."

Maggie knew that had to be true. And she also knew that everyone at the table was reminding her that Harrington could not teach her how things were done at the track while sitting on a bale of hay in the barn. He might never be able to show her how to run a racing operation at the track.

That information wasn't new. So why had she turned so cold just now? Was she already too dependent on him?

"But it must be awfully expensive racing up here," Maggie protested, stoking her throat with rigid fingers.

Both Clint and Cassie smiled. "We will only charge you our costs," Cassie said. "There will be no trainer fees."

"What! Why would you do that? I'm no charity case," Maggie fumed.

"Now don't get stubborn on us," Cassie cooed. "We can afford to help out in this way. And we want too."

"But why would you? You hardly know me."

"There are lots of reasons," Clint answered soberly. "We've struggled before, like you. It's good to see a woman with grit and determination doing what she can to save a piece of her heritage for her family. Reminds me of another woman I know fairly well." He flashed a smile at his wife.

"And," he added, nodding in Harrington's direction, "it's good to see someone give another human being a chance to prove himself. It's simply the right thing to do. Don't turn us down, Maggie Anderson. You don't want to deal with my wife's Irish temper."

Maggie gave him a weak smile and reached to cover her twitching cheek.

"It's good business, Maggie," Harrington said softly. "For them, as well as for you. If you succeed, and I fully expect that you will, you'll be back to buy more horses. If you get in over your head, you'll risk losing the farm. And these folks will have one less buyer."

She didn't know if his logic was correct, but Maggie knew when she was surrounded. As gracefully as possible, she lifted her orange juice glass and declared, "To the Anderson Racing Stable based in Chicago." She paused, catching her breath and soaking up the warmth and hope of the three beaming faces regarding her intently. "I hope you know what you're doing. I'm not at all certain what I've gotten myself into, but it's too late to turn back now."

"That's my girl," Harrington murmured.

Clint and Cassie swallowed, busying themselves by soaking up syrup with stray pieces of pancake and leaving Maggie to stare questioningly at Harrington, who seemed completely unaware that he'd vocalized what was so evidently on his mind.

"They're nearly ready to load," Cassie said, looking toward the Arlington Park starting gate. "We just want the filly to run a clean race without injury."

Maggie nodded, listening intently. It wasn't easy to do. There were so many distractions. The excitement of the crowd thrilled her. Everything was so colorful, from the jockey silks to the characters analyzing racing forms or peering through binoculars at the horses warming up.

It didn't matter to Maggie that she knew nothing about handicapping. She was here to learn about the business of horse racing. And Cassie Travers was a very astute instructor.

Maggie's temples throbbed with anticipation and apprehension. As they stood by the rail at the finish line, she knew they were in the process of buying a horse. There was no seller present; there would be no handshake between buyer and seller. Yet she was definitely buying a race horse.

Twenty-five thousand dollars of her money lay in a box in the stewards' office which would go to the owner of horse number three, Jill's Pride, in the upcoming race. It was called claiming. The owner of the horse had entered the filly in a twenty-five thousand dollar claiming race, essentially saying if someone wanted to buy the horse for that price, he was willing to sell.

Cassie thought the animal would make a good claim since she believed the current trainer had dropped Jill's Pride out of the allowance ranks to pick up a relatively cheap win. The bettors thought so too—the filly was the current betting favorite. Yet there was also the possibility that something was physically wrong with the horse.

Crossing her fingers and toes, Maggie thought time stood still while the horses entered the starting gate. She knew unless there was a competing claim, she'd own Jill's Pride when she crossed the finish line. win or lose, or even if the horse dropped dead out of the starting gate. She didn't want to think about that.

Although the winning time for the sprint would only take about a minute and twelve seconds, for Maggie it might as well have been an hour and twelve minutes. Mercifully, the race came to an end with Jill's Pride finishing a respectable second.

Maggie followed Cassie to the track where she placed her lead rope on the horse and led her toward the barn area.

"She won't do her best until she can race around two turns, I know it," Cassie said. Jill's Pride pranced lively beside her new owner and trainer, as if she hadn't even been in a race.

"I think you're going to like this one," Cassie said, running her hand down the horse's shoulder. "She's got the spirit."

Maggie nodded, hoping she would soon be able to identify horses that had *the spirit*. She hugged herself, trying to comprehend fully the magnitude of the day, of the Chicago trip. There was no more questioning it—she was up to her ears in thoroughbred horseracing.

If she had been seeking some adventure in her life, which she admitted she had been, then she had found it at the track. Horseracing was filled with emotion, from bitter disappointment to breathtaking elation.

The pulse of the crowd stimulated her senses. The horses strutted around as if they knew they were among the most powerful athletes on the face of the earth. And those small people, the jockeys, moved about with tremendous pride. Cassie had told her that jockeys had tested out to be more in shape than any other group of athletes. Maggie didn't doubt that.

As they watched Jill's Pride cool out on a hot walker, Cassie explained some of the workings of shedrow. Maggie paid close attention. She couldn't wait until she could have daily hands-on experience. Looking at the filly, she said, "They sure are majestic looking creatures, aren't they?"

"Yeah," Cassie responded, grinning at Maggie. "They can quickly get in your blood, can't they? Though being involved with race horses can be almost as nerve racking as a love affair."

"So, Harrington raced horses here?"

"Sure. Here, and at Hawthorne in the city. When we raced at Hawthorne, his string was usually stabled down the same row but in the next barn. I often thought he was too close for comfort."

"Oh." Her eyes clouded. If it hadn't been for his misfortune, she would never have met him. Nor would she have met the Travers. And she wouldn't be standing here, a neophyte horse owner. And she wouldn't be pulling her hair out trying to decide what to do about Harrington.

Observing Maggie's faraway look, Cassie's features softened. "You've got it bad, don't you?"

"What? What do you mean?" Immediately on guard, Maggie wished her face wasn't so damn expressive.

"Harrington is coming to mean more to you

than a way to learn how to handle race horses."

"I don't know what you mean," Maggie stammered, bending to remove bits of straw from her slacks.

"It's okay. I don't intend to pry. Give yourself time. He's a good man, who, with your help, is overcoming a lot of pain."

Maggie stared at her trembling fingers. Could it really be happening? It had been so long since she'd felt anything for a man, she couldn't trust her memory or her emotions. What would he be like? She listened to her bones, but they were silent.

Oh my God, she groaned to herself. Here she was away from her children, spending money like it had no end, fantasizing about things she had no business imagining.

He's a good man. How good?

With the sun lingering on the western horizon, Maggie leaned against the rail fence contemplating the next day's trip back to Iowa. She was looking forward to going home. And it had been a fruitful trip.

Maggie glanced quickly over at Harrington, standing beside her. What was he was thinking? Was he as satisfied as she was?

The two yearlings and a couple two-year-olds in the next paddock would provide him with the raw materials he needed for teaching her about training race horses. A four year old gelding and a six year old mare needing rest from their racing campaigns grazed in the paddock closest to the Travers barn. The six horses would be loaded into the trailer early the next morning.

What would the kids think of the horses? She'd talked to them daily. They seemed to be enjoying themselves, maybe too much. Wait until they got back with the horses — then the work would really begin for everyone.

Maggie closed her eyes, asking herself for the millionth time whether she'd gone certifiably crazy. What if she failed? She couldn't fail. She wouldn't allow that to happen.

Besides, she had Harrington. Right. He was a top-notch trainer. How long would he stay with her if the Chicago stewards lifted their ban against him? Likely not any longer than it would take him to pack his bags.

"You've done very well, Maggie." Harrington broke into her reverie. "A good dozen horses to start with. I'm looking forward to working with the young ones. They have nice racing pedigrees and are well conformed and should do you proud. We can spruce up the gelding and the mare some before sending them back to the track. I expect the horses Cassie's training for you will do well here on the Chicago circuit. They'll have off days and poor racing luck, but they are good looking contenders.

"And that regal looking black mare grazing to your left, she'll be an excellent foundation broodmare, if you want her."

"Is she for sale? She's gorgeous." As if in

response, the mare lifted her head and broke into a trot, showing off an elegant stride. "She's so fluid. There's something about her that's more striking than any of the other horses we've seen."

"You're developing a good eye," Harrington praised. "That's class you're seeing. That mare is well bred and was an excellent runner. The question is whether her offspring will be. Chances are good. You don't have to make a decision about buying her until the fall. For five thousand, Clint will give you first choice before he sells her to anyone else. That money will be ten percent of the purchase price if you decide to buy. She'd be a super broodmare for you."

Maggie beamed. "For that price, she'd better be. But if her offspring take after their mama, they'll be first rate. Sounds like you think she's worth the initial investment."

Harrington nodded.

Taking a deep breath, Maggie scrunched her toes together. "Let's do it. I believe in destiny." She turned and spoke directly to the mare. "Our paths crossed for a purpose. We'll make a good home for you come fall, young woman." The mare pricked her ears forward, listening intently.

"Ed, do you know her name?"

"Midnight Dancer. She has some Northern Dancer in her bloodlines, and she's as dark as midnight on a clear, moonless night."

"That she is. We'll call her Dancer for short. She's as graceful as the most accomplished ballerina. It's a lovely name, and fitting too."

Harrington shrugged. "Guess so, if you're into names."

"Come on, Ed," she cajoled, "she's a creature of beauty. You can see that. She deserves a name worthy of her heritage and presence."

"Yeah," Harrington agreed. "I just didn't know you were such a romantic. Remember, I've warned you about getting too attached to your horses."

"I know. I know. A horse can die from eating a poisonous plant, from twisting in its stall, from heat exhaustion, seemingly from crossing its eyes." Maggie sighed heavily, clasping her arms across her breasts. "Sometimes I think all of this is too big to get my head around. Four months ago, I hadn't even heard about horse racing. Now, I've read more than I ever imagined was written on the subject. I've gone to a track for the first time. I own nearly a dozen thoroughbreds. We've selected a fantastic foundation broodmare. I've got Cassie and Clint working for me here in Chicago. And I've got you. It's almost too much for an Iowa country girl."

She turned to face him, holding his gaze steadily.

"Damn, woman, you have the most kissable lips I've ever seen," Ed mumbled, keeping his hands stuffed deep in his pockets.

A brief smile tugged at the corners of Maggie's mouth. "Looks may be deceiving. Maybe you should find out for yourself." Standing on tiptoes, she leaned into him, offering her parted lips.

"Oh, shit." Ed's hands leaped out of hiding to pull her against his body. He settled his mouth atop hers.

Behind closed eyelids, Maggie luxuriated in their delicious kiss. She traced his lips and invaded his mouth. She warmed to the sensations of his hands roaming her back and buttocks. Clasping his taut shoulder muscles, she marveled at his firmness. She could feel his arousal pressed against her pelvis. Even her fantasies were not this good. Her brain turned to soup. Her body tingled all over. His tongue played with hers. They shared an intimate game of oral tag.

And then he pulled away abruptly. Ed glared at his hands as if they had betrayed him.

"I'm sorry," he stammered. "I shouldn't have done that. It'll never happen again. You can count on that."

Maggie gasped at the terror in his eyes. She started to sputter a response, "But..."

Ed spun on his heel and moved rapidly toward the barn. Only the horses heard her protest.

Breathless, slouching against the fence for much-needed support, Maggie let the tears flow. What was wrong with her? She had seduced her hired man. He'd wanted her, but had more restraint that she did. Thank God for that.

How far would she have gone? She had kids. She was a widow. She had a farm to save.

But why couldn't she have a life too? Why did she have to deny her emotions—yes, even her sexual needs?

God, she loved the way he'd crushed her to his hard body. She thought she'd been well loved before, but never had she felt so desperately, passionately needed. She had been a source of new life for him, yet he walked away from her without even glancing back.

For how long? Once a bubbling spring burst above ground, it was next to impossible to push it back underground. And she wasn't entirely convinced they should try the impossible.

- o -

Ed was much less ambivalent.

"Son of a bitch. You damn fool," he harangued at himself, pacing back and forth in the barn driveway where he'd found a badly needed retreat. "What do you expect from that woman?" He slammed a fist into an empty stall door. He pulled back in pain. Hell, she should fire him on the spot.

She'd picked him out of the gutter, and he'd nearly taken advantage of her excitement about buying race horses.

He closed his eyes and pinched the top of his nose. A headache threatened to make a bad evening worse.

Maybe she did feel some attraction to him. God knew he couldn't understand why. But if so, it was only how the rescuer felt for the person being rescued. He'd even heard stories of female volunteers falling in love with prison inmates.

94

Maybe she'd been too long without a man. But when it was time for her to get involved romantically, Maggie Anderson needed a real man, not some empty shell she'd collected outside a Des Moines flophouse.

Ed crouched down on his haunches. He tried to catch his breath. Damn, never had a more delicious taste crossed his lips. All her curves seemed to fit so naturally. Even now his heart skipped several beats. She'd tasted like crushed mulberries. It was her tongue that had entered his mouth seeking, exploring. And he'd suckled it like it was the only life force available to him. He could still smell her lavender scent and feel her quivering body. Where would it have ended if he hadn't walked away? *Run away* was more accurate.

He'd have to be extra careful, for both of them. Surely, giving her time to think would help her see the futility of what she'd begun. They had no future together — not romantically.

And to think they had nearly jeopardized their chance of building a racing stable. He had an opportunity to reconstruct a career. She had a shot at saving her precious land. None of that would happen if they succumbed to raging hormones like a couple starry-eyed teenagers.

There would be no more kissing those delightfully kissable lips. He couldn't allow that to happen. He wouldn't.

The next morning, Ed felt like he was caught in

the jaws of a vise, only the vise was the sides of Maggie's truck cab. He drove while Maggie sat far away on the passenger side. That single kiss hung heavily between them.

He didn't know how to repair that fiasco. And he couldn't quite get rid of the enticing taste of mulberries.

He toyed briefly with the idea of quitting, but quickly thought better of that. He desperately needed the job. No way was he going to slip back into a place like the Resting Arms.

He checked the side-view mirrors to see how the trailer was riding. Everything looked fine. Out of the corner of his eye, he spied Maggie glowering straight ahead. So much for everything looking fine.

Now, because of him, she was very committed to the business of horse racing. She had just spent thousands of dollars refurbishing the barn and purchasing some damn good horses. He'd feel like a heel to pull out on her now. But he'd feel even worse if he let himself get involved with her personally. The only thing that could come from that was suffering, and he'd had enough suffering to last two life times.

- o -

Equally stiff, Maggie resolved not to give up on the man beside her; he might not be a flaming romantic, but he was what she wanted. She'd come to that conclusion during a night of tossing and turning. She couldn't quite forget the promise of his body pressed against hers. Moreover, she didn't want to forget.

While she had not set out to find a man, she'd found one. Her bones were humming a lyrical, romantic tune. That kiss had been as hot as a branding iron. She hoped it was as effective on him as it was on her.

As they crossed the Mississippi River at the Quad Cities, Maggie could stand the silence no longer. "I'll bet the kids are getting anxious to see the horses."

Ed jumped as if she'd popped a balloon near his ear. He scowled before responding, "Yeah, Johnny's probably been sitting on the steps watching for an hour or more already."

"He sure is excited. Carolyn is too, but she won't be as transparent about it. She's too grown up for that."

"Yeah, I know. It'll be interesting to see how much they like horses once they see how much work's involved."

"If I know my kids, I think they'll be enthralled. Both of them. Neither one's afraid of work, as long as they know what's expected of them."

"Guess that's my job."

Glancing out the passenger window, Maggie watched the farms come and go. Some were working farms; most were only shadows of what they once had been. "Yeah, that's your job." Turning her gaze toward her driver, she asked, "How good are you at teaching, Ed?"

"Don't know," he responded with a half groan. "I've had to train a lot of grooms and owners over the years. Seemed to work out okay most of the time. Guess we'll find out soon enough. Results might depend some on how good my pupils are."

"Maybe I can find a delicious apple to give my teacher," Maggie teased, warming to the idea of having Ed as her teacher. "Or is that what Eve did for Adam?"

Ed turned several shades of pink and coughed, redirecting his attention to his driving.

Maggie smiled to herself. Once she made up her mind about something, she seldom changed. Her mind was made up about Ed Harrington. She could bide her time; she might even try ignoring him for awhile to see what he'd do. But no matter what he did, Ed Harrington would be pursued like he'd never been pursued before. Maggie Elizabeth Magee Anderson was not known for giving up.

CHAPTER SIX

"Boy, they sure are big," Johnny declared, his eyes bulging.

"That they are," Ed agreed. It pleased him to see the boy's enthusiasm. It was Johnny's turn. He'd waited two weeks watching his mother and Carolyn being instructed on the fine points of grooming and exercising horses.

Ed had done some initial teaching with all three of the Andersons, but he much preferred working with one student at a time so he could devote his total attention to the horse and one other person. And that also meant he wasn't always surrounded by the smell of lavender.

Leading an older chestnut mare, Ed said to Johnny, "Horses aren't like a pet dog or cat. For one thing, they weigh a heck of a lot more than we do. One wrong move and you can be stepped on or kicked. Horses are naturally skittish. Most anything can startle them. Even if you do everything right, someday you'll be stepped on or kicked. Hurts like hell, but you'll survive."

Ed glanced down at Johnny, whose stare was fixed on the horse's rear feet.

"This mare," Ed said, tying the lead rope to a hitching post and running his hands up and down the horse's front legs feeling for swelling and heat, "should be a good one for you to begin with. She's mild mannered. Likely close to the end of her racing career. She'll make a good broodmare someday."

"When will we have babies?"

"Not until late next winter or early spring. We'll have to buy their mothers in the fall. You think you're going to like the foals, huh?"

"Oh yeah." Johnny shot a quick smile at Ed. "They'll be great. I can hardly wait."

"I can see that. Maybe by then you'll be calm enough with them to help me with the foaling." Ed stifled a grin as the towheaded boy puffed his chest. "Now let me show you how to brush this one. Remember, there's no time for daydreaming when you're around a horse. First, we'll let her get to know you."

Ed guided the boy's hand toward the mare's muzzle. Johnny's eyes widened. With a mild display of interest, the mare sniffed and then rubbed her large lips his hand.

"That tickles," Johnny giggled, pulling back. The mare followed the boy until her head rested against his chest.

"Think she wants to be scratched liked this." Ed ran his fingers along the horse's neck and between her ears. "She's having a good time. Notice her ears — they're tilted toward you. Now she's got one forward and the other back. Horses talk to you with their ears."

"No way," Johnny said in hushed tones. He stared intently at those ears twitching back and forth, listening.

"Believe it. If you see a horse with its ears pinned back, you better do something to calm the animal or get out of its way. That horse is telling you it's frightened and will likely kick or run off, or do both. This old chestnut is having too much fun right now for any of those shenanigans.

Ed ran a brush across the mare's belly; the animal dipped its back asking for more. "Some horses are social like this one, but some aren't. You can't take anything for granted with a horse. It's always good to hum or speak softly when you're grooming. That way a horse will know where you are. Keeping a hand on its body as you walk around also helps them keep track of you. Horses don't like surprises. They like very predictable, slow moving routines. You think you can do that?"

Johnny reached for the brush in Ed's outstretched hand. "I'll sure try," he said earnestly.

Ed smiled inwardly at the squeak in the lad's voice. The kid was likely wondering if he had a slow speed in his body. That was one thing about horses—they taught you how to slow down. They taught a person how to be alert and relaxed at the same time.

- o -

On the concrete washing pad next to the barn, Maggie and Carolyn scrubbed a gray gelding that was away from the track for a rest. Maggie refilled a water bucket with a hose and looked over to see Ed working with her son and the mare.

Ed's patience often surprised her. He had the patience of a good father. She closed her eyes, blotting out the intimate scene that conjured up. Where had that idea come from? But she was right. He would make a good dad, although that was probably the furthest thought from his mind.

Routines were settling in at Anderson Stables. Ed had taught each of them how to muck out a stall well enough for it to meet his approval. He was very finicky about such things. Every morning after one of them thought they had done it just right he'd would come by and inspect. Too often, he discovered a wet spot. "You can't have a race horse with bad hooves," he would intone. Without any display of anger, he'd reinstruct the embarrassed worker in the proper way of cleaning the stall until it was done right. There were fewer mistakes each day.

Cold water penetrated Maggie's tennis shoes. She peered down at the overflowing pail and lurched backward, jerking the hose away. The spray caught Carolyn full in the chest.

"Mom!" the girl shrieked, dodging from the cold water.

Instantly, the gelding shied back and forth, nearly stepping on mother and daughter.

Maggie pulled the lead rope sharply, getting the nervous gelding's attention. "It's okay, big guy. Nobody's going to hurt you. Sorry, Carolyn, I guess I was daydreaming."

"What the hell is going on here?" Ed uttered the demand through clenched teeth, obviously trying not to further excite the horse.

"I'm sorry," Maggie stammered, her cheeks flushing rosy pink. "It was an accident. I was thinking...what to have for supper."

Seeing irritation flicker across his face, Maggie stood her ground, wondering what had made his patience evaporate so rapidly. He seemed to exercise much more tolerance with the kids than with her. The entire Anderson family stood with slumped shoulders waiting for Ed Harrington to burst.

Ed glared at the three of them. Maggie watched his Adam's apple rise and fall as if he were trying not to shout. At last his words came out of an icy calm.

"This isn't a game you're playing. These are high strung thoroughbreds, not Shetland ponies. They can step on you, kick you or bolt if you startle them."

Holding her breath, Maggie tried not to react to his insinuation that she and Carolyn had been playing a game. She watched Ed approach the gelding and run his hands softly over the animal's withers. Clinching her teeth, she fumed at his disregard for her ability to calm the unnerved horse — and at his fingers soothing the horse's flesh.

Stepping back from the horse, Ed sighed, "Okay, no harm was apparently don this time. But none of you can let your minds wonder. You'll screw up, and the next time you'll be flat on your back or worse."

"I'm sorry," Maggie mumbled, unable to make eye contact with her hired man.

"Sorry doesn't cut it with horses. They don't know the meaning of the word. You'll have to do better than that."

Maggie nearly wilted under his paternalistic glare. Remembering who she was, she squared her shoulders in defiance. Damn, she was the boss. It was her money that paid this guy. Her cheek twitched. What a farce. She was trying to run a business she knew next to nothing about and was catching abuse from a man who didn't care one iota about her.

"Another thing," Ed thundered. "How many times do I have to tell you to wear boots when you come down to the stables?"

Maggie gulped and peeked down at her offending sneakers. He was right; she'd been in such a hurry to help with the chores she'd forgotten to change shoes.

"And, you, young lady," he groused at Carolyn, who took a step backward, "get yourself dressed the next time you come down here." With that demand hanging heavily in the air, Ed stomped into the barn leaving his workers to gape at each other.

Oh, my. Maggie clamped a hand over her wide open mouth. He was right again. Damn him. Carolyn hadn't worn a bra. Her pert nipples and small round breasts were on full display through the soaked yellow tank top.

"I don't think horses give a damn what I wear," hissed the fourteen year old, finding her voice.

"Don't look so mortified. Ed's right, you forgot to put on a bra this morning." Maggie's mouth turned up slightly. "Besides, there aren't any boys out here to attract."

"Mom!"

Watching her teenage daughter stalk toward the house, Maggie wondered why Carolyn hadn't put on a bra. The only male to see her was Ed Harrington and he was old enough — she shivered — to know better, that was for sure. A mother daughter talk was in order, most definitely.

She and Ed Harrington would at least agree on that. His overreaction earlier began to make more sense. He'd been enraged at Carolyn's brazenness. That was understandable, yet he did seem overly protective of all of them. Yes, each of them would probably be stepped on or kicked at some time. Ed couldn't prevent that from happening.

Turning to speak to Johnny, Maggie shrugged seeing the boy had already returned to brushing the mare. Ed stood next to him clucking about something. Damn, she was getting tired of the tension. She knew it wasn't all caused by the horses, saving the land, or girls without bras.

Whether he'd admit it or not, she'd gotten under his skin just as he was definitely under hers. He was like an itch that wouldn't go away; trying to ignore the annoying ache didn't seem to be working at all.

Later that evening, Maggie sat across from her pouting daughter in the small room she affectionately called her office retreat. After Mason's death, she'd turned a tiny bedroom into a den of sorts. Slouching piles of bills and ledgers sat on one corner of an oak desk. A computer took up space on another corner. Dust across its keys attested to the amount of time she devoted to learning how to use it. That was the problem. It took less time to enter the figures in a ledger than it did to learn how to manipulate a spread sheet. On the floor beside the desk and in front of the small sofa across from it, where Carolyn sullenly waited, sat piles of tattered magazines and books on horseracing.

Supper had been a silent affair. Ed stayed away; no one seemed in the mood for conversation.

Reluctantly, Carolyn had joined her mom. She sat rigidly, refusing to soften her defiant stance.

Maggie glanced at the framed picture on her desk. It had been taken at a family picnic three years earlier. Everyone seemed so happy then. Did the picture lie? Just a little? Sure, there had been conflicts. Most families had some, just like most family pictures lied, a little bit. Three years ago no one could have foreseen what was to happen — Mason's death, Anderson Racing Stables, a haggard stranger becoming her hope for saving the land, that same stranger wreaking havoc on her mind and body. The picture remained an important memento of the past; it had nothing to say about the future.

Frowning, Maggie wondered what Mason would have said to his daughter about her untoward behavior. She shook her head. It didn't matter what he might do. She was the only one there to deal with the situation. Patience. She needed patience.

"Well, what were you trying to do going down to the barn without a bra on?" Maggie inquired gently, trying not to accuse. "You've grown to be a young woman. You have to dress like one."

Carolyn's sulk deepened. Was this the beginning of the dreaded teenage rebellion? They had been spared most of that, so far. She'd always enjoyed their mother daughter confidences. Now, she feared part of who they'd been was slipping away. "We've always been able to talk. I'm more upset with your withdrawing from me than about the show you put on at the barn."

A trace of a smile crossed Carolyn's lips.

"Not wearing a bra was a deliberate choice wasn't it?"

Her daughter's eyes went wide with fear; then she nodded hesitantly.

"Why? Surely, you don't think Mr. Harrington..."

"Oh, Mother," Carolyn interrupted, crossing her arms across her chest. "You don't know what it's like to be ignored. Boys don't seem to notice me. You had Dad, and now Ed can hardly keep his eyes off you."

107

Maggie blushed.

"I just wanted him to notice me. I'm not stupid. God, he's old enough to be my father. I just wanted to be noticed. He hardly ever looks at me."

Moving to hug her daughter, Maggie murmured, "Guess you got his attention. Promise you won't pull a stunt like that again."

"You don't have to worry about that," she said biting her lip. "I'm so mortified. I didn't think he'd freak out, though. I thought women were supposed to tease men."

"Not all men like to be teased. Especially men like Ed Harrington."

Maggie watched her daughter try to stifle her sobs. "You know, I do remember what it was like to be fourteen. Boys my own age seemed so immature. I dated a senior briefly, but he wanted much more than I was ready to give."

"But at least you were noticed."

"Yeah, but not particularly for the right reasons. Any way, boys your own age will start paying attention real soon, I expect. I'll probably have to use a broom to keep them at bay. You'll be lucky if Ed doesn't use a shotgun."

Carolyn nodded, half smiling. "He sure does seem to think he has to protect us all."

"Must be some kind of macho instinct."

Chuckling, Carolyn wiped tears away. "Mom, are you involved with him? Romantically, I mean."

"I know what you mean. I don't think it's something a mother ought to be discussing with her daughter."

"He's kind of old fashioned in some ways, but God, he *is* handsome."

"You can leave God out of this. But you don't think I should be involved with him?" Maggie probed cautiously.

"It's not that. It's just, he seems so, so manly."

"Manly! You mean you don't think I'm woman enough for him?"

"Mom, you're my mother," Carolyn gasped. "But you do look cute when you get angry with him."

"Well, this concludes our mother daughter conversation, young lady. You must have something else you need to do."

"Okay, I'll let you off the hook," Carolyn said, standing to leave. "In case you're still curious, I think you're woman enough for any man."

Maggie's mouth stayed open long after the door to her daughter's room closed.

She stood and walked to a bookshelf. After absently perusing her library of contemporary novels, she glanced at the clock. It was not too late, only a little after eight. Through the office window, she saw a light in the loft apartment.

They had to talk about the events of the day. Ed could not be so interfering in her family's life. She might need him in a lot of ways, but the family disciplinarian was not one of them.

The damn woman would drive him crazy, but she wouldn't drive him to drink, Ed assured himself, raking his fingers through his hair. He'd been sitting in his cushioned chair for over an hour stewing, rehashing over and over how he had gotten himself into such a mess.

It had been over two weeks since *the kiss* and he could still taste the crushed mulberries of her lips. Why did they always seem to pucker in such an inviting fashion?

And what was with Carolyn? How had her mother let her out of the house without a bra on? Good God, didn't they know what boys and men could do? The sight of taut nipples brought out the natural predator instinct in the male, young or old. If she were his daughter, he'd have the young flirt fitted with a chastity belt. But she wasn't his daughter. Maybe he'd overreacted some...but not by much.

Damn, he needed this job. They'd been able to pick up some good horses to work with. Clint had told him he hadn't given up on clearing his name. Maybe he could yet get back to the track. He missed it so; it was almost like breathing. He'd do most anything to get back to the Chicago circuit. It was heady stuff working with horses worth more than he'd ever make.

And there was the lifestyle of the track. That was where rarefied air truly existed. Greeting the sunrise, breathing in the heavy early morning mist, dreaming of the next big horse — that was what shedrow was about. The only scent rivaling that of shedrow was the lavender of Maggie Anderson.

Ed shook his head trying to clear it of her scent and taste. Hearing the light rap on his door, he groaned. There wasn't much doubt who that was, and she was likely madder than a wet hen.

He opened the door.

Looking somewhat hesitant and sheepish, Maggie asked, "May I come in?"

"Might as well," Ed said curtly, "you're here." Had the little woman come to read him the riot act, or to apologize for her careless behavior earlier in the day? The latter was unlikely. He wasn't duped by her apparent meekness. Might as well start packing his bags. It'd been a nice dream, but like so many dreams this one had turned into a nightmare. He slumped back down into the winged chair without offering her a seat.

Maggie remained standing. "You look pretty haggard. Are you okay?"

"You don't have to worry about me climbing back into the bottle, if that's what's bothering you."

"I'm worried about you. I'm worried about all of us." She folded her hands together, as if to steady herself against the tension whirling between them. "We have to talk, you know."

Ed sighed. At least she wasn't going to fire him on the spot. Damn woman. Damn kids. Damn himself for getting involved with them. Why couldn't they listen when he told them to be careful around the horses? Any one of them could be seriously maimed or worse. "I know," he finally replied. "Guess I overdid it some today. Sorry about that. How's Carolyn?"

"She'll survive. We all will," Maggie said forcefully.

He shook himself. He was close to falling over the edge. What the hell was wrong with him? Those blue ovals staring narrowly at him looked so innocent and so filled with worry. Had he ever had anyone this troubled over him? It made his skin crawl and his heart crack open.

"Do you know why she did it? Why she wasn't wearing a bra?" Maggie inquired, bending over to straighten some magazines on a small round table next to Ed's chair.

Ed shook his head, trying not to notice the casual bobbing of the woman's breasts.

"She wanted you to notice her."

"What the…"

"Not so much sexually. She seems to think you ignore her."

"She's sort of difficult to ignore. Pretty, like her mother. I'd have her on a tight leash if she were my daughter." He regretted his remark as soon as it escaped his lips.

"You don't think I'm a good mother?" The calm voice belied the anger reflected in her twitching cheek.

"It's not that at all," he corrected quickly. "You're a fantastic mom. But I'd make a damn poor dad. Men are predators when it comes to women."

"You don't think we women can defend ourselves?" Maggie asked, crossing her arms under her breasts.

"You might, but Carolyn…"

"Most of us females learn about the mating dance when we're young. Many of us choose not to follow all the steps until we're older. In fact, I would suggest that women are often in more control of that dance than men."

"Oh." Ed fumbled with his fingers, not liking at all the direction of their conversation.

"Besides," Maggie chastised in a sultry tone, "women can be predators too. Don't you agree?"

"Don't know." He shrank inside his skin as the blonde pixie leaned over and brushed her lips lightly against his.

"Don't," he protested, and then her tongue touched his. There was that intoxicating mulberry taste again. He floated in its familiarity as Maggie settled on his lap, wrapping her arms around his neck. She was as light as a feather. He knew she had to feel his erection pressing against her bottom. He felt her shift her position to gain more leverage. Then, she aggressively invaded his mouth.

"Don't talk. Don't run from me," Maggie muttered against his lips, catching her breath.

He couldn't run if he tried. Ed clutched her tight, not wanting to ever let her go. She felt like a life preserver being thrown to a drowning man.

Again her lips bruised his; breasts crushed against his chest. He stroked her neck leisurely, then her back, and then her buttocks. She moaned encouragement.

Maggie reached for his hand and guided it up the length of her bare inner thigh. Her skirt already lay bunched at her waist. His fingers froze when she placed them on her straining mound. Not breaking the kiss, she pulled aside her bikini panties and pressed his fingers against her sensitive skin. The throbbing in his ears was deafening. Her tongue probing his mouth and her swaying hips pled for him to enter her.

Mesmerized by her tongue, Ed committed to memory the satin texture of her skin hidden from view. Her curly hair was moist from wanting. Her fingers pressed against his until they were inside. He probed tentatively. She was wet and hot to the touch; she pushed upward, taking him further in.

His fingers began their own exploration. Her muffled pleasure reverberated against the insides of his mouth.

She opened for him and he plied her with two fingers, searching deep and then nearly withdrawing. Her breath shortened. He worked in and out, slowly, then faster.

She hunched up on her knees, giving him even more space. And then she began riding his fingers as if it were the most natural thing to do. Her gasps were audible as his thumb glided over her clit. Her grip tightened. She was closing in on a massive climax. Her tongue slipped from his mouth. Her body shook and she buried her head against his shoulder, as if trying not to disintegrate.

Ed kissed her hair, helping her find herself. Too soon, his head started to clear from the erotic fog that had overtaken him. He grimaced. Maggie had given him a great gift that he could neither claim nor keep.

He sensed Maggie gradually drawing back into her body. Her hands fumbled at his belt. She had the buckle undone and was reaching for him.

"You've got to get out of here," Ed hissed, shoving her hand away. "Now!"

Her eyes rounded. Her face filled with shock and disbelief. "But don't you…"

"Now, Maggie," Ed mumbled, roughly pulling down her skirt and unceremoniously standing her on her feet. "We've got to get on top of this, woman."

Without a word, Maggie straightened her clothing. Moving toward the door, she turned and smiled like a wanton temptress. "I certainly expect to do that, Mr. Harrington. Sooner or later. I like being on top."

As she shut the door quietly, Ed leaned against it emptying his lungs of air. She had clearly laid down the sexual gauntlet. The woman would drive him crazy. Damn, she smelled delicious. Her sticky heat still warmed his fingers. But she needed a decent man. A man who would make a decent husband and decent father.

Her scent hovered, teasing, enticing his

hormones. She would be devastatingly delicious.

- o -

On the other side of the door, Maggie caught her own breath and gingerly made her way down the stairs on wobbly legs. She hadn't planned on seducing Ed, not tonight, but she was a firm believer in spontaneity. Again, he'd left her only partially satisfied, wanting, needing more. Next time she wouldn't be denied. And what about that parting shot? Being on top. She smiled broadly.

Two days later, Maggie paused from doing her morning chores to watch a white Con-Ex Farms van pull down the driveway. "Here comes trouble," she grumbled. Her stomach knotted even before the tall, dark-haired man stepped away from the van. Determined to show no fear, she left the sanctuary of the barn and headed toward her uninvited guest.

She recognized him—she'd seen his picture often enough. It appeared in the local newspaper whenever there was a store opening, a county fair, or a church bazaar. He looked too confident, too tall, and definitely too handsome. Hiding behind polarized sunglasses, Mr. Taylor Fallon in his dark suit seemed very out of place standing in front of a barn. He was vice-president in charge of acquisitions. At least they weren't sending a water boy.

Taking off her gloves, Maggie extended her

116

hand in the mandatory greeting. "What can I do for you, Mr. Fallon?" she asked, squaring her shoulders.

"Have we met, Ms. Anderson? I'd never forget such a pretty face."

"No," she said, ignoring his comment. "Your picture has been in the paper a time or two, that's all."

"Thank goodness, thought I might be slipping."

Not liking his subtle sexual innuendo, Maggie said, "Let's get to the point, Mr. Fallon. I'm not interested in anything you might be offering."

"Testy little thing. Josh Prater warned me about you. Guess you've earned your reputation for being a ball crusher." Fallon folded his arms, then continued, "I'm only interested in your farm, Ms. Anderson."

"It's not for sale."

Scowling, the man tugged at his tie. "You haven't heard my offer yet."

"Doesn't matter. Farm's not for sale. Not to you or anyone else."

"There must be a price we can agree on."

"This farm doesn't have a price tag," Maggie snarled through compressed lips.

The Con-Ex Farms man cast her a knowing smile. "Everything has a price tag, Ms. Anderson. Sometime it takes longer to discover what it is, but I can assure you, everything has a price."

"Prater said about the same thing, but you're both mistaken. This land has no price tag, Mr.Fallon." She spoke distinctly, in case the man was hard of hearing.

She reached a hand to her cheek, trying to still its jumping. "I don't want to be rude, but I think you found what you needed to know. Best you be getting on with your day. I've got plenty of work to do."

Disbelief etched across his face. "But…"

"Don't think there are any more buts," Ed offered as he strolled easily out of the barn with a pitchfork in his hand. "Sounds like the lady's made up her mind. And I can assure you she doesn't change her mind easily."

"Who the hell are you?" Fallon retreated a step.

Maggie swallowed a giggle—the vice-president's take charge attitude had slipped a little. He hadn't expected running into a man like the one threatening him with a pitchfork. Probably neither Fallon nor Prater knew about Ed yet—well, they sure knew now.

This was a new Ed, relaxed on the outside but coiled on the inside, ready for whatever happened next. She wasn't positive she liked being protected in this way, but this wasn't the time for that discussion.

"Name's Harrington. Just happen to be here." Ed spat within inches of Fallon's shiny black wing-tips. "Thought you were leaving."

"I'm out of here." Glowering at Maggie, Fallon declared, "But this isn't the end, Ms. Anderson. You can count on that. I'll have this land yet. Everyone has a price. Don't stretch yourself too thin, you might just snap. You better hope we get some rain soon, or your crops will dry up before you can name an asking price."

Annoyed, Maggie watched the Con-Ex Farms van tires spin in Fallon's rush to leave. "So, what do you suppose he meant by that? Not stretching too thin."

"Does this place have a mortgage on it?" Ed lean heavily against the pitchfork, his gaze focused on the disappearing van.

"Not much, given what it's worth."

"Can you pay it off? That's what matters."

"I could. It would eat into what I could invest in the stables, but it wouldn't be a severe dent. The mortgage is less than thirty-five thousand. It's a loan left over from when Mason wanted to start a trucking business. That didn't work out too well."

Ed gritted his teeth. "I don't want to know how much you have in reserve, but getting the mortgage paid off seems timely. Sounds like the suit who just scurried back to town is in cahoots with the local banker. If it was me, I'd pay the loan off, even if I had to cut back on the horses. You don't need anybody having that kind of leverage on you. Makes you too vulnerable."

"I agree, but Fallon's right too." Maggie picked up a handful of dry dirt and let the powder fall between her fingers. "If we don't get rain fairly soon, we could be in deep trouble. A lot of money is going out. I might have to borrow against the land or the horses to make it through to next spring's planting. Or maybe put off buying the broodmares."

Ed fixed his gaze on her.

She knew he was trying to determine how long she could and would stick to the plan for the stables. She didn't like the fact that he doubted her courage.

"In the long run, the broodmares will likely be your cheapest investment," he said, without censure. "They can help you make a profit without depending on the luck of the track. But that will take time."

Maggie watched the man remove his dusty ball cap and run his finger nervously through his hair. He wasn't speaking his mind. Ed was clearly on edge about her financial situation. She couldn't blame him, she was too. And he did have a lot riding on her being able to make it.

"I never advise anyone to borrow against their horses," he said. "That's too damn risky. The value of a horse is only one race or one bad step away from plummeting."

"Can't that value also go up?"

"That doesn't seem to happen as often." Ed fell silent.

Maggie watched a hopeful robin tap the ground with its beak, trying to entice a worm to rise. Maybe it was too dry for a worm. Yet, shortly the bird was pulling on a long worm, extricating it from its home.

"Think I'll run into town this afternoon and pay that mortgage off. If I have to borrow later in the year, it will be from a different bank. Prater doesn't know I have the bulk of my husband's insurance money in the Walker bank."

She noticed Ed flinched at the word *husband*. No matter, that was his problem. If he wanted to be hung up on the fact that she had been married and was the mother of two children, she couldn't do much about it.

"Maybe I should make a deposit in a Des Moines bank and pay the loan off without exposing the existence of the Walker account."

Grinning, Ed drawled, "You hang around me long enough and you'll become a suspicious person, Ms. Anderson. But I do believe that's an excellent idea. Devious, but superb."

Maggie curtsied gracefully, returning his smile. "Well, I am pleased that I please you, Mr. Harrington. Sometimes I wonder."

"It doesn't take much to please me," Ed said, looking down at her. "It's you I worry about."

Ed sauntered back to his work without waiting for a reply, leaving Maggie sputtering to herself. Pleased! He'd pleased her immensely. Why the hell couldn't he see that? Why wouldn't he let her please him?

CHAPTER SEVEN

Color drained from the teller's face when she saw the amount of Maggie's cashier's check. "It'll take me a little bit to pull together the necessary paper work. Would you like to take a seat over there?"

Maggie nodded at the mousy haired woman with the honey sweet voice. She knew what was coming next. She'd prepared herself against the forthcoming onslaught. She hardly had time to settle on the slippery vinyl chair before Josh Prater stormed out of his office looking for her. Spying her, his eyebrows arched and he made his way quickly across the foyer.

"Maggie, you don't have to do this. We want your business. You don't have to borrow from another bank to pay us off." He scowled. "I know Mr. Fallon was out to your place. He told me how rude you were to him."

"Rude. Rude? Me?" Maggie pounced off the chair and Prater took two steps back. "You tell Mr. Fallon if he wants to see rude, just come back without an invitation."

Maggie thought Prater was going to burst. His face looked as red as a vine ripened tomato.

"You sure are a chip of the old block. Your father thought he was bigger than his britches, too. Didn't get him far." Glaring down at her, he stood ramrod straight and hissed, "You'll get your comeuppance, young lady, just wait and see."

Maggie glared at the back of the banker practically dashing toward his office. The slamming of his office door echoed across the lobby. Tellers who had been discreetly observing the scene quickly found something else to do.

"I'm ready for you, Ms. Anderson," the teller handling her transaction said.

With a flourish, Maggie signed all the necessary papers. Seething, she walked through the bank foyer, hurrying for some fresh air. She'd never thought her dad had an enemy in the world. Sometimes she could be naïve, though. She groaned. It wasn't difficult at all to imagine Ed Harrington agreeing with her about that.

As she stepped out onto the sidewalk, Maggie glanced skyward. Hardly a cloud could be seen. Worry lines strained many of the faces she saw in town. It was mid June already, and tender new crops were starting to wilt. If they didn't get rain soon, they'd all be in trouble. Of course the bank and Con-Ex Farms were big enough to ride out even weather difficulties. They'd be major beneficiaries of a prolonged drought.

"So how's life treating you, Maggie?

Maggie turned to greet Ben Templeton with a wisp of a smile. "Just made the banker unhappy by paying off a loan. I'm surviving. How about you?"

"I'm doing fine. Join me for a glass of cold

lemonade in my outer office?"

"Sarah is going to start charging you rent one of these days," Maggie replied, allowing herself to be guided toward Sarah's diner.

After Flo Zimmerman set two tall glasses of icy lemonade at their table, Ben asked, "Did you ever find Harrington?"

Taking her cue from Flo, Maggie cocked her ear and heard Patsy Cline's _Crazy_ playing on the jukebox. She'd have to sort that out later, maybe. "Yes," she replied to Ben. "Harrington's working for me now." Maggie kept her tone steady, certain that Ben already knew about her hired hand. So what did her old friend really want to know?

"Drove by the other day. Saw a few horses, but not enough to qualify as a racing stable. Figured you'd found some help."

"It'll take time. Actually, I have a half dozen horses racing in the Chicago area."

Ben's jaw dropped. "That's got to be expensive."

"So far they're holding their own. And some of Ed's friends cut a real good deal for me."

"You can trust them?"

"I'm wondering these days who I can trust, but I know I can trust them. They have long standing roots in the horse industry, and they're good people."

Maggie looked quizzically at Ben, a question forming in her mind. "Say, do you know any reason why Prater at the bank hated my dad? I thought everyone liked him, or at least tolerated his quirks."

Sipping his lemonade, Ben closed his eyes. His skin darkened. He looked like a man in a trance.

Maggie started to fidget. "Don't withhold anything from me. I feel like I'm all of a sudden stumbling around in the dark. The man's intense dislike for me makes no sense. I've never done anything to harm him."

Ben opened his eyes and put his glass down carefully. "No, it's not you specifically. Prater is superb at nursing a grudge, always has been. We were all graduating from high school. Prater, your dad, your mom, and me. Your mom had been dating Prater for six months or so.

Maggie gasped.

Nodding, Ben continued, "He thought Iris was going to marry him. She thought otherwise. Apparently, she was using Prater to get your dad's attention."

Maggie grinned — how like her mom!

"Anyway. Prater was bragging to the guys about how he was going to ask Iris to marry him after the graduation party. He never had the chance — your dad and mom eloped to Las Vegas with their diplomas in hand."

"Oh, my God!" Maggie gasped, covering her mouth.

"Prater never spoke to your mom again. Never forgave your dad for taking what he claimed was his."

Maggie's eyes widened. "So he's been after the farm ever since."

"Ever since. Your mom would have died before letting that land go. Your dad did everything he could to hold onto it through bad years as well as good. Even though the land had been in your mother's family for generations, it was often used as collateral. That was the case with most family farms. I think Colt paid it off maybe five years before his death." Ben chuckled softly. "There was a lively celebration that night."

"I remember that. I'd never seen my folks so happy. But I didn't fully understand. I never had the background information. So Prater never married."

"Nope."

"Not much of a life, living to hate."

"You got that right. Everybody needs somebody to love."

Maggie knew Ben was thinking about his deceased wife. She leaned over to pat his hand. "Thanks for being honest with me, Ben. I don't know why my folks never shared that story with me. They weren't evil—they were just in love."

"Don't know why they didn't tell you, either. Maybe they felt some shame about it. You can bet Prater would disagree with you, though."

"How's that?"

"About what's evil and what's love."

"Suppose you're right. So what did you want from me, Ben?"

Ben reached into his coat pocket and pulled out a letter. "I need to talk with you and your brother about this. It just arrived yesterday."

Her brother. Why on earth? "What is it? What's wrong?" She didn't like the sound of terror coming from her throat.

"Nothing's wrong, Maggie." Ben handed Maggie the letter. "It seems that your folks took out a life insurance policy in Las Vegas the day they got married. They never told me about it. Of course, I wasn't in the insurance business then. Seems that it was an endowment policy that they lost track of once it was paid up."

Maggie stared at the piece of paper. "How could they forget about this?"

"Happens all the time. People pay up insurance. Never tell anybody. Forget they ever had it. Sometimes the companies don't spend a lot of time trying to find the policy holder. Your folks dealt with a reputable company. As you can tell from the letter, they contacted me because I sell insurance in this region."

"So what now?" She knew the answer. They'd have to contact her brother.

"It's not a lot of money, though a hundred thousand sounded like all the money in the world back when your parents married." Ben reached for his reading glasses. Retrieving the letter, he said, "I guess since I was the executor for your parents' estate, I have an obligation to let both their children know there are still proceeds to be divided between them."

Shivering slightly, Maggie pursed her lips trying to remain calm. The last thing she wanted was another blowup with her brother like they'd had when the will was first read.

"My recommendation to both of you," Ben said, "is to simply divide the money equally. There's little doubt about the court doing that if they got involved, since these monies were not part of the original will. Going to court over this would be a waste of money."

Maggie sneered. "Tell Brad that."

"I intend to, but I don't know how to get a hold of him. I need your help with that."

Maggie grabbed her purse. She'd just as soon leave her brother lost in his own California world, but she couldn't do that. He was her kids' uncle. And they did like him a lot, even if they seldom saw him.

She scribbled Brad's address and telephone number on a slip of paper. Handing the note to Ben, she said, "This is no guarantee. He moves a lot. We don't often hear from him. Maybe there will be a forwarding address."

"Thanks, Maggie. I'll get back to you on this as soon as I can. I'm sure you're like everyone else: you could use the money as soon as possible."

"If it comes about, I won't turn the money down." Recalling her brother's taste for money, Maggie added, "But I won't count on it either."

Wrestling with ghosts of past and present, Maggie drove back to the farm. She replayed recent conversations with Fallon, with Prater, and with Ben. Her folks had eloped to Vegas. Her heart raced. That must have been love without limits. Her parents must have been thrilled with the danger and the abandonment of it all. Wow, she'd never done anything that wild, that unconventional. And these were her folks, not some Hollywood characters playing out a script.

Yet they had taken time to invest in life insurance. Why then? Maggie swerved into the middle of the road and back again. They must have known that her mother was already pregnant. She'd been an early baby — or so her mom had said. And Maggie had never seriously questioned that information. Now she knew it wasn't necessarily true. No couple eloping to Vegas would purchase life insurance...unless. Unless they knew their family was enlarging. Goodness. She didn't want to think about that any longer. She couldn't.

Maggie rolled down the pickup window, wishing the truck had air conditioning. Damn, it was hot. And summer only promised to get hotter.

So, there was more behind Prater trying to get her to sell to Con-Ex Farms than the land. His animosity made more sense now. She'd bet the second party eager to buy the farm was none other than the bank.

Damn! Prater could have been her father if her mom had not fled to Vegas.

Now *that* was sobering.

He wanted her land — he wanted revenge on her parents.

"Never!" she screamed to no one.

She smiled warmly, mulling Ben's words over

and over: *Everybody needs somebody to love.* Surely, that included the recalcitrant Mr. Harrington.

Was she being too forward with the man? She'd had no interest in any other man since Mason's death. Why now, all of a sudden? Life was already complicated enough without a man. Was she really throwing herself at him like some hard up woman?

No—she just knew what she wanted. And she expected he wanted the same thing, but lacked the courage and self-esteem to acknowledge that fact or act upon it. Obviously, he was attracted to her. She could still feel the promise of his arousal against her bottom.

Maggie nervously ran her fingers up and down the steering wheel. Dust from the gravel road made it impossible to see anything in the rear view mirror.

Was she simply trying to rescue him from the bottle? Definitely not. She'd read enough about co-dependence. She'd left him standing on the crummy sidewalk to make his own choice. And he'd sobered up and come to her. Well, he came for a job. But he came to her, nonetheless. She hadn't expected or wanted to respond to him as a man, but she had. It was too late to retreat now. She wouldn't give him up without a good fight. Even if that fight had to be with Ed Harrington, himself.

Ed took a swig of root beer and scratched the lazy tomcat sitting on a bale of hay beside him in the barn walkway. He'd needed a break, but that simply meant more time for thoughts of Maggie Anderson to torture his body and soul.

Why couldn't he simply get up off his duff and walk away from the damn woman? He didn't owe her anything; not anymore. There must be other jobs around he could get now that he was sober. Hell, the Travers would hire him in a heartbeat. He always appreciated what they did for him, but it felt too much like an obligation. He wanted a job that he'd earned.

And he had indeed made a promise of sorts to help his perky, hardheaded, mush-hearted boss establish a racing stable. They'd never discussed a timeframe. Hell, it could take years. Or he could tell her he'd done enough after the purchase of the broodmares. She'd be minimally set up then.

Though he doubted she'd ever foaled horses before. He couldn't just up and leave her, or leave those mares to her mercy. Ed Harrington honored his promises. He might not have much left, but he still had his pride.

Stroking the cat behind its ears, Ed mumbled, "Your damn mistress has enough pride for all of us, Tom. That's a large part of the problem. She can't accept no for an answer once she gets her claws into an idea — or into a man.

Maybe he'd get lucky and it wouldn't take so

long to make the stables competitive. After all, Cassie was running some horses in Chicago, and she was damn good. If they could set up the foundation of a contending racing stable, then he might be able to reestablish himself in the racing world. Maybe Maggie might even let him buy in on a horse or two after she got to know him better. Like it or not, this was the best game in town for him; it was the only game.

He shook his head—that wasn't all of it. He didn't *want* to leave. He didn't want to leave behind that lavender scent or walk away from the mulberry taste.

The calico tomcat stretched to his fullest extent before leaping from the hay bale. Ed chuckled. "You wouldn't have a second thought about what to do, would you, Mr. Tom?" The cat walked on without ever looking back. "Maybe that's what separates us. She deserves more than just having an itch scratched. And I have nothing more to offer than that. Nothing but pain and heartache. Surely, that woman's had enough of that to last a lifetime."

- o -

Forty-five more days passed without a drop of moisture, not even early morning dew. The ground cracked like so many broken mirrors. Corn leaves had long since curled. Alfalfa grew to about four inches and then turned brown. Even if a drenching rain occurred now, farmers would be lucky if the land would yield forty percent of a normal crop. Not enough to cover expenses. Not enough to purchase seed for the following year.

Maggie knelt at the edge of the corn field west of the barn. Parched dirt sifted through her fingers like desert sand. Anxiety furrowed her brow. "Damn this heat wave," she muttered. It couldn't have picked a worse year to happen. Her financial reserves were rapidly shriveling up like the corn, which should have been towering over her head this late in July.

If things got much worse, she might have to consider cutting back her investments in horses in order to make it through to another spring and another season. At least she had that option. Other small farmers would only make it if they could find work in town. When the weather failed to cooperate, there weren't many jobs available in communities whose economies depended upon the cash crops the land produced.

At least she had the horses to fall back on. They weren't making a lot of money by any stretch of the imagination. The Chicago based contingent was showing a modest profit; she expected that was largely because the Travers were not taking out training fees. Still, Cassie was very high on the three-year-old, Capote's Dream. He'd already won a mid-level allowance race. Cassie had nominated him to run in a modest stakes race at Prairie Meadows over Labor Day weekend.

A lot could happen by that time. If there was any major calamity, she might need to borrow money. Never from Prater. Maybe her parent's insurance money would arrive in time — if Ben could ever find Brad. And if her brother didn't behave like a greedy snake. Hell, it might even rain.

Maggie stood and squeezed herself tightly. The scorched landscape seemed lush compared to the blistering wasteland her body was becoming. He hadn't touched her for too long. Had it all been her imagination? They'd been polite enough; too polite. The kids made most of the conversation at mealtime. Ed disappeared most evenings. She imagined he'd found more meetings to attend. Once he'd spoken briefly about working the twelve steps. He was anxious about completing some of them. He had a sponsor; she was thankful for that.

The last thing she wanted was for Ed to start drinking again. That would be the end of everything, for him and for her.

Maybe he was seeing another woman. Maybe the meetings were just a ruse. Maggie shivered in the heat. Her loins tightened. Removing her cap, she ran dusty fingers through her hair. No, he couldn't be involved with another woman. He couldn't.

Shaking her head, Maggie hoped and prayed for rain. This heat wave couldn't go on forever. Much longer and it would drive her batty.

As Maggie left the field and approached the paddock area, she heard voices coming from the round pen. Heading in that direction, she heard

Ed giving instructions to Johnny and Carolyn.

Leaning against the fence rails, Maggie smiled. Ed was showing her kids how work a yearling filly on a longe line. Things had improved greatly between Ed and Carolyn. He no longer seemed so shy around her, and she wasn't trying to be sexual in the least. Thank God for small favors. Johnny worshipped the man. Ed Harrington could do no wrong in the boy's eyes. "He understands horses like that *horse whispering* guy," he'd boasted just the other day. Johnny was up early each morning to help with the horses. He certainly spent more time listening to Ed than to his Walkman.

Just as his connection with the kids was improving, the relationship between him and her was stagnating. And that was being kind. Not that they were ripping each other apart — it just wasn't going anywhere. At least it wasn't going where she wanted it to go.

She'd always hated running in place in gym class. This by far was worse. Ed Harrington might be like that horse whispering guy, but he sure had a lot to learn about romancing a woman before he could challenge Robert Redford.

Finished with the morning lessons, Ed led the filly over to where Maggie was standing. Her children followed.

"You've got a couple bright kids, Maggie. Hope you know that," he drawled.

Maggie wished she had a camera to capture that moment of beaming smiles. Ed was not big on praise, so when it came, it merited a celebration.

"Hey, Mom," Johnny piped.

"Hey, yourself." Maggie pulled her son's cap over his eyes.

"When are we going to the fair? There are only two more days left."

"Wondered if you were going to forget this year!"

"When, Mom?" Johnny pleaded.

"Tomorrow is Saturday. Why don't we go in time for lunch? Then we can see some of the animals. And the rides won't really start until later anyway."

"All right!"

"Mom, can I invite Amy Ramsey?" Carolyn asked.

"Sure, why not?"

Johnny dragged his boot, making a deep line in the soft corral dirt. Looking up at Ed, he said, "You're going to come with us, aren't you?"

"Now, boy," Ed began, "I've got things to do. I'm not much of a fair person."

"But I want you to come and watch the 4-H kids show their horses. You said you might have time this winter to teach me how to ride the correct way."

Ed frowned at the boy.

Slumped shoulders, turned down mouth, doleful eyes—Maggie could see Johnny's entire body arguing his case. What would Ed do? Maggie watched the internal chaos churning inside him. He really didn't want to go, that was perfectly evident. The fair would probably place him too close to her. But he clearly didn't want to let Johnny down. In the end, tough Mr. Harrington was a cream puff. There must be much she could learn from how her children handled him. And wasn't it nice to know that he intended to stay through the winter?

Shoving his hands in his pockets, Ed grumbled, "Oh, all right. We'll go see some horses. It's not like we don't see horses everyday."

Maggie saw him glance at her. She tried not to look too triumphant.

CHAPTER EIGHT

Johnny, Ed and Maggie munched on hot dogs and potato chips while watching the equitation classes. For a change, Maggie welcomed the late July sunshine warming her skin. Today she would forget about the drought. Instead, she relaxed, sitting on backless wooden benches looking watching 4-H kids chasing their dreams. Johnny would most likely be out there in the arena next year. That would be much more nerve-racking; she'd enjoy this mellow day while she could.

Ed remained quiet, no doubt wishing he was somewhere else, but he did comment to Johnny now and then about a particular horse or rider. Maggie appraised her men and knew that this was as close to being a family as they had experienced since Ed came on board. The only one missing was Carolyn, who was off somewhere with her friend. Fourteen-year-olds didn't do the fair with their parents, Maggie had been informed.

"I only want to ride western," Johnny said to Ed. "No eastern riding for me."

"Can't blame you on that. 'Course, jockeys can do both." Ed cleaned his fingernails with a penknife.

Johnny wrinkled his nose. "Well, maybe I should learn just in case."

"Um, we'll see," Maggie interjected. One thing

she didn't want to happen with all this racing business was for her son to become a jockey. She couldn't think of a much more dangerous sport than sitting on top of a twelve hundred pound beast running as fast and often as wildly as it possibly could. Maybe Johnny would grow to six foot tall and two hundred pounds — considering her frame, that seemed unlikely.

"Look Mom, here come Dave and Mike. Can I go with them for a while? I think Ed and I have seen all we need to see here."

Ed's jaw jutted out and he turned white and then red. Was that fear in his eyes? She gave him a coy smile. Ed looked at the boy as if about to speak, then shrugged his shoulders and directed his attention back to the show ring.

"Sure, son," Maggie said. "Run along. Remember, we're meeting Carolyn at the Ferris Wheel at six o'clock."

After watching her son dash off with his friends, Maggie said to the still-stunned man sitting beside her, "Kids can be fickle without even trying. Don't take it personally. He has really enjoyed being with you."

She stretched, thinking a nap would provide a nice interlude. No, he probably wouldn't like that suggestion. Well, he wasn't getting away from her this time. Even if it was hot enough to fry an egg, they would see the fair — together.

Maggie pulled the pink tank top she was wearing away from her skin in an attempt to garner some cool relief. Maybe they should find a shade tree and make out. She chuckled at her teenage memories and then directed her attention to the man who was doing his best to avoid her.

"Guess we have nearly four hours to kill until the Ferris Wheel rendezvous," she said. "What do you want to do?"

- o -

Ed drew a blank. Maybe crawl under a rock? Or better yet, take a four hour nap. *No, don't go there.* Not with Maggie Anderson beside him. Four hours with her hounding him was not going to be much fun, but there was little choice. They'd come together; they'd leave together. She'd stick to him like a burr to a dog. He'd probably be lucky if he could go to the bathroom alone. Ed inhaled deeply. Damn kid. Maybe he'd get sick on the rides and they'd have to go home early.

Unlikely. Cool would be the best way to play this situation. He wasn't going to show Maggie Anderson that he was unnerved about spending an afternoon with her. It wasn't like there weren't a lot of other people around. "The showing here is almost done," he said. "Guess we could walk through the other animal barns. Maybe something is going on at the grandstand."

Two hours later, Ed had to admit that being with Maggie for the afternoon was turning out to be quite a bit of fun. He hadn't been to a county fair since he was a kid. Their conversation was less strained than at the farm. They laughed at the odd looking caged birds with unpronounceable names. They oohed at lambs suckling their mother's teats. They watched enviously as a sow received a cold water bath. Maggie seemed so happy and carefree. You wouldn't know the problems she carried on her shoulders. He guessed a small break from worry was what they both needed.

She often glanced at him with an impish *come play with me* look. Damn, he wanted to kiss those lips; they seemed fuller than usual. He only remembered them being so full after he'd bruised them badly with his own.

"Ah, a day at the fair," Maggie said, turning to face him. "Isn't it fun?

"It's okay."

"Come on, Ed. Loosen up. You'll get a day older each day no matter how you live it. We still have more than an hour before we meet the kids. Let's go ride the Octopus."

Ed scowled at those wide blue eyes. Surely, he must have misheard. No, he'd heard right. "You got to be kidding. At our ages?"

"Well, you old fuddy duddy. There are people on the rides who are a lot older than us." Rising on her toes, she barked, "I dare you. I say the Octopus. You can pick the next ride."

"Okay, lady, you're on." Grabbing her hand, he almost dragged her down the midway. She scrambled to keep up.

Awkwardly, Ed sat alone on the left side of the Octopus cart. Maggie grinned, as if telling him he couldn't prevent her from sliding tight against him once the machine started.

The Octopus arm lifted and then dipped. He squinted. Sure enough, here she came like a cannonball, screaming her lungs out. Ed swung his arm down to protect her. After making sure she was safely tucked in, he looked away. She looked far too satisfied with their situation.

Well, she'd angered him with her smug dare — he shouldn't have reacted so instinctively. But she did feel good snuggled up against him. One thing he had to say about her, she had guts. She must know that the whole damn county would be talking about them after this day. Those country phone lines would be at risk of burning up from overuse. He smiled. *Wait till she sees the next ride.*

As they stepped off the Octopus, Maggie pleaded, "Let's take a short break. It's been awhile since I've done this. Got to get my legs back."

"Okay. How about some cotton candy?"

"Damn, you are getting into this."

"Haven't been to a county fair in decades, but used to go a lot when I was a kid. Always liked it when a girl dared me to take her on a ride."

They ate their cotton candy while strolling across the midway. Bright pinks, oranges, reds, purples, and yellows splashed across the carnival booths, in front of which hawkers shouted at Ed trying to cajole him into winning a stuffed bear for *his girl*. Over their shouts blared music and recordings enticing folks to sideshows and monumental rides. The scents of hamburgers, hot

143

dogs, corn on the cob and elephant ears wafted on the air. There was no escape from the assault on the senses.

Ed watched Maggie light up as she immersed herself in the whirl of the midway. They walked for nearly a half an hour laughing at the clowns, at the barkers, at people leaning every which way in their attempts to land quarters on slanted glassware.

Ed pulled Maggie to a halt none to gently and reached down to pluck a piece of cotton candy from her hair. Her upturned smile sent warmth radiating throughout his body. His pulse raced. The familiarity of such a simple act thrilled him like no carnival ride ever could. Yet touching her terrorized him, if he allowed himself to think. He tried desperately not to think.

"I'm ready for more. It's your choice," Maggie said, running her fingers lightly across his forearm.

"Come on, then. It's a ride from my youth. They used to call it airplane, only it doesn't look like one. Looks more like baskets."

"Oh God, I remember." She took a step back. "I was never very good being upside down." Bravely, she squared her shoulders and handed her ticket to the attendant.

Ed stood aside letting Maggie climb in and sit down on the narrow, hard bench. "Damn, I remember these baskets being bigger than this," he muttered, trying to find enough room on the bench for himself.

"Seems comfy to me," she said, with her head somewhere between his chest and shoulder.

The tall machine purred, their basket rose like a chair on a Ferris Wheel. He knew that would change quickly. With one strong arm holding Maggie securely, Ed began to rock the basket.

"No…" she breathed.

The heat of her wet lips seared his bare arm. He spun the basket. Over and over they went.

"Oh, my God," Maggie cried out. She bit his arm. "I give up," she screamed. "You win. Whatever you want. Just stop the spinning."

The ride ended. Bemused, Ed watched Maggie stagger toward a nearby tree. Without even the slightest touch of class she tossed her hotdog, fries, cotton candy, and soda.

Ed didn't know if he should laugh or cry. This was not what he'd intended.

"Sonofabitch, Ed, don't just stand there looking like you swallowed a frog! Give me your handkerchief." Moaning, Maggie leaned hard against the tree trunk. "Damn, I may yet live. Wow! What a ride. You must have been something in your youth." He turned away as her stomach lurched again. "I may be older than I thought," she gasped.

"I'll get you some water. Don't go anywhere."

"Don't worry about that," she retorted.

"How are you?" Ed asked, handing Maggie a tall paper cup filled with ice and water.

"Better. I'll make it." She sipped the water and

rinsed out her mouth. "This helps. Thanks. Let's move over there," she said, pointing to a tree some thirty feet away.

"I'm sorry, Maggie." Ed put his arm around her waist to help her to the tree.

Relieved, Maggie promptly sat down and leaned back against it.

He removed his cap and sat down beside her. "I didn't mean to hurt you. I just wanted to scare you for getting me into such a pickle like this."

"I know. I should've been more forceful about my sensitivity to hanging upside down." She met his gaze. "This is a small price to pay to see you finally loosen up some. Damn, that was good. If I hadn't just thrown up lunch, I'd kiss you."

Sliding away from her, Ed said flatly, "Thanks for small favors."

"Is that you, Maggie Anderson? You're looking a little peaked," Sandy Singer asked. She was a longtime schoolmate and friend who, with her husband, managed the local motel.

"It's me," Maggie groaned. She smiled weakly. "Seems like my stomach isn't much better than it was when we were kids."

Sandy laughed. "You always did have a weak stomach when it came to rides." She winked at Maggie before glancing at Ed. "Looks like you're in good hands, though. Are you going to introduce me to your handsome friend? Is this the hired hand I've been hearing so much about?"

Maggie frowned. Ed scowled. "This is Ed Harrington, Sandy. Ed, this is an old friend, Sandy

Singer. She's good people, even if she is nosey."

"Pleased to meet you, ma'am," Ed said, rising to his feet.

"Likewise. I'd really like to stay and talk, but I have to get over to the garden show. I'm one of the judges and can't be late. Good seeing you both." Sandy smiled broadly and waved a bejeweled hand at them as she turned to leave.

"Knew it wasn't a good idea to come," Ed said.

"No need to pout. We've had some fun. Sandy isn't going to say anything to hurt us. She's a friend. She'll talk, but I'll have to be careful to keep the other women off you now that they'll know you're here."

"I'm not pouting. I just don't want anyone getting the wrong impression, that's all."

"Come on, Mr. Hot Shot Trainer," Maggie teased, "I'm not worried about impressions. Come sit back down beside me under this old oak tree and regale me with stories of winners and losers while I try to get these tennis shoes cleaned up some. I'm done with carnival rides, until maybe next year."

Ugly dark clouds raced across the western sky. Maggie stepped off the porch to get a better look. She hadn't seen a cloud in weeks. *Please be filled with rain*, she begged. Swirling dust devils sprouted everywhere ahead of the gusty winds.

Running headlong toward the paddocks to check on the horses, Maggie heard screams even before she rounded the corner of the barn. Panic

147

clawed her heart.

Turning the corner, she witnessed, to her horror, her son being buffeted about like a bag of fluff by an hysterical mare. Somehow Johnny hung suspended from the horse's halter. As the animal repeatedly reared, the boy's body was flung up and down. Maggie ran, but felt as if her legs were stuck in concrete. No noise issued from her clogged throat. The terrifying scene of horse and boy moved in slow motion.

She saw Ed dash from the barn doorway to grab the lead rope. He moved gracefully, seeming to know what to do and say to steady the horse while lifting Johnny's legs in his arm so her son's weight no longer pulled on the mare's head.

She saw Johnny pull away from the horse and place one arm around Ed's neck, his other arm dangling helplessly by his side. As she neared, hardly able to breathe, Maggie counted five fingers on his hand. "Thank God," she murmured.

"Here, take the boy," Ed commanded when he saw Maggie. "Head for the truck. I'll be right behind you. We got to get him to a hospital. Keep talking to him. Don't let him fall asleep."

She nodded dumbly; Johnny cried silently on her shoulder.

Ed led the skittish horse toward the barn and called to Carolyn, who stepped out of the doorway with a quizzical look on her face. "We've got to get Johnny to the hospital. He'll be okay," Ed added quickly. He saw Carolyn fight back a rush of tears.

"See that the horses are fed. We'll call you."

"I'll do it." Carolyn's knuckles on the pitchfork turned white. "You take care of Johnny and Mom."

"Right."

Ed ran toward the truck and sprang in behind the steering wheel. The boy sat in the middle propped up against his mom. Truck tires spun gravel every which way as Ed made his way toward the road. He didn't want to think about what might be wrong with the kid or of what might have happened if they hadn't gotten to him right away.

He gave Maggie a quick glance. Her face was almost as pallid as Johnny's.

"You got to keep talking to him, Maggie. Otherwise he might go into shock. That'll only complicate things. As it is, the doc will have to pop his shoulder back in place."

"Tell me what happened, Johnny," she asked, taking her eyes off the speedometer.

"Dunno," was the plaintive response.

"Did the horse spook?"

"Yeah. Some paper flew in the wind," Johnny sobbed. "She got scared."

"Why didn't you let go of the halter?"

Johnny shook his head. Tears rolled down his cheeks. "Ed will be mad at me," he mumbled.

"What?"

Concentrating on his driving, Ed never looked at the boy. He knew what Johnny meant. The kid had screwed up, and he hadn't seen Johnny quickly enough to prevent an accident. Now the kid was paying the price. And his mom.

Johnny exhaled. "I had two fingers through the halter ring."

Maggie rocked back. "My goodness," she gasped. "You could have lost both fingers."

"I know. Maybe. If Ed hadn't been there, maybe I would've."

"Oh, my." Maggie brushed the locks of hair from the boy's forehead and kissed him over and over. Johnny didn't complain.

It was early evening before Dr. James entered the waiting room to talk to Maggie and Ed.

"He's going to be okay. No lost fingers. No permanent damage. It'll take a few weeks for him to heal fully. A dislocated shoulder, two broken fingers, and pulled ligaments are nothing to sneeze about."

Breathing freely for the first time in hours, Ed felt like a huge anvil had been lifted from his chest.

Tears crept down Maggie's cheeks. "Thank you, Doctor," she mumbled through a shaky smile.

"From what the boy tells me, you two took some quick decisive action that probably kept him from going into shock and suffering any permanent damage." The young, dark-haired physician smiled. "I imagine you know it, but you've got a lad who thinks you both walk on water. We don't see kids relating to their parents that well very often."

Glancing at his clipboard and then at his watch, the doctor continued, "Well, I've other patients to see. I want him to stay overnight. Just a precaution. We have him on pain medication. He should sleep pretty much through the night. He'll be able to go home in the morning."

Maggie started to speak.

"Yes, you can spend the night in his room."

An hour later, Maggie stared at her son sleeping soundly in his hospital bed. The room was quiet and semi-dark. She tried not to think of what might have happened. He could have been maimed, or crushed under the horse's hooves. They all knew there would be accidents, but she hadn't counted on this.

"Thank you," she whispered to Ed, who sat next to her on the small couch. She placed her hand in his.

He didn't pull away. She was relieved at that. She needed his comforting, and she also needed to give comfort. She squeezed his fingers; he squeezed hers in return.

"I wish it hadn't happened," he stammered. He had hardly spoken a word since they arrived at the hospital. "I should've been a better teacher. One of the first rules of being with horses is never wrap a rope around any part of your body or put your fingers through halter rings or in places where they might be caught. I didn't see what he was doing until it was too late." Ed dropped his head into his hands and sobbed.

Maggie stroked his neck and looked at the haggard man as if for the first time that day. He'd been through hell. He thought he was responsible for Johnny's mistake. And he cared. A lot. A new kind of warmth claimed her body. She didn't want to name it — not now.

"Don't whip yourself, Ed. You told all of us rule number one over and over again: never place your fingers in halter rings or rope loops. Maybe we really don't learn until something like this happens. We got off easy."

"This time."

"We got off easy this time because you were there and knew what to do," she asserted. She smiled weakly. "You surprise me, Ed. In some matters you have more courage than any five men combined, and then in others you seem so timid."

She'd give anything to know what the man was thinking. But he so seldom shared any inner thoughts or feelings. At least he wasn't running from her touch. But he looked so drained by the ordeal. "You know," she said, "you've been through a lot. More than me. Why don't you go home and get some rest. I can…"

Maggie stopped mid-sentence under his withering glare. It was clear Ed Harrington was not about to go home until he saw for himself that Johnny was okay.

Curling up on her end of the couch, Maggie laid her head on his thigh. Did he realize he was stroking her hair?

As Maggie and the boy slept, Ed tried to sort things out. He seemed to be a danger to Maggie and her family if he stayed or if he left. With the crops dying, the horses were the only realistic hope she had for saving the farm. But he couldn't protect them from every conceivable danger. Risks came with the horse business. But would they learn to do everything they could to prevent accidents? Johnny had done a very stupid thing. Ed knew it. Maggie knew it. And so did Johnny. Ed shuddered at what might have been.

If he stayed, he'd have to deal with Maggie more directly. She wanted more than his body. It was hard to believe she even wanted that. But eventually she'd want commitment. She needed, deserved someone a lot more reliable than him. What did they say—a recovering alcoholic was only one crisis and one drink away from the bottom of the bottle.

He had to build a stronger shield around his heart, that was for sure. Johnny's accident had proven that. He never cried, and here he was blubbering over people he hadn't even known a year ago. Sometimes he missed the drink—at least it was good at blurring emotions. You didn't feel as deeply. Not pain, not...he shook his head.

He had no business thinking about such things. That was another thing about a good drunk, you didn't think so much. His skin crawled at the thought of it. Booze had kept him from being who he really was and what he wanted to be. It had provided a fragile shell of a reality. He wasn't going back there, no matter what.

Ed slowly opened his eyes to see sunshine pouring through the hospital window. The storm squall, long gone, had delivered no rain. Still asleep, Maggie was slumped beside him on the small couch, his arm resting on her shoulders. When he stirred, she yawned and pulled herself up to a sitting position.

"Mommy."

Maggie turned her head toward the hoarse, sleepy voice. "Yes, Johnny. Yes, baby. How are you?" She moved to the bedside and rubbed his uninjured hand.

"Mom, you said you'd never ever call me baby again."

Ed chuckled.

"I'm sorry," she murmured with a catch in her throat. "I forgot. Forgive me this once. Okay?"

"Okay. Only this once."

The towheaded boy's smile reminded Ed of a ray of moonshine on a clear, cold wintry night. In fact, he hadn't noticed until now that Johnny had his mom's smile.

"So, how are you, young man?" asked Ed, a bit more gruffly than he had wished.

"Fine," was the whispered response. "You're not going to keep me away from the horses, are you?" Johnny's voice became stronger, his eyes widening in fright.

Grimacing, Ed took the boy's good hand and squeezed it. "No, of course not. Don't think you're going to get out of doing chores that easily. Reckon you won't make the same mistake twice. But we will have to spend some time going back over the basics of safe horse care. Okay?"

"Okay. I know I screwed up, Ed. Thanks for helping me."

"Yeah."

"Hey, you guys — it's nice to see this male bonding thing. But what about the mother? Don't I get to say if he continues with the horses?" Maggie arched her eyebrows high.

"No." Both males responded in unison.

Maggie beamed broadly. "My men. You guys are going to gang up on me."

Ignoring her possessive reference, Ed kidded, "It'll take a lot more than a couple guys to gang up on you."

Johnny giggled and then sobered quickly. "Mom?"

"Yes."

"Will I still be able to go to camp? It's two weeks away."

Ed studied the boy and his mom. They were now communicating on a level he didn't know. He suspected the boy was pulling on his mother's heart strings. And she was weighing the merits of clinging to her son or allowing him to grow up.

After a very long pause, Maggie responded, "If the doctor says it's okay, then you'll be able to go to camp."

"Hurrah!" cheered the boy, pounding the air with his uninjured arm. "I asked him last night before they gave me the shot. He said he'd bet I'd be able to go."

"No swimming," Maggie demanded. "Crafts may be difficult, but I'm sure you'll manage. Guess we'll have to see what you can do in two weeks time."

"Time can heal most anything," growled Ed. "At least that's what folks say."

Maggie stared at him quizzically. "Does it heal broken hearts and shattered egos?"

Ed gave the blond sphinx the blankest look he could muster.

CHAPTER NINE

Drip...drip...drip. The kitchen faucet droned on.

"Dammit. Ed, would you fix my dripping faucet sometime today?" Maggie sighed heavily. "It never stops. Between it and this stifling August heat, I think I'm gonna go batty."

Ed drew his attention from the pedigree books spread out across the kitchen table to look over at Maggie. He didn't know if she was more likely to faint from the heat or jump out of her skin. It had been like that since the kids had left for camp. Ed wiped moisture from the end of his nose. He hoped the kids were cool by the lake.

"I'll get a pipe wrench after we're done here. Hip Number sixty-six looks promising," he commented, running his finger down a page in a fall auction catalogue.

He glanced back at Maggie. Her eyes had glazed over as if she didn't give a damn about Hip Number sixty-six. The heat wave was causing humans to wilt as well as plants.

He didn't have to be a mind reader to know she also worried about her family's future. And she had every reason to worry. The crops were essentially a bust, though he knew she did have crop insurance. The horses were holding their own in Chicago, but that could change in a flash. She had to develop a credible, quality breeding program in a short amount of time.

They had to select some broodmares at the major fall sales to go along with Midnight Dancer, who he still hoped she'd buy. *That* was one fine piece of horseflesh.

"I don't know, Ed. Maybe we're just fooling ourselves." Maggie wiped her brow with the back of her hand. "I can't use up all my reserves buying horses. I have to keep some aside for making it through the winter and next spring's planting."

"That's understandable, but broodmares are the best way to go for the long haul. If you can't afford them this fall, so be it, but what you're learning now about breeding and pedigrees is important whenever you buy."

"Suppose you're right. But if something good doesn't happen fairly soon, I'm not even going to be able to afford Midnight Dancer."

Ed saw the disappointment on her face and winced. He'd been wondering about Dancer and whether Maggie would be able to swing that deal. Ignoring a warning gong clamoring in his head, he closed the pedigree book. "Tell you what, Maggie, if you can come up with half of the price for Dancer, I'll come up with the other half. We'd split all costs and profits right down the middle. What do you say?" He couldn't believe how rapidly his heart pounded.

Maggie cocked her head sideways. Slowly she started to grin. "Harrington, you've been holding out on me. I thought you were down and out when I found you."

Ed's lips thinned. He had no plans of sharing his life story with this woman. "Let's just say I have a fair amount of reserves that I never drank up. Or maybe you got to me before I sank that low."

She shook her head.

He didn't like the fire he saw building behind those blue ovals. "Well, do you want to buy the Dancer or not?"

"Of course, I do. And I like the idea of being your partner." Her teeth looked especially white and gleaming. "I like that a lot."

"I'll call Travers later today and let him know. I'd like to get the mare purchased before he gets too antsy. We won't move her down here until later in the fall. I just don't want you to lose the Dancer."

"Thanks, partner." Maggie reached over to shake his hand.

Ed dropped her hand like it was diseased. The biggest problem he had working with Maggie Anderson was keeping his hands off of her. And now he had just muddied the waters further because of a damn good broodmare. Well, it was one way to get back into the business.

Yet, she was the boss. He didn't really mind that, but she was a landmine waiting to explode in his face. She wanted him to be more than her hired hand. But if he succumbed to her wishes and his sexual urges, what would they have then? It wouldn't work. You just couldn't screw around with the boss. He knew that. Sometimes his body wanted to forget.

And now they were partners.

He reached for another sales catalogue and began thumbing through it. Usually he could ignore Maggie when necessary — it was painful walking around half aroused much of the time. He doubted she had any clue how easily she turned him inside out.

Try as hard as he might, Ed couldn't shake the memory of her in his arms, of her taste, of her scent, of her scorching heat burning his fingers. Avoiding her overtures was harder now that Carolyn and Johnny were away. There was little to stop a tryst from happening, except his certainty that it wouldn't work. Maggie wasn't the type of woman who would be satisfied with a fling. Nor was she the kind of woman with whom he'd want a fling. She was too innocent. Too serious. Too fragile. Too strong.

Ed peeked at Maggie. Was she unaware, even now, of the provocative, impish picture she presented sitting across the table from him in a faded print sun dress with the top three buttons undone in surrender to the intense summer heat? Curves of soft ample breasts made the plain dress the most seductive he'd ever seen. Perspiration outlined shadowy nipples.

Large blue baleful eyes caught him staring. They looked soft, filled with innocence and surprise.

Ed slouched more, unable to look away.

Her brain had nearly turned to mush listening to Ed's lecture on pedigrees. It was too damn hot for much of anything to penetrate her brain. Yet his startled stare just had. What had set him on edge—something he'd said, or something she'd done? She liked the idea of sharing Midnight Dancer with Ed. For one thing, it meant they could afford to buy the mare. And for another, partners had a harder time avoiding one another.

Even with the kids gone, he'd made no move to take her to his bed. Maybe he didn't find her attractive or interesting after all. But no, she remembered vividly his stiff arousal the evening she'd visited him in the loft apartment. He wanted her. So why the hell didn't he do something about it?

Unsettled by her own yearnings, Maggie colored slightly, glancing away under his inquisitive stare. Had they come to this? Paralyzed by the sexual tension hanging between them?

"Damn this heat. Damn that faucet." she said, standing up and pushing her chair away. She went to the refrigerator and opened the door wide, closed her eyes and turned around in front of it, lifting her short cropped hair off her nape so the coolness could reach her skin as quickly as possible.

Opening her eyes gradually, she saw Ed turning red, gawking at her. Oops. She'd given up wearing a bra on these hottest of days. If it

161

bothered him, so be it.

Ed's gray eyes turned to slate but failed to mask smoldering emotions. She had his attention. Maggie marveled at his self-control.

This sexual impasse could not continue without resolution. Breathing shallowly, Maggie decided to find out where she and Ed were headed. Enough waffling. One way or the other, she had to know. Now!

Returning Ed's gaze boldly, she stuck her tongue out playfully and cupped a breast in each palm. In a low hushed voice, she muttered, "Well, well, Mr. Harrington. Cool Mr. Harrington. Have you finally noticed something you like?"

He choked. She thought his eyes were going to pop.

"I don't know what you're talking about. What do you think you're doing?"

"Don't you, now?" Pretending to pout, she bent at the waist and rotated her upper body suggestively. Silence enveloped the kitchen with the exception of the steady drip of the faucet.

His ragged breath sounded like that of a drowning man. She watched his eyes narrow and focus on her nearly bare breasts.

Maggie straightened and tousled her hair, glancing at the *God Bless Our Home* plaque on the opposite wall. "I know one thing," she said, "I'm hot as hell, and I need to cool off."

Reaching into the freezer compartment, she retrieved several ice cubes. Swiftly, two cubes disappeared down the inside of her dress. She shivered as her breasts soaked up the frosty moisture.

Frowning at her own daring, Maggie spread her legs and pressed two more ice cubes against the dress fabric covering her crotch. With half shut eyes but keeping her gaze glued to Ed's, she swirled the cubes around and around until only a large wet impression highlighted her mound.

Shutting her eyes completely, Maggie resolved to continue her brazen act of seduction. It wasn't an art she'd ever learned much about, but then she'd always considered herself a natural learner. She'd mourned long enough. For too long she'd been alone and unloved.

Slitting her eyes open, she was pleased with Ed's perplexed scrutiny. Giving him a lopsided grin, smoothing her dress, she marveled breathlessly, "That may help some...You want some?" She extended her palms, holding more cubes.

- o -

Ed's brain buzzed trying to log in Maggie's words and actions. Had she finally gone over the edge? Was it just the heat? Why would she pursue an old broken down horse like him?

Doubts notwithstanding, his arousal was immediate, hard and painful. He ducked, cringing at the too innocent-appearing woman skipping toward him with devilment filling her eyes and three more ice cubes in her hands.

Frigid fingers grazed his bare arm, sending goosebumps chasing each other. Maggie placed herself behind his chair and then let ice cold water drip through her cupped fingers onto his neck. Ed opened his mouth to protest; words evaporated in the heat.

Chuckling softly, Maggie slipped one small cube down the back of his blue work shirt while sliding her cool moist lips across the base of his nape. "Maybe this will help you cool down some."

Closing his eyes, Ed tried to relax, certain her words were far from true. Even the relief of ice against heated skin could do little to ease the conflagration consuming his body.

Bobbing from foot to foot, Maggie reached around and placed another cube down the front of his shirt. Her hand followed, rubbing the slippery cold into his upper torso.

He tried not to shudder.

"Don't run from me again."

Ed shivered. There was no way he could run — his legs had liquefied. The feel of her breasts crushing against his back had his toes curling. His too-obvious erection spoke louder words than he could manage.

Maggie moved in front of him and knelt down to rub the last ice cube with great care along the length of his rigid arousal that strained against the denim.

"Don't reject me, Ed. This is okay. We'll work the implications through as we go. I've known for some time this was inevitable. I think you have, too."

Ed grabbed her by the shoulders and pulled her roughly against his chest. That corner of his mind which usually blew the bugle of retreat when Maggie pursued him was eerily quiet. He spoke hoarsely into her hair. "I can't deny I've fantasized about you for a long time, ever since that day on the sidewalk. You looked like such an angel then. You still do. But you shouldn't have to settle for a guy like me."

"Humph," she grumbled into his shirt, "shows you how much you know about women, particularly this woman. And I'm no angel. Don't try putting me on some pedestal with *off limits* signs posted all around it. I'll have none of that. I want to be kissed. I want to be touched. I want to be loved."

"You sure it's not just the heat or that cranky faucet that's got you all riled up?"

Leaning back to look him straight in the eye, Maggie smiled thinly, tracing a finger across his lips. She whispered, "No temperature, no drip could make me feel what I'm feeling right now. I have a thirst that only you can quench. No ice cube is going to succeed at that."

He nodded, lowering his lips to meet hers. She tasted as tart and sweet as he remembered. Her tongue sought his. He reciprocated. She put her arms around his back and held him tight. He lifted her until she sat on his lap.

The kiss had gone from testing to bruising. He wanted to climb into her delectable mouth. She arched her back, pressing harder against him.

He broke away from her lips gasping for air. Her lips were full. There was a bruise on her neck. Had he been that rough? He gulped in air trying to slow down, not wanting to be a Neanderthal. But she continued rubbing her bottom against him like they were running out of time.

Unable to withstand more of that, he abruptly stood her on her feet. Then he licked beads of perspiration from her throat. He laved first one earlobe and then the other. He bore into her ear suggestively.

Ed stopped. Maggie froze.

"Where?" he asked, gruffly.

She groaned, clutching him tighter. "Why not right here? The tiles are clean and cool."

"Babies?"

Chuckling, Maggie unwrapped herself from his arms, kicked off her flats and stepped to the counter, where she rummaged in her purse. She let out a sigh of relief and handed him a thin disk. "I'm told this is quite effective," she whispered, with a catch in her throat.

"Thought the man was supposed to be prepared."

"Figured you might never take the initiative, and, if you did, lack of this kind of preparation would be another convenient excuse for you to back off. So," she giggled, "I took things into my own hands."

"So I've noticed." Her half smile and shimmering eyes spoke loudly of her conniving.

He'd had no more chance at escaping her charms than a fly caught in a spider's web. Why had he struggled so hard for so long?

Her fingers reached for the buttons on his shirt, then spread across his bare chest. "Yes," she purred, "the kitchen will do just fine."

Stepping back from him, she unbuttoned her dress to the waist, shrugged her shoulders, and bared her upper torso.

Ed held his breath as two exquisitely round breasts greeted him. Plopping back down on his lap, she rubbed taut nipples across the hairs of his chest.

Drip...drip...drip. The only sound to be heard was the steady tapping of water slamming against the stainless steel sink. They clung to each other for a long moment.

Finally, Maggie stood again and stepped out of her dress. She slid her hip hugging panties down to the floor and stood with her gaze fixed on his.

"You're beautiful." His mouth dried. He'd never realized just how perfect a female specimen she was. And now the sexy woman who had tormented him since the moment he'd seen her approach on the sidewalk outside the Resting Arms Hotel stood before him with palms turned upward, inviting him home.

Maggie moaned softly when Ed easily picked her up and laid her on the kitchen table. Sale catalogs and pedigree charts tumbled every which way.

Ed leaned over to kiss her lips, her neck, and

then her breasts. Each breast received equal oral attention: each orb washed, each nipple stroked to full extension, each crown suckled.

Clasping her bare legs tightly around his bottom, Maggie rocked back and forth. Ed smiled when she pressed his head gently downward. He needed no more encouragement. With his tongue he traced a trail across the rivulets of perspiration forming on her flat stomach.

"I'm not a yearling filly to be gentled," she squealed huskily. She applied more encouraging pressure to his head.

"I'm not very calm," he muttered, moving his tongue lower still. Her sex opened before him. The soft fleece of golden ringlets was already soaking, and not just from the humidity.

He breathed deeply, sucking her scent into his lungs, never wanting it to escape. She tasted slightly salty. He would never get enough of her. His tongue searched further. Her legs jerked; her thighs squeezed. He paused for air.

"Oh my God," she screamed. "Don't stop now!"

In response, Ed slipped two fingers into her cleft. Spreading her thighs wide, wiggling her bottom, she offered him a better angle. He probed deeper while his tongue tapped her clit. Repeatedly, he rhythmically grazed and licked her engorged flesh.

- o -

Through the hazy fog of her mind, Maggie became aware of what Ed was doing. His subtle, sensual movements matched the beat of the faucet drip. Excruciating. Exhilarating.

She waited. He flicked his tongue and plunged his fingers. Maggie moved closer to the edge. As the faucet dripped, he continued his excruciating pace. This was different. She'd never before been played like some erotic instrument. The edge was near. She was the edge.

Shaking uncontrollably, she felt her release cascade through her body.

When at last she hunched forward on her elbows to peek through teary eyes at Ed's head resting on her belly, Maggie ginned lazily. "What a way to beat the heat." She yawned, stretching like a satisfied cat. "Why did we wait so long? But what about you?"

Maggie didn't have to wait long for an answer. She watched Ed stand and unbuckle his belt.

In a manner of moments, Maggie straddled her lover's thighs, smiling down at him. Ed didn't seem bothered at all by the kitchen tiles. Again, he was letting her assume the lead. She leaned over and kissed him lightly. "I've dreamed of this often. Have you wondered?" she asked.

"Yeah, I've thought about it once or twice," Ed deadpanned, lacing his fingers under his head.

"I should leave you hanging for that," she said, tickling his ribs, "but I won't, because I finish what I start. Unlike some people I know."

"You're not going to let me forget about that

night in the loft, are you?"

"Never. It's too much fun to threaten to leave you in the lurch, so to speak. But enough of this chatter." Maggie raised up and moved forward. Positioning herself over him, she began an unhurried descent.

Settling back on his torso, she luxuriated in the touch of him pressing against her inner walls. It had been so long. Too long. Maggie pulled on her nipples and rocked slowly back and forth. She bent forward to run her tongue across his lips and then pulled back, grinning broadly. "You like?" she asked.

- o -

Ed nodded, not trusting himself with words. Her heat surrounded him. Ed waited for Maggie to set the pace. She was more patient than he had expected. She looked so in control, so powerful. Waiting. Squeezing him with her inner muscles. Waiting again.

He watched her inch up his shaft in tiny spirals, her tempo painfully slow. A devious smile crept across her face; her eyes remained fixed on his. And then it dawned on him: she was doing the same thing he'd done. She was slithering up and down to the cadence of the drips falling from the faucet. When a drip splashed in the sink, she crashed to the floor, swallowing his shaft deep inside.

Ed squinted at their juncture, praying for the

drip to pick up speed. It didn't.

Shifting her weight slightly and placing her hands on his knees, Maggie sparked yet a different sensation, as if she were testing a new prize possession. Ed didn't care. There would never again be a first time for them.

Grinning broadly, Maggie sat back up and stretched her arms high about her head. "Two can play this game," she whispered merrily, continuing to match the pace of the dripping faucet.

"Ah." Ed smiled back at her. "And you play it so well."

Maggie rode him steadily. He started to tense. They both knew it was only a matter of time and friction. She rode on.

"Oh hell," Ed moaned, his torso straining toward completion.

He began to pulsate and rumble. At last he grabbed her hips and slammed her to his loins, draining himself. He felt Maggie shudder with her own release. Ed's entire body quaked with aftershocks. He hugged her tenderly as she settled against his chest.

Maggie mumbled somewhat incoherently, "You know, if I had any energy left, I'd get us some ice water. There'll be other times. I bet you're going to be around a long time."

Reality burst through his sated haze. A long time? Hardly. Eventually, he'd become a millstone hanging about her neck. Later. Later, he'd worry about that. For now, he permitted himself to wallow in the pleasure of her body pressed atop his.

It had been a fantastic day, Ed acknowledged grudgingly. To have a woman to love like Maggie who worked as hard as he did and shared similar dreams was an uncommon experience. Oh, there had been women before, plenty of them. But no Maggie Anderson. Most of the women he'd been with weren't interested in getting their hands dirty, and he'd never shared his hopes and dreams with any of them.

He glanced down at Maggie nestled in the crook of his arm. They sat on the porch swing gliding rhythmically back and forth, letting the day wash gently over them. Robins chattered and finches chirped as the sun settled for the night. The evening seemed so right. That humbled and frightened him.

"This is pretty good." Maggie said, peering up at him.

"Yeah, this is pretty good," he agreed, pulling her closer. He wouldn't allow himself to wish that it could last. They had some time before the kids returned from camp. That might be enough for her to tire of him or to wake up and see the fatal flaws that marred his character. But for now he wasn't going to dwell on the inevitable. Now was a time to enjoy and to fill his senses with Maggie. He leaned over, breathed her scent deeply and kissed the top of her head.

He watched her look up at him inquisitively.

Her faint smile would confound any man's heart. Her eyes were misty with tears of joy. He shuddered — they were only harbingers of tears of a different kind.

"I'm glad we finally got our act together, Mr. Hot Shot Trainer," Maggie teased. "There for a while I thought you were running a marathon, and I didn't know if I was going to keep up."

"Humph. You have enough stamina and courage — you could run any man into the ground."

"No, not just any man," she disagreed. "You're the only man I'm interested in. And I'm a one man woman."

"I never doubted that a bit, Maggie." Ed stood abruptly, leaned with his back against the porch rail, and faced those sky blue eyes.

He saw her swallow hard. Fear flickered across her features before she folded her hands in her lap. She was probably wondering if he would even stay the night.

Ed shoved his hands in his front pockets. "Woman, you've gotten to me, I have to confess that. Yeah, I know you're a one man woman. I don't know if I'm a one woman man. It's been so long I'm not sure about anything when it comes to women. Fair warning — just don't get your heart set on anything long term."

"I didn't ask for promises."

"Your body speaks louder than any words can. Ah, Maggie." He pulled her off the swing into his arms. "It's hard as hell to be with you, but it's even harder without. Just remember, I warned you. Your roots are deep in this rich Iowa soil. And I'm a rolling stone."

"It's okay," she moaned into his chest. "I don't have a crystal ball either. But be forewarned, I collect stones."

Gliding his hands over her buttocks, pulling her closer, rubbing his lips tenderly across her forehead, Ed whispered, "Maybe we ought to find a bed this time. My body's getting a little too old for tile floors."

"I think your body is just the right age, but I bet a bed can be arranged." Placing her hand in his, she tugged him through the kitchen doorway toward the stairs leading up to her bedroom.

- o -

Five spectacular love-drenched days sprinted by far too quickly. Maggie lay in her bed watching rays of the sunrise peeking through lacy curtains. She gazed at the lined face of her sleeping lover and her eyes watered. She couldn't remember a more delicious five days in her entire life.

Daily, she and Ed had risen early to make love, cook breakfast and then go work with the horses. In the evening, they would sit on the porch and listen to the twilight sounds as nature prepared for bed, and then they too retired to make fabulous love again.

Ed had surprised her with his attentiveness. She'd soared so often in a sensual orbit of fulfillment there weren't enough hours in the day to do all that needed to be done.

She greeted each day as a blessed gift. Never had she expected she would be fortunate enough to find love twice in a lifetime. Wasn't that what fairy tales were made of? Could it last when the kids returned from camp? It had to.

Yet as her spirits climbed new heights, Ed was less talkative, more glum and at times downright rude. Was he struggling with commitment? Did he wonder about how the kids would react to him as their mother's lover?

Or did he regard her as not good enough for the long haul? He was probably used to flashier women in the big city. Maybe he'd quickly tire of a plain farm girl.

And it wasn't like he had pursued her. But he was such a considerate lover. He'd matched her passion. She didn't doubt his love for her. Still, there was something troubling him, and he wasn't talking about it.

- o -

Through narrowed slits, Ed cringed at the sight of radiant bliss on Maggie's face. How had he allowed things to get so out of control? She was the most beautiful women he'd ever been with. She was stunning on the outside, but even more especially, she was beautiful on the inside. He didn't want to see her hurt, but pain was inevitable now. He'd failed at protecting her —

from him.

She would do okay. She was a survivor. Behind her air of innocence stood a steel-trap will. The woman had more grit and determination than most men he'd known. If she set her mind on something, she seldom failed. She exercised a sharp sense of judgment that would take her far in the horse world. How had her powers of discernment had gone so far awry with him?

Flashing a half smile, Maggie ran a finger across his furrowed brow. "Don't play possum. I know you're awake."

Ed grunted, feigning sleep.

Maggie bounced playfully on the bed and tossed the sheets to the floor. Kneeling beside him, she leaned over and used her tongue to trace tiny circles around his nipples, first one and then the other.

"Damn, woman, can't you let a man sleep now and then?" he groused, stroking her corded neck muscles.

"Not this man." She worked her hand around his erection and up and down its length. "Feels like you're more than a little awake."

With Maggie licking his belly button and moving lower still, Ed sank into a pleasurable abyss. How could he escape a whirlwind? How could he protect Maggie Anderson from herself? Quickly, the questions were forgotten.

CHAPTER TEN

Later that same day, after the horses were cared for and supper dishes were finished, Maggie and Ed sat comfortably side by side on the porch swing. She worked a crossword puzzle and he caught up on racing news from the Daily Racing Form. Frogs croaked, announcing the approach of evening. The blood-red sun rested atop the western horizon.

Both Maggie and Ed glanced up at the sound of a vehicle entering the driveway. It was a white compact, the kind popular with rental car agencies.

Maggie scrutinized the familiar figure getting out of the car and walking stiffly toward the house. "Oh, shit."

"Who the hell is that?" Ed asked, picking up on Maggie's distress. The man approaching them had on a blazing Hawaiian shirt, khaki shorts, and the whitest patent leather shoes Ed had ever seen. He didn't know whether to laugh or cry.

"That's my brother."

"Your…"

"Brother. Guess I didn't get around to mentioning him," she said weakly.

"No, guess not." Ed stood aside and watched Maggie move to greet her brother. Neither sibling appeared all that eager. This didn't look like a grand family reunion. He decided it was best for him to simply lay low. This was Maggie's place. And it was her brother.

The man dressed for the beach opened the screen door. "You don't look all that pleased to see your dear brother, Sis. Wonder why?"

Ed observed the man's smile, which never reached his eyes. His resemblance to Maggie was remarkable. The same straw-blond hair, turned-up nose and oval face. But he was of medium build. Thankfully, her brother's eyes were brown. Ed's dislike for the sneering intruder was immediate and intense. Not only had Maggie failed to tell him about her brother, neither had she indicated the pain she carried because of him. Ed took a step closer to Maggie.

She swung an arm behind her back as if to keep him from interfering. "Do you want some coffee, Brad? Or maybe some lemonade?" Her inflection was flat and toneless.

"Not even a *good to see you, long time no see, why are you here?*"

Clasping her hands loosely at her waist, she replied, "I figure you'll tell me soon enough. If you don't want anything to drink, at least have a seat. And oh...this is Ed Harrington. He works for me." Motioning toward Ed, she added, "This is my brother, Brad."

Ed extended his hand, quickly took the shorter man's and shook it firmly. "Pleased to meet you," he lied.

"I doubt that." Moving to sit on the edge of a

chair, Brad frowned at his sister. "So this is the man you've been shacking up with."

Maggie squeezed Ed's thigh tightly as he started to rise up off the swing to go after her brother.

"It's all right," she whispered to him. Turning to Brad she said, "Ed and I are lovers. So what is that to you? You've been married and divorced more times than I can remember, and I sure wouldn't know what came in between."

"Hell, I don't give a damn how many men are screwing you, Sis. I just think it's a hoot. I wish Mom and Dad were here now. You were always the perfect one. The hard worker. The good student. The perfect wife and mother. And now look at you—a single mom with the hots for a man who can hardly limp past a bottle. Yeah, I've heard about your good Mr. Harrington. Sis, you never could walk past a stray dog."

Ed throttled his anger. How could the usually bristling Maggie just sit there and take crap from such a fancy dude?

Maggie sat ramrod straight.

Brad studied his manicured fingernails.

At last, Maggie broke the silence. "So what do you want, Brad? Why are you here now? I've sent a check each month since the will was read. It'll take time, but that was stated clearly in Dad's will."

Ed's brow furrowed.

Brad shot him a look of contempt. "So you don't know that I'm a silent partner in this operation of Maggie's? I own twenty-five percent of the place."

"You did own twenty-five percent. That's down to less than twenty now. I should have just paid you off in a lump sum with Mason's life insurance money, but Dad's instructions were to pay you over a fifteen year period."

"He wanted me tied to my sister's apron strings, that's why."

The bitterness in her brother's voice bothered Ed. Why would a father want to dictate family loyalty from the grave?

Maggie crossed her arms under her breasts. "And you have no say in what I do with the land. You own a portion, but you can't sell it to anyone but me. I not only own over eighty percent of the land, Dad made clear in the will that he wanted you to have no say in the operation of the farm. That's why you got so much cash when Mom and Dad were killed. I can't help it if you go through money like it's toilet paper."

"Ah, yes. Saint Maggie. Maggie—Daddy's girl who had dirt under her fingernails and sand in her veins. I never could understand why you loved this damn farm so much. I couldn't wait to get away from it, and you seem to wear it proudly like a millstone around your neck."

"We always have had different interests."

"That's putting it mildly. Anyway, I understand from the banker that we have a significant offer for the farm. I want to sell!"

Ed thought the man's neck veins might pop.

Well, at least he finally knew what was going on. Sort of.

Maggie laughed a dry laugh. "You've certainly wasted your time coming all the way from California to tell me that news. You've wanted to sell from the moment our parents were in the ground. I'm not selling. No chance. I'm sure Prater went to a lot of effort to track you down. But it won't do any good. You can't make me sell. I wish I could just pay you off and be done with it."

"Who the hell is going to sue if you did pay me off? Dad's not coming back, you know."

Ed watched Maggie recoil from her brother's words. He was surprised by pain flashing across her brother's face. Maybe he hadn't meant to hurt his sister after all. How much of Brad's performance was an act? Or maybe it was the twenty-fifth act of an old play between brother and sister.

"For your information," Brad's voice lowered, "I happened to be coming back from a business trip to Minneapolis. And Mr. Prater keeps me informed now and then about my Iowa investment and the carryings-on of my sister." He paused. Ed received the brunt of the man's glare. Looking back at Maggie, Brad said, "And I don't like one bit you chasing some damn foolish fantasy regarding racehorses. You'll screw everything up yet. If you go bankrupt, I stand to lose right along with you."

"I understand." Maggie exhaled slowly. "Your position is clear and always has been. If I can get ahead enough, maybe I should go ahead and pay you off. But until then, I'm afraid your investment in the farm, as small as it is, remains at the same risk as mine. In any legal proceeding, I out vote you eight to two. And there is the binding will, which you have already unsuccessfully contested. So?"

Ed crossed his legs at the ankles and relaxed a little. That was some good news. This was better than any soap opera he'd ever seen, which wasn't very many. This was the determined Maggie that he knew so well. This was the Maggie who could scare him at times — and no doubt her brother, too.

"So. You never were able to take sound advice." Brad visibly shed some of his anger and relaxed a bit. He gave Maggie a genuine smile. "Well, as long as I'm here I'd kind of like to see my nephew and niece. They've probably grown a lot since I last saw them."

"I'm sorry, Brad. They're not here. They're away at summer camp and won't be back for another three days."

"Oh, isn't that just handy," he said, balling his hands into fists. "I've got some time coming. I guess I'll wait a few days to see them. Maybe I can find out some information from Prater or Con-Ex Farms that will convince you to sell."

"Don't count on that. Has Ben Templeton reached you yet?"

"No, but I've been on the road for weeks. What does that snake-in-the-grass want?"

"You'll have to ask him, but it is important. He

can explain." Letting out a sigh, Maggie said, "Brad, it's nice that you want to see the kids. They do miss you. They've always liked the funny stories you tell. And you know you're welcome to stay here."

"No. No way. I haven't slept in this house since you inherited it. And I certainly wouldn't start now when you have your hands so full with horses and your hired man." Brad stood and sauntered toward the door. "No, I'll stay in town. Maybe look up some old buddies. I'll be around."

Ignoring Ed entirely, Brad Magee stepped out into the darkening night.

- o -

Maggie felt Ed place a comforting arm around her shoulders. When all they could see of the compact was its red tail lights in the distance, she shuddered against the cool breeze and the despair her brother left behind.

"You want to talk about it?" Ed asked softly.

She turned and buried her tears in his chest. "You sure got an ear full. Bet you didn't know I was such an evil person. Most of the time I try to forget I have a brother."

Maggie stepped away from Ed, leaned against the porch wall, and shook her head. She stared past Ed out into the dark.

"He was Mommy's boy and I was Daddy's girl." She sighed and flopped down onto an overstuffed porch chair. "Maybe it would have

183

been different if I had been the second born. But I was first born. And I listened well to my dad. I accepted his philosophy and work ethic. He taught me to love the land, and that nothing came to anybody without hard work. He taught me to be strong because I had Magee blood coursing through my veins."

"You're nothing if not strong," Ed commented. "Sometimes too damn strong for your own good."

"I doubt that," Maggie muttered. "Four years younger, Brad always resented his older sister. Maybe for good reason. I don't know. He didn't naturally take to the land or to farm work. He hated the hogs. He'd rather have his nose in a book."

Maggie smiled a half smile. "There's nothing wrong with being studious. But it didn't meet Dad's expectation for a son. Dad kept forcing me on Brad as the role model. *Work as hard as your sister and you'll be fine. Your sister can work the land and still get good grades, why can't you? Why do you want to go off to college, your sister didn't. Your place is here on the farm with your sister.*"

"Oh, I'm sure I had to have been a real pain in the ass for Brad. I was active in 4-H; Brad didn't want to join. And Dad was furious. When we were young, I don't imagine I really appreciated what was happening, or wanted to. If anything, I was probably smug about being the favored child. And I probably worked hard to maintain that status."

"Where was your ma in all of this?"

"Oh, she tried to protect Brad the best she

could. But she seldom took Dad on directly. Few people did. He was a good man, but he was set in his ways. And he did have a temper."

"Sounds like somebody I'm getting to know," Ed said.

Maggie glared at him and then broke out laughing. "Yeah, I suppose you're right. I take after my Dad, but I hope not in all ways. He was much more controlling that I ever understood when he was alive.

She hunched forward, rubbing her shoulders. "Anyway, Brad did as little as he could around the farm and then only grudgingly. He only did things he was told to do. He'd never volunteer to do more. He couldn't wait to escape to college. And Mom encouraged him to go. She knew it wouldn't ever work for him to stay on the farm and work with Dad. Their personalities clashed. There seemed to be no way around that."

"And there never was a reconciliation?"

Maggie tucked her legs under her body. "No. Never. Brad joined a fraternity and lived the good life: beer, women and partying. It took a while, but he finally did graduate in computer science. He only came home to visit—mainly Mom. Never stayed long. And then he was on his way. He's gone through almost as many jobs as women. But he's never had much difficulty finding another of either." Maggie frowned. "He's not big on permanency."

Ed nodded. Maggie saw a flicker in his eyes she couldn't recognize.

"Let me get us some coffee," Ed said, getting up and moving toward the kitchen.

She heard him banging around in the kitchen and was comforted to have a break. It was difficult talking about her family. But maybe now Ed would say more about his. He certainly was learning that her family was no model. She worried that her crack about Brad and permanency might have struck too close to home for Ed.

"Try this," he offered, returning with two steaming mugs.

She sipped the butternut flavored coffee and grinned. "This is soothing. Thanks."

Ed sat back down. "So your father didn't trust Brad with the land even in the will. He seems to have gone to some fairly extreme measures so you would control the land."

"Yes, he did. I was shocked by the will and the letter of instruction. Brad was livid. While he liked the extra cash that came to him, he still wanted me to sell the farm. For him, it was almost a matter of principle. The farm had been such an onerous thing for him. Obviously, I wouldn't sell, and he knew that. So did Dad. That's why he wrote the will the way he did.

"Right or wrong. Fair or unfair. I don't know." Maggie sipped her coffee and glanced at Ed, wondering what he was making of all of this. Now that she'd begun, it was important that he understand. "I've been paying Brad off bit by bit. I wish I could have paid him off with the insurance money, but I don't trust my brother—no matter what he says. If I violate the letter of the will by paying him off faster than it states, what's to prevent Brad from contesting the entire will again?"

"You two do seem to be bound together by parents from the grave," Ed said. "I know it happens a lot, but it seems eerie."

"Dad always said blood was thicker than water, and Mom always wanted us to be more of a family. I imagine both of them thought the way the will was written would mean we would at least have to deal with each other. That may be true. But I don't think the will has helped brother-sister bonding. Sometimes I don't know what to do with him. He is my only brother. And he is the kids' uncle."

- o -

The next day, hoping to avoid Maggie's brother, Ed stayed busy with the horses. That afternoon his luck ran out.

Glancing up from inventorying medical supplies, he saw Brad Magee enter the barn. At least the man was more appropriately dressed today with jeans, a tan polo shirt, and tennis shoes. He hadn't come ready to work, but then Ed hadn't expected that.

"Good morning," Brad said cheerfully.

Immediately on guard, Ed responded, "And how are you today?"

"I've been worse." Brad glanced at the vast array of bottles, syringes and bandages Ed had spread out on a work table. "So you were quite successful in Chicago?"

"You could say that."

"But things went sour."

"You got that right."

"How'd you get linked up with my sister?"

"She found me."

"Why doesn't that surprise me more?" Brad paused, taking a second look at his surroundings. "Looks like you've got quite a set up here."

Ed lifted his eyes from his checklist to peer directly at Maggie's brother. "Your sister wanted me to help her set up a competitive racing stable. We've done some things that make that a possibility."

"I'll just bet you have."

"Do you have a problem with something?"

Brad raised his open palm quickly. "Not at all. Ben Templeton vouches for you as a horse trainer. I'm sure you know what you're doing. I may not trust the man, but he wouldn't do anything to harm Maggie. As far as my sister goes, anybody who can take her on is a better man than me."

Reaching into his back pocket, pulling out a flask, Brad paused to lift the container to his lips.

As the sweet smell of whisky invaded his nostrils, Ed watched Brad's Adam's apple rise and fall, measuring greedy swallows. The man was in ecstasy. Ed's stomach lurched; his entire body tensed.

"Want a pull or two?" Brad asked, holding out the flask toward Ed.

Repulsed by the man's devilish grin, Ed stopped long enough to visualize his latest sobriety chip. "No, thanks. I don't touch the stuff. It can be dangerous to your health, but then you probably know that."

"Yeah, heard tell that Sis was trying to reform an alcoholic. Our dad always believed she could work miracles."

Brad shoved the flask back into his hip pocket. "So tell me about betting horses. Craps has always been my game, but I've had a run of bad luck recently. I hear money can be made at the track, though."

"For some. But trainers are about the last folks who can talk about betting. They get too attached to their own horses to handicap objectively."

"But you know something about handicapping?"

"Of course. You have to make similar judgments when placing your horse in appropriate races."

"So how do I learn? Where do I get the inside tips?"

Ed stood grinning at the shorter man. "You want an edge? There is no edge other than some hard-headed work and a good bit of luck. Now, I've got to go work some horses. Hopefully, with a bit of luck, we can make some money at the track that way."

"So you won't help me?" Brad sneered. "Hard

work and luck—that's what I've heard all my life. I'm doing pretty well, and I don't have to sweat much doing it."

"I can loan you a book or two if you like," Ed offered. "With your background in computers, you might be quite interested in speed handicapping. Now I have to get back to work."

"Don't you walk away from me when I'm talking to you!" Brad shouted at Ed's back.

Ed turned slowly. "I'd suggest that you not use that tone of voice with me, mister. Your sister may feel that she has to tolerate it—I don't. I've tried to be polite with you because you're Maggie's brother, but enough is enough. It's probably best for both of us if you leave the barn area now."

Brad sputtered. "That's fine with me. The stench is overwhelming."

Ed knew Brad was following him, but he didn't turn around. He didn't want a physical confrontation with Maggie's brother.

"I'll let you get back to planning how to wheedle your way into my sister's pants and money."

Ed tensed when he heard mocking laughter. He turned and stared at the smaller man, who had come to an abrupt halt just out of arms reach.

"Looks like you're doing fine with both." Brad put his thumbs in his belt loops.

He didn't look nearly as tough as he probably thought he did. Ed wanted to laugh.

"I sure don't know what she sees in you. You've got no future, only a past. One of these days she'll come to her senses and dump you on your tarnished ass." Brad ginned a victorious smile. "Maybe then she'll sell."

Ed's fingers flexed involuntarily into fists. In an earlier time in his life, he would have bloodied the man's nose long before now. He took a half step toward Brad and stopped. Maggie would be mad as hell if he threw a punch. Instead, Ed turned and walked away, leaving her brother cussing at him and the entire world.

Seeking relief, Ed saddled a horse and trotted him out across the meadow and the old pasture land. He wondered why Maggie's father had never plowed it under for planting crops. It didn't make much sense to use the valuable land for a few beef to graze when it could be planted with cash crops. But then a lot about the Magee-Anderson family didn't make much sense.

He felt like he was being sucked into some vortex that had no name and was governed by rules unknown to him. Why hadn't she told him about her brother? Was it shame, or did she think he might perceive her brother as a monkey wrench in the stable plans? Who was playing whom for a fool?

Ed squeezed the horse into an easy canter. He loved being on horseback. Often he could think more clearly atop a horse than on the ground. Images of Carolyn and Johnny flashed through his mind. Damn, they'd be home shortly. Then what?

A lot of things were crowding him all at once.

Life would get worse before improving. Why had he succumbed to her wiles? That was what was making everything so sticky. If they hadn't become lovers, Maggie's brother would have less ammunition to use against her. Brad might be a rake, but Ed didn't want Maggie to be regarded in the same light.

Did anything hold brother and sister together other than resentments and admonitions from the grave?

That stupid ass for a brother had seen through him quickly enough. What had he said? *You've got no future, only a past. One of these day's she'll come to her senses and dump you on your tarnished ass.* Ed didn't doubt that at all; he never had.

- o -

Two days later, Maggie sat on a hay bale watching Ed repair a longe line. He looked so focused braiding the rope to fit a gun metal snap. She loved to observe him when he was totally engrossed. The cat in her lap stood, arched its back and leapt to the floor.

It was hard not to worry. There was her brother, and she and Ed were working through their relationship, and then the kids would be home the next day. They'd be pleased about Ed and her, but she still was a little embarrassed. It wasn't every day that she could tell her adolescent daughter and pre-adolescent son that she had taken on a lover. They would be delighted; she just hoped they wouldn't smother Ed. He'd balk at that. No doubt about it.

He'd become even more quiet and pensive since her brother showed up. Maggie had tried to get Ed to talk about the future, but he was so adept at sidetracking the conversation. Their lovemaking, if anything, had become more intense, more urgent. Her body warmed just imagining them entwined in the aftermath of passion.

With a satisfied smile, Ed looked over at her. "There," he said, pulling on the longe line and testing its strength. "That ought to last a while longer. Okay, what now? I can see the wheels spinning in your conniving little head. You're up to something."

"So…you're Eddie Travers' godfather."

Ed frowned. "Where the hell did that come from, and what else has Cassie been telling you behind my back?"

"All your secrets and more. I was touched by the story of Eddie's birth. Don't be so grumpy about it. You should be honored that they wanted you to be his godfather."

"I am," he responded. Exhaling, he said, "I'm just not very damn good at it now, am I?"

"What do you mean by that?"

"Would you want your son to grow up like me?" He laughed caustically, as if he had told a bad joke.

"I would be delighted if you were the father of my son. You'd make a super dad," Maggie said, jumping to her feet. "We all make mistakes, Ed. None of us is perfect. The question is, what will we learn from our mistakes? I hope Johnny turns out as caring and loving as you."

"Bullshit!" He started to walk away.

"I think you should move into the house."

- o -

She might as well have hit him over the head with a sledgehammer. Like a trapped animal, he growled and backpedaled. "No, that won't work. What we've had has been nice, but it's got to end. Your kids are coming home tomorrow."

"Nice!" Maggie rapidly closed the distance between them. "Won't work? Why the hell not? I love you," she said, pounding her fists on his chest. "You love me. We'll make it work."

"I never…"

"I know you never used those words—you don't have to. They are in your eyes and on your fingertips when we make love and when we're sitting on the porch swing. You can't deny it."

Ed simply glowered at her, then turned his back on her so she wouldn't see his pain.

"So why won't it work?" she asked in a low, hushed voice. "Anything worthwhile will work if you set your mind to it. And we have love working for us."

Ed spun around.

Maggie took a step backwards.

"Don't tell me what I feel. You've got it all

194

wrong. Pollyanna doesn't work in real life. You pick a drunk up out of the gutter and think you can remake him and do whatever you want with him. It won't work. Even your brother is smart enough to figure that out."

"Ed…"

"Don't try to color things different than they are. We've had a damn good roll in the hay these last several days, but that's it." Ed grabbed gloves from his back pocket. "You've proven you can still attract a man, of sorts. Now go out and find a decent one who can give you what you need, love ever after."

Not waiting for a response, Ed stormed out of the barn toward his truck. He climbed in and twisted the ignition key. The engine sputtered and stopped. "Not now, Mabel." He slammed a fist against the steering wheel. "Don't do this to me." He tried the key. Again the engine sputtered, then seemed to catch new life. Without looking back toward the barn, Ed gunned Mabel and himself out of the driveway and out of Maggie Anderson's life.

- o -

With mouth ajar and tears streaming down her face, Maggie ran to the barn entrance to watch his beat up truck lurch down the dirt road. How could he run away from her like this?

Brushing away tears with the back of her hand, she screamed, "No!" Her balled fists banged against the unyielding rough boards of the barn wall.

With her energy drained, she stared down the empty road. Could he be right? Had she merely used him to see if she could still attract a man? Had she misread what she thought were signs of love—his and hers? Ed wasn't big on talk. She often was left to read between the lines. Well, reading between these lines wasn't difficult at all—he didn't want her anymore.

Squaring her shoulders, Maggie marched toward the house. She'd move on. She'd always been able to pull herself together after a crisis. It was doubtful he'd want to continue working for her. Not that she wanted or needed him. She'd have to find someone else to help with the horses.

Going through the doorway leading into the kitchen, Maggie sank to the floor, her newly found reservoir of determination seriously sapped. It was here where they had first made love. The kitchen table would never allow her to waltz back to a time before Ed Harrington as if nothing of incredible import hadn't transpired on that table and this floor. She could sell the table, but what about the floor?

She cried until there were no more tears. How had she screwed up so badly? Moving on would be extremely difficult. The horses were one thing, but Ed was quite another. She rested her head in her hands. Whether he loved her or not, she had come to love him profoundly. And that was the problem. He was meant for her. Her bones still sang that fact clearly. So how could things get so desperately out of whack so quickly?

Like a sleepwalker, the next morning Maggie dragged herself though the chores that had to be done. She fed the horses, made sure the water tanks contained fresh water, turned out a couple horses for exercise and rubbed them down afterward. The same routine as usual — but nothing was normal.

Ed had not come back, not even for his clothes. She expected he'd do that when he thought she'd be away.

The kids would be home sometime in the afternoon. How was she going to explain to them what had happened when she didn't really know herself?

Hank had been by to begin plowing under the parched, stunted corn in the forty acre field bordering the road. There was no hope left for that crop. The best it could offer now was fertilizer for next year's planting, if there was to be a next year planting and a next year harvest.

She leaned heavily against the barn door and watched Hank methodically drive the tractor and plow back and forth turning over the dry soil. Would this heat wave, would this drought ever end? Other fields might yet yield some kind of crop, but as each day went by to be followed by yet another parched day, the chances of any harvest became increasingly remote.

A dry wind blew her hair but brought no relief

from the heat. How long would Mr. Fallon of Con-Ex Farms wait before returning with a check in his hand? And what about Prater? He was no doubt praying for the drought to continue. And her brother? Ah, yes, her lovable brother. What had he said to Ed? He'd probably drop by to gloat before long.

Maggie rubbed residual tears from her eyes, questioning her own sanity. Had she put too much faith in the land? Would the land be her ultimate downfall? No, her family had survived worse over the decades. She would make it.

"Damn," she mumbled, "why couldn't he stay and work things out?"

CHAPTER ELEVEN

Johnny and Carolyn ran toward the house loaded down with sleeping bags and duffels. "We're home!" Johnny cried, grinning from ear to ear. "Mrs. Murphy didn't have time to come in."

Both children dropped bags and duffels to the floor and ran to hug their mother.

"It's great to see you," Maggie squealed, hugging them. "You look so tan. How was camp? Were your fingers a problem, Johnny? Was it cooler by the lake? Tell me all about it."

"Not very," Johnny said. "Even the water was warm. But it didn't matter none. My hand didn't bother me. Camp was great! Wait until you see the rocks I found."

"Have you been sick, Mom?" Carolyn asked, squinting at her mother. "You look puffy."

"No," Maggie said heavily. "I'm not sick. So tell me everything."

Peering more closely at her daughter, Maggie gasped. Four metal studs adorned Carolyn's left ear. "My goodness, Carolyn what have you done to your ear?"

"Don't have a fit, Mother. All the girls are doing it. Even some of the guys."

"But we never talked about it. You could get an infection. This is serious."

"Mom. It's my ear. I can do what I want with it.

Besides, the girl who did the piercing knows what she's doing. She has five studs in each ear."

Maggie's hand flew to her ear. "Good God."

"You're always telling us not to bring God into things like this. I'm almost fifteen, Mom. I can do what I want with my own ears." Carolyn grabbed her duffle and stalked toward the stairs.

"Please stay, Carolyn, and tell me about camp. We can discuss this later.

Carolyn's lower lip quivered before she dropped her bag and pulled up a chair at the kitchen table.

Maggie looked at her daughter. How could so much happen in two weeks? Not only did Carolyn have the studs, she wore so much eye shadow that her eyes almost disappeared.

It took nearly two hours to hear the highlights of two weeks of camp and to see all the crafts and memory books. Johnny was more forthcoming than his sister. Maggie wondered what else her fourteen year old daughter was concealing. They'd never really kept secrets.

Right. Well, a mother should keep some secrets from her daughter. She wasn't so sure it should work the same the other way around. But then, she hadn't told her mom about all her own teenage escapades, either.

"I'm gonna run tell Ed about camp," Johnny announced, jumping off his chair. "I've missed him, too."

Maggie nearly gagged with dread. She reached for her son's arm as he started to race by. "Ed's not here," she managed to mumble.

"Oh. Did he go to town?"

"I don't know."

"Mom." Carolyn straightened her posture. "What aren't you telling us?"

Maggie shook her head, fighting desperately for control.

"You two had a fight, didn't you?"

Blanching at her daughter's accusation, Maggie retorted, "That's none of your business." *Great. Now I'm shutting out my own kids. Get a grip.*

"Will he be back? Mom, will he be back?"

Johnny's plea ripped at Maggie's soul. Tears formed in his eyes. Maggie wished she had an answer. She desperately wished she could make those tears go away. But she could only say, "I don't know, son."

Carolyn sneered. "What did you do to send him away?"

The blaming words didn't surprise Maggie. Even though somewhat prepared for them, she still struggled to stay on top of her temper. Her children were shocked and grieving. She didn't want them to deny their feelings, but neither did she want to shoulder the entire blame for their loss.

"I'm sorry, Mom," Carolyn muttered. "I didn't mean to be so crappie."

"I know, honey. We all came to depend on Ed. And maybe even love him a bit. But sometimes things don't work out the way we hope they will."

"Well, I'm not giving up hope yet," Johnny

declared. "He promised he'd teach me how to ride this winter."

"I know. We'll just have to wait and see what happens." Maggie stood and gathered her children in a giant hug. She sensed their reluctance. "We'll be okay," she whispered.

While no one challenged her words, Maggie expected that three doubters stood in that small circle clinging to each other, and maybe to unrealized dreams.

A half an hour later, Maggie continued to sniffle while berating herself. She hadn't handled the kids' homecoming and telling them about Ed leaving well at all. But then she wasn't handling his running out on them very well, either.

At least the house sounded normal again. Carolyn was watching music videos on MTV while Johnny played with a noisy electronic game. Maggie looked down at the larger and dirtier than usual piles of camp clothes she had readied for the laundry. Yeah, some things were back to normal.

Maggie glared at her brother sitting uncomfortably on the chair across from her. She'd had difficulty not confronting him about Ed all evening, and he knew it. Even now Brad wouldn't meet her eyes directly.

He'd come out to the farm to spend some time with the kids. Both Johnny and Carolyn enjoyed seeing their uncle. Maggie often marveled at how easy going and humorous her brother could be with them.

Looking away from Brad, Maggie traced the upholstery pattern of the davenport with her index finger. It had been a good evening for the kids. At least for a moment, Johnny and Carolyn had been able to forget the man who had left without ever saying goodbye.

Now with the kids upstairs, Maggie and her brother sat in the living room sparring over the past, present and future. That was one thing that never changed.

"What did you say to Harrington that made him leave?"

Brad looked sharply at her. "What makes you think I did anything to make him go?"

"Because guilt is written all over your face. And you were shocked to hear how much Carolyn and Johnny miss Ed."

A red glow worked its way up Brad's neck. When it reached his ears, he cleared his throat. "Well, I may have said something about him not measuring up to my sister's standards. And that you would wake up someday and send him packing. I don't remember exactly, but something like that. I guess." He crossed his arms over his chest. "But I don't assume for a moment that I made him leave. He had to be leaning that way anyhow. Maybe I just nudged him a bit. At first, you know, I thought he was trying to take advantage of you. A lot of men would do that."

"Yeah, thanks a lot. That's all I need is one more man trying to protect me," Maggie said softly, tucking her feet under her. She let out a deep sigh. "No, you didn't make him go all by yourself. Ed's a man who is struggling with his own sense of self-worth. You just tapped his sorest spot. But he'd been digging at that ache for days."

"For what it's worth, after hearing from the kids, I'm sorry Harrington left. He must have been good for them...and for you." Brad frowned. "You know, sometimes Sis, I wish you lived on the moon so we wouldn't have to cross paths at all, and then there are moments when I wish you lived closer so we all could be more of a family. That's what Mom longed for, you know."

Maggie's eyes widened. Had she heard correctly? Was her brother seeking some kind of reconciliation after all these years? Or was this one more scam to get her to sell?

"I don't know how many computer jobs there are in the area, but there must be a lot in Des Moines, or Chicago, or the Twin Cities." She smiled, hoping he was genuinely concerned for her and her children. "Who knows, you might like the Midwest, as long as you didn't have to live on a farm."

"Maybe. Don't worry. I wasn't expecting you to move to California."

He looked like he wanted to say more, but he didn't. Maggie had never seen her brother look so tired. Maybe he *was* looking for some kind of change.

"Did you ever stop in and see Templeton?" Maggie didn't want another fight over money, but they had to talk about the insurance proceeds.

Brad nodded. "Not to worry. I think Templeton's plan of splitting the money evenly between us is fair and equitable." He grinned at her knowingly. "You may be surprised to learn that my rage about the will had much less to do with you than with Dad. We were compensated equally. They saw to that. But I still resent him, and I'm sure Mom just went along so as not to make him angry, trying to govern our lives from the grave."

Maggie's eyes widened as she listened to her brother. "Dad could be quite demanding," she acknowledged. "But he was a good man in his own way."

"Well, I've got to catch an early plane in the morning," Brad rose to his feet. "The boss seems to think I've been away long enough."

"Don't stay away so long this time," she said. Their family never had been big on hugs. She wasn't about to go that far, though she wished she could discern the emotion registering in her brother's eyes. Something had just transpired between them, spoken or unspoken, that had made a difference. She decided to take a next step. "You're always welcome at Thanksgiving or Christmas. The kids would love to see you."

"My company has a contract that brings me to Chicago a fair amount. Maybe I will stop by more often. I'll think about it. Sorry if I screwed things up for you and the kids. I didn't intend to do that, you know. I just wanted you to get out from under this albatross," he said, gesturing at the house. "Just wanted you to sell."

"I know. But I won't sell." Maggie pursed her lips and laced her fingers at her waist. "You should know that by now."

Brad smiled self-consciously. "Maybe I'm a slow learner. Anyway, good luck, Sis. I think you're going to need it."

"I don't doubt that."

She watched him step down the porch stairs and walk toward his car. Why hadn't she asked more about how he was doing? She had just assumed that he had come to hassle her like he always had in the past. Contrite was a word she'd never used to describe her brother. Was he just softening her up?

In any case, Brad hadn't chased Ed away. Her brother might have pushed him over the edge, but Ed had been more than halfway out the door anyway.

She was alone again. Maggie's stomach knotted and her heart shrank, but there wasn't anything she could do about Ed Harrington if he was bound and determined to leave. She wouldn't beg for anyone.

- o -

Ed didn't blink, staring at the single shot-glass of whiskey and a stein of beer sitting on a tiny, circular table. He gripped its pedestal between his knees. The darkened corner of Mel's Tavern in

206

Beaverhill provided a welcome hiding place. Almost as good as a cave.

He'd driven for hours after leaving the farm — after running as quickly as he possibly could from that menacing woman. That night was spent in his car. The next morning he'd poked around Clarion, his hometown.

Apparently, not only didn't he have much of a future, he didn't have much of a past, either. The building in which he'd grown up no longer existed, long since succumbing to progress and growth. An elementary school sprawled across half a block where several mom-and-pop stores and an apartment building had stood. It wasn't much of a loss. The town had grown a fair amount, but it still was a small mid-western town.

Sadly, the train station was pretty much gone. When he was a kid, he'd sit by the railroad tracks and count train cars numbering well over a hundred. There'd been a roundhouse for turning and repairing engines. Both the Rock Island and the Great Northwestern ran over those tracks. Trains still ran through Clarion, but probably not nearly as many as in his youth, and it was doubtful that any stopped. Such was progress. It made him feel like a dinosaur — maybe he should be in a museum.

What the hell did she want with a broken down dinosaur?

Kind of like the way a horse would return to its stable when given its head, his truck had led him back to Beaverhill. He'd have to find a way to slip back into the loft and pick up his personal items.

He frowned. The head on the beer had nearly disappeared. Likely it would be warm to the taste by now. Didn't really matter; it was beer. It was juice for the despairing. He knew it well, could savor its taste without even tasting.

Thoughts tumbled across his brain. He wondered how many hours his dad had spent in bars and taverns across the Midwest either raising hell or drowning sorrows. How many hours had he, himself, frittered away in similar places seeking release from pain? He'd always thought of himself as a hard fisted social drinker, until the rug was pulled out from under him in Chicago.

Then the booze had become a bosom pal, not easily ignored or set aside. He hadn't liked how it ran his life when time was measured from one drink to the next and fun was a twenty-four hour happy hour, when work was something to survive until he could leave for the nearest bar.

He'd tried to quit, or at least back off, dozens of times. He was no fool. But the brew was seductive, more seductive than any woman he'd encountered, with the exception of one. There were days when he would have done most anything to get the next drink. That scared him when he was sober, so he drank to avoid the fear.

What would she think if she could see him now? Would serve her right — putting her faith in a drunk. What did she really expect of him?

Without flinching, Ed ran a finger around the rim of the shot glass. Long moments dragged by while his mind resembled a blank slate. He knew if he drank enough he could make those blank periods last longer. Blackouts — they enticed him and terrorized him. He would be able to function, but not remember. Was that bliss, or a coward's way out? It wouldn't take long, if he only had the courage to take that first drink.

Hah. So many people in those meetings he'd been attending talked about the courage necessary to avoid that next drink. Here he was asking himself if he had the guts to lift a single glass to his lips and let the stinging, hot whisky glide down his throat. He could practically feel the familiar burning. So why didn't he just gulp the damn stuff down and get on with it?

He could leave them all behind. No Maggie harping at him, wanting more than he could give. No worrying about which kid was going to get injured next. No wondering when they'd all figure out he didn't measure up — that he was some kind of fake, a figment of their imagination.

Ed glanced furtively around with renewed awareness. His senses sharpened. How long had he been sitting like that, gawking at his future? The waitress and bartender stared at him as if he were an alien. He scratched the two-day growth of beard. He swore inwardly at the booze. He swore at the memories.

Why couldn't he just walk away from her? He didn't owe her anything. Not anymore. He'd paid his debt. But she wanted more, much more.

The bouncy, buxom waitress stood in front of

him. "Listen, Bud, if you're gonna drink, drink up. We're gonna be closing soon. And don't forget my tip." Leaning over, jiggling huge breasts, she whispered, "Or maybe you've got something else in mind. You've got possibilities. I can see that."

She withered under his icy glare. "Okay, I get the message, Bud. Why don't you just get out of here? You give me the willies. Any man who buys whiskey and beer and then just stares at them for more than an hour can't be much of a man in my book." The waitress brushed back curly brown hair and then flounced off to serve other customers.

Ed hardly knew she'd left. He wet his lips. Trying to steady his hand, he reached for the whiskey glass. Lifting it, he paused, and then slammed it down, splashing its contents over the scarred table.

He might be able to run from all of them, but he knew he'd never be able to run from himself.

Pushing his chair back, Ed stumbled getting up. He threw some coins on the table and rushed toward the exit.

Outside, Ed gulped for air. His hand shook like some ancient reminder of what used to be and could so easily have been again. He placed a hand in his pocket and curled his fingers around the ninety day chip.

Sobriety was a daily battle. Everybody said it. He knew it. And this day, he had been victorious—so far. He had not been that close to a drink since he was accosted by the tiny blonde woman in Des Moines. Dangerously close. Wiping his mouth with the back of his hand, he staggered, bone tired, down the alley toward his truck.

"Not so fast, Mister," thundered a stocky man dressed in dark clothing. Grabbing Ed by his open collar, the stranger jerked him nearly off his feet.

Ed kept his mouth shut. His senses went into overdrive. He was keenly aware of a second man standing behind him ready to pounce.

"Rushing back to take care of the little babe?" The man laughed derisively, pushing and pulling Ed back and forth as if he were a rag doll.

Ed went limp; he'd been rolled before. It didn't pay to put up a fight. Let them take his money. Wasn't much anyway.

"We just want to help you on your way, friend. But we want to make sure you're going in the right direction. Crawl back to Chicago, to New Orleans, to California. Anywhere but back to her farm. You don't want to get caught up in Maggie Anderson's battles." The burly man jerked him again. "Nothing good can come to you from that. Just in case you have a short memory from all the booze you drank, we're gonna tattoo the message clear...on your body."

Ed felt himself being pushed backwards into the waiting arms of the second stranger who stretched him out like a helpless scarecrow. And then the fists started pelting his body. First the solar plexus. Then the rib cage. The man holding him managed to do damage to Ed's kidneys.

"You won't go near that farm again, if you

211

know what's good for you." The only man to speak pounded until Ed could no longer see through bruised eyes. A blow to the jaw loosened some teeth.

Through a haze, Ed felt cartilage in his nose break. Then, mercifully, he was on the pavement. The smaller assailant kicked him in the groin repeatedly. Ed tried vainly to roll into a ball.

"That bitch is more than you can handle anyway, cowboy. You better heed our message," the little man wheezed. "The next one won't be near so gentle."

Vaguely, Ed heard their footsteps retreating. There was a hysterical internal laugh when he realized that they didn't get his money. Then there was blackness. Total blackness.

- o -

The kitchen phone rang at eight a.m., jangling Maggie's already frayed nerves. She grabbed it on the second ring.

"Yes," she said warily.

"Maggie, it's me, Flo. How are you?

"I'm okay. What's up?" Maggie knew her attempt at cheerfulness fell flat. Her throat was so dry it was a wonder she could talk.

"I'm not sure I should have called." Flo hesitated. "Does that man, Harrington, still work for you?"

Maggie ran fingers through her hair wishing she knew the answer to that question, but she was no sphinx. "I don't know. He stormed out of here a couple days ago."

A deafening silence ensued. Finally, Maggie could wait no longer. "What have you heard, Flo? Why did you ask?"

"Well, Mel was just in for breakfast. Harrington is the talk of the town, but I don't know how much is rumor."

"Will you just spit it out?" Maggie struggled to control her rising temper. What could the bar owner possibly know about Ed? Oh, no!

"Ed was beaten up last night outside Mel's place."

Stunned, Maggie gasped, slumping against the wall.

"Maybe I shouldn't have said anything," came the weak whisper over the phone.

"No. No. You did right," Maggie assured her friend. "I've just got to think, that's all. I'll get back to you later."

After hanging up the phone, Maggie leaned against the sink. Acid gnawing on her stomach threatened to escape. She lowered her head onto the cool sink. What to do?

What to feel? Guilt for pushing him too far. No, he was already running before she ever suggested he move into the house. Anger. Damn right, she was angry. They'd had so much to look forward to. Now there was nothing but memories. Relief? Maybe eventually. Right now there was too much numbness to experience any relief.

Whatever she might feel, even if she did want

213

to crawl under a rock and hide, she had to know what really happened. My God, who would stoop to beat him up, even if he was drunk? She had to determine if the idiot was okay. If he was, then she could give him a quick kick in the ass and send him packing.

First things first. She'd call Mel and find out what had really happened.

- o -

Ed sniffed lavender. God, it was such a lovely smell. He recognized her scent before he could force an eyelid open. Her touch on his fingers was warm and comforting.

"Where..." he managed to murmur.

"You're in the hospital," Maggie said. "Mel found you in the alley by the tavern when he left for home. You've been beaten badly, Ed."

Behind closed eyes, Ed winced at the quiver in her voice and tremble in her fingers. He figured he didn't look so good.

"Doc says no internal damage. But you're going to hurt like hell for days." Maggie picked up a paper cup of water with a bent straw. "Here, try to sip some water."

With great effort, Ed swallowed twice and then pushed the cup away. He squinted his eyes open and sighed. It hurt like hell to even breathe. "You look a mess," he said at last. Actually, he'd never seen a more attractive sight in his entire life. With mussed up hair, no makeup, and a rapidly thrown together appearance, she looked more bewitching than ever. Nor did he fail to notice the worry lines marring her forehead.

"Well, you're not going to win any beauty contest for awhile," she countered, squeezing his fingers gently.

"No, don't suppose," he muttered, nodding off.

- o -

Maggie waited as he slept. She always seemed to be waiting for this man to do something: to come to work for her, to love her, to come back to her. Of all the possible men out there in the universe, she couldn't fathom why her heart had been captured by a tumbleweed like Ed Harrington.

She had more confidence in the man than he had in himself. Was he wrong, or was she? Tearfully, she contemplated their bleak future. Would he come back and reclaim his job? He couldn't really go anywhere else for a while, given the shape he was in.

Tracing her fingertips across the hairs of his forearm, she wondered if he would ever come back to her. She didn't think she could stand working next to him without also loving him. She could turn a clock back, but she couldn't figure out how to do the same with her heart. Would he run away again? Would he run from anything that smacked of commitment?

Right now, all she wanted was for him to

215

recover and to own the love that she knew they shared. She had to be in his arms. The rest could wait.

Maybe she was being foolish. She'd spent most of her life not being foolish. What was it her mother used to say when quoting the Bible? "There is a time for everything." Maybe it was time for being foolish.

Maggie smiled, imagining some of the whimsical things she wanted to do with the man lying in the raised hospital bed. He looked so pale, and the room so sterile. The man who could work miracles with horses and with her kids and with her body looked so out of place lying bruised and battered against white hospital sheets.

- o -

An hour later, Ed wrenched himself into a half sitting position. "There," he declared with a degree of satisfaction, "I'll be out of here in no time." He grimaced at the alarm darkening Maggie's features. So she didn't share his assessment of his physical well-being.

Ignoring his comment, Maggie said, "Cops are going to want to talk with you about what happened as soon as you're able."

"Nothing much to say," he grunted.

"They know it wasn't robbery. Your wallet was intact, even with cash in it."

"Yeah, it wasn't robbery," he agreed grudgingly. Ed closed his eyes. How could he

216

keep her from knowing why the guys beat him up? Should he? Was she in danger? The kids? He doubted that.

Maggie pre-empted him. "You were beat up because you helped me, weren't you?"

Her words were like another blow to his solar plexus. He didn't want to tell her, to add fuel to her fears. But she sat erect — so defiant — on the edge of the bed. Her face appeared frozen in worry. He'd never be able to elude her. She'd know immediately if he lied.

"You're too smart for your own good at times, Maggie." He closed his eyes seeking darkness. "Just let it lie. Let me get out of here, out of your life, and you'll be all right."

"No," she said with a dry chuckle. "You're not going to get away from me that easily. And whoever beat you up, or whoever paid to have you beaten, will not be satisfied until I go belly up. I have no intention of doing that. Magees don't cave in while there's an ounce of fight left in them."

She placed her small hand on top of his large one.

"You are coming home with us. We'll help you heal, Ed. You are a very good man, a decent man. Please don't throw yourself on a garbage heap."

The glitter in her eyes mesmerized him. He wanted to cry. What did this woman see in him? Over and over, he'd let her down, and she was still there goading and egging him on. She left him little choice. Had he ever really had a choice about her? At last he spoke. "Maggie, I didn't drink." A tear eased its way down his right cheek.

Maggie leaned over to brush it away with the tip of a finger. "I know you didn't. Mel told me. If you had, I wouldn't be here." She gave him a weak smile. "Despite what you may think Ed, I didn't save you. You saved yourself."

Even with cracked ribs, he let out a huge sigh. Gazing up at the tear-streaked woman, he managed a trace of a grin. "You're right, Maggie."

He saw her lips thin. Then she took in large gulps of air. She squeezed his fingers too tight, but he wasn't about to tell her stop. He knew she was measuring what to say next.

"You should know that I've done a lot of thinking—about us," she said softly. "I love you, you battered oaf." Her declaration sounded almost defiant.

She stopped speaking to pull the blanket up tighter over his chest. "You need to know that. I don't know what you will do. But you gotta know. But maybe then you're not ready for a strong woman in your life."

Closing his eyes, Ed tried to feel nothing. He failed miserably. His lungs expanded and he felt a deep urge to cry. Why did she have to name it? Why couldn't she let things be? No, not Maggie. She wouldn't settle for anything less than the sun, the moon, and the stars. She wanted it all, including him.

"I want you to come back," Maggie pressed on not waiting for a reply. "The kids and I will help you heal. You'll continue to help me build a racing stable. And I promise…" Her voice rose, faltered and caught in her throat. "I promise," she sobbed, "that I will not seduce you again. If we are to be together in that way, you'll have to take the lead."

Ed slouched back on the pillows, deeply gratified by the effort Maggie was making to place all their lives back on some sort of even keel. How could he resist?

He nodded at her. "Okay," he whispered, frowning. "I don't know what to do with you." He flashed her a feeble smile. "You deserve so much more."

Maggie remained at his side, shook her head and tenderly stroked his hand.

He waited several moments, reveling in her touch, before asking, "But what about the bad guys?"

"Let's just take it one step at a time. They may give up."

"They won't give up."

"Well, neither will we. We're survivors, Ed." Maggie brushed the tips of her fingers across his cheek. "Somehow, we'll make it."

He'd never grow tired watching Maggie's emotions skip so vividly across her bright blue eyes. He found her strength contagious; she gave him an emotional transfusion.

Still groggy, Ed drew in upon himself. He could no longer see her, but Maggie's presence was no less powerful. Grudgingly, he acknowledged that love was a much more powerful force than drink.

Love was demanding, requiring patience and much more than he ever thought was possible. In the long run, though, love endured. He had heard of such a truth, but never before had he experienced it.

So why did he still feel like a fake waiting for her to see through the illusion?

CHAPTER TWELVE

Johnny gawked at Ed lying on the bed in the loft apartment.

Ed squinted back at the boy and managed a lopsided grin. The fear and disappointment writ so clearly on Johnny's crestfallen face troubled Ed. He regretted bringing more danger to the lad and to his family. But Maggie was probably right: they were in danger, with or without him.

"Gosh, you look terrible," the boy mumbled, not able to take his eyes off Ed's multicolored welts. "How did you let them beat you up so bad?"

Chagrined by the boy's shaking faith, Ed understood Johnny's disappointment. Clearly, his hero now had clay feet. "They surprised me, and they were huge," Ed grunted in response. "Wait 'til next time."

"Okay." Johnny grinned broadly and gave Ed a high five.

"You look sort of like a Picasso. Somber colors mixed with purple and yellow, lines sharp, bold even in defeat," Carolyn said. A hint of a smile crossed her lips.

Appreciating the girl's attempt at humor, Ed chuckled softly. Damn, the ribs still hurt when he laughed. "Don't think anyone has described me better. How are you doing, girl? Are you keeping the horses exercised?"

"Of course. What did you expect?"

"Nothing less." He grinned. She sure was plucky — she'd turned out to be a first rate hand. Good natural horse sense and patience could take her a long way in this business, if she wanted. Maybe she'd be a racetrack veterinarian.

"Hey," he said, catching Maggie's eye. "Looks like your daughter is trying to gain some weight.

Both mother and daughter frowned and looked at Ed as if his medicines were making him nutty.

"Sure, isn't that a lot of new metal in the ear?"

"Oh," Carolyn responded. "Do you like it?" She giggled, bending her ear closer for him to inspect. "Mom doesn't. But then she'll just have to get used to it."

Ed scowled. "I'm not going to get in the middle of that one. I take it this is a cry for independence."

Carolyn ignored him, jutting her chin out just like her mom did when she was upset with him. Maggie had mentioned that she thought a boy might be entering the girl's life. Problems. Maybe. She might not have as much time for horses. But at least in the short run, a boy would help boost her confidence. Closing his eyes, he hoped she wasn't as passionate as her mom, at least for another decade.

Finally, Ed said, "Guess the horses won't be bothered by your new jewelry."

"Thanks, Ed," Carolyn murmured. She squeezed his fingers lightly. "Thanks for understanding."

"Why don't you and Johnny run along now and finish the evening chores?" Maggie instructed, getting up from a chair. "I'll be along after I've had a chance to see how much of this chicken soup our patient can handle."

As her kids hurried down the stairs two steps at a time, Maggie leaned over and plopped a wet kiss on Ed's forehead.

"Hey," he gasped brusquely. "Thought you said no more seduction on your part."

Maggie raised her eyebrows. Placing her hands on her hips, she announced, "Mr. Harrington, by now you should know me well enough to understand that a little buss on your hard head is no attempt at seduction." She snaked a finger down his bicep. "If I were in the seducing mind, you'd know it, and we wouldn't be standing her conversing like we've got all day. Nope, that was just good nursing skills. Didn't your momma ever kiss you on the forehead when you were sick?"

Shaking his head, trying not to laugh, he teased in a low, sexy voice, "You're right. I forgot. If you were seducing me, you'd have that blouse undone and you'd be pulling on a taut nipple. Your blue eyes would glaze over like a high mountain lake. And that rosebud mouth of yours would be puckered in a bewitching pout. Your other hand would be sneaking its way inside your jeans."

Maggie slapped at his hand. "Enough. Now who's seducing? And you not able to do anything about it even if you wanted to."

"Ah, Maggie," he groaned, inching himself up into a sitting position, "you look good enough to eat when you get your dander up."

He saw her make a face, but he ignored it. "We're safe for the moment; you're right about that. You know, you are an enigma. How does someone who can hardly stretch to five feet get to be so brassy?"

It was Maggie's turn to laugh. "You never knew my dad."

"He must have been quite a character."

"Apparently, more than I ever realized."

"So he made you think you didn't need balls to get what you wanted."

"It never mattered to him that I was a girl." Maggie chewed on her lower lip before continuing. "He always said I could do whatever I wanted as long as I didn't turn my back on the values of the land. *Work hard,* he'd say, *and the land will reward you. Try to stay in step with the seasons — time marches on, you can't hold onto it, you can only go with it like trying to ride a horse. Put your trust in the land and it will repay you like you were a princess. It may rip you apart with hail, or flood, or drought, but in the long run it is more dependable than any damn human ever will be."*

Sighing, Maggie glanced out the window at the parched lawn and premature drying of the trees. "I hope he's right. This heat wave is a test of our commitment to the land."

Maggie held out the soup spoon towards him.

"Life has not been easy, that's for sure." She hesitated. "I imagine the land tempers a person, like the old timers used to work a plowshare on an anvil. Besides, I'm not as strong as you think. If I were, how come you can turn me inside out by just touching me? Or just saying those sexy words to me?" She blinked. "Why can't I just let you walk out of my life? Now *that* would be strength."

"You may be right about that," he admitted, separating his lips for the proffered spoon. "I've certainly given it a lot of thought, and I sure don't understand why you insist on keeping me around. You'd be much better off if you'd just send me packing. I've endangered your family by coming back here."

"Would you stop saying that? Please," Maggie countered quickly. "We're in danger as long as I don't fold up and sell out. You just got in the middle of things. You'd be out of trouble entirely if you hadn't come back. Maybe I was unfair insisting that you return to the farm. Maybe I'm too selfish."

"Nonsense. I couldn't just walk away leaving you vulnerable. Might not have come back to the farm if you hadn't been so damn stubborn about it, but I never would have left the area until this thing was settled." Ed touched the swelling under his left eye. "When someone gives you a beating like I got, things become personal in a hurry."

Grimacing, she removed the empty soup dish and sat on the side of the bed. "Here you are hovering about trying to protect me," she said, "and I hardly know you."

Ed smirked sheepishly. "I'd say you know me better than most."

"I don't mean in that way," she scoffed, brushing back a clump of hair from his brow. "Who are you? You call me an enigma, but you're the real enigma. How did you get into horse racing?" Glancing away, she whispered, "Why should I trust you?"

"Do you always close the barn door after the horse has dashed off?" Ed scowled. He wasn't one who liked revisiting the past. The past was best buried. But he also knew that once Maggie got her claws into something, she hung on until she was satisfied. He didn't have the reserve energy to fight her.

"There's not much to tell," he began reluctantly. "I grew up above a crossroads grocery store near Clarion. My ma ran the store. My dad traveled a lot, selling whatever he could get cheap." Ed halted.

"That's it?" Maggie's eyebrows arched. "That's not much of a story. Obituaries are longer than that. Did you have brothers and sisters?"

"Yeah. One brother. Last I heard he was in jail somewhere in the east. We don't talk much."

"Oh. So did you work in the store when you were a boy?"

"Sure. That's how I got spending money, and Ma needed the help."

"Didn't your dad help when he was home?"

Ed glanced away from her intensity. "Seldom.

He was too busying chasing around the bars."

"Oh."

"Are you finding out what you wanted to know?" Ed mumbled sourly, folding his arms.

"Yes." Maggie would not be deterred. "I want to know who you are. We can't select our families, you know; they come with the package. However difficult things were, you've done well for yourself."

"Right," Ed spat out in disgust. "I'm just a shining example of success — poor boys rises to the ranks of the wealthy only to piss it away through scandal and booze."

Maggie's eyes blazed at him. "So, are your parents still alive?"

"Nope. Ma worked herself to death by the age of fifty-five. Dad was quicker. By fifty-one he'd drunk himself into the grave."

Her face fell. "Damn. I'm sorry."

"No need to be. Like you said, we can't select our families." Ed flashed a sarcastic grin. "Ma taught me a lot about survival, and Dad taught me more than I ever needed to know about escape. What else does a kid need to know?"

"Love."

"Huh?"

"A kid needs to be taught about love," Maggie said, shifting her weight uneasily on the mattress. "How to receive love and how to give love."

"I suppose Ma loved me," Ed replied thoughtfully. "There just wasn't much time for her to show it. Dad? Dad was likely afraid of love."

"And you're not afraid of love?"

Ed closed his eyes, kicking himself for not seeing the trap the wily female was setting. He'd been too focused on avoiding the past to realize the greatest danger sat right next to him in the present.

Maggie pressed on. "Why did you leave Clarion? How did you get to Chicago? I'll lay odds it was a woman."

Ed's eyes sprang open.

Maggie laid her hand over his. "Tell me about her."

"Why?" he grunted, annoyed by her perceptiveness and persistence. "It's ancient history. Nothing good can come from rehashing it now."

"I want to know," Maggie insisted, jutting out her chin stiffly. "You know all about me. I want to know about you."

"So maybe you like to talk about yourself more than I do."

She squeezed his hand.

His eyes closed, but he did begin to speak. "I was twenty-one; Amy was nineteen, the daughter of a lawyer from a neighboring town. We met at the community college where we were both taking some courses part-time. Her family wanted her to go to a private school in the east, but her grades weren't good enough. She was trying to get her grade point up and I was just taking some courses in agriculture for the hell of it. I was working for a hog farmer at the time who owned three farms. He encouraged me to take the courses and planned on having me manage one of the farms."

"Really. You wanted to be a farmer? And here you are."

Ed frowned. "Please, don't bounce on the bed."

Chastened, Maggie muttered, "Sorry."

He watched her sit very still, pleading with her eyes for him to continue his story. "Anyway, it was love at first sight. She was my dream girl: tall, long blond hair, former cheerleader, zestful. And I guess I was her dream guy. It turned out to be a nightmare."

Ed paused. Maggie held her breath until he went on.

"We decided to marry. The day before the wedding, she telephoned to inform me that she couldn't go through with it. As a girl, she'd set her sight on someone higher than me. Amy had gotten so wrapped up in the whirlwind of romance that she forgot what she and her family wanted and had overlooked who I really was and what kind of future was likely for us. In short, I wasn't good enough for her."

Ed shifted to his side and placed a hand on Maggie's waist. "Call it acute wedding jitters for the bride or that her parents had finally gotten through to her — call it what you want — the wedding was off. She had relatives already in the air coming from all across the country to attend the ceremony. Instead of a wedding, her family held a big party in the place where we were to have had our reception. They celebrated Amy's nerve to dump a guy that didn't measure up before it was too late."

"How terrible," Maggie whispered, leaning over to brush her lips across his creased brow.

"Not looking for sympathy. It happened a long time ago."

"Just good nursing skills," Maggie reminded. "So you left for Chicago."

"You bet. I left the very next day. I only regret not being able to give Mr. Hobson enough notice. He seemed to understand and wished me well."

"How did you get wrapped up with horseracing? That's quite a leap, from hogs to horses."

Absently, Ed stroked Maggie's arm as he responded to her question. "When I was ten, my dad took me along on one of his sales trips. He took me to the old Arlington Park track. I was bitten hard by the bug. I dreamed a lot about horses, about being a jockey, about owning them. But those were a kid's dreams. Until I got pushed out of Iowa."

"Out of adversity comes the light."

"Maybe. Anyway, when I got to Chicago, I hooked up with a trainer. I started as a groom and worked my way up." Ed shrugged. "End of story."

"Women?"

Chuckling, Ed winked at his inquisitor. "Are we going to leave any stone unturned?"

"No."

"Sure, there were women," he admitted, idly

pushing back a strand of Maggie's hair. "Plenty of them. Too many, I guess. But none serious. Being dumped once was one too many times."

"Ah. Are you afraid I'll tire of you and dump you?" Maggie asked, her voice dropping half an octave.

Ed thought long before replying. He'd hoped he'd shared enough so she would realize there was no lasting future for them. Maybe she'd have enough sense to back off. Common sense when it came to her and him seemed to only come from one direction—his.

"I don't know about that," he said cautiously. "But you and I are very different. You're rooted in the soil; I'm a rolling stone. And that's the way I like it."

"I appreciate your honesty, Ed."

Ed watched her debate the wisdom of taking him on about their difference.

"What about the Travers?" she asked. "Where do they fit? Was Cassie one of those women you chased around with?"

"Hardly." Ed chuckled softly. "She didn't want to have anything to do with me beyond swapping information between trainers. I was in my carefree stage when I met her. Too much beer, too cocky, and too footloose. Besides, she was in the middle of a cross country affair with Clint shortly after I met her. He had a ranch and raised thoroughbreds in Utah. He's part Ute. I didn't like him at all at first. But turns out he's really a solid fellow. They're madly in love—still. Renews one's faith in marriage, a bit."

"Oh." Maggie swallowed hard.

"Yes. They're both good people and deserve each other. I'm pleased for them and they've become good friends. Turns out they stick by you when most friends dash for cover if things start to turn sour," he went on bitterly.

"I'm sorry. You know I won't dash for cover when the going gets tough," Maggie asserted, her eyes glistening.

Ed nodded. "I know. You're a tigress masquerading as a sexy female of the human species," he muttered, cupping her chin. "Now, why don't you get off my bed before I do something I might regret later on?

- o -

The corner of Maggie's mouth turned up. She heard the emotion contained in his words and saw the tent forming in the sheet between his legs. He was in no shape for romance. She stood. She'd learned a lot, perhaps more than Ed realized. There was much to think about.

She still trusted her bones and her heart; this was her man. She understood more about why he ran when things seemed to be at their best. Funny, in him she had a man who tried to escape her love, but would return to protect her from danger. He might run far, far away at the first whiff of personal success, yet he'd do all he could so she wouldn't fail.

He was definitely worth waiting for. She was beginning to think she had more patience than a cat staring at a dormant mouse hole.

As if he could read her mind and didn't want her to hold onto a single illusion, Ed said, "Don't get that faraway look of yours, Maggie. I'm just going to hole up here and heal some. Then we'll find out what's really going on here about your land. And then I'll be moving on."

Maggie clenched her fists at her sides. Was she furious, or was she beyond such a mundane feeling? Dazed, she picked up the dishes and started to leave.

"You've known all along that I'm the drifting type," Ed said to her back.

Maggie ignored his strained words. She struggled to keep her balance in her rush down the stairs. Getting away from Ed Harrington was her most important objective of the moment. If she didn't place some distance between him and her, he might wind up dead. And she had no desire to see the inside of a prison.

Later that afternoon Maggie was on her hands and knees scrubbing the kitchen floor. Her arms were tiring. She'd been at it for over an hour. The soapy water had long since turned cold. Her tennis shoes, cutoffs and light blouse were soaked. The yellow bandana around her head couldn't keep perspiration from flowing down her tear-streaked face.

She sat back on her haunches assessing her

clean floor. "Good," she muttered. "Now all I have to do is get rid of the idiot." She'd a belly full of Ed Harrington. She had a farm to save. There was not enough time to mess up her life with false hopes of romance. Spying a tile that didn't look clean enough, Maggie grabbed the sponge and started working on the recalcitrant spot.

She never heard the door close.

"Are you nesting, or trying to tear the house apart?"

Maggie glanced up to see Flo Zimmerman staring down at her with a look of awed disbelief. "Neither. I'm just cleaning the damn kitchen floor. Is that okay?"

"Oh." Flo took a step backward toward the porch. "I just brought by the medicines you wanted me to pick up at the pharmacy. You can pay me later."

"Don't go," Maggie said, rising to her feet with sponge in hand. "I didn't mean to be rude. It's just not been a very good day. Thanks for bringing the stuff. I'll get some money."

"No, you're all wet and in the middle of something. Pay me next time you're in town. How is your hired man? Mr. Harrington."

"He could be dead as far as I'm concerned." Maggie twisted her mouth and stared at the floor. Looking back at Flo, she said, "He'll mend. And then he'll move on."

"Oh." Flo clasped her hands behind her back. "You know, at first Brad thought your hired man was just trying to use you. And then he changed his mind. Just before he left town, Brad came by the diner. He thought the kids really liked the man and that you were all gonna be a family. Brad actually seemed quite happy about that."

"Shows you what my brother knows." Maggie glanced sharply at Flo standing in the doorway looking like she was trying unsuccessfully to keep a secret. "So what is my brother doing confiding in you?"

Flo's skin turned rosy pink. "Nothing. He just likes to come in and have a cup of coffee at the counter." Her fingers twisted at the knot of the belt of her skirt. "He's changed a lot, you know."

Closing and opening her mouth, Maggie shook her head. "Oh my God. Not you. Sensible Flo. You know he goes through women like water comes out of a spigot." She looked quickly at the sink faucet; her hand flew to her mouth. "You can't be too careful around my brother. Well, he won't be around often."

"He'll be back for Thanksgiving. He said you invited him."

Maggie frowned. "Right, I did. I forgot." She scrutinized her friend. "Be careful, Flo. You're my dearest friend, and he's my brother. Be very careful."

"Nothing's going to happen," Flo stammered. "I think."

"So why do you flush and stutter every time you speak of him?" Maggie regretted her words immediately. Flo's pained looked needed no elaboration. Maggie kicked herself for hurting her friend. "You'll do fine, Flo. You've got a good head on your shoulders. You can keep Brad at bay if you want to." Maggie wished she believed that.

Seeing yet another blotch on a tile, Maggie stooped to wipe it up.

"I best be going, Maggie," said Flo. "I'm sorry about Harrington."

"Yeah, well everything works out for the best." Maggie's heart tumbled, belying her confidence. "He'll be on his way shortly, and then maybe life can return to normal."

"Normal isn't always so good." Flo blinked and wiped perspiration from her brow. "But he is a lot of man."

Maggie's brain exploded. She stood and hurled the wet sponge at the kitchen table. "Why the hell does everyone think I'm not woman enough for Ed?"

Flo retreated to the middle of the porch. "I didn't say that."

"The hell you didn't!" With hands on hips, Maggie glared hard through tears. "You might as well have."

"It's just that he's so mysterious. He's a stranger. You're doing what a lot of women dream about."

"And you think those kinds of dreams turn into nightmares."

"I dunno—romance doesn't happen here in Beaverhill. That's Hollywood stuff."

"Maybe I should be warning Brad to stay away from you." Instantly alarmed at her own bitterness, Maggie said, "I'm sorry, Flo. I didn't mean that. Maybe you'd best be going. I'm not very good company today."

Casting a horrified look over her shoulder, Flo moved swiftly down the steps toward her car.

"Thanks for bringing the medicines by," Maggie shouted at her friend's back. The slam of a car door was the only reply. Maggie fell back onto the porch swing and sobbed. Belatedly, she realized that Flo had never mentioned what country western tune was playing on the car radio when she drove into the driveway.

Within an hour the phone rang. Maggie answered.

"I'm sorry, Maggie," Flo said. "You're woman enough for three men."

"Whoa." Maggie laughed. "I don't want to go there. But I do appreciate your confidence. I'm glad you called. I know I was upset and rude earlier. I'm sorry."

"It didn't matter. We've been through a lot worse."

"Guess you're right about that. What are old friends for if they can't get ticked at one another now and then?"

"Stop by the diner when you're in town next. Love you."

"Of course I will. Love you, too."

CHAPTER THIRTEEN

The next morning, standing before the loft window, Ed watched the slouched form of Maggie carrying his breakfast. He supposed he should have gone over to the house; he could have managed. But he wasn't sure he was ready to handle Maggie yet.

There was no question in his mind that he'd hurt her badly the day before. He'd spent most of the remainder of the day and night trying to explain to himself why he had felt it so necessary for her to grasp that he would be leaving. There was plenty of time. He wouldn't be going anywhere for a while. And it would take some time to figure out who was trying to scare Maggie off her land.

He never intended to hurt Maggie, yet every time he said something or did something he wound up hurting her anyway. Ed scowled at the memory of her leaving his room.

How had she deceived herself so? She couldn't really love him. Maybe she loved some reformed image of him, or of herself as his reformer.

He squared his shoulders, readying himself to withstand her latest strategy for getting him to change.

Maggie knocked, entered and set down the tray of scrambled eggs, bacon, juice and coffee. At last she looked at him.

Ed's stomach lurched. Sunken eyes greeted him. Where had their spark gone? Each eye sat back over a darkened, fleshy bag. Maggie didn't wear eye-liner. Dammit to hell, he screamed to himself. No words came from his dry throat. His hands began to shake.

"We've got to talk," Maggie said, her voice little more than a hoarse whisper.

"I'm sorry," Ed replied. His words were shaky. Only with a strong will was he able to keep from hugging the woman to his body. "I didn't mean to hurt you."

Maggie's eyes grew cold. "It doesn't matter. You did. But it doesn't matter. I'm over that now."

Like hell. Ed had been lied to by women many times. Some of them had been experts. Maggie was not. He started to speak.

Maggie interrupted, "Eat your breakfast. It'll get cold."

Sitting down on the edge of the bed, Ed reached for the fork. He didn't feel any more like eating than jumping from a twenty story building, but it was important to Maggie.

She plopped down on the chair across from him. He had other memories of her in that chair.

Speaking to him as if he were a cardboard image, she said, "We've got to get to the bottom of who had you beaten up. I'm sorry you suffered because of me. You're free to leave now if you wish. In fact, I'd like that. But you're probably too stubborn to do that."

240

"Look who's calling me stubborn."

Maggie showed no sign of responding to his bait.

Ed reached for his coffee. She was more hurt than he had imagined. "You're right. I'm not about to go anywhere, yet. As far as my suffering goes, I've been hurt worse when a horse kicked me in the knee. A couple days and I'll be hobbling around okay. Another week and I should be as good as new."

"I sure hope so; I want to get this resolved quickly."

Maggie stood and paced back and forth while he ate. Ed was pleased to see some of the old fire returning to her body. She stopped three feet away from him. "Apparently some creep out there is very serious about taking over this land. We've got to find out who it is before anyone is hurt even worse. Could Con-Ex Farms be this ruthless?"

"Maybe." Ed relaxed some as they turned to a common purpose. "I doubt they're used to losing or having a woman stand up to them. How about Prater?"

"He's twisted enough. He could be behind it all," Maggie agreed, sitting back down in the chair. "Prater also mentioned a second party was interested in the farm. Never told me who."

Ed hesitated, scowling. "You're not going to like this thought, but what about your brother?"

"Brad?" Maggie squeaked with a start.

"Yeah, he's got a lot to gain. Clearly, he doesn't want you to hold onto the farm. And I don't think he ever quite signed up for my fan club."

Maggie shook her head rapidly. "No. We may have our differences, but he wouldn't stoop that low." She caught her breath. "Oddly, I might have considered him before our last conversation. I think he really wants to have a better relationship with me; part of that is because of the kids. But still..."

"Okay. I accept your opinion. Yet he strikes me as a very crafty guy, capable of concocting quite a story if he wants to."

"There's no doubt about that." Maggie riffled her hands through her unkempt hair. "What do we do now?"

Ed tried not to notice how the simple action of running fingers through her hair lifted Maggie's breasts in such an alluring manner. He wished those were his fingers entwined in that soft hair and that his lips were caressing those beading nipples. *Whoa.* In spite of what he might say to convince himself otherwise, he missed the feel of her under his body and of her fragrance filling all his senses.

"I'm thinking I'll talk with Ben Templeton again," Maggie said. "The insurance man is all over the area and has a good ear. It doesn't look like the police are particularly helpful."

"That seems clear. They just look at me as a drifter involved in a fight over a woman. The area would be better off if I disappear, was their thinly veiled message." He paused. "So how does it feel to be the woman guys are busting bones over?"

"I wouldn't trust Deputy Harris as far as I could throw him. He tried to break up Mason and me when we were juniors." Shuddering, Maggie added, "He came on to me three months after Mason died. I told him about the facts of life."

Ed chortled. "I'd liked to have seen that. So the Sheriff Department might have a vested interest in my taking a hike. Guess we can't rely on them for much."

"I don't know about Sheriff Hampton. He always seemed fair enough, from a distance. I never had any dealings with him, but he's one of the good ole boys. If a friend wanted you to move on, I'm not sure he'd get very worked up over a beating."

"Maybe I'll give Clint Travers a call," Ed stretched, testing the recovery of his shoulder muscles. "He's got a good nose for these kinds of things. Don't remember if I told you he has a degree in criminal justice. He's actually a partner in a Chicago based detective agency."

"No! Really? I thought he kept busy buying, selling and trading horses. Sounds like he still spends a fair amount of time in Utah. When can the man find time to be a detective?"

"I don't think he does any of the actual leg work. He's more of a silent partner."

"That reminds me," Maggie said. "Cassie will be coming down the middle of next week. With all that's happened, I almost forgot. You remember we're running Capote's Dream in the Inaugural Stakes at Prairie Meadows Labor Day weekend.

I'm looking forward to working with her at the track."

"That'll be great." Ed grimaced, hesitating. "Sorry I haven't been able to help you out there."

"We knew from the start you wouldn't be able to go to the track with me." She stopped. "At least not until your name is cleared. There's no way I'd be on the verge of a competitive racing stable without you. Apart from anything else between us, I think you know how grateful I am."

Ed nodded. "The pain of not being with you on race day, to smell shedrow, to swap stories, to hear the announcer's call, is a hundred times more severe than what those two goons inflicted on me with their fists."

- o -

Maggie kept her gaze on the floor. Desperately, she wanted to stay angry at Ed until he left her and the farm. But she couldn't do it. She had as much if not more to do with their personal difficulties than he did. Maybe she didn't have to stay angry. Maybe she could just hold her emotions in check better. "I know being away from the track is tough on you," Maggie responded meekly. "I hope and pray that the truth is found out, and soon."

"Thanks." Ed returned his empty coffee cup to the tray and stood awkwardly. "Okay tiger, let's go get 'em. We'll win our share of the races, and we may even be able to foil a bad guy or two."

Maggie slowly descended the loft stairs. *Yes, races and bad guys, but what about us?* What us? In his judgment, she was just as much banned from his life as were tracks and booze.

"Now, Maggie."

"Don't *now Maggie* me, Ben Templeton! My business is nobody else's concern," Maggie said, sitting on the edge of a cushioned chair across from the oak desk of her old family friend.

Ben held up his hand to silence her.

Grudgingly, she held her tongue.

"You know all about the character of rural communities, Maggie. You grew up here. You went to school here. Your roots are here. People are nosy. They talk. There's a reason why our paper only comes out once a week. We don't need a daily."

Maggie groaned. What he was saying was true. She'd given the folks of Beaverhill more than a little to talk about lately. Unable to contain her curiosity, she leaned forward. "So what are they saying about me?"

"Don't you have any friends, girl? Am I it?"

He looked uncomfortable. What was he holding back? "Mason and I were childhood sweethearts. There wasn't a lot of room for many others. Most of our friends were his. Of course there's Flo, though she's usually too afraid to tell me what's really happening because she doesn't want to see me hurt. Dolly Thompson and I used to be close, but she thinks I should build a shrine to Mason and grieve for him the rest of my life."

"Don't do that, Maggie," Ben said, staring at the picture on his desk of his deceased wife. "Whatever you do, don't do that. Loneliness is a disease you never quite get comfortable with. I was an old man already by the time my Hazel died." Ben coughed and rubbed his chin. "I didn't want another partner. Looking back on it, I should have at least looked around. Sometimes life is too long without someone to share it with."

Maggie nodded, feeling oddly uncomfortable about a man of his generation sharing such intimate information with her. Yet she was also honored that he cared enough to expose his own vulnerability.

Still, she wasn't about to pursue his train of thought further. "So what are they saying about me?"

Ben fidgeted with a pen. "Well, some folks think you're in way over your head. That it's just a matter of time before you have to fold your cards and sell out like so many others have."

"Uh, huh. That's not surprising. What else?"

"Of course, everyone knows about Ed Harrington helping you out and living in the loft in your barn."

Maggie slid back in the chair. Her legs stuck to the sticky vinyl and her feet failed to touch the floor. "So what do they say about him?"

"Again, nothing that would surprise you, I'm sure." Ben steepled his fingers, eyeing her intently. "Most seem to think he's taking advantage of you.

Everyone knows of his history with the booze. Beyond that there are a lot of rumors about who he really is. A drifter. A cowboy from the west. A horse trainer. A con artist. You name it and it's probably been mentioned. Naturally, your mother-in-law claims to be aghast from these rumors, but she also seems to be adept at promoting them."

"No doubt. I never was quite good enough for her son. Okay," Maggie said, clenching her hands tightly in her lap, "what else do these good citizens have to say?"

"Oh, some believe," Ben peered over his glasses, "that Colt Magee's daughter is finally showing her true colors, shacking up with the first stray tomcat that happens by."

"Son of a bitch," yelped Maggie, jumping from her chair. "What right do they have to judge? And we're not shacking up."

"Well, I suppose the only right has to do with their sense of being in the right." Ben shook his head. "Maggie, I don't care what you're doing as long as you're not setting yourself up to be hurt. But it doesn't help any that you keep the fellow cloistered out at the farm."

Maggie looked blankly at her friend. "What do you mean—cloistered at the farm?"

"It's a lot easier to put horns on a person you don't know than one you do know."

"Hah, I seem to grow my own easily enough. And everybody knows me."

Ben smiled. "Some of that is inherited. You may

247

have thought your dad was loved by everyone, but his independent ways ticked off a lot of folks around here. Colt Magee was a man who never believed in the majority rule idea."

"Guess you're right about that," Maggie conceded. "And I don't imagine I do things the way the little wife and mother ought to do them. But Mason was never much into farming. And I've had to be a mother and a father these last two years. Frankly, I don't care much about what people think of me. But I do care about how they treat my kids."

"If you're serious about keeping Harrington around, in whatever capacity, why not bring him out to a few of the social events? So people can meet him and learn that he's not such a bad apple after all."

Maggie gave the insurance man a crooked smile and sat back down. Five days had lapsed since her unsettling truce with Ed Harrington. Did she want to keep him in any capacity? A not-so-tiny voice screamed from a corner of her brain, *Yes*.

"So tell me, what do people really think is going on out there at the farm? Do they know about the horses, or do they think we spend all our time in the sack?"

She grinned when Ben coughed and sputtered.

"To be honest, since the county fair, there hasn't been much doubt about whether the two of you are...ahem...intimate," Ben said, his cheeks turning rosy.

"Boy, that's a good one," Maggie responded.

They hadn't made love until after the fair. "Goes to show you what the common consensus knows. What about the horses?"

"Folks can't seem to figure it out, and it's not for lack of trying. I've honored my pledge of secrecy. But it's just a matter of time now. Because you have so few horses at the farm, people can't believe you expect to generate sufficient income to live on from that enterprise. Of course, they don't know about the horses you have stashed in Chicago. By the way, the next quarterly premium is about due on those animals."

"And what about Ed being beaten to a pulp on the streets of this good town? Does anybody wonder about that? Do they give a damn?"

"Shock, mostly. That's not something that's supposed to happen in our small town. Most have concluded that riffraff attract riffraff. Many are still concerned for your welfare, Maggie, but they don't know how to reach out to you. They feel you've turned your back on them."

"Me!" Maggie couldn't believe her ears.

"If you want them to ever accept Ed Harrington, then you better start ushering him around and introducing him about." Ben Templeton stared directly her. "That is, if you still plan on living here."

"Of course I'm going to stay here," she retorted. "What would ever lead you to think otherwise?"

"If you really succeed in the horse business, Maggie, won't you outgrow little Beaverhill, Iowa? There are much more lucrative racing circuits than Prairie Meadows. And I'm told that you have one of the best trainers in the business with your man, Harrington."

Maggie tried to think before responding. Ben was raising a question that had never crossed her mind. Of course, she would stay in Beaverhill. The whole thing with race horses was to save the farm, not to move beyond it.

She rubbed her nose thoughtfully. "You may have a point, Ben. I hadn't thought about bringing Ed to social events. It just seemed right to focus on the horses, and Ed's a private sort of guy anyway. But what about the sheriff—is he going to do anything about looking for the guys who beat up Ed? I've got the kids to worry about, too."

Ben rolled his chair back from his desk. "I wouldn't count on much help there. If you or your children were attacked, that would be a different matter all together. Even though people here may not understand you, you still are part of this community."

"But not Ed."

"No, not Ed. People don't even know who he is. Maybe someone was settling an old score with him. The town wouldn't want to make that their business." Ben raised his palms upward. "Who knows who did it and why? Or who hired the guys to do the job? But I don't think the sheriff's office is going to bust a gut digging around for clues."

Maggie's brow furrowed with suspicion. "Does Con-Ex Farms own Sheriff Walker?"

"No, I don't think so. But the sheriff and Prater are close. You know, his wife is Prater's sister. That banker runs around here like a bull in a china shop whenever your name comes up. You certainly are not making the man happy. If he could have you tarred and feathered, he'd certainly supervise the task."

Maggie grinned. "I think we gave that up, even here, sometime in the last century or so." She frowned and kept her gaze steady at one of the few people she trusted. "So are you saying you think Prater is behind Ed's beating? Would his dislike for my dad and for me go that far?"

"I wish I knew. What your mom and dad did all those years ago is forgotten by most folks, but I'm not certain it just hasn't gnawed on Josh all this time like some open wound that won't scab over. I don't think he'd do anything to really hurt you or the kids. But Ed? Who knows? Harrington is helping you save the farm, or at least that's the plan."

"So what do you suggest, Ben—do we just sit tight?"

"Be vigilant. Be cautious. I expect Harrington's being beaten had more to do with the land than with any relationship you may be having with him. I wouldn't be surprised if somebody isn't intent on trying to scare you off the land, but it's not a large amount of property. Shouldn't really be worth that much to anyone. Certainly, that somebody will tire when they realize you're not easily frightened. Maybe I'm just rambling and maybe I'm just hoping, but can't imagine Con-Ex Farms or Prater or anyone else who would wish to do you physical harm."

Maggie nodded, hoping he was right, and rose to leave. "Thanks, Ben," she said, hugging the slightly embarrassed man. "You've given me a lot to think about."

As she opened the door to step out of the office, Ben said, "Why don't you think of bringing Harrington out to the Harvest Festival in October? That would be a natural opportunity for folks to see that the man is human — that he probably breathes and laughs pretty much like the rest of us."

Maggie turned, smiled and waved. She walked toward her truck. Why not invite Ed? As long as he realized she wasn't trying to seduce him, maybe he would be willing to go. It might be fun. If nothing else, it would be fun to watch some of the town gossips trip over themselves trying to get the scoop on what was happening out at the Anderson farm.

For that matter, she'd like to know what was going on out at the Anderson farm herself. Maggie chuckled and her step became lighter.

"So, your friend Templeton thinks I ought to come out of my hole, huh?"

Maggie glanced at Ed, who sat at the kitchen table while she started supper.

Running the palm of his hand over his head, he said, "I knew something like that was coming.

Once you took me to the fair, people were bound to ask questions or figure on their own that one plus one makes two."

"Do you mind?" Maggie quizzed, cutting up chunks of ham for a casserole.

"Not on my account. I don't give a damn what people think of me. But I do care what they say about you." Ed paused. "And what about Johnny and Carolyn? Will they get hassled at school?"

Maggie turned and leaned against the counter. "Don't ever think," she insisted, waving the knife, "that what we have had or may have in the future is something that bothers me. I would shout my love for you from the rooftop if I didn't think it would scare you off."

Ed's cheeks flamed and Maggie grinned in response. She was done being angry with him — and with herself, for that matter. He might bring her more pain, but damn if she was going to run away from him or from her feelings. Subtlety and escape had never been her strong suit. He would just have to deal with her, one way or the other. "Don't worry, I'm not about to climb the roof. Though it is a thought. Apparently the kids are handling whatever is coming down at school. Both of them confide in me when they're having trouble."

"I wonder how long that will last," Ed quipped. "Aren't teenagers supposed to be at odds with their parents? I thought that was part of growing up."

"I'm sure they'll have their moments. Carolyn

is probably testing the limits as we speak. Won't be long and it will be Johnny's turn. Sometimes I wish they could stay just where they are and never grow up."

"Some wishes aren't possible. Peter Pan found that out."

"Well, you old faker," Maggie chided, returning to her work. "You know more about kids than you like to admit."

"In case you forgot, I was one once." Ed rose to begin setting the table. "I was close to an owner and his family for awhile back in Chicago. He had three of the cutest little girls you'd ever see. We all went to watch *Peter Pan* on stage. I guess it made a lasting impression."

"Do you miss not having your own?"

Ed nearly dropped a plate. "Kids? Me? Nope. Doubt I'd be a very good father over the long haul. They'd want more than I have to offer." He filled a couple water glasses. "I like other people's kids, though, in small doses."

Maggie turned to look directly at the man who was slowly healing physically. Would he ever heal emotionally? At least enough to recognize what he wanted and what he had before him. "Cassie Travers seems to think you do great with her kids. I heard them calling you *uncle*. And that little Eddie is going to think you're real special as he grows up."

"Maybe. He's just a little thing now."

"You seem to get along very well with my kids. Johnny worships you and Carolyn says you're the greatest teacher."

"That's different," Ed protested, looking away from Maggie. "They're Johnny and Carolyn — my students, my helpers."

The pride and pleasure in his voice as he spoke of her children reassured Maggie immensely. Ed Harrington might not realize it yet, but he was gradually becoming comfortable with his situation at the farm. She sensed that he was even becoming more at ease with her. While she didn't want to be as comfortable as an old shoe or petted like a family dog, she welcomed this period of calm reconnecting without the tension of the chase. Would he ever be ready to pursue her, to love her?

The sudden spasm of heat shooting through her loins caused Maggie to gasp audibly. She saw Ed turn and look at her suspiciously. She sneezed, trying to cover up her response to those delicious images cascading through her mind of him pursuing her and them making love until overcome by exhaustion. Maggie turned and wiped the sink and counter.

At last, when she was more under control, Maggie asked, "So what about getting out into the community socially?"

- o -

Ed jarred himself from his own reverie. She'd been so quiet for so long it was difficult not to simply focus on her body. Maggie Anderson had to have the tightest little butt he'd ever had in his hands. Unwanted memories let him feel again her firmness and her electrifying response to his touch.

Shaking his head, he tried to refocus on her words. What the hell had she said? "Probably wouldn't hurt much. Folks know I'm here. Templeton's right. It's harder to tell stories about someone you know — well, maybe not really a lot more difficult."

"Yeah, they've known me all my life."

Why did she have to look so pained? What did she expect when she invited a drunk into her life? "We both know small towns and rural communities, Maggie. I got away from one once. What I like about the big city is you can be anonymous."

"But people die in the cities and no one shows up for their funerals."

"True. There are advantages both ways, I expect. I do love the peacefulness of this place." He closed his eyes, reconstructing the open fields, the canopied maple trees, and the refurbished paddocks. He hesitated. "I think getting out more might help the uneasiness that sometimes exists between the two of us. Maybe it'll help being around other people. And it'll give me an opportunity to develop my own impressions of your neighbors. After all, one or more of them aren't behaving very neighborly toward you and your friends."

"Okay, Dick Tracy," Maggie said, looking amused, "by the time the Inaugural is run, you should be fairly well healed. We'll start taking you out of your dog house and show you around a bit. The town holds a Fall Harvest Festival Dance. That should be fun. I love to dance."

Ed scowled at her. Dance! She had to be insane.

"If any other female so much as breathes on you," Maggie scolded, "I'll chain you back on your leash."

"I didn't have dancing in mind when I thought about socializing. Besides, I don't dance."

"I bet you will by the time the Festival gets here," Carolyn teased, strolling into the kitchen.

"Maggie," Ed complained half heartedly, "how come your kids have ears like elephants until I want them to do something?"

"I don't know. Somebody once said that's the way teenagers grow up."

CHAPTER FOURTEEN

On the following Wednesday, Maggie sat beside Cassie Travers in the pickup truck pulling a horse trailer down the Prairie Meadows shedrow. In the trailer rode Capote's Dream, who would run in Sunday's Inaugural Stakes.

Cassie turned toward their assigned barn. Maggie tried to take in everything around her. A groom bathed a high-strung bay. Other horses walked methodically in circles on hot walkers. Clumps of men and women gathered here and there huddled in discussion.

Maggie could hardly contain the excitement and the tension coursing through her body. "It's hard to believe we finally have a horse running here. Thanks for bringing him all the way from Chicago," she said, turning toward her companion. "I'm sure you could have found a race for him up there."

Cassie shook her auburn curls vigorously. "We've been aiming Dream for this race since you bought him. It's a very credible stakes race, and you need to become familiar with the operations at your home track." Cassie directed a warm smile at Maggie. "Being here is a nice change for me; it'll be good to get away from the pressure of the home circuit for a few days. Clint is picking the kids up from their grandmother this weekend. So where else would I rather be? This will be fun. I'm eager to show you around."

After getting Capote's Dream settled into his stall, Cassie guided Maggie through the stable and track area explaining what was happening and trying to prepare her for her first big race. "I always use the same groom when I run a horse here at Prairie Meadows. Juan can gentle a horse as well as anyone I've ever worked with.

"Saturday night, Jessica Wilder will arrive. She's the jock I've told you about. She and Dream have a beautiful relationship. Jessica works him in the morning and has taken the time to get to know the animal. It's one thing for a rider to hop on the back of a horse during the afternoon races; it's another for her to exercise the horse during workouts and to develop an understanding for how the mount reacts to different race conditions. I wouldn't trust anyone else to ride Dream in such an important race."

"Will she join us back at the farm for Carolyn's birthday party Sunday evening?"

Cassie grinned. "She'll have to head back right after the race. Of course, we'll be celebrating a victory as well as a birthday."

"I wish I could be that confident."

"Don't worry. We all go through race jitters. Wait till the day of the race — you won't be able to sit in one place for longer than a minute."

Maggie couldn't decide if Cassie's words were comforting or simply added to her own anxiety. As they walked over the grounds, Cassie continued to impart useful information, but Maggie had difficulty concentrating and remembering.

The place pulsated an earthy, sensual allure. Smells of horse sweat, leather, hay, sour mash, rubbing alcohol, and manure blended into an aroma as scintillating as many essential oils. Occasionally, Maggie heard the echo of hammer meeting metal as farriers worked to protect the hooves of the high priced runners. And there was the low murmur of chatter coming from groups of trainers, grooms, and exercise riders plotting courses of action.

The backstretch area resembled a small town. Many of the grooms and some of the jockeys stayed in large dormitories. A sign over the café doorway promised good food at cheap prices. Over a thousand horses were stabled on shedrow during race season, requiring considerable coordination and cooperation among all who worked and lived on the grounds. And the area was restricted to licensed owners, trainers, and workers.

Maggie brushed a palm against the owner license ID suspended from her blouse pocket. This was her world now. A chill skittered up her spine. She belonged here, though that was still difficult to accept. Would she ever really belong?

"Horses going for their morning workout enter through that gate," Cassie said, pointing to a small contingent of horses and riders making their way along a lengthy path leading from the barn area to

261

the track. "We'll give Dream a brief workout over the track Friday morning. Nothing too serious. I just want him to get a feel for the dirt surface under him. All tracks may look the same, but each is different, has its own character in terms of the mixture making up the dirt, sharpness of turns, and buildings and towers around the perimeter."

"Do you think he really has a chance to win?" Maggie asked again as they retraced their steps toward the parking lot.

Cassie rolled her eyes skyward. "By the way, there's the tack shop. You can get anything imaginable for a horse or rider in there. How many times are you going to ask that question? Yes, I think Capote's Dream has a very legitimate shot at winning.

"Horses are coming in from around the country for this race. A hundred-fifty-thousand-dollar purse attracts owners and trainers who don't use this track as their home base. But Dream will be competitive at this level. He's already won some decent allowance races at Arlington.

Cassie waved to an acquaintance leaving the parking area. "If he wins here, we'll probably leave him with you and Ed for the winter. Dream deserves some rest. We'll start again in early spring, if you still want me to handle him for you."

"Of course, I want you racing him where he'll do his best. But," Maggie insisted, grabbing Cassie's arm bringing them both to a halt, "if we win here, I want you to start taking your ten percent trainer's fee. It's only fair. Our share of such a large purse would make my life secure, at least until another crop is planted."

Chuckling, Cassie patted Maggie's hand. "Okay, I know how important that is to you. But the word secure is not one usually associated with horse racing."

"But you do all right."

"Sure, but it's the sale of breeding stock and promising young prospects that's our base; any profit from racing is whipped cream on top."

Apprehension suddenly overtook Maggie as they neared Cassie's red pickup. "I don't know if I'll ever be able to do all the things you have to do at the track. Placing your horse in the right race to win seems to be a skill developed over long years of experience. And how do you decide to take the risk to drop your favorite horse into a claiming race where anybody with enough money can take him away from you?"

"Whoa, girl," Cassie cautioned, climbing into the truck. "You don't have to do it all at once. You have Ed to help. I don't plan on dropping out of the picture. If you don't want to do the track management piece of the business, you can work with the horses on your farm and then turn them over to other trainers. Or, hopefully, the ban on Ed will be lifted soon and then you'll really be set up nicely."

"Do you think that's likely?" Maggie asked hesitantly. That'd be wonderful news for Ed — but what would prevent him from simply moving back to Chicago, with nothing resolved between the two of them? She instantly felt guilty for the selfish thought.

"One of Clint's contacts is chasing down a new lead. Clint's fairly optimistic. And he doesn't usually lean toward optimism in these kinds of matters."

"That would do so much for Ed," Maggie said, brightening. "Sometimes he behaves like a free and easy spirit, and then he just clouds over, sinking back into his depression. You know then he's remembering what he had and how he lost it."

As they drove back to the farm, Cassie returned to the topic of Ed Harrington. "You all looked like a real comfortable family last night. Ed seems to be fitting in quite well."

Glancing at Cassie, Maggie tried not to blush. "You could say that, but he was on his best behavior last night." She paused. "The kids adore him."

"And you don't."

Maggie couldn't hold back a chuckle. "I didn't say that. Ed's afraid of commitment. He doesn't think he's good enough for me. He thinks I deserve better. I think he's a fool."

"Wow. You just said a lot. If he lets you go, he's a double fool in my book," Cassie said, pulling around a slow driver. "Though men and women seldom move at the same pace in these matters. Guess there has to be a pursuer and a pursuee."

"So which were you?" Maggie giggled.

"Oh, well, with us?" Cassie wrinkled her nose. "Clint was definitely the pursuer in the beginning. Then, I almost did too good of a job of getting away and I ended up having to chase him all the way to California to corral him."

"I'll bet he wasn't hard to catch."

"It had its moments," Cassie whispered, giving Maggie an unhurried smile.

Maggie smiled. "I'll guarantee you my man is not going to get away, no matter what he might be thinking. I'm not pursuing at the moment. I agreed to a truce — temporarily. But I'm scheming."

"Ah, a woman after my own heart. Men may usually be stronger than us physically, but if we want 'em, they don't even come close to matching our cunning. I'm putting my money on you, girl."

Maggie peered out at the track from a box seat in the clubhouse. The days leading up to the Inaugural had flown by too rapidly. She'd loved talking with Cassie about horses and men. They agreed that both had a number of things in common. While a horse was a gregarious animal typically found in herds, he was also a wanderer, resisting human notions of confinement. When the horse sensed imminent danger, he'd flee. And horses lacking in self-confidence were particularly prone to spook at the slightest provocation.

She'd miss Cassie when she went back to Chicago on Monday.

Maggie and Ed already planned a trip to the

Travers' farm in October to purchase their long awaited broodmares. Midnight Dancer was at the top of her list, if she could still afford the beauty. Given everything the Travers were doing for her and Ed, Maggie wanted to give them all the business she possibly could.

She had readily agreed with Cassie's suggestion to go directly to the clubhouse rather than standing by in the saddling paddock. Her bundle of jangled nerves would not help Capote's Dream one bit.

Both kids were off getting food. How could they eat with the race coming up? She warmed remembering Ed wishing all of them good luck before they drove to the track.

"Good luck," he'd said, before kissing her on the top of the head. "Remember, we can't win them all."

She hadn't missed the moist glaze in his eyes. He badly wanted to be with them for the race. But that wasn't possible.

Obviously, he was concerned about how she might handle the disappointment of losing. Cassie was confident. Jessica Wilder, who she'd met earlier that morning, was thrilled to have the ride and believed in Capote's Dream. And Maggie's own bones were humming with enthusiasm. Still, her nerves were strung out tight, as if she'd been on a caffeine binge.

Maggie watched Johnny climb the concrete steps balancing chips and cheese dip and a large pop. Maggie's stomach roiled in protest.

Smiling bravely, she welcomed her birthday girl back to her seat. Carolyn clutched a large salty pretzel and a pop. She was so excited by the crowd and by the prospect of seeing one of their own horses race.

"Mom. Take a moment, bend over and take a deep breath or two," Carolyn counseled. "You don't want to pass out and miss the race."

Although not wanting to, Maggie took Carolyn's advice. It would be totally embarrassing to keel over before her horse ran. *Good God, when will this race start? Why is it taking forever?* Slow motion was a flash compared to this waiting. She'd never been very good with waiting.

Her nails dug into her bare thighs. Even with the air conditioning going strong, she was pleased she'd finally decided on shorts and a tank top for the day. People came to watch the horses, not her. Any more clothing and she would've suffocated.

This was big. This race could make a huge difference for Anderson Racing Stables. It could make saving the farm a pure fanciful wish or a plausible reality.

At last the horses stepped onto the track for the post parade. Fidgeting with her program, Maggie peered closely at the number six horse. Capote's Dream looked splendid. His coat gleamed, announcing to all to take notice. He looked proud and ready to do battle for honor and glory. The four year old seemed so big compared to the horses they'd been working with on a day-to-day basis at the farm. And there was Jessica Wilder with her game face on decked out in black and red colors — Anderson Racing Stables colors. Scottish colors; her dad would have liked that.

"He's up on his toes nicely," Cassie said, scurrying to sit down. "Dream is going to run a big race."

"I'm sure he'll do his best," Maggie managed to murmur. "I just wish it was over. The pit in my stomach is terrible."

"You'll get accustomed to it," Cassie said, chuckling. "Sort of."

Maggie stared so hard at the starting gate her eyes hurt. At last the gate sprang open and the horses were racing. She was surprised at how quickly Capote's Dream raced to the front of the pack. Front running horses had won nearly every race that day. Crossing her fingers, she urged her horse on. He entered the backstretch four lengths in front. This was a critical juncture in the race — would he maintain his speed around the turn? Or would the closers pass him by?

Maggie stood and screamed encouragement along with her kids and Cassie. Not able to see around the burly man in front of her, Maggie stood on her seat in time to see the finish.

No one would catch Capote's Dream this day. He continued to stretch his lead, crossing the finish line six lengths in front of his nearest competitor. Maggie's ears went temporarily deaf from her children's screams and her own. She hugged herself and then her kids. This couldn't be happening. But it was. It most definitely was.

"Hurry," Cassie shouted. "We have to get to the winner's circle. Follow me."

Cassie led them to the winners circle. After their picture was taken with Dream, Carolyn protectively carried the yellow and blue Inaugural Stakes blanket in her arms. Johnny couldn't stop jumping up and down. And Maggie felt like she could spend a week in bed without ever waking up.

Maggie stopped at a betting window to collect her winnings. Ed had asked her to put a hundred on the horse to win and she'd done likewise with twenty of her own money, which included five dollars for each of the kids. With the horse going off at three to one odds, the payoff was simply an added bonus for the day.

While Cassie led Dream toward the test barn where winners were examined for illegal drug usage, Maggie and her kids headed back to their seats. She even bought drinks and pretzels for herself and her children. "This must be the most weird birthday you've ever had, Carolyn."

"It's the greatest," Carolyn squealed. "I just wish Ed could've been here, too."

"Yeah," Johnny chimed in. "He would've cheered louder than anybody."

"I don't know about that," Maggie responded lightly, "but it would have been nice. Maybe someday."

"Fifteen. And I got to stand in the winner's circle. Can you believe it?" Carolyn wiped her hands on a napkin and then very carefully brushed the Inaugural Blanket. "You know, when I become a vet, I might specialize in horses."

"That's a grand idea," Maggie said, "but let's not rush things. You're already growing up too fast."

"Mother," Carolyn scolded, "I want to dream big just like you. Just like Ed. Just like Cassie."

"I know. I know." Maggie reached for her daughter's hands. "We all grow up. Hopefully, we all have dreams to chase. And I dearly hope that you and Johnny will reach for and fulfill your own dreams, whatever they might be."

Later that evening the celebration of the day's victory continued in Maggie's living room. After expenses, Maggie would clear about seventy thousand dollars for the day. Her mind swirled trying to grasp those numbers and their implications. She was used to eking things out over the course of a year from cash crop to cash crop. She might be permanently bruised from the number of times she had pinched herself since the completion of the race. She sobered some, remembering Cassie and Ed's cautionary words— *one race does not make for a competitive stable.* But it would do a lot to assure them they could stay afloat until another growing season.

In January, the foaling season would begin. Maggie looked eagerly toward that time. That would be the best yet. She'd helped many sows give birth beginning when she was little, but this would be even more special. Ed had shared the awe of foaling in words, but she wanted to experience it herself. How could any man be so sensitive about horses and kids as well as being a considerate lover, and not imagine himself good enough to be a husband and father?

Maggie smiled at her daughter, who was blushing slightly, apparently searching for words. She was far too rapidly becoming a young woman.

"This has been the best birthday ever," Carolyn finally said. "Thank you everybody for all the gifts."

Maggie nodded with satisfaction. It certainly had been a memorable birthday. She'd given Carolyn cute dangling earrings and a silver bracelet. A very stout riding croup came from Cassie, who had leaned over to remind Maggie about the tack shop at Prairie Meadows. Johnny had given his sister a huge book on horse injuries and diseases. He'd confessed that Ed had helped him pick it out. Even Brad had sent a funny card and two videos on training colts. And Ed had probably shocked them all by presenting her with custom made eastern riding boots. They must have cost a small fortune. He insisted that every vet ought to have a pair.

Their house hadn't witnessed such a celebration for some time. This was the way it ought to be more often. Tonight everyone and everything was mellow. She liked that very much.

The next morning as Cassie prepared to drive

back, she exchanged hugs with Maggie and Ed. "Let me know when you're ready to come up and look for broodmares. You're staying with us, of course."

"I'm looking forward to it," Maggie said.

Ed frowned and said, "Let Clint know I'll be calling him soon. Want to talk with him more about the troubles we've been having down here."

"I'll do that." With furrowed brow, Cassie clasped Maggie's hand. "I do hope your troubles will end now that people know you're serious about keeping your land." Winking, she added, "And good luck with the cantankerous one here. His bites are not as bad as his growl."

They watched Cassie's pickup pull out of the driveway. Ed muttered, "What the hell did she mean by the cantankerous one?"

"How does she know about your biting skills, is what I want to know." Maggie teased.

Ed squirmed. "She doesn't know a damn thing about what she's saying, and neither do you," he bellowed, stalking off toward the barn.

Maggie grinned at the man fleeing her tongue. He wouldn't go far. She trusted that now. Things were on the improve all the way around. And she was very happy.

CHAPTER FIFTEEN

"Look at this!" Johnny shouted, skidding to a halt in the middle of the kitchen.

"Slow down, Johnny," his mother urged. "Why so excited? I thought going all the way to the road for the paper was a big chore for you."

"Look, Mom. You're in the paper. We all are! Front page. Even our picture."

Maggie grabbed the paper and moved quickly to the table. Carolyn and Ed, who had been working a puzzle in the living room, also rushed in to see what the commotion was about.

Leaning over the table, Maggie gawked at the paper. She read the front page headline aloud: "Local Girl Scores Big at PM." With awe and pride, Maggie read the sub-title: "With Big City Connections, Anderson Stables Races to Inaugural Stakes Victory."

"Oh, my God," Maggie groaned, "if what we were doing here was unknown before last Sunday, it isn't anymore."

"Nice picture," Ed said. "You all look real happy."

"It was fantastic," Carolyn responded.

"Yeah, next time you'll be there, too," Johnny declared.

Ed blinked and nodded at the boy. "We'll see, pardner."

Maggie cleared her throat, and continued reading aloud. "Maggie Anderson, daughter of the late Colt and Marilyn Magee, owner of Anderson Racing Stables, pulled off a major coup in her first entry at Prairie Meadows. Capote's Dream, a four year old, won the $150,000 Inaugural Stakes running away from the field.

"Turns out, surprising to most folks around here, Anderson has been racing a number of horses in the Chicago area with Cassie Travers, a trainer well known throughout the Midwest. Capote's Dream was shipped in special for this high stakes race, like so many of his challengers. A purse of $150,000 attracts horse people from all over the country.

"Folks locally are abuzz about their new found heroine and her future plans. Is this a rags to riches story, or what?

"Mrs. Anderson is not without help. Mr. Ed Harrington, a former horse trainer from the Chicago area, is reportedly helping her set up a first-class racing stable and handling her younger horses and broodmares. While Harrington is banned from entering any horse track because of being implicated in a betting scandal in Chicago, his expertise no doubt is providing the foundation for Anderson Racing Stables.

"A graduate of Beaverhill High School, Mrs. Anderson is the mother of two children: Carolyn, 15 and Johnny, 10. Her late husband, Mason Anderson, died tragically of cancer two years ago. Mrs. Anderson has been active in the Crossroads

Community Church and in a number of organizations here in town. Sources tell us that her level of participation has fallen off of late, probably due to her working with Mr. Harrington and her horses."

Maggie slapped the newspaper down on the table. "*Her level of participation has fallen off of late.* Now is that catty or what? Sounds like Mrs. McPherson. And is *working with Mr. Harrington and the horses* sexual innuendo?"

"Mom, what's sexual innuuu…whatever?" Johnny asked.

Maggie blanched at the look of wonder on his face. How could she explain this one? "Ah, that will become clearer as you get older." Sometimes you just had to duck.

"Great, Mom. Must be pretty bad, or you'd explain it."

Pulling out a chair to sit, Ed said, "It's not that it's so bad, as that someone is trying to diss your mother some. But I expect we can handle it." Then he grinned at Maggie, "Don't know whether that was what was meant. But the headline is a mite suggestive: *Local Girl Scores Big At PM.*"

"Damn, didn't even notice that one."

"Mom, you're slow," Carolyn chided. "Wow, this is going to be all over school. You're a celebrity. *We're* celebrities."

"You don't mind the sexual overtone?"

Carolyn gave her a simpering smile. "Just makes you more glamorous. Since when do Magees and Andersons care about what other

275

people think?" she squared her shoulders.

Maggie didn't correct her daughter, but there were some Andersons in the area who cared a lot about what others thought. There was no reason, however, to widen the gulf between her in-laws and her children. Mason's parents wanted to stay involved with their grandchildren, but couldn't understand why Maggie wasn't trying to disabuse her daughter of becoming a veterinarian. That was a dirty job for a man and ill suited for a lady. And how could she allow Carolyn to wear four metal studs in her ear? That had to be unhealthy and too provocative. And Johnny, being small for his age, never quite performed in sports as well as his grandparents hoped. Both children had shared their disappointment and the pressure they felt to be perfect like their dad was remembered to be.

She'd loved him, and she knew he was never as perfect as his folks thought. He'd been in her pants from the time they were seniors. She expected his parents would have regarded that behavior as slightly flawed, but would have explained it away easily as Maggie leading their son astray.

That was history. She had the present to deal with. Looking at each individual standing around the table, she let out a breath she hadn't realized she'd been holding. "Okay. Guess there's no need to pretend anymore about our plans for the farm. Each of you can talk openly about what we're doing with the stables. If Con-Ex Farms or whoever wants to get their back up about it, so be it. We're ready to fight. There is no place to retreat to now."

"That a girl." Ed grinned broadly. His pride and his willingness to join the fight were obvious to Maggie.

Resting her head against his chest, Maggie wondered if he was aware of what he was doing. Then their hug was joined by Carolyn and Johnny, laughing and hurrahing. Could life be better than this? It was a family hug. They were prepared to stand by each other.

- o -

Staring out the loft window toward the house in mid October, Ed could only guess at what she was plotting now. Maggie Anderson was full of surprises. Even after pledging not to seduce him again, she constantly made it clear in small ways that she wanted him. It might be the crook of her smile. The gleam in her eyes. The way she arched her body. The sultry voice daring him to react. Or the way the woman embraced life. Seldom was she depressed. He'd never been around anyone so hopeful and determined.

No matter what she said, she hadn't given up on him — or on them.

That pleased him immensely, and it made him break out in a cold sweat. Her boldness sometimes lit him up like a Christmas tree. Tension snaked across his lower back. He wanted her, pure and simple. He missed her touch, her smell, her taste.

Somewhere along the line he was either going to have to leave for good or find a way of being with her, totally. Thinking of life without Maggie and her kids made him cringe.

He placed his forehead against the window. The cool glass pane provided welcome relief. A strong wind blew about the brown, red and yellow leaves from oaks, maples and aspens. The seasons were changing. The heat of the summer was finally gone, replaced by cool crisp mornings. It wouldn't be long until winter would arrive with its brashness.

They were ready for it. Most of the horses would winter all right, with access to one end of the barn or to other outbuildings. He'd just finished constructing stalls for the broodmares. That was a task requiring much care and patience. Those stalls were larger than the average stall and there could be no tiny protruding objects that might hurt a new born foal. Within the next week or two they would go to Chicago to purchase Maggie's broodmares. He was eager to bring back Midnight Dancer. Every time he thought of that mare, his pulse quickened.

Foaling season would begin in late winter and early spring. He smiled, anticipating the family's reactions to the arrival of babies. They hadn't seen anything yet.

Ed pressed his palms against the window. He was weary from running — from Maggie, and from himself.

He broke into a sweat. Why did he have to run?

There was no way he could leave these people. They'd become his family, as important to him as breathing. Equally impossible would be staying and watching Maggie with another man. His skin crawled at the thought of anyone else running fingers over her body. He still believed Maggie deserved much better, but he guessed she was too stubborn to change her mind.

Stepping back from the window, Ed grinned, satisfied. If he and Maggie were ever going to be a real couple, then they were going to go about it his way. There would be room for romance. The Harvest Festival was the following Saturday, and he planned on having a date for it. *Maggie, what will you do when it's my turn to pursue?*

- o -

"I can hardly believe it, Mom," Carolyn giggled, standing next to her mother in the bathroom and fluffing her long blonde hair over and over. "A real date. I'm so nervous."

"We've talked a lot about boys," Maggie began. She watched her daughter roll her eyes toward the ceiling.

"Please, Mother. Not tonight."

"Oh, okay." Maggie placed an arm around Carolyn's shoulders. "I'm sure we haven't left anything out. You're a responsible young woman, and I hope you have lots of fun. Running gloss across her lips, she mumbled, "When is your date supposed to pick you up?"

"Seven o'clock, but Bobbie Humphries was probably late for his own birth. No one in that family is ever on time." Carolyn threw her mom a pained look and then smiled. "But he is the best wide receiver on the football team. And he chose me!"

As Maggie added a touch of eyeliner to herself, she smiled at her delighted daughter. Her own memory was not so poor that she couldn't remember her first date—a mixture of pure excitement and nagging fear.

"How about your date, Mom? When is Ed picking you up?"

Maggie saw color rise on her cheeks as she continued to examine herself in the mirror. She wasn't used to dating, and she certainly was not used to imagining herself on a date going to the same dance as her daughter. But such was the way things were in a small community. It would be okay. She didn't know which would be worse: trying not to pay too much attention to her daughter and Bobbie, or trying to ignore the stares and comments of her neighbors when they saw her being escorted by Ed Harrington.

He had surprised her—no, shocked her. He'd hung around after breakfast one morning hemming and hawing until he finally blurted out, "I'd like it if you'd go with me to the Fall Festival Dance Saturday night."

Well, she'd expected that she would be taking him along. After all, it was a good opportunity for him to meet people. But he clearly intended on making something more of it than the two of them being at the same place at the same time and sharing the same vehicle for transportation.

Ed had left no doubt in her mind—he'd said he was asking her for a date. Smiling, she remembered actually blushing before saying yes. "Good," was his ecstatic response. Then he'd strolled out the door to the barn as if nothing important had transpired.

And then the next morning a bouquet of yellow and red tulips greeted her on the dining room table. The card read: "Looking forward to Saturday night."

He'd warned her that it was time for some romance in her life, and he was certainly delivering.

Flattered by his renewed attention, Maggie wondered if this meant that he was preparing to commit to her or whether he was simply physically well enough now to have some fun. Having a good time was okay with her, but they would be carrying on this romantic intrigue publicly, on her turf.

While he might choose to walk away if things didn't work out, she couldn't. What would folks say if she was jilted by the drifting horse trainer, about whom many thought the worst? *That Maggie Magee finally got burned*, Mrs. McPherson would snipe with her nose turned up. *That's what happens to moths when they get too close to a flame, and that's what happens to wayward women.*

"Mom, I asked when Ed would pick you up?"

Maggie gave her daughter a blank look. "Oh, I'm sorry. Around seven thirty. We won't go until we're sure you're on your way okay. And be home by midnight."

"Yes, Mom. How about you?" she teased, sticking her tongue out.

"Carolyn!"

"I know. Just wanted to make sure you were still listening. I've got to go put on my dress."

Maggie shook her head. Carolyn sure had a free spirit. Even give the anxiety of a first date, she remained confident and eager. Sighing at her own reflection in the mirror, Maggie wished *she* could be so carefree and confident.

Did he plan on them making love? Would he take her to the loft? Should she invite him to her bedroom?

Why did she suddenly feel so out of control? Trying to rub the chills from her bare arms, Maggie shrugged at her image in the mirror. A strap of her slip fell away, nearly baring a breast. She closed her eyes and felt his lips nuzzling her skin. His teeth pulled the thin fabric away and her erect nipples strained under the caresses of his tongue and lips.

Shaking, Maggie opened her eyes wide. She leaned against the vanity. Her entire body was on edge. Heat gnawed at her loins. The uncertainty of the evening had her coiled like a tight spring.

Romance was supposed to be lovely and delicious. Then why did she feel so imperiled? It was only a dance. It wasn't like he held her life in his hands.

Frantically, she brushed her hair. She felt like a billiard ball completely at the whim of the careening cue ball. Maggie laughed aloud — it must be tough being a billiard ball, especially if you were used to being the cue ball. She tried to imagine what her personal cue ball was up to. A whisper of a smile flitted across her lips. Was he as nervous as she was? Or was he simply taking the evening in stride?

- o -

Ed buttoned his dress shirt feeling quite pleased with himself. He'd thrown Maggie off balance a time or two. She hadn't expected his formal request for a date, and she certainly had not known what to say about the flowers. She'd been flustered, and he liked that. Her vulnerability needed to surface more often, or she'd give him a complex for sure. Maggie was so in control — of herself, and too often of him. There were occasions when he wondered just how much her pride was covering up. She'd known a lot of pain and loss, but she always seemed to pull herself together and hold up her chin, prepared to take on the next hurdle. Ed tugged at the string tie. The woman had to be more vulnerable than she let on.

God knew he was vulnerable enough — maybe enough for both of them. Yet, he'd come a long way. Seldom did he have the classic drinking nightmare anymore, where he'd wake up sweating because he dreamed he'd fallen off the wagon. Even most crises didn't cause him to shake. Still, he never underestimated the risk of drink and its danger to his life. Chaos remained only one drink away. He was determined never to test that theory.

Maggie Anderson had thrown him a lifeline, but it was his own hand that had reached out and grabbed what was offered. And now he was beginning to think he might actually have a life to look forward to again. He wanted that life to include Maggie, but he still wasn't sure how that could happen. Maybe he'd just try to be her escort for a while and see where that led.

Tongues would wag, that was for sure. But then they were already wagging. He and Maggie both deserved some fun. They worked hard. She was driven to save the land, and he guessed he was driven to leave his past behind. In order to have some fun, they'd have to get away from the farm now and then. Could he ever get away from his past?

He hadn't formally asked a woman for a date in years. Whatever had possessed him to do so now was beyond his comprehension. They could've just gone to the festival together, and his nerves would be less jumbled. What did she expect of him? Would she want him to take her to his bed?

Ed shivered. Damn, he'd always hated dating as a kid. And his entire adult life was made up of a smattering of one night stands; not a lot of confusion there. But Maggie was not a one night stand—never was, never would be. And he certainly wouldn't want her any other way.

Grabbing his billfold and keys off the night stand, Ed glanced around briefly. The place looked orderly enough, not that Maggie would mind a mess particularly. He wasn't certain that taking her to bed was such a good idea. They needed time—well, at least *he* needed time—to sort things out bit by bit. Glancing down at his arousal, he realized that part of him required no more time for sorting.

The red numerals on the digital clock gave him his immediate marching orders. "Well, little lady," he drawled, picking up his Stetson, "guess it's time to see where this dancing thing takes us. Romance I promised, and romance it will be." With a swagger in his step that he hadn't felt for a long spell, Ed made his way down the loft steps and across the driveway toward his quarry.

"My, my," Ed said, appreciating what he saw when Maggie greeted him at the door. "Carolyn informed me if I was getting you a corsage that it had to be for the wrist. I didn't tell her I'd never buy a woman a flower to cover up her breast, particularly if we were going dancing. But...you look spectacular."

"Thank you," Maggie shyly demurred, turning around slowly before his gaze.

His eyes swept over her body. She wore a baby blue dress, matching her eyes. It clung to her shapely curves like a well fitted glove. Tiny shoulder straps held it up while showing suggestive soft cleavage. If she wore a bra, it was sure hard to tell. The dress stopped well above her knees; he figured the slit in its left side was the only thing that enabled her to move some. Tiny pearl earrings and a matching choke collar made her appear somehow more feminine.

He'd never seen her in heels before. These were low and matched the color of her dress. They looked practical, well suited for dancing. Maggie remained a sensible woman, but was still the sexiest female he'd ever seen.

Carolyn was right—there was only room for a wrist corsage, and he liked it that way. He hoped he didn't appear too eager.

- o -

Maggie bit her lower trembling lip while carefully placing the corsage on her wrist. She had to slow down her heartbeat somehow. He'd surprised her again. A corsage. And an orchid, at that. It looked so fragile. She sniffled, trying to hold back tears. At thirty-four, she'd just received her first orchid. She peered up at Ed. Could her body and soul withstand much more romancing?

"I guess we'd better go," she managed to say. "Carolyn was picked up fifteen minutes ago, and I deposited Johnny at Adam's house late this afternoon."

She took a step toward the doorway and then stopped. "No, not yet. I've got to tell you, Ed," she said, reaching for his hands, "you look terribly handsome tonight. You look nothing like that shadow of a man I remember meeting on the sidewalk in front of the Resting Arms. You must've gained at least twenty pounds since then—and all of it in the right places, I might add." Her small hand squeezed his hard bicep.

Ed flinched. "Must be all the good food and hard work," he finally mumbled.

"And determination on your part. I'm so proud of what you've been able to do. I know it's not been easy, particularly when things go badly."

"I used to believe alcohol was a friend in my times of greatest need. It blotted out the memories. Now I know it was my worst enemy." Ed sighed and grabbed Maggie's hand. Tugging gently, he said, "Let's get out of here before we get too mushy. I want this to be a fun evening."

"Me too," she agreed quickly, flashing him a smile. With her nerves tightly under wraps, Maggie said gaily, "Lead on, Sir Knight, your damsel awaits your command."

Ed laughed while offering her a deep bow. "That'll be the day."

CHAPTER SIXTEEN

The Beaverhill High School gym doubled as a community social hall. With its bleachers folded against the walls, Ed thought the gym looked like most any small town high school gym characteristic of the Midwest. Autumn decorations of brown and orange crepe paper hung from the basketball hoops and from the ceiling. Fall leaves and shocks of corn stalks decorated a corner of the room. A few oddly shaped pumpkins that had survived the summer's heat sat on the stage next to the five-member band.

Band members ranged in age from maybe thirty to seventy. He'd been told the four men and one woman were quite versatile performing pieces from the thirties to the present. As long as there was plenty of country and soft rock and roll, he'd be satisfied.

Ed sensed the tension gnawing at Maggie as soon as they entered the building. At first she seemed uneasy to meet anyone in the eye. When he reached for her hand, her palm was sweaty. In a matter of minutes though, she'd relaxed.

Smiling as if she possessed a secret, she introduced him to old friends and neighbors. There was plenty of small talk about the welcomed change in the weather, poor crops, and getting by. A few folks asked him about Maggie's horses, but most didn't broach the topic. And none asked about what might be going on between him and his beautiful boss.

Most of the party-goers sat at cloth-covered card tables. As soon as he and Maggie entered the gym they'd been spied and waved at by Ben Templeton. Clearly they'd been expected.

Ed liked Ben. He was genuinely interested in their horse business, but he didn't pry. And he had a dry sense of humor that many probably missed. Ben had invited a widower, Gladys Mays, to join him for the evening. He'd whispered something to Maggie about taking his own advice. Maggie's cheeks had pinkened in response, but neither she nor Ben had provided further elaboration.

"So what do you think or our little town, Ed?" Templeton asked, lifting a glass of punch to his lips.

"Seems like most small communities, I guess. I'm from Clarion—but you probably knew that. There's good and bad in small and large. I do appreciate the relative quiet and slower pace."

"That's true enough. Say, that was quite an article in the paper a while back. Do you think our Maggie is going to succeed in the horse business?"

Ed glanced at Maggie, who sat beside him listening intently. He smiled. "I think Maggie will succeed in whatever she sets her mind to.

Templeton nodded. "Think you're likely right about that."

"Right now," Maggie said, reaching for Ed's

hand, "I simply want to succeed at dancing. If it's not too much to ask, I'd like a partner."

"I'm willing," Ed declared, looking into those sparkling eyes. He didn't fail to notice Templeton's eyebrow flash and approving smile at Maggie's vague use of the word partner.

With a hand resting on her back, Ed guided her to the dance floor. Somehow in that brief moment he'd passed inspection by one of Maggie's oldest mentors and protectors.

It was a slow song, just the kind he liked best. They moved together easily. She snuggled against him with one hand holding his at his chest and the other resting on his shoulder. He encircled her waist, holding her tight and resting his chin on top of her head. Ed breathed deeply of her scent as they glided gracefully, oblivious to others on the floor.

Seemingly without skipping a beat the music changed to a Texas two step. With ease, Ed quickened the pace and Maggie followed as if she'd been following him all her life.

Leaning back to look at him in surprise, Maggie chided, "Thought you said you couldn't dance."

Ed grinned. "Sometimes I'm overly modest. Knowing that should keep you guessing."

"I think you like to keep me guessing," she teased, laying her head back on his chest.

He wondered if she could hear his heart pounding. It was so easy to imagine her scrunched up against his body forever. Damn, he'd missed making love with Maggie; mostly he missed simply holding her and being held by her.

"Keeping you off balance is the only way I'm going to have a chance," he muttered, twirling her about as if she were a rag doll.

- o -

As Ed escorted her back to their table, Maggie noticed a few individuals staring at them with disdain, but she didn't care. This was good. Taking time to dance, to have some fun, to be together. It was the right thing to do.

Thank God Ben had suggested bringing Ed to social functions. Sometimes you had to get away from the land, or it would wear you down.

Some who stared were simply curious about him — and probably about her, too. There'd been a few questions about the horses. No one had yet claimed she was insane, although a few likely thought it. It was good to see old friends; she *had* been neglecting some of those relationships. With the approach of winter, the pace at the farm would likely slow down and there would be more time for catching up on social happenings.

Mildred Woodson grabbed her arm. Maggie stopped and smiled at her old friend, dressed in a brightly colored muumuu. She'd never been able to control her weight and had apparently given up on trying. They'd known each other since they were in diapers. Mildred's smile was radiant.

"I hope this means we'll see more of you at church," Maggie heard her say. "I've missed you,

Maggie. Too much work is bad for you."

"I know, Mildred. I'll be around more. Johnny should start confirmation in January. I've missed seeing you, too. Oh, this is Ed. He…"

"Pleased to meet you," Mildred said, pumping Ed's hand in greeting. "I read about you in the paper. I'm sure pleased that Maggie found you. She needs a steadying influence from time to time." Her eyes were full of mischief. "Bye now. See you, Maggie."

Watching in disbelief, Maggie shook her as Mildred squeezed her way between chairs making her way to the desert table.

She redirected her attention to Ed, who stood there belly laughing.

"*A steadying influence?* Maybe on a horse, but I don't think anyone has ever described me in that manner regarding a woman."

Annoyed, Maggie didn't know if she should laugh or scream. The idea that she needed a steadying influence! Mildred must have been remembering their junior high school days. Admittedly, she'd been a little wild then, but now there wasn't time for adventure. And she didn't want Ed to think she was used to cavorting around like someone who required being reined in. Then, she recalled her efforts at seducing him. She blinked. Her thighs warmed as she remembered his probing fingers that night in his loft and her brazen attempt at cooling off in the kitchen.

She headed for their table. She could use a cool

drink with plenty of ice cubes.

After they sat down, Carolyn brought her date by to say hello.

"Good evening, again, Ms. Anderson," Bobby Humphries mumbled, shifting his weight from foot to foot.

"I'm having a great time," Carolyn buzzed. "Are you?"

"I'm glad." Maggie gulped the cooling punch. "Yes, I am. A delightful time." Maggie glanced at her watch and then at Ed. How soon could they leave? They had until midnight, when Carolyn would be back.

"What about you, Ed?" Carolyn asked.

Maggie was a little embarrassed that Carolyn couldn't better conceal her pleasure in seeing the two of them together. Anyone watching would certainly know that the teenage daughter posed no problem for her mother and her hired hand.

Ed winked at Carolyn. "Couldn't be better. Thanks for all the advice."

"Right," she smirked. "I can see you didn't need any. I knew you'd be a terrific dancer. And the corsage is so beautiful."

"Well, we better be getting back to our table," interjected Bobby. "I'll have her home by midnight. You can count on that."

"Great," Maggie said, trying to be as serious as the boy.

After the young couple was out of hearing, Maggie whispered in Ed's ear, "I'm surprised Bobby can drive. He looks much more nervous than Carolyn. I'm pleased about that."

"Oh," Ed whispered back, "is the male supposed to be a nervous wreck to inspire confidence?"

"Only for mothers."

"Oh." Ed's eyes danced brightly. "Then this Sir Knight doesn't need to sheath his sword and put on a subservient act in order to win his damsel's favors."

Maggie couldn't control the tremble in her lips. She bit her tongue and then leaned closer to his ear. "Have you thought about possibly unsheathing your sword before it gets rusty? We have two hours before Carolyn gets home."

His body jerked. His jaw strained. She knew he could feel the heat of her words swirling in his ear.

- o -

Before he could respond to Maggie's suggestion, a voice reminding him of fingernails on a chalkboard interrupted his erotic musings.

"So this must be the mysterious rogue about whom I've been hearing so much."

Ed turned to see a thin, smallish woman with steel gray hair glaring at him. If the woman ever smiled, he expected her lips would crack.

"Ah," Templeton bellowed from across the table, "I wondered how long it would take you to sniff out our foursome. Ed, may I introduce you to Mrs. Mary Jane McPherson, who prides herself on knowing all there is to know about Beaverhill, and then some."

Ed nodded. He appreciated Templeton's attempt to buffer what could be an embarrassing situation for Maggie. He figured it was the *then some* that they had to worry about. "Pleased to meet you, ma'am," he said warmly, not giving away his feelings of distaste and distrust. "Hope you're enjoying yourself this evening. I know I am."

"Don't have time to enjoy myself, young man. Never do. Enjoyment is for those who have no motivation or sense of duty."

"Guess that must include everybody here but you, Mary Jane," Templeton commented smoothly. Turning to Ed, he confided, "In case you didn't know it, Mrs. McPherson isn't here to enjoy herself. No sir, she's working on her weekly newspaper column, and on keeping the oral communication channels well greased."

"You're an evil man, Ben Templeton."

Ed watched Mrs. McPherson stand even more rigid, her eyes boring into Ben.

"You were evil as a child, and still are."

"Now then, Mrs. Anderson," she called out imperiously, "tell me about this scheme of yours to raise race horses. What a ghastly business for a young lady to involve herself in!"

Maggie, who had been chuckling at the interplay between Templeton and McPherson, stiffened her back and spoke softly, "There's not much to tell, I'm afraid. Ed does most of the work with the horses, though he is coaching me and the kids. And the horses currently racing are being trained by friends in Chicago."

"Well, you certainly seemed to have developed a batch of new friends of late. What does Greta Anderson think about her daughter-in-law mucking stalls? Or her grandchildren, for that matter?"

Maggie blanched. Ed knew she was drawing on every ounce of her strength to remain calm.

"I don't know," Maggie managed to say. "Not that I particularly care. You'd have to ask her."

"You don't seem to care about a lot of things that affect your reputation," Mrs. McPherson sniped, looking down the tip of her beak-like nose. "I don't know how you can let...someone like this," she sputtered, gesturing toward Ed, "live on your property. You, a widower. And with a susceptible teenage daughter."

As the woman worked her mouth, trying to catch her breath, Ed clinched his fists, but before he could utter a word, he heard Maggie's icy voice.

"Mrs. McPherson, I believe your concern is misplaced. I'm quite capable of making decisions about how I will live my life. And my children's interests are always a high priority for me."

"Humph, you don't seem to be thinking straight now," Mrs. McPherson retorted. "I have a mind to talk to child protective services."

Ed grabbed Maggie's arm as she rose out of her chair with a stricken look on her face. Ben Templeton's mouth fell open.

Maggie sat back down in her seat, clearly still fighting to quell her anger. Ed wanted to defend her, but he knew this was Maggie's battle and she would not appreciate his interference.

"Mrs. McPherson, I hope you aren't serious. But if you are," Maggie paused and then spoke sharply, "you need to know that if you do anything...anything...to harm my children, I will see that your reputation is irreparably harmed. You will lose whatever meager status you have left in this community as the keeper of high morals."

Gasping, Mrs. McPherson flung a trembling hand to her throat. "Well, my word, threatening an old woman like me. What do you mean by that?"

"Just remember, I am my father's daughter." Maggie smiled thinly. "I have all his mementos. All of them. Do you recall *Roses are red and violets are blue...?*"

"Oh, my goodness." Mrs. McPherson grabbed hold of the table edge, barely maintaining her balance.

Ed thought the woman was about to faint. But she revived.

"Like your father, Maggie Magee, you have a tendency to over-react. I didn't mean to threaten you or your children in any way. I only had the best interest of your family in mind."

"Of course, Mrs. McPherson," Maggie responded smoothly. "And I appreciate that."

Ed frowned trying to figure out what had just

transpired. Mrs. McPherson's sweet words didn't match the undisguised hostility on her face. And there seemed little doubt that his Maggie was a blackmailer. She had something on the old gossip, and it must be good — damn good.

"Well, it was nice meeting you, Mr. Harrington," Mrs. McPherson offered meekly, preparing to make her exit. "I do hope you'll like our town and will be pleased to call it home."

"I surely am pleased to do that, Mrs. McPherson," Ed drawled. "Now you enjoy the rest of your evening."

He felt the heat of Mrs. McPherson's withering glare before she turned and walked rapidly away.

Ed covered Maggie's shaking hand with his own. "Wow," he ventured to no one in particular, "poisonous snakes can be friendlier than that. Does the woman have a husband?"

"Not anymore," Ben explained. "She no doubt henpecked Jethro to an early grave."

Maggie snuggled against the warmth of Ed's body as the truck made its way toward home.

"So what do you have on old McPherson?" Ed asked. "It must be a powder keg, the way that woman backpedaled."

Maggie nodded. It had started to rain as they headed out of town toward the farm — far too late to save any crops, but welcome nonetheless. Raindrops pelting the cab made her believe for a moment that they were encased in their own small world, impervious to what others thought or said.

Maggie sighed. "You bet I do."

"Well?"

"You won't tell?"

"Of course not. She means nothing to me."

"Okay. Apparently, she and Dad were an item back in high school before he got involved with my mom. In fact, they made it during a church camp between their junior and senior years."

Ed blinked. "You mean...Mrs. McPherson and your dad. Together. In bed."

"I don't actually know about whether it happened on a bed, or a floor, or on the ground, but they knew each other carnally, shall we say." She couldn't contain her glee.

"Wow! And you have proof."

"Uh, huh. Dad gave me what are supposedly a pair of Mary Jane's panties. But most damning is a note she sent him in her own handwriting. I have it stashed in a box, and in my memory. It goes like this:

"Dear Colt, my love,

Roses are red and violets are blue.

You are the absolute best in bed; my loins ache for you.

I can't wait to feel your colt tickling my insides again.

Maybe on the way home from school. Or after church Sunday.

Tell me when. I'm more than ready.

Love, Mary Jane N.

"Naylor was her maiden name. Dad told me to hold onto that note because I might need it someday. Mary Jane never forgave him for leaving her for Mom. As she aged, she seemed to become even more vindictive. And Dad wouldn't have put it past her to direct her resentment at me or the children someday. Giving me the note was his way of protecting me, I suppose."

"And you never let on about it until tonight?"

"Nope."

Chuckling, Ed said, "Seems like your parents stirred up a hornet's nest when they up and eloped. And people in Beaverhill have very long memories."

Maggie nodded in agreement. "Some of them sure do."

"And you really are a chip off the old block, or so the old saying goes. No wonder folks are ambivalent about you. They're just worried waiting to see what you'll dredge up next."

"Yeah, and some must wonder how many secrets I really do know," Maggie whispered, nestling tighter against his body. "I like it that way."

Drenched from dashing through the heavy rain, Maggie stood in the middle of her kitchen confused and cold. Tension hung between the two of them like a heavy blanket. He hadn't invited her to the loft. She kept reminding herself that it was his call. He had to take the initiative; that was their agreement. She was sure he'd been ready to love her again before old biddy McPherson stopped by.

Would he even kiss her? It had been a lovely evening, and now she was acting like an inexperienced teenager again. She looked quickly at the sullen man, who seemed as out of place in her kitchen as she felt. Oh my, they were making puddles where they had first made love.

"Wonder if she's home yet?" Ed grumbled, obviously out of sorts, holding his Stetson with both hands.

"Huh?"

"Carolyn. Hope that Humphries kid is more reliable than he looks."

"Oh." Maggie brushed rain out of her slick hair. Good God, he'd remembered Carolyn before she had. Her little girl was still out there in that storm. She rubbed warmth back into her bare arms. Clearly neither she nor Ed had a will for romance tonight. Such was the nature of parental responsibilities.

"If you can wait a minute, I'll brew some coffee," she said. "I've got to get out of this wet dress. Why aren't you as wet as me?"

"Something to be said for a broad brimmed Stetson, I guess. Go ahead and change—I'll start the coffee."

- o -

As Ed measured out the scoops of coffee, his mind jumped from thought to thought. How

302

could Maggie put up with such nasty people as Mary Jane McPherson? Would the woman leave her alone if he weren't in the picture? Probably not.

What was keeping Maggie so long changing clothes? He tried without success not to imagine her upstairs slipping out of the wet dress, rubbing herself dry with a thick towel, and slipping into something soft and warm. He glanced down at the sink only to be startled because the pot he was filling was running over with water. "Damn," he groused. "She's like a sand burr that refuses to get unstuck."

"And where are those kids?" Ed slammed the pot in the coffee maker just before the hot liquid began to pour out. He hadn't realized how time could be so excruciatingly slow. He'd watched races that seemed to move in slow motion, but this waiting was even more painful. Where the hell had those two bonehead teenagers disappeared to? It was twelve-thirty in the morning.

"Thanks for making the coffee."

Ed jumped back from the counter. He hadn't heard Maggie come down the stairs. Looking over at her, he didn't know whether to laugh or cry. There she stood with a long pink robe buttoned up to the base of her neck. On her feet were the most god-awful slippers he'd ever seen. Were they supposed to be squirrels or rabbits? Pink rabbits, he assumed, given the long ears.

He started to speak, but couldn't. He wanted to take her in his arms, but didn't.

Maggie moved toward him like some wood spirit he'd read about as a kid. She floated, making no noise. Her hand touched his chest. A hot iron couldn't have seared more.

"She's a half hour late," he grumbled.

Maggie winced. "Damn, don't you think I know that?" She chewed on her lower lip. Worry lines stretched her brow. "I hope they haven't had trouble on these slick roads. I don't think they'd deliberately break Carolyn's curfew."

"No," Ed concurred. "Looked to me like the boy wanted to please you so much he would have had her home and hour early if he could've."

Moving to the table with a cup of coffee, Maggie sat down only to immediately jump up and begin to pace. "It's hard letting them go, letting them try their own wings. You want to hold onto them, to protect them from all that's out there, but you can't. You can try, but in the end, you can't."

Ed sat in a chair at the table, from which he would see any headlights turning into the driveway. "Well, that kid she's with better have a damn good excuse."

Before Maggie's hard stare, Ed dropped his gaze. His right knee bobbed up and down and his hands quivered as they cradled the coffee cup.

"Ed," she admonished, "don't you be thinking about getting in the middle of this. If something needs sorting out, I'll do the sorting."

He nodded at her blankly. "You're right, Maggie. I'm kind of a spare tire here. Guess I ought to be hauling my ass off to bed."

Maggie gasped. "I didn't mean it that way. I need and want your support, particularly now." She hesitated, then plopped down in her chair, taking a gulp of the coffee. "This is all new for me, too. Having a dating teenager. Having a man I care about. I just don't want you to do some crazy macho thing with the boy." She sniffled. "Can't you just hold me?"

All of Ed's emotions drained into a single puddle. Without speaking, he stood. She rose to meet him. He placed his arms around Maggie tightly, as if she might evaporate. Her fingers dug into his back, but he wasn't about to complain. His chest muffled the sounds of her sobbing. He stroked her back in small concentric circles.

Bending, he kissed her hair. Lifting her chin with a finger, he covered her lips with his. Her lips were wet, her mouth warm. He kept the kiss gentle, yet prolonged. This was no prelude to sex. His body shook as he recognized it for what it was—a prelude to love.

Maggie's body likewise shook in his arms. Was it simply fear for her children? As her tongue slithered into his mouth, he had her answer. Yet she, too, seemed fully satisfied with the kiss. No more was needed.

At last breaking the seal, he whispered, "Everything will be okay." He continued to massage her back.

"I know," she replied. "I'm just tired of waiting."

"I think I hear a car slowing down now."

Moving away from the comfort of his body, Maggie rushed to the porch with Ed right behind her. Sure enough, the Humphries' car was inching down the driveway.

- o -

"I'm sorry to worry you, Mom," Carolyn said, immediately hugging her mother. Quickly moving on to hug Ed, she explained, "We had a flat on Highway Twenty Six and Bobby had to change the tire in a downpour."

Maggie looked at Bobby for the first time, as if he hadn't been standing there from the moment Carolyn entered. She saw a totally soaked and very muddy young man.

"There's no doubt you've been playing around in the mud," Ed acknowledged.

"Come on into the kitchen, Bobby. Let me make you something hot to drink and dry you off some," Maggie offered.

"No thanks, Ma'am," the boy replied. "I best be getting on home. My folks will be worried something fierce. The car heater works."

"Okay. I understand. And I'll call them so they won't have to worry anymore."

Maggie called the Humphries as Bobby drove out the driveway.

"What a night!" Carolyn chirped gleefully. "My first date! Bobby could use some dancing lessons, but my toes made it. Jackie Hennessey said all her date could do was stomp on her feet. So much for football players being agile. And then the flat tire…I was so afraid you'd be mad."

"Those things happen. But not on every date," Maggie cautioned.

"It sure is hard making conversation with a boy for an entire night."

Maggie laughed. Ed choked on his coffee.

"Well, it wasn't so bad at the dance. There were other girls to talk with, but alone in the car…" Carolyn rolled her eyes.

"I'm not sure that'll get much better," Maggie observed, glancing in Ed's direction. "Men seem to like to listen to themselves think a lot."

She grinned at Ed who was making a show of trying to ignore her.

"And then with the flat and all and having to rush right in, he didn't even try to kiss me," Carolyn complained, crossing her arms over her chest.

It was Ed's turn to laugh. "Don't want to disappoint you, but, looking at the lad, I don't think he would've tried that on a first date anyway."

"You may be right. Bobby's not a real romantic guy, but he did ask if I wanted to go to a movie next weekend. Can I go, Mom? Can I?"

Setting aside all the worry she'd just gone through, Maggie said, "You may go. But remember, I'll put the brakes on your social life if your grades go down."

"Don't worry about that, Mom," Carolyn called

out over her shoulder as she headed for the stairs. "Boys aren't going to come between me and what I want to do with my life. I know I have to have good grades to become a vet."

Listening to the muffled sound of her daughter's bedroom door closing, Maggie wondered aloud, "How much of a chance is there that she will stay that focused over the next several years?"

Ed's face lit up. "Oh, she may vacillate some, but Carolyn seems to have a strong dose of her mother's stubbornness. I'd put money on the girl doing what she wants."

"Aren't you an interesting odds maker," Maggie teased, feeling much more relaxed than an hour earlier. Would she ever get used to being a mother of a teenager? She looked at Ed. So what did he have in mind now?

"So, I'd best be going," Ed said, rising from his chair. "It's been a stressful night. You need to get some rest. Morning will be here before you know it."

Maggie folded her arms and pouted. "Aren't I even going to get a goodnight kiss from my date? I'm not sure I could sleep if I wanted too."

Ed grinned down at her. "Guess I can manage that," he said. "Must have been an oversight on my part."

She felt his finger tip brush lightly across her lips before his mouth settled on hers. She waited, applying no pressure, more than a little curious about how her man was going to handle this goodnight kiss.

His tongue traced her lips. She loved the care he was taking with her. This would be no peck, nor was it a kiss to comfort.

In a moment, his tongue moved across the roof of her mouth, teasing, caressing. Maggie held back no longer as she joined her tongue in their play. His hands cupped her butt. God, he had wonderful hands. She stood on her tiptoes to grind her crotch against his stiff arousal. She felt him tense and begin to withdraw; she held on firmly. Without thought, she jumped up into his arms and swung her legs around his rear. She rubbed against his erection, wanting more.

Finally, Ed succumbed to her rhythm. Maggie bit his shoulder and stifled a scream. He braced himself, holding her steady. She rocked back and forth, slowly at first and then more rapidly. When relief came, it threatened to shatter her soul; she was awash with fire. And then there was nothing—almost no feeling.

Limp. It would have taken a Herculean effort to move a single muscle. She was grateful that somehow Ed knew all she wanted was to be held.

How much time went by she didn't know, but her head eventually cleared some. Her muscles strained. Aware of Ed still holding her, she lowered her feet to the floor. How could it be possible they still could hold her up?

"I've got to go, Maggie. Your daughter just went upstairs, and here we are making out like a couple randy fools."

With the back of her hand, Maggie wiped the heat from her lips. As her eyes regained the ability to focus, she said, "You're right. I didn't plan to seduce you again."

He chuckled. "I know. Let's just say this one was mutual. It must be those damn rabbit ears."

"What!"

"I've been turned on ever since you came down with those rabbit-eared slippers on your feet. Never thought I'd be involved with a bunny."

"If that's what it takes, I may never take these slippers off." She dropped her eyelids briefly. "I had a great time tonight, Ed. I hope there will be many more. You are full of surprises. I didn't know you could be so romantic."

"Oh, there are plenty more surprises. You haven't even begun to sample my repertoire." Setting his Stetson squarely on his head, pulling the brim down some, he promised, "Till next time." And then he stepped out into the night and made his way toward the loft.

Maggie watched him disappear in the darkness, feeling suddenly alone and chilled. It had been a marvelous night. And he *was* full of surprises. But he hadn't asked her out for another date. Turning off the kitchen lights, she grumbled, "At least Carolyn got a second date."

The next morning Ed arrived early for breakfast, his body rigid and his face ashen.

"Didn't you get any sleep? You look like hell," Maggie mocked, glancing up from cracking eggs into a large mixing bowl.

"Put the eggs down, Maggie," Ed said firmly, "I've got some bad news."

"What?" Maggie wiped her hands on a towel. The smoldering anger in his eyes chilled her body. "What happened?"

"The tomcat." Ed breathed deeply. "Somebody slashed the tomcat's throat. I found him this morning in the barn crosswalk when I went to feed the horses."

"Oh, my God," Maggie murmured. Collapsing into a chair, her body shook. "Poor Tom. Someone was here? Someone is trying to scare the hell out of us. Someone is very serious."

Ed moved behind Maggie and began massaging her shoulders. "No question, and very sick. Any bastard who'd kill a cat has to be sick. I don't know if it happened while we were at the dance or later."

"He could've been killed while we slept. Thank God Johnny or Carolyn didn't find him first." Maggie struggled to quell her roiling stomach. She gripped the tabletop; her knuckles whitened. "What next?"

- o -

Ed bent to kiss her ear. He'd never seen her so devastated. She'd always been the strong one — now she needed someone to lean on, and he wasn't sure he ought to be that one. But no one else was available.

311

"I don't know." He continued rubbing her neck. Maggie leaned forward, giving him more access. He could feel the strain in her neck muscles seeking release. "You should report this to the sheriff. He might do nothing, but at least there will be a record. Killing a cat goes a long way beyond vandalism. I'll call Clint later today and bring him up to date."

Ed worried whether they would find the bastard before any further damage could be done. He cringed at how vulnerable everyone in the household was—as well as some promising, pricey horses. How could he protect them all, isolated from neighbors by a half mile in either direction?

Maybe he'd go into town later in the morning and buy a gun. He wouldn't tell Maggie—she'd just be more alarmed. But they had to do something to protect themselves.

"We can't leave the kids here alone, singly or together," Maggie said. She pressed a hand against her throbbing temple. "What if..." Maggie closed her eyes.

Opening them again, she said, "Who is safe anymore? What is safe?" She turned to look sidewise at Ed. "Are you safe in the barn? Are we safe in the house? There's a rabid person out there. We've got to be careful."

"I wholeheartedly support you on that. I'm not sure we can afford a lot of security. The cost of an alarm system for the barn and house would be prohibitive."

Maggie laid her head down on the table. She was comforted by the warmth of his large hands resting on her shoulders. What would she do without him? She would survive; she knew that. But this was so much better — sharing the good and the bad with someone you loved. Still, none of them were safe.

She sat back in the chair. "You're probably right about the cost of an alarm system, but I should at least check it out. We can't just sit here and be easy targets for any sicko who happens to want this land." Maggie's shoulders slumped. "What would compel a person to kill an innocent cat?"

"I don't know, but if we're lucky we're going to find out."

Maggie rose to continue preparing breakfast. Regardless of what else was happening, they had to eat. Squirting oil on the frying pan, she couldn't shake the feeling that her safe cocoon was in danger of falling completely apart. What if they weren't lucky? She couldn't imagine anyone she knew stooping so low. Could she really have an enemy that hated her that much or who coveted her land that much?

The hate in Mrs. McPherson's eyes last night had been raw and intimidating. But could she really be behind the killing of the tomcat? Maggie knew better than to rule out that possibility, but she found the idea preposterous, even for Mrs. McPherson.

Maggie shuddered. Squaring her shoulders, she focused her attention on what needed to be done. Ed would notify Clint. She had more faith in the Chicago-based detective agency than in the local sheriff's office. She'd make a report to the sheriff, though. Then she'd see about a security system for the house. There was no way she could afford an electronic system for the barn; a night watchman was out of the question. No matter what they did, they would remain vulnerable to anyone determined to cause trouble.

Maybe she should get a gun. She grimaced. She didn't know the first thing about shooting a gun. Her family would likely be at greater risk if she owned one.

Glancing from the stove to where Ed remained at the table pretending to read the same page of a magazine over and over, she thanked God that she had his help. How long would he put himself at risk for her and her family? Could he be scared off? She would be so much more vulnerable if he fled.

Was the land really worth all of this? Maggie stared out the kitchen window toward the paddock where horses grazed and beyond, toward the corn fields that had failed her this season. Who was she without the land? What kind of future could any of them have if they were separated from the land?

CHAPTER SEVENTEEN

Two weeks later, Maggie sagged against the mail box, her eyes fixed on the certified letter she held in her trembling hands. The envelope was addressed to Edward H. Harrington; its return address was the Illinois Racing Board.

If it contained what she thought it did, she should be thrilled for him. So why was she shaking like a leaf? If it was the good news he'd been so afraid to hope for, would he leave her? If it was bad news, would he retreat to the nearest bottle?

A week earlier, when they'd been in Chicago picking up four broodmares, Cassie had hinted at a possible breakthrough in Ed's case. She hadn't been at liberty to say more. Given the glare from her husband, she'd likely already said more than she was supposed to.

Because of the tomcat being killed, Maggie had insisted on taking the kids with them to Chicago, school or no school. Hank looked after the stock while they were gone and nothing had gone wrong. Her children had been awed by the skyscrapers, though neither Carolyn nor Johnny seemed particularly enamored with big city life.

Maggie hefted the weighty envelop gingerly. It even felt important. If the Board had decided to reinstate him, Ed would go back to his old life.

Why wouldn't he? This backwater community had to be small potatoes for a trainer of his skill and stature. Cassie had told her about his burning desire to be on the level of a Baffert, a Lucas, a Zito. He'd been on the verge of making the leap to that next plateau when the scandal hit. Maggie knew he'd never make that next level training her horses in Beaverhill, Iowa.

She sighed, turned and slowly walked toward the house. It had been a good run with Ed and the horses. Smiling, she remembered the close camaraderie they'd shared remodeling the barn and constructing new fencing; the thrill of buying those first horses and then sharing that initial kiss; his running, only to be caught. Her muscles ached recalling each moment that morning in the kitchen when neither one of them could run anymore. She took a deep breath remembering his laughter, his arms holding her securely during a waltz, his body speaking to her own in a language unique to them.

It was over. With the dead cat and the trip to Chicago with the kids along, there had been little time for romance. And now he would scurry off to Chicago as fast as his beat up old truck could haul him.

No need to prolong the agony. Maggie walked toward the barn. If this wasn't a good news-bad news event, she'd never known one before.

Maggie stood rigidly watching Ed rip open the certified letter with shaking hands. Holding his breath, he scanned it quickly. A smile spread wide across his face. It grew broader. It became his entire face. She heard him hoot, "They did it! I'm cleared. I'm reinstated."

Ed threw his cap toward the haymow. He grabbed Maggie by the waist and twirled them across the barn driveway. "I can't believe it, Maggie. Two so-called witnesses changed their stories and the circumstantial evidence collapsed."

He kissed her on the top of her head; she clung tightly to him as if they were aboard a Tilt-A-Whirl.

"I can dream again," Ed shouted. "There is life after death. This is cause for celebration, Maggie — get your best dress on. We're going to go to Des Moines to the fanciest restaurant they have. It might not be like dining at the Pump Room in Chicago, but it will do for tonight."

Not wanting to burst his bubble, knowing that she owed him at least this much, she set aside her own fears to celebrate with him. She celebrated wildly, maybe even drank too much wine. He insisted she have the best wine in the house even though he had none. They ate and they danced. She felt so secure and so afraid in his arms. He didn't seem to notice the tears in her eyes. Or if he did, he must have written them off as tears of joy and pleasure. They weren't.

Maggie tried desperately to guard a portion of her heart as she waited for reality to hit — waited for him to announce when he'd leave for Chicago.

This might be their last night. She was determined to enjoy the ride as best she could for as long as it lasted.

There was little conversation between them during the return trip from Des Moines. Maggie even found it difficult to appreciate the late October full moon. Maggie shrank farther into the corner of her seat.

Ed drove down her driveway and said quietly, "I'd like you to come to the loft, Maggie. Let's check on the kids, and then come and stay the night with me."

"Okay," she whispered. She wanted one last time. She needed one more memory to tuck away.

"Leave the lamp on," Ed said, pulling the blankets off the bed.

Maggie warmed under his unabashed appraisal.

"I want to see you. I want to memorize your shape. Your taste and smell are branded into my mind. I intend to memorize every square inch of your body, woman. I'm going to accomplish that with my tongue."

Maggie's eyes widened and then glazed over.

"Every square inch," he reiterated. "Nothing will ever be forgotten."

His intensity impaled her to her very core. The firmly set jaw, the gleam in his eyes, the burning of his touch. She wanted him now; she wanted him deep inside. His look disarmed her, turning her body to soft clay to be molded however he desired. Normally, she'd struggle with him for control. This time she willed herself to receive and to follow his lead. She willed herself to be patient.

Quickly, Maggie discovered that she didn't have to work at waiting, at being patient. Her body could do no other.

He started by pulling one of her hands to his lips. He nibbled and suckled each finger before moving to her wrist. She sighed heavily as his tongue traced her earlobe and then lapped at her nape. His lips brushed her eyelids, then her nose; Maggie smiled as her nose twitched in response. His tongue traced the outline of her smile before moving to her chin.

She started to put her arms around his back. Ed raised his head and looked at her. "Not yet," he whispered. "I'm not near finished." He placed her arms back on the bed. "Just receive. We have all night. Who knows about tomorrow?"

Maggie tensed, nearly panicking. "Tomorrow can wait, and so can I," she managed to say before her heavy eyelids shuttered.

She luxuriated in his quest to know and remember her body. Ever so lightly, his tongue advanced from the crown of her breast to its nipple, which ached in anticipation. He twirled the nipple with his lips and teeth. Maggie's back arched in response.

He moved on.

After swirling his tongue around her navel, Ed paused, easily rolling her over on her stomach. Lying there surprised, Maggie felt even more exposed, more naked. He started at the base of her neck. She nearly dozed off.

This was beyond any sexual experience she'd ever had. That smooth rough tongue communicated much more than lust and desire. Love. Pleasure. Delight. Warmth. She was an object of adoration. She'd been loved before, but she couldn't remember ever being adored.

His lips graced her buttocks; her skin puckered as he suctioned her flesh. Her loins cried out for attention, but she waited. This was his night. Smiling inwardly, she rephrased that thought — this was very definitely becoming *her* night.

She had never known how sensitive the back of her knees were. At last, he turned her over again and his tongue inched its way around her waist, down her inner thighs, and then back up to that ultimate prize.

She was so wet there was no need for further preparation. Undaunted, Ed continued to explore and apparently memorize. All her senses were drawn to that one singular tingly spot. Maggie could wait no longer; she bucked in response to his probing tongue. She was about to explode into a thousand pieces. She felt him press his open mouth firmly against her straining sex, as if by doing so he could keep her from dismantling. Maggie grabbed his head, pulled his ears, locked his body to herself with her powerful legs; rapidly, she lost herself in an exquisiteness so rare she hadn't even known it existed.

Minutes later, Ed still smiled into her wetness. He savored her nectar clinging to him like a protective shield. Had he become addicted to Maggie Anderson's taste?

If there was but one truth in his life, then he knew what it was—there was no way he wanted to live without Maggie. Memories, while powerful, would never be enough.

At last, Maggie's legs loosened their grip on him. "I want to feel you in me, Ed," she panted. "No more exploring. Please. Just love me."

"What do you think I've been doing?" Ed teased, easing her over onto her stomach.

"It was great, but I need more."

Climbing to her knees, Maggie wiggled a steamy target for him. Ed didn't miss his mark.

"Ah, yes," she sighed. "That's where I want you."

He felt her squeeze his erection while pushing back against his thighs, pulling him deeper into her interior. As if both of them wished for time to be suspended, they waited. After what seemed like minutes, she squeezed once more. It was his signal. He began flexing his hips to and fro.

He reached to cup her breasts. Maggie's breathing quickened. Ed sensed the gathering at her sexual center.

"Faster," she called out, raising her head. "Now. Don't wait. Don't hold back."

Her command acted like a trigger. His hips

traveled at a speed unknown to him. Maggie howled and mewed.

He knew the moment her climax began. He felt her shatter beneath him, her fluids wetting his thighs.

Maggie's release sparked his own powerful response. His hips ceased moving. He kissed her back.

"My God, Maggie, what am I going to do with you?" he moaned, collapsing, pinning her body to the mattress.

Ed felt her shudder beneath him and he rolled them to rest on their sides, her rear tucked firmly against his thighs. Still intimately joined, he couldn't imagine life getting any better. He had his life as a trainer back, and he'd at last found a woman to love.

Yes, dammit, he'd admitted it. A woman to love—if she'd have him. Maybe she'd seen more than enough of his indecisiveness. She would never leave the farm; he'd never ask her to. Somehow they could work things out. He hadn't come this far and overcome so many obstacles to lose her now.

"A body can't feel better than mine is feeling right now." Maggie cooed faintly.

Half asleep, Ed cuddled her even closer and grazed her neck with the tip of his tongue. "Me too," he whispered.

Loud banging on the loft door and insistent shouts jarred both lovers awake. Ed grabbed his pants from the chair, slipped them on and rushed to respond.

Instinctively. Maggie pulled the sheets and blankets over her nudity.

When Ed opened the door, a man dressed in bib overalls stood there with raised fist screaming as loudly as he could. "The barn's on fire! You got to get out quick."

"Oh, my God!" Maggie shrieked, overlooking modesty and clambering to get out of the bed.

With their eyes straining, both Maggie and Ed pulled on boots, threw on clothes and rushed down the stairs. They headed toward the broodmares, who were housed in stalls at the other end of the barn.

Maggie had recognized the man who sounded the alarm as her neighbor, Randy Jackson. He already was leading one broodmare out of the barn by the time she and Ed got down the stairway. That left three broodmares in the barn and several younger horses in a nearby shed. The fire seemed to be located in the feed and storage area, but it was spreading rapidly. Flames climbed the wooden walls toward the haymow. It was already too late to save the barn. She turned her full attention toward the mares. They were stomping furiously and whinnied anxiously.

Ed was already putting a rope around Midnight

Dancer's neck and trying to convince the balking animal to leave her stall. With a halter in hand, Maggie entered the stall of another frightened horse. The mare threw her head about so much that Maggie could only get the halter strapped around the animal's neck. "It'll have to do," she muttered to herself, tugging hard on the halter. At first the mare only pulled back. The animal's wide eyes mirrored the terror which was happening around her.

Without a second thought, Maggie pulled off her blouse and used it to cover the mare's eyes. She didn't know what she'd done to win the animal's trust, but at last the horse stepped forward following Maggie's lead.

The heat singed her breasts. Flames spit out dangerously close to the mare's tail. Slowly, but determinedly, Maggie walked the mare down the center of the barn toward safety. She refused to look up at the ceiling above her. She didn't have to look; she knew it was ablaze.

Grateful for the coolness of the night air, Maggie led the mare toward a paddock and safety. She removed her blindfold-blouse, soaked it in a water tank and slipped it back on. Later, she would attend to her burns; now there was more to be done.

She dashed back toward the burning barn. Ed caught her at the entryway. "Get back," he shouted. "The second floor is going to collapse at any moment. That guy who warned us is still in there trying to free the last horse. I'm going back in. Stay put." The fierceness of his eyes invited no debate.

Maggie withdrew back into the nearest paddock. She tried not to think. She tried not to feel. She squinted, trying to see through the thick smoke and flames. It might as well have been opaque.

At last she made out the dark figure of a horse. The animal was pulling against the men who were holding one arm over their mouths trying not to breathe in the burning air while coaxing the mare to continue stepping forward. The mare threw her head to the left trying to turn around, nearly knocking Ed off his feet.

As Maggie watched, standing on her toes, leaning this way and that to get a better view through the smoke, she saw the horse rear and then kick back, knocking Randy to the barn floor. She feared that the panicked horse would trample Randy if Ed couldn't get the animal away from him. Cajoling, pleading, Ed got the frightened mare to inch its way out of the barn doorway.

Maggie ran forward and grabbed the rope hanging around the mare's neck. Without hesitation, Ed scrambled back into the barn in search of Randy.

She watched with growing horror as four-by-sixes and beams that had been strong enough to hold the barn roof through generations began to crumble like a child's game of blocks. The end of the barn closest to the house — the end where she and Ed had been so recently — had collapsed. Her hand flew to her mouth. And then she saw Ed step from the barn. He had Jackson swung over his shoulder like a bag of feed.

"Thank God," Maggie squealed when Ed laid Randy Jackson on the ground beside her. Neither man spoke. Both heaved and gasped for more air. Both had singed hair and eyebrows, but both men were alive. Maggie could breathe again.

First she heard sirens, and then the fire trucks started to roll into yard. But it was too late to save much of anything of the barn. They had saved the horses, and they had saved each other. Thank goodness for neighbors.

She look at her companions and then down at herself. Maggie laughed; she couldn't stop from laughing. The three of them were so smudged with black soot they could easily pass for chimney sweeps.

Then Maggie started to cry. She shook her head, trying to clear it of fiery images. She didn't want to appear hysterical, but she couldn't stop crying. There was no telling if she cried because of the tragedy that happened or because of the tragedies that might have happened or might yet happen.

She thanked God for life as tears rolled down her cheeks. And then she pounded the ground with her fists. Who would endanger lives to get her land? She stood. She flopped back down on the ground and closed her eyes attempting to blot out the sights, the sounds and the smells of the firestorm destroying her dreams.

If Ed asked her to, she would take the kids and go with him to Chicago. Tonight would not be too soon. Enough was enough. Even the land wasn't worth the lives of those she loved.

Ed and Randy both lay nearby trying to catch their breaths. She moved over to tenderly brush Ed's hair with her reddened fingers. They exchanged no words. Words were not necessary when their eyes spoke so eloquently. They had each faced death; they had each survived a descent into hell.

"I owe you my life, young man," Randy said, struggling to get to his knees. "It was dumb thing to do, to come back in after me." He paused, brushing tears back from peeling skin. "But I thank you."

"You owe me?" Ed was incredulous. "We owe you, mister. If you hadn't banged on my door..."

"Well, maybe things sort of canceled out. Sure glad I drove by when I did and saw your light on." The older man leaned over to wink at Maggie. "Don't go worrying about what I'm gonna tell people. What you do privately is your own business."

"Thanks, Randy," Maggie murmured. "I appreciate that. And thanks so very much for helping with the horses. The future of Anderson Stables could have evaporated here tonight, if it weren't for you."

Grinning sheepishly, the man replied, "Just remember to give me a hot tip at the track now and then."

"You can count on that."

Maggie turned and held out her arms as Johnny came running at her from across the yard.

"Did he really do it, Mom? Did Ed save Mr. Jackson's life?" her son cried, clinging to Maggie's side.

Maggie chastised herself for forgetting about the children during all the commotion. They'd been awakened by the fire engines and had heard the story from one of the firemen.

"He sure did, Johnny," she said, tousling his hair.

Ed appeared genuinely embarrassed when Johnny ran and jumped into his arms. "It wasn't all that much, pardner," he said to the boy. "You would've done the same thing, if you had been here."

Johnny shook his head, his eyes bulging. "This is bigger than winning a fight. Wait until I tell Dennis Baxter. He thought you were a coward because you let two men beat you up."

As the barn continued to burn behind them, Maggie watched Ed set her son on the ground. She watched him place a hand on each of Johnny's shoulders. His admonishment was clear, and she knew it came from his heart. "Don't ever measure a man's courage by the outcome of a fight, son. There are many more important things that are a true test of a man's grit."

Maggie's heart warmed. How she hoped Johnny would listen to and remember that wisdom. She wondered at how easily the man called her boy *son*. Shaking her head, she reminded herself of Ed's letter and how he was free to reclaim his life without her, without any of them.

Maggie sat alone on the porch swing the following morning, the stench from soaking, smoldering wood and leather permeating her entire world. There was no way to avoid its heaviness. Neither could she escape the icy despair strangling her heart.

With the stewards in Chicago clearing Ed's name, he was bound to leave for the big city. The barn was a total loss. At least no horses were lost—and no humans. Maggie shuddered. They'd come so close.

Every muscle in her body ached. She'd applied aloe to her burns and those suffered by Ed and Randy. They should have gone to the hospital, she supposed, but neither she nor Ed wanted to leave the farm. And a volunteer fireman drove Randy home.

Her eyes ached from staring at the gray-black scene—and from tears that refused to come. Maggie realized she was still in shock, but knowing that didn't help a damn bit.

One by one, the rest of the family emerged as if from a shared nightmare. Maggie managed a half smile in greeting. She had her children; things could be much worse. *Buck up, girl,* she ordered, *people still depend on you and your strength.*

After murmuring good mornings, Johnny and

Carolyn sat down on porch chairs; both children remained uncharacteristically quiet. Each appeared lost in disbelief as they, too, stared at where the barn had stood only hours before.

Maggie watched Ed's bent form moving toward the house. He could hardly place one foot in front of the other. He'd stayed up all night and into the morning, checking along with the firemen for hot spots in the dying embers. The last fire truck had left about an hour earlier. Several of the men indicated they would return later to make certain everything was still safe.

That was a bad joke. How could their lives ever again be safe?

"Carolyn," Maggie said softly, "bring out the coffee pot, please. Ed will want some."

Ed entered the porch and collapsed into the chair across from her. He shut his eyes and kept them closed for a long moment. Then he opened them, brushed soot off his forehead, and gave her a look filled with concern. "How are you holding up, Maggie?"His voice was scratchy, probably from swallowing so much smoke and from lack of sleep.

She shrugged. "I'll survive. How about you? You lost everything in that fire. Your clothes, money, mementos."

He coughed and then smiled weakly, reaching for the cup of coffee Carolyn offered. "Thanks, Carolyn. Don't know how many gallons I've drunk since last night, but this is still a lifesaver." Turning back to Maggie, he continued, "You're wrong, Maggie. I didn't lose everything. What I lost is replaceable. We are extremely lucky not to have lost more. Extremely lucky."

Maggie bit her lower lip. She couldn't stop trembling, no matter how hard she tried. She noticed her children listening intently, trying hard not be noticed. They didn't have to try so hard — she wasn't about to send them away. What she had to say, they all needed to hear.

"You're right. We were terribly lucky." Maggie sighed heavily. "We took a risk — or I forced us all to take a risk." She ignored Ed's eyebrow flash. "I took a risk that we were dealing with a reasonable person who merely wanted some land that wasn't available. I didn't know we were dealing with someone so crazy he'd stoop to killing cats, burning barns, and not caring a whit about life — animal or human."

"At least this should get the attention of the law," said Ed, jumping in when Maggie was forced to pause for breath. "I'll call Clint later today."

"Why bother?" Maggie's voice shook and her cheek twitched wildly. "I'm done. They can have the land. It's not worth the price of human life."

"What?" Johnny and Carolyn gasped in unison.

Ed showed no evidence of surprise. "Why don't we put off major decisions for a day or two, Maggie? Give it some time. Let's reassess our resources — practical and emotional — and then go from there."

Laughing out of control, Maggie slumped

331

further in her chair. "That's easy for you to say," she accused. "You've got a career to go back to now. I don't know what I'll do. After I sell, maybe I'll take Ben's advice and go back to school. There must be some skill I can learn."

"Mom, I don't want you to sell the farm," Carolyn cried, jumping to her feet.

Johnny grabbed his mother's hands, tears sliding down his cheeks. Watching him, Maggie thought her heart would surely break. "No way, Mom. I'm not scared. Ed can take care of us. We'll beat those bad guys. Don't give up, Mom. We can do it."

Maggie could feel herself losing it. Her spine, her muscles, her strength unraveled. She might have cried in front of her children, but she'd never bawled. There was little doubt that she was on the verge of a full scale bawl. "You two have been great throughout all of this, but I don't think I can fight anymore. And Ed has his own life to live. We can't expect him to stay and help us now."

She paused, trying to focus on her kids through a rainbow of tears. "With the fire and all, we never had a chance to tell you that Ed has been cleared by the Racing Board in Chicago. He can go back and pick up where he left off now."

Speaking calmly, Ed did not take his eyes off of Maggie, "Carolyn, Johnny, I know all of this is very important to both of you. But I think your mom and I need to talk about some things privately. Would you mind leaving us alone for a little while? We'll bring you up to speed when we're done."

"Fine," Carolyn declared, "maybe you can help her find that Magee backbone she's always telling us about."

Disheveled and exhausted, Maggie tried to focus on Ed. Why didn't he just leave? She didn't need his pity. She felt defenseless now that the kids had left. Why had he made them go? Squaring her shoulders, Maggie prepared for the worst.

"Did I fail to live up to your expectations?" Ed leaned forward. His gray eyes burned with an unfamiliar emotion. "I'm sorry your barn burned down, Maggie. Maybe I should've done more to protect it and to protect you."

"No, no," Maggie blubbered. "You do too much protecting. But you got what you wanted. The Board reinstated you. Now you can go back to Chicago and pick up where you left off."

"So you thought I was going to leave you and go back to my old ways?"

Maggie didn't know what to make of his smugness. She was missing something. "Yes, of course," she replied hesitantly. "Weren't you?"

Ed shook his head slowly. "What did you think last night was about? Before the fire. Was that just a farewell kiss to you?"

"But...but you wanted to memorize my body."

His pained look haunted her, making her speechless.

"Good God, Maggie, I wanted to memorize your body because I can't stand ever being apart from you. I want to be able to breathe you and feel you when I'm in the barn and you're in the house. But you didn't trust me."

Maggie was speechless. She'd been terribly wrong.

"Did you believe I was so fickle that I'd play with your emotions until something better came along?" Ed stood and passed to the end of the porch.

Her eyes widened as she realized that she'd hurt him while trying to protect herself — her pride had not only led her to believe what he would do when he was reinstated, but worse, prevented her from asking him directly. So she'd been content to skip along in her presumptive world, making him much less than the man he was. He wouldn't break his word. Clearly, he'd stay to help her rebuild the stable, if that was what she wanted.

"Don't you have anything to say for yourself? You're usually much more verbal than this. Or is it still the shock of the fire?"

"I don't know what to say," she murmured. "I'm sorry, I underestimated you. I'm glad you're willing to help, but I'm still not sure I want to rebuild."

"Help! Haven't you heard anything I've been trying to say?"

As he stood before her, Maggie stiffened. It was her land, dammit. And if she wanted to sell, she would. She began to speak, but he pressed a finger across her lips.

"Woman, I have no plans of leaving, now or

later." His voice was deep and guttural. "It never seriously occurred to me that you would be willing to leave this place. I won't leave you, Maggie Anderson, until you kick me out. I love you too much for that."

"You what?"

"Do I have to draw you a picture? I love you. Last night was about love. It wasn't about a last tumble in the hay. And I think you love me. People who love each other don't walk away when things get rough. They work together. They work things out, *together*."

Maggie's heart raced, her breathing stilled. She moved her lips, but no sounds came out. His eyes had turned to liquid gray; his features softened.

"I'm saying, if you'll have me, I'd like to grow old with you, Maggie. Sometimes I don't know why..." he brushed a tear from her cheek. "You can be as stubborn as a mule. And you can totally misread people, but I love you as you are. I..."

"And I love you as you are," Maggie finally burst out. He looked so calm; *her* hands were doing the shaking. Closing her eyes, she breathed deeply, wanting to imprint this moment on her memory. If she wasn't mistaken, Ed Harrington had just declared his love for her. Stumbling out of her chair, beaming, she clambered into his arms.

His lips against hers were tender, cool against her burning mouth. "Maggie, you wouldn't give up on me when I was crumbling, when I was nearly down for the count. Don't give up on me now. Don't give up on us. We've got so much going for us. Give us a chance."

Eagerly, Maggie placed wet kisses across his soot-stained face. Giggling, she said, "I won't give up, I swear — ever, ever."

"Then, you'll marry me?"

Maggie's eyes widened; her breathing became as ragged as it had in the midst of the barn fire.

"I love you. Marry me."

She could feel the tumblers of her brain tipping over and spinning. He was completely sincere; this was not a response to their loss. He'd reached this point before the fire. The letter had freed him up to move forward. He was waiting for her response as patiently as if he was working with a weanling. *Marry me.*

This was what she had wanted. This was her hope and her dream. Why wouldn't words come? Was she still afraid he'd flee? She'd just given him that opportunity, and he hadn't taken it. *Marry me.*

And then she felt a broad smile split her face. "You better believe it, cowboy. I'll marry you today, if you want. Or next month. Or whenever." Laying her head on his chest, she offered, "We'll make quite a team."

"That proposal wasn't as romantic as I'd planned, but it will have to do."

"It did real fine," she responded, luxuriating in his arms. "What a twenty-four hours we've had."

"That's for sure." He set her back down on her feet. "Now that we know I'm staying, how about backing off on selling the farm? I know how important the land is to you and to your family.

Give it some time. Okay?"

"Okay," she murmured. "We'll work it out...together. I love you so much. I can't believe our good fortune. The kids will be ecstatic. Wait till I tell Flo." She glanced up to see him frowning. "Well, it is okay to talk about isn't it? This isn't some secret we have to hold onto for the next forty years."

"Of course not," he conceded. "Guess I'm just not sure how to proceed. I'm looking forward to telling the kids, but I'm not so sure about the neighbors." He leaned away from her and spread his arms out wide. "I can see the local headlines: *Big City Drifter Lassoes Local Maverick Girl.*"

CHAPTER EIGHTEEN

By late afternoon following the fire, casseroles, salad bowls, cake pans, pie tins, wax paper, and plain boxes overran the Anderson kitchen. Maggie couldn't fathom how her neighbors had come up with the volume and variety of food. There was ham, chicken, beef, fish, cooked and raw vegetables, and more deserts than she figured were healthy for any family. One person even brought Chinese and another, frozen pizza. Maggie knew this was typical for small rural communities in times of crises. Lord, she'd cooked many a dish to take to a home when someone had been ill or died.

A wave of weakness flooded Maggie — her community still accepted her. It felt good to belong; it always had. Some of her neighbors could be royal pains at times, but all in all she wouldn't trade any of them for the big city.

She stopped putting away food to savor the moment. Even in the face of what was a dark, tragic moment, she was thrilled about the future.

Without a word, she stepped over to kiss Ed lightly on his head, then quickly stepped away. He wanted her, and she didn't have to move away from Beaverhill to have him. The kids were excited about having him for a real dad.

Ed pulled his eyes away from the charts he was

working on long enough to ask with a curious glint in his eyes, "What was that about?"

"Nothing more than a little *I love you*," she said, returning to the task of finding room for food.

The soft response, "I love you, too," came before he resumed reading.

Maggie wished everything could stay as comfortable as it was in the familiar warmth of her kitchen. It wouldn't. The cloud of danger still loomed over all of them. They would remain wary of strangers and be on alert, but Maggie was confident that together they could face anything. She'd regained her composure and her mettle; no way would she be frightened into selling.

The fire marshal had already determined the barn fire was the work of an arsonist. Although the sheriff continued to scratch his head in wonderment about the whole situation, Ed had told her that Clint Travers had a private investigator nosing around in the area.

It still amazed her that the man who seemed so at ease with kids and horses operated a detective agency on the side. Mainly, he was a silent investor, but it sounded like he had taken a personal interest in their case.

A knock on the porch door elicited a groan from her. "Not more food. There's no space for it."

"Hi, Maggie," Ben Templeton said, stepping through the doorway carrying several folders and pamphlets. "Do you have a minute or two?"

"Of course. Come in. I'll get you a cup of coffee. Sorry, I forgot to call you about the insurance

340

claim."

"That's only part of the reason I'm here," he said, nodding to Ed, who had put aside his paper.

"Why the catalogs, Templeton?" Ed asked as Ben pulled up a chair and Maggie set a cup of coffee in front of him. "You planning on building a barn?"

"Sort of," Ben replied. His grin was tight. "Actually, you two are."

Maggie wondered why Ben was nervous. He seldom appeared to have a worry. Pulling up a chair for herself, she said, "We haven't decided what to build. We need more time. And even with the insurance, I'm not sure we can afford to rebuild. The costs are much higher today than when we took out the policy."

Ben sipped his coffee. He glanced at Maggie and looked quickly away. He paused. At last he spoke, "Yes, that might have been a problem, but not anymore."

Maggie scowled. "What do you mean?"

"I've already gone over the insurance papers. You'll do okay, but it won't pay for the kind of facility you need. However," he hesitated, fingering one of the pamphlets, "people in town and your neighbors out here in the country have been keeping the phone lines hot all day."

"So?"

"So, folks around here don't like it when someone is out to hurt one of their own. You should know that, Maggie." Shoving the catalogs across the table to her, he said, "Your friends and

341

neighbors want to help out. They want you to pick out a barn design that will meet your needs. Quickly, before winter sets in. They'll provide the labor. We have carpenters, plumbers, and electricians prepared to donate their labor. You'll only have to cover the cost of materials."

Maggie reached a hand to her forehead trying to steady herself. Ed gave her a knowing smile. She started to speak, but Ben continued on.

"The insurance money probably won't cover even that, but an anonymous donor appeared on my doorstep first thing this morning. That donor is prepared to cover any costs in excess of insurance up to $100,000."

"My God," Maggie gasped, "I can't take that. Nobody around here could afford to do that."

"I know it's a bit of a shock, Maggie. But the money has already been deposited into an escrow account that I'm empowered to manage. All bills are to come directly to me."

"But how can we take the money? I'm not a charity case." Maggie clenched her fists.

"Of course not, but you *are* part of a community that does not want to be pushed around by anyone. This is more than helping a neighbor in need. It is a statement to whoever is trying to bring you down. We will not stand by and allow that kind of vigilantism to win out. If you fold under that kind of pressure, who will be next?"

"But who can afford that kind of money?"

"I can't tell you that. But I can assure you that the money is available for the sole purpose of helping rebuild Anderson Stables. So what are you going to do about it?" Ben peered over the top of his eye glasses, which as usual had slid down his nose. "Are you going to let your neighbors down and run?"

"Oh, my goodness." Maggie giggled into her cupped hands, glancing back and forth between Ben and Ed.

"What do you think, Ed?" she asked softly.

"It's your call, Maggie."

"You don't get off that easy," she chided. "Remember, we're doing this together."

Ed frowned. "I'm committed to rebuilding. I don't know about the community thing. That seems bigger than even us. Maybe in time we could pay it back."

"That's it! Can we treat the extra money as a loan, Ben?"

"The donor anticipated your response. The money cannot be repaid to the donor. But," Ben steepled his hands, "if you wanted to give some of it back to the community later on, the donor suggests setting up a college scholarship fund at Beaverhill High School for kids who want to study agriculture or related subjects."

"Guess we can't argue with that," Maggie said pensively. "A lot of kids could benefit from the money." She nodded at Ed. "Looks like we've got some planning to do in short order."

"That's for sure," Ed agreed. "Winter could hit us most anytime. With luck, it'll hold off another six weeks or so. That should give us plenty of time to build and settle the horses. I'm most concerned about the broodmares. We're darned lucky none of them aborted during the fire."

Reaching for his hand, Maggie murmured, "I think we're just plain lucky to be alive, to be a part of this community, to have the kids, and to have each other."

Ed leaned over to brush his lips across hers.

Clearing his throat, Ben said, "I expect there's more going on here than I knew about."

Maggie felt herself blush a little. "Yes, we're going to get married after the first of the year. Hopefully, things will be back to normal by then so we can actually have a honeymoon."

"All right! Congratulations to both of you," Ben said, grinning broadly. "I'm pleased for you, Maggie. I sure didn't know when I referred you to a horse trainer that I was playing matchmaker."

"Neither did I, but you couldn't have done a better job if you had tried."

The days flew by. Maggie and Ed selected a design for their new stable. The building was designed specifically for horses and would make a better all around horse facility than the old remodeled cattle barn. An enclosed riding arena would also meet their winter training needs.

Maggie stood at the kitchen sink staring out the window. Where there had been only charred ruin a week before, many men and a few women were scurrying about checking off supplies, unloading lumber, and pacing out the new barn dimensions.

It looked like what she might imagine to be a beehive having a fire drill. She wondered if that made her the queen bee. What a thought.

A clear division of labor existed. The older women worked in the house helping her with food preparation. Many of the younger women were swinging hammers beside the men. When had the feminist movement subtly hit Iowa?

Chatter and swapping of news droned among the women in the house while they sliced vegetables, peeled potatoes, and cooked meats. The warmth and odors of the kitchen soothed Maggie's nerves some, but it was difficult to concentrate on gossip while so much was taking place outside that would alter her life.

Could things really be turning around? How many times had she heard and even said that old phrase, *Out of darkness comes light.* She felt good; really good. But her bones seemed less certain. Maggie's brow furrowed. She wasn't about to let even her bones disturb her good mood.

Ed had moved into the house, since the loft had gone up in smoke with the rest of the barn. Having a fair amount of money tucked away in a savings account, he was able to re-outfit himself without any difficulty.

They'd agreed for him to sleep in the downstairs guest room rather than share her bedroom. She shook her head softly. Ed was somewhat old fashioned about some things. With the kids in the house, he thought they should maintain some semblance of decorum.

Maggie chuckled at the memory of Carolyn's response: "Why not share the same bed? You're sleeping together anyway. We're not stupid, you know."

Maggie shuddered at her lame excuse: "That's just the way we want it to be." Right! Well, that was the way it was.

Living arrangements aside, there had been plenty of opportunity for lovemaking. She'd never before given much thought to the amorous advantages of having kids in school. It had been pure pleasure to make unhurried love with Ed. He was such a considerate lover; there would never be enough time to get her fill of him. But she certainly was willing to work very hard at trying.

"How many pots of coffee do you have brewing?" Ed asked, sticking his head through the kitchen doorway.

"Four pots. I borrowed two from the church and one from the school. Hope that's enough."

"We'll need them all. It's chilly, but the sun is burning off the frost. Can't expect much better for November. There must be twenty people working on the barn. I'm told more food should be arriving shortly. At this rate, the barn will be raised by the end of the weekend. These folks came to work." Ed brushed his lips across hers and squeezed her butt before turning to go back to the construction site.

Maggie felt her skin warm; she glanced furtively around at the other women helping in the kitchen. If they noticed that little love statement, no one was letting on. She worried a little about what her neighbors might think, but damn, it was good to have a man in her life again.

"You seem to have found quite a man for yourself," ventured Amanda Jackson, smiling knowingly at Maggie. "Randy can't say enough good things about him."

Maggie returned the worn stocky woman's smile. The woman had given birth to nine children and worked many hours beside her husband to raise her family. Yeah, she knew something about having a man in her life.

"Thanks, Amanda. I think he's pretty great, too."

"Well, many of us want you to know that we're right pleased for you, Maggie." Drying her chapped hands on a dishtowel, she added, "It was past time you found another husband. We should honor the dead, but the dead don't keep you warm on a cold winter night."

Maggie felt a lump of emotion constricting her windpipe. Somebody actually understood. Unable to speak, she nodded. Lunch time approached. Maggie hoped they were prepared. Tables had been set up in the living room, dining room and on the porch as well as in the kitchen. All the women had agreed that paper plates would suffice. There was no need to take this community togetherness to the point of having to wash piles and piles of dirty dishes. The workers wouldn't mind what they ate off of as long as there was plenty of food. And it was unlikely that Mrs.

McPherson would be by. She always complained at community dinners if china was not used.

An air of determination and happiness hung over all who shared the noon meal. Maggie moved from table to table bringing more food and thanking each person for helping out.

People were glowing with pride. Ben was right. While her friends and neighbors were sacrificing much to help her out of a difficult time, they also were the beneficiaries. Each of them was reminded that they were part of a larger community, and when their turn came for a crisis, their friends and neighbors would stand by them, too.

As she made a second round of pouring coffee, Maggie looked up in time to see Mrs. McPherson marching up the steps like it was an everyday occurrence for her to be entering the Anderson house. Maggie pasted the most welcoming smile on her face she could manage. It shouldn't be such a surprise to see the old shrew. After all, the news of the day was happening at the Anderson farm.

"Welcome, Mary Jane," Maggie chirped, determined not to let the woman put a damper on the day. Maggie accepted the layered cake which Mrs. McPherson handed her with outstretched arms.

"I came because it is the neighborly thing to do," Mrs. McPherson explained. "And I understand your rogue is actually going to make an honest woman of you. How nice of him."

"Oh, I don't know about that," Maggie cooed, brightening. "Quite the contrary, I just about had to lasso and hogtie him in order to make an honest man out of him."

Mrs. McPherson raised her chin and stalked rigidly through the kitchen to the living room, probably seeking a friendly face. Maggie smothered a giggle. When she turned around, several of her neighbors gave her sly approving looks. Most folks wouldn't dare to tweak the gossipmonger of Beaverhill.

Two weeks later Maggie walked proudly through the new stable. While finishing touches remained to be done here and there, the facility was operational. Four broodmares, appreciating their new surroundings, stretched their necks over stall doors to greet her and search for a carrot or an apple.

Maggie reached out to scratch the ears of a bay. A few more months, she told herself, and they would have little ones dashing about. She and the kids could hardly wait. Even Ed, who like so many horse folks kept emotions secreted away, couldn't keep awe from creeping into his voice when he spoke of foaling season.

Half a dozen horses on R and R from the Chicago tracks also benefited from the more spacious stalls in the newly constructed building. The two-year-olds that Ed had been training during the summer and fall were now with Cassie; she would finish their gate training at the track. Maggie and Ed had not decided where the remaining horses would race. Certainly some would stay in the Chicago area, and she and Ed would race others at Prairie Meadows. No doubt some would shuttle back and forth, depending on purse sizes and race conditions.

As Maggie walked toward the end of the stable, she was particularly pleased with the adjoining enclosed arena. There she would continue to learn the nuances of horse training even when it was cold outside. Ed had said that they would be able to work the horses fairly well until the outside temperature dropped below zero. At that point, horse, human, and tack could be too stiff and resistive to accomplish anything positive.

Still, a lot of training would take place in the arena year around. Ed was even considering the idea of giving riding lessons to interested 4-H youth. He'd promised to teach Johnny, and a few additional students wouldn't matter. She knew he believed that was one way he could help pay back a community that had reached out to him as well as to her. Did he realize how attached he'd become to the land and to their neighbors?

As she finished making her rounds, Maggie noticed the too familiar white Con-Ex Farms van coming down the driveway. "Damn," she cussed, "what a way to spoil a perfectly good day. What the hell does corporate America want now?"

The van came to a stop only a few yards from where she stood. Taylor Fallon, dressed in his standard dark suit, stepped out of the vehicle.

"Good morning, Ms. Anderson," he said somewhat shyly, looking away from her glare. He glanced around at the spacious stable area. A lopsided, satisfied grin settled on his face. "Looks like you've done well with your new barn."

Maggie ignored the admiration in the man's voice. "What can I do for you?" she asked abruptly. "As you can see, the land is still not for sale. And it never will be."

"No, I don't suppose it is or ever will be."

Why did Fallon seem so amused? Hadn't he expected her to fold in front of his corporation's demands?

"If I may say so, you've got a lot of guts, ma'am. I respect and appreciate that."

Almost as if at attention, Maggie stood her ground, waiting for the man to state his business. Whatever he had on his mind, she wasn't going to like.

Fallon frowned. "I'm not here to give you a hard time. I just wanted you to know that while Con-Ex Farms was interested in purchasing your property, it isn't anymore."

"Oh." Maggie's curiosity was piqued.

"Nope." Fallon paused and shifted his feet, his voice cracked. "We want you to know that Con-Ex Farms is not into beating up people, killing cats, or burning barns to make anyone sell what they don't want to sell."

"You're not?" Maggie swallowed.

"Absolutely not. We might do things some folks in the local community don't like. We do try to turn a profit as efficiently as we can. But we like to think we also help build the community up,

351

giving it a better long run future by providing jobs and a healthier tax base."

"You don't have to do a public relations job on me, Mr. Fallon."

The executive winced. "Sorry, but it's the truth. We've helped communities with building and maintaining roads, with getting their products to market, with providing scholarships to kids interested in careers in agriculture."

"And you've also driven people out of their homes," Maggie snorted. "Oh, I don't mean deliberately," she said, waving off his protest. "Still, they leave. For all the good you might do, you wreak a lot of havoc and ill feeling."

Maggie stopped speaking. Her hand flew to her mouth; she shook her head in disbelief. It couldn't be, she shouted to her five senses. Her stomach shriveled in response. "Oh, my God," she gasped. "You're the donor. The hundred thousand dollars came from Con-Ex Farms."

Fallon blanched. Shaking his head, he started to speak.

"Don't lie to me," Maggie said, hardly breathing.

"Okay. So what if we did?" Fallon growled. "We don't want to be brushed with the paint of criminals. And we hope we don't do anything that incites others to do evil deeds."

"Do I detect a little guilt behind that goodwill?"

"I won't deny it." Fallon pulled on his tie and loosened his collar. "I...*we* don't like the way things have been going here in Beaverhill, and the way people point fingers at our corporation as if we're responsible."

"But why didn't you go public with your concerns and your donation? Broadcast to the world that you helped save Maggie Anderson from the jaws of humiliation and failure," Maggie said, flailing her arms.

"Now don't get all riled up. We wanted to help quietly. You wouldn't have accepted the money otherwise. And I understand you plan on paying the money back over time into high school scholarships. So everybody wins. And you've used the money well. This is a beautiful racing facility."

"I suppose you're right." Maggie scuffed one booted toe across the other. She felt her cheeks heating. Looking up at the man who she'd thought was her nemesis, Maggie had a hard time saying what she knew needed to be said. "I guess I owe you an apology...and a thank you." She paused. "So what can I do for you? You know I'm not going to sell."

"You're welcome. And of course you won't sell. I said we weren't interested. But maybe you can do two or three things. First, don't always assume that Con-Ex Farms is the bad guy. Second, don't trust that banker, Prater, for anything. Third, hold open the possibility of selling me some shares in a racehorse." Fallon flashed a brilliant smile. "And I'm a very happily married man, Ms. Anderson, or I might be looking for more. You are a remarkable woman; I hope Harrington appreciates what he's getting."

"Well, thank you. I think." Maggie wasn't about to get into a discussion of Ed and what he was getting. Still, Fallon had said something that nagged at her. "We'll keep you in mind regarding the horses. We may be interested in partnerships as we grow the stables." She hesitated. "I'm curious. More than a little, actually. Do you know anything specific about Prater being behind our troubles?"

Fallon should his head. "If I did, I would have said so," he said grimly. "All I know is that your name causes him to go into tirades that border on insanity, at least from my point of view."

Maggie felt a chilling darkness creep through her veins. What had she ever done to send anyone into tirades bordering on insanity?

Fallon opened the door to the van. Getting in, he said, "I'll let you know if I hear anything specific, but I don't expect to have much to do with the local banker. Let me know when you're ready to sell a piece of a promising horse." He grinned broadly. "Good luck, Ms. Anderson. With the farm, the horses, and with that hired man of yours. See you."

Every emotion imaginable raced for attention throughout Maggie's body as she watched the Con-Ex Farms van pull out of her driveway. She wanted to be angry at Fallon, at Con-Ex Farms, at Ben for duping her about the money, but she couldn't.

Truthfully, she'd been awed by Fallon's

genuine concern. How much of him was behind the donation? And she was pleased that through her and Con-Ex Farms, a lot of local kids would get much needed assistance for college. He'd been right. In the long run, the money would be a good investment in the community. In the short run, that money made Anderson Stables more viable than it had ever been before. Biting her lower lip, Maggie admitted she was grateful.

Maggie scowled and walked back into the barn thinking about Fallon's advice regarding Prater. Obviously, the list of those possibly wanting to see her succumb to failure had been narrowed by one. Con-Ex Farms no longer belonged on that list. Who did that leave? Prater. McPherson, maybe. And a possible second party Prater had alluded to in the spring but never mentioned by name. Someone else or some other company interested in the Magee property. Would this assault over her land ever end?

Maggie looked around the table and smiled easily. The Thanksgiving meal had never been better. Remains of turkey, mashed potatoes, yams, cranberries, cooked carrots, and homemade bread adorned the table while fresh pumpkin and cherry pies sat on the kitchen counter.

"Maggie, everything is delicious. Again, thank you so much for including Gladys and me on this special day," Ben Templeton said, lifting his wine glass in a salute to his hostess. The gray haired woman sitting beside him nodded her head in agreement.

"We're happy you could join us, Ben. Both of you. This Thanksgiving Day wouldn't be nearly as filled with bounty if it hadn't been for your help."

"Yeah, I sure didn't know what I was getting you into when I referred you to Harrington," Ben quipped. "I'm glad it worked out, though. I'm pleased as punch for the both of you."

Ed cleared his throat. He looked briefly from Ben to Maggie and then addressed Ben. "Well, I don't hardly know where I might be if you hadn't sent her to me. Expect I wouldn't be eating turkey and all the trimmings. And I certainly wouldn't have a family and my career. Doubt that the Illinois Racing Board would have found me, and if they had, they would never have wanted me back in the condition I was in."

"Now don't go getting mushy on me, Harrington," Ben cautioned. "I may have started the snowball, but you and Maggie, here, made the snowman."

"And snow-woman," Maggie chuckled. "Still, Ben, you've been there for us throughout — with the community, after the fire...you've been a very loyal friend." As her eyes glistened, she lifted her glass to make a toast. "To a dear man who listens to quirky females who can't seem to ever get Iowa soil out from under their fingernails."

After sharing some wine, Ben countered, "To a young, spunky woman who still takes time to listen to the wisdom of the land. I'm real proud of you, girl. You know your dad and mom would be, too."

"Yeah, sis, I want to get in on this too," Brad said, lifting his glass. "Ben's right. Mom and Dad would be proud." With a shaky voice, he added, "I am, too. Best of luck to both of you."

"Thanks," Maggie mumbled. Her brother had shown up two days earlier. Her kids were thrilled at his arrival. And she had to confess he'd been very conciliatory. Several times he'd started to engage her in what she thought was an important conversation, only to have it fade away. They'd both agreed to let Ben process their insurance money without going through lawyers. Thank goodness for that. And thankfully, too, Brad and Ed had behaved civilly with each other. She couldn't expect more than that.

"Can I have some more turkey, Mom?" Johnny piped. "Before more speeches."

Everyone laughed except Johnny.

Ed passed the boy the turkey platter while Maggie asked, "So what are you thankful for, Johnny? And how about you, Carolyn?"

"Food," Johnny blurted out. "And for the horses and Ed. And that we don't have to move."

Maggie nodded and looked across at her daughter.

Carolyn frowned. "There's so much. All of what Johnny said, including the food." She grinned. "Happiness. I think I'm most thankful for everyone being so happy. Even when things go bad, we seem to be able to find some happiness."

"So that's different, huh?" Maggie pressed.

Shrugging as only teenagers could, Carolyn responded, "I know you always wanted us to believe you were happy, Mom. But you couldn't fool me." Glancing around the table, she said, "This is good."

"Yeah, you're right." Maggie sighed. "This is good. May we always remember this moment."

With his mouth half stuffed with turkey, Johnny sputtered, "I'm not so sure everything is so great."

"So what's your problem, son?" Ed asked.

Johnny turned several shades of pink and shook his head.

"Well?" Ed encouraged.

"Kimberly Johnson thinks I'm too small," the boy complained, his voice unsteady. "But she won't leave me alone. One day she hates me and the next day she wants me to be her best friend. Go figure!"

"Sounds like you got girl problems."

Johnny bobbed his head. "Yeah, big time."

Ed stroked his chin thoughtfully. Sending a knowing look at Maggie before returning his complete attention to the troubled boy, Ed said, "You'll have to learn to have a lot of patience with girls, young man. They tend to be kind of flighty. Sometimes they do one thing and you think it means this, but it really means that."

Johnny nodded rapidly. His eyes widened. Maggie wondered if he'd be more impressed if the Wizard of Oz had just spoken.

"Sometimes they want you to chase them," Ed

continued. "And sometimes they don't. Seldom will they ever tell you straight out what they want. You'll have to use your powers of observation." Ed tapped his temple. "Patience is the word, son. Patience."

Johnny thought a moment. "Sounds like working with a skittish horse."

Chuckling, Ed replied, "You're not far off on that, Johnny. Not far off at all."

Maggie tried not to laugh, but enough was enough. "Well, if you men are finished analyzing women as if they are mere horses, perhaps you would like to help clear the table so we can have desert."

"Yes, Mom," Johnny replied meekly.

As they stood, Maggie whispered in Ed's ear, "Am I like a skittish horse, cowboy?"

"You better believe it," he whispered back. "Like a skittish, contrary broodmare. But you're more than worth the time and effort."

"Look. There they go again," Johnny shouted. "Mom's kissing Ed again."

Not at all embarrassed, Ed pointed to the mistletoe hanging over the oak door frame between the dining room and the kitchen. "I hung the mistletoe myself. So you better watch out before the women start kissing you."

"Yuck!" Johnny exclaimed, rushing through the doorway.

Maggie laughed. She couldn't shake the tingly feelings that peppered her chest; she didn't even want to try. Ed fit so well into her life, into her

359

family's life. Oh, there would be difficulties, those were expected. But she was confident that no matter what happened, their love was strong enough to carry them through the darkest of times.

Counting her blessings, Maggie suddenly felt old. Perhaps the weight of brooding about the land, about the horses, about Ed, about her kids was finally catching up with her. She knew, without looking, that her skin was not wrinkled and there were no gray hairs.

Shouldn't she be feeling younger now because so much of that weight could be set aside? Maggie closed her eyes briefly. Had she become so accustomed to worrying that she just naturally worried? No, of course not—there was still somebody out there who wanted to destroy all that was hers.

After she heard the soft snoring of her children, Maggie slipped into her robe, padded down the hallway and then down the stairs to Ed's room. As she entered, his heavy breathing greeted her. Maggie smiled—he'd been unable to stay awake for her. Must have been all that turkey.

Sitting on the edge of the bed, she leaned over to run her moist tongue across his upper lip. The stubble of his mustache tickled. He stirred. Her fingers played in the thatch of his chest hair. Moving to curl her tongue in and around his ear, Maggie edged her fingers lower across his abdomen, which was as taut as a skin on a kettle drum.

Aware of his strained passiveness, she whispered, "Play possum as long as you want, cowboy. This woman isn't skittish around wild beasts, asleep or awake."

Maggie traced his neck muscles with her lips, then chewed gently on his pebbled nipples. Back and forth between them she moved, leaving traces of wetness. Her fingers wrapped securely around his erection, squeezing and tugging.

His muscles tensed. His hips moved upward almost imperceptibly. Maggie grinned and moved her hand deliberately but cautiously, not wanting to bring things to a premature conclusion. His loins and hips tightened.

Becoming suddenly still, she murmured, "Not yet, my love. Wait for me."

She kept her eyes open while swishing her tongue around his crown. He jerked. She caught him between her lips and swallowed him into her mouth, then bobbed several times as if dunking for apples. He strained for completion; she stopped.

His eyes slit open when she abandoned him. Smiling dreamily, Maggie tugged her nightgown over her head and canted her body to straddle him.

"Ah," she mumbled to the silence. For a small eternity, she sat there letting his pulse resonate through her body from her center to her extremities.

Then she moved — at first, simply swaying from

side to side. Next, she rotated her lower body in small, tight circles. Maggie rocked leisurely back and forth on her knees. "Delicious," she moaned, biting her lower lip. Her eyes remained closed.

Her body coiled around his shaft. Her entire focus, her breathing, her movement centered on that single, simple point of intersection. Pulling on her own aching nipples, she rapidly levered up and down.

Ed's eyes popped wide open and his hips joined hers, propelling them toward completion.

"Now. Now," Maggie panted in rhythm with their movements.

A humming throb burst within and Maggie felt first her release showering him and then his quickening, pulsating response. Like a hot air balloon severed from its tether lines, Maggie floated slowly out and above her body. A luscious light wrapped her in warmth and security.

Collapsing to his chest, she savored the heat of her lover's skin and his strong arms encircling her. "Hold me, please," she whispered. "Don't let me go."

"Don't worry about that, lady. Not in this lifetime."

Maggie's lungs filled as she savored his hoarsely spoken words. She drifted asleep atop of him, still joined at their center.

- o -

Ed tenderly played with strands of her wheatstraw hair. Every once in a while, he sensed the sleeping woman stir. Was she trying to assure herself that he was still there? "Maggie, Maggie," he moaned. He knew she still possessed vestiges of fear that he would yet run from her intimacy. He guessed she had every right to wonder.

But he knew running was no longer possible. He had worked hard not to run. He'd learned much about himself and his natural tendencies to escape when faced with risking too much of himself. He'd already risked more than ever before.

If nothing else, working the twelve steps taught him about his weaknesses while at the same time providing him with a foundation upon which to hope. And with Maggie, there was lots of room for hope.

Ed smiled. Christmas was coming. It was about time to drive to Des Moines.

CHAPTER NINETEEN

Twenty-four hours later, at three in the morning, Maggie heard loud pounding at her porch door. She wasn't asleep. Nearly consumed by worry, she hurriedly put on a robe and raced down the stairs and through the kitchen.

Dread laced her heart like a myriad of heavy manacles. Ed had not come home since he'd left for Des Moines that afternoon. He'd seemed nervous before leaving and had been very vague about why he had to go into the city. And then he hadn't returned.

The strained, blank look on the deputy sheriff's face through the storm door glass confirmed her fears. Something terrible had happened.

Maggie shuttered her eyes briefly, seeking strength. Breathing shallowly, she reluctantly opened the door.

The deputy removed his hat and stepped into the porch. "Sorry to have to tell you, Maggie," he began, "but your hired man's pickup was found in the ditch off of Highway 47. Looks like the vehicle went out of control on the dusting of snow we had early last evening."

Maggie's body stilled from shaking. "Is he..." She gagged. "Is he alive?"

"Don't rightly know, ma'am." The officer shifted his considerable weight from foot to foot.

He was trying to focus on something just above her without being obvious. "We can't find him," he said at last.

"What?" Digging her fingernails into her shoulders, Maggie squeezed with all her might trying to hold on, trying to concentrate on what the deputy was saying. Nothing made sense.

"We can't find him anywhere. Tracks lead away from the accident and then disappear. Somebody must have picked him up."

"Then he's okay," Maggie reasoned. "Or maybe someone took him to the hospital."

The deputy shrugged his shoulders. "He hasn't been at any of the area hospitals. We checked. I'm sure he's actually not feeling much of anything right now."

"What do you mean?" Maggie asked. All her senses went on alert, knowing this story was only going to get worse.

Scowling, the officer said, "Maggie, there were lots of empty and broken beer and whiskey bottles in the cab. The interior stinks to high heaven."

"Oh, my God." Maggie felt herself falling and would have sunk to the floor if the deputy had not reached out to grab her.

Had someone placed a large anvil on her chest? Her teeth chattered. Thoughts whirled about her brain without coherency. She allowed herself to be led to the kitchen table.

Maggie slouched over the table an hour later with her head resting on her arms. She was alone.

Completely alone. There were no more tears to cry. That reservoir had been drained.

She remembered the deputy sheriff handing her the keys to the pickup before he left. It would be towed to the farm in the morning. That was all that was left of Ed Harrington. That, and memories.

"He won't come back," she murmured to the kitchen walls, which no longer held any comfort. Somehow she'd scared him away again. Worse than that, she'd chased him back into the bottle.

What had she done? Things had seemed so right between them. How long had he been planning his escape? They had just made such satisfying love the night before. Did he know then? Or was it a spur of the moment thing? She shuddered. Ed Harrington was not a spur of the moment kind of guy. How could he have given up on them after all they had been through?

Maggie raised her head, rubbed her eyes and stared at her hands wishing they could turn back time. What should she have done differently? Had she been too determined, too driven, too strong? Did he want to get back to Chicago, to his old life? Why was he running from her?

Well, he'd better just keep on running. She rose and kicked the chair across the room. She wouldn't let the louse back in the door if he came back all contrite and begging. He'd betrayed her. He'd betrayed himself. He'd betrayed the children. Good God, how was she going to tell them?

Maggie started making a pot of coffee. She was up; there was no going back to bed now. As she filled the coffee pot from the spigot, a horrific realization overtook her mind like a tidal wave. Ed had been driving dead drunk. He could have run into an innocent couple and killed them — just like her parents had been killed. Ed Harrington was no better than the drunken animal who had mercilessly murdered her own parents.

She jerked a hand toward the spigot; she didn't know how long the coffee pot had been overflowing.

Why had she been such a stupid fool?

"I wish I never knew him!" Johnny cried for the tenth time that morning. Then he stumbled off the kitchen chair and raced out the door toward the stable. The slamming of the door added one more exclamation point to the air.

Maggie had told her children without holding anything back. She believed they deserved to know the truth. The sooner each of them was able to forget the rugged horse trainer, the better off they'd all be.

Her heart had shriveled over the last several hours. Maggie sat at the table staring into a cold cup of coffee.

Not surprisingly, Johnny took the news of Ed's desertion hardest. He had wanted a dad real bad. Ed had seemed like the right man for him, but that was when the trainer was sober.

Perhaps more like the teenager she was,

Carolyn seemed more aloof about the whole thing. She'd held back the tears, but was unable to hide her disappointment and anger. Maggie shook her head sadly — her daughter had tried to explain everything away like some kind of fairy godmother. When would her teenager learn that fantasies were just that, fantasies.

Glancing warily at her daughter still sitting across from her, Maggie felt Carolyn's fury. Maybe with Johnny outside, the girl was going to let her feelings out. Then Maggie realized that Carolyn wasn't angry at Ed; she was furious with her mother. Maggie braced herself.

"Are you sure the two of you didn't have a fight or something?" Carolyn accused.

"How many times do I have to tell you? No, we didn't. He just left. I can't tell you why. He never told me."

"It doesn't make sense that he would just up and disappear. He loves you, Mom. He loves us." Carolyn moved her shaking hands under the table. "I know he does."

"Maybe there was too much love for him," Maggie ventured softly. "Some men can't stand to be loved."

"Well, I don't think Ed Harrington was *some men*," Carolyn claimed. "You must have done something to send him away."

Maggie lowered her head slowly, shaking it back and forth. She had no clue what else to say or do.

"Or," her daughter's eyes grew huge, "maybe

somebody beat him up again and hid his body. Maybe somebody tried to finish him off this time. But you don't care anymore. Do you?

Maggie's eyes narrowed watching the backside of her daughter disappear rapidly up the stairs. Maggie clenched her fingers. It had never occurred to her that Ed might again be the victim of foul play. She'd simply assumed he'd run away from her.

Why had it taken her daughter to raise that possibility? Why hadn't the deputy mentioned that? Could Carolyn be right? An icy chill spread through her bones. She didn't know what to think or feel. She'd been so angry, felt so abandoned, she had merely accepted the obvious, that Ed Harrington did not love her enough. Could there be truth in her daughter's words?

Chewing on a fingernail, Maggie tried not to panic. If Ed was in trouble, he would eventually call. She wouldn't know where to begin looking for him. And if he'd gotten drunk and driven into the ditch, she didn't want to see him again anyway. About all she could do was wait and take care of the horses.

She still had the farm. The stable was viable, at least for a while. Cassie would race the horses, if need be. Maybe she should contact Clint; he would know how to find a missing person. She desperately needed to talk with somebody, but she didn't want to tie up the phone or leave the house.

Unable to force herself away from the table,

Maggie didn't know which was worse: believing that Ed had fallen off the wagon, or that someone had threatened his life. Rubbing swollen eyes, repressing a scream building deep within her lungs, she knew with certain agony the answer to that question.

The phone rang. Maggie glared at the noisy intruder debating whether to answer or not. There was a world out there. She didn't want to have to deal with that world. She wanted to roll into a ball and stay hidden from sight and sound.

Reluctantly, she picked up the receiver. "Hello." She hardly identified the squeaky voice as her own.

"Maggie, is that you?"

Maggie slumped against the kitchen counter. "Yeah, Flo, it's me. Guess you heard."

"I'm sorry."

"Well, it's over. That's the way it is. Sometimes you just lose."

"Are you sure he's not coming back?"

"If he knows what's good for him he won't."

The ensuing silence gnawed at Maggie. What was her friend not saying?

"Okay, Flo. Spit it out. What's really on your mind?"

"I just think you need to know the first song I heard this morning."

Maggie groaned. Why did she have to have loony friends? Maybe they thought she was just as loony. "Well, what was it? You're not going to be able to go on with your day without telling me."

"Tammy was singing *Stand by Your Man*."

Maggie closed her eyes and counted to three. "Then I guess you better go find a man and stand by him."

"Maggie!"

"Why don't we talk later, Flo? I'm tired and I'm grumpy. Thanks for calling. Love you."

"Love you, Maggie. Take care of yourself."

Maggie didn't know whether to laugh or cry as she hung up her phone. Stand by your man, indeed. Kick your man's ass down the road would have been a better tune.

It was noon. Still no word. She congratulated herself for surviving that long. Maggie pulled her windbreaker tighter to ward off the early winter chill as she stepped of the porch and walked across the driveway. Ed's pickup had been towed into her yard earlier that morning. From a distance, Mabel looked the same as always: worn, but reliable. Up close she told an entirely different story.

The deputy was right. Maggie could hardly breathe when she stuck her head in the cab. The stench was beyond words.

For a couple hours after her daughter's tirade, Maggie had held onto the shred of hope that maybe Carolyn was right. Maybe Ed had not left voluntarily. But once Maggie saw the wreckage of liquor bottles in the pickup, there was no doubt left in her mind.

Ed Harrington preferred the comfort of drink to any comfort she could provide. There were no more tears. She just wished she could let him know she thought he was the most despicable creature that ever stepped on the face of the earth. He was just damn lucky he hadn't killed anyone in his hurry to get away from her this time.

She stood by the truck trying to decide if it was best to clean the stuff up now or wait. The easiest thing to do would be to drop a match in the gas tank and watch it burn. Putting a match in the cab might be just as efficient.

Concentrating on what to do, Maggie did not at first hear a car coming down the driveway. When she did, she looked up quickly, only to want to run and hide. It was her brother. He would no doubt gloat and have a grand time at her expense.

"Hi, sis," Brad said, getting out of the car. "I came as soon as Flo told me what was happening. How are you? How are the kids?"

Maggie scrunched her mouth. She hadn't expected those questions. "The kids? Johnny is mad as hell at Ed. Carolyn is just as mad at me. She thinks I chased him off. Or that somebody beat him over the head again."

Brad nodded. "How do you know they didn't? I understand he hasn't been located yet."

"Just get a whiff of this cab," Maggie replied, opening the pickup door.

Brad stuck his head in and pulled it back quickly. "Whew. I've been in breweries that don't smell that ripe."

"So, you see? He fell off the wagon big time. Success must scare the guy. And he could've killed anybody on that road that night." Maggie placed a hand on her brow. "Just like Mom and Dad were killed."

Brad looked curiously at his sister. "Maggie, I think you may be mixing a lot of different things up here. Ed didn't kill our parents. As far as I know, no one was hurt the other night."

"But that doesn't excuse him."

"No it doesn't. Not if he was driving drunk."

"Of course he was driving drunk. Look at all of these broken bottles."

"You don't know much about drinking, and apparently neither does the sheriff's department."

"What do you mean?"

"In the first place, I doubt there is a human being alive who could consume this much booze and not be comatose. Secondly, a heavy drinker, particularly an alcoholic, is not going to smash these bottles like this. A time might come when a guy could almost kill for a swallow. And one of those bottles might not have been completely drained. Or he might be able to pour just a little water into a whiskey bottle and still get a taste."

Maggie tried to think through a heavy mind-fog. What did her brother mean? He certainly had more experience with alcohol that she did.

"So what are you saying?" She heard a trace of hope in her own question.

"I'm saying all of this evidence is a set up. Why, I don't know. What happened to Harrington, I don't know. But this truck cab is to make you and the authorities believe that Harrington was driving drunk. I doubt very much that he was."

Maggie slumped to sit on the running board of the pickup. Looking up at her brother, she said, "So you agree with Carolyn? That somebody got to Ed. That he might be hurt." Her hand flew to her throat. "Or worse."

Brad stooped down on his haunches. "It's too early to jump to conclusions. But I expect Ed's in trouble."

Maggie held her head in her hands. "This is too much. Why didn't I trust him? Why is it Carolyn and now you?

"I know it's hard for you to believe that I am actually on your side, but I am." Brad coughed and pulled the zipper of his jacket up to keep out the wind. "You have a difficult time accepting that I no longer harbor ill will toward you, Maggie. My issue was always much more with dad than with you. I haven't told you, but part of the reason I know this is I'm in therapy. I've been working hard on my shit."

Maggie's mouth fell open. "Really?" she squeaked.

"Really." He blinked. "You might wonder a little bit about why you don't trust more easily. Dad always set you up as the perfect kid. But he wasn't doing you any favors—not really. You wound up having to stay on the farm to measure up, while I got to run off to college. On the surface I was the loser, but I'm less certain anymore."

"But this is where I've always wanted to be," Maggie protested.

"But whose idea was that? You were brainwashed from day one to inherit the land, to protect the family legacy. Since Mom and Dad were killed, Maggie, you've been obsessed with this land. At first I wanted you to sell because I was so angry with Dad that I didn't want a trace of him left. Then, since Mason died and since some of my own head work, I've wanted you to sell because I thought it was unhealthy for you to stay. But Harrington changed my mind about that."

"He did?" Maggie struggled to concentrate. She'd never known her brother was capable of caring about her.

"Yeah, with him, certainly more than with Mason, you've been able to share a dream where the land serves you rather than always the other way around." Brad smirked. "Harrington is the only person with whom I've seen you willing to share equally. Maybe it's the first time you've encountered a man who is man enough for you." Brad glanced toward the barn. "I've probably said more than you wanted to hear. I'm sorry, but I think you needed to hear it."

Maggie sighed deeply. "Don't be sorry. You're right in more ways than you may know." She paused a long time before continuing. "In ways I didn't want to face, I guess. This farm has been a mixed blessing for me. I did resent you running off without a care in the world, leaving me to cope with family expectations. I blamed you and held our parents faultless. Maybe I've had too much pride in what this place means."

Maggie struggled to her feet. "I need to be alone for awhile. Why don't you go on into the house? Please don't leave."

"I won't. You can count on that."

Approaching the barn, Maggie felt warmed by the now familiar smells of horse and leather. She walked to Midnight Dancer's stall. The mare stuck her head over the stall door, encouraging Maggie's touch.

Maggie smiled through her tears. "You'll always be here, won't you Dancer?" The horse's ears twitched forward.

"Why is it so hard to admit when you've been wrong?" Maggie stared at Dancer's soft eyes. "I guess you wouldn't really know about that."

Running her fingers up and down Dancer's neck, Maggie tried to name and confront her own demons. All these years she'd seen Brad as the bad boy. And he had been a hellion in many ways, yet she'd been guilty of so much tunnel vision and so much pride. How often had she puffed up her chest when her dad listed her successes to egg on her brother? And had she ever really treated Mason as an equal? It'd always been her family's land. Her land.

Why hadn't she ever questioned the sacrosanct status of the land? Both her mom and dad had coached her over and over about her responsibility to the land — to nurture it, value it, and at all costs protect it as her children's legacy. When had it become an icon, to be worshipped?

Maggie closed her eyes as if in prayer. No more, she vowed. No more would she let an obsession with the land run her life. "Dancer," she murmured, "I like the idea of land furthering my dream, for a change. I can still nurture it, or I can sell it and move on. The family will survive. Maybe a new legacy will emerge. Maybe you're part of that new legacy, Dancer. What do you think about that?" Maggie stood back to stare at the mare. "You're not going to give me a clue, are you? Well, maybe I'm done struggling to live out other people's dream. It's about time, huh?"

Dancer nickered softly.

Maggie plopped down on a bale of hay. Dancer retreated to the far corner of her stall.

There was still the matter of Ed. She clasped her knees tightly to her chest. Why had it taken her daughter and her brother to see what was happening?

Maggie rose and walked with renewed purpose toward the house. Her bones hummed an unfamiliar but upbeat tune.

When she entered the kitchen, the first person she saw was Brad, standing by the sink.

"Give me a hug, will you Brad? I think I need that, a lot."

"Gladly."

"What about Ed?" Maggie's voice shook. "I feel so terrible. I was so quick to judge him. Will he ever forgive me? God, how can we find him? Is he alive? I can't give up. Not now."

Brad chuckled in her ear. "That won't happen, Sis. You have the tenacity of a badger; you always have. Before this is over, though, you may need the patience of a cat. I expect we'll hear from Ed soon. He's not going to leave you stranded here facing danger by yourself."

- o -

Thirty-six hours later, Ed Harrington struggled to open his eyes. Had someone glued them shut? His head pounded as if some damn idiot was trying to open a coconut with a dull knife. His too-heavy tongue wouldn't move. His heart sputtered. Something was terribly wrong.

Like an amateur cameraman trying to bring a blurred image into focus on a projector screen, Ed focused and refocused his brain. His eyes slit open. A TV silently stared back at him. Flowered wallpaper covered the walls, just barely. The background might have been white at some time. Where did people grow brown tulips? The shag rug might have been orange once—now, it matched the walls. The only furniture he could see was a dresser and the bed on which he lay.

His eyelids fell shut. The place smelled musty. Where the hell was he? Memory traces glacially emerged. His fingers traced the shape of the lump on his head.

He ran his tongue across dry lips. Images

379

started to surface. He remembered walking down the sidewalk from the jewelry store to his truck when something slammed him from behind. Faintly, he recalled being dragged away. He'd felt the prick of a needle in his right arm. That was all he remembered.

No, not quite all. He pressed his finger against his front pocket. The ring was still there in its box. Ed sighed. Now what?

He swung his legs off the bed, one at a time. On his third try, he was able to stand. Walking unsteadily, he moved toward the window of the cheap hotel. He must be about four floors up. He could make out a half empty parking lot below; he assumed he was looking out of the backside of the building. The next block contained two apartment buildings, a gasoline station, and a couple nondescript businesses. He looked toward the horizon, shading his eyes from the glare of the rising sun. He cussed softly as he recognized in the distance a very familiar skyline.

He was back in Chicago.

His nose twitched. Was he dreaming, or what? His clothes smelled like they'd taken a bath in a brewery vat. But he knew he hadn't been drinking.

That he wouldn't forget. And while he thought someone must have hammered on his body long and hard trying to reshape it, he did not have a hangover. Ed rubbed a hand roughly across his whiskers. He most assuredly knew what hangovers were like; this was not one of them.

Ed collapsed back onto the slumping bed. Reality materialized — only in droplets at first, and then in torrents threatening to overwhelm. He'd been beaten and drugged and then his ass was hauled to Chicago and deposited in this hellhole. Somebody was trying to send a strong message: Chicago was where he belonged.

Ed rose to a sitting position. Bent over, he held his head in his hands trying to put the pieces together.

What was Maggie doing? Where was his truck? What the hell day was it, anyway? He checked his watch, which still kept time as if nothing out of the ordinary had happened. He'd been out about two days. "Holy shit," he muttered.

No doubt he'd been set up to take a fall, but what kind of fall? What did Maggie and the kids think happened to him? What did they think he'd done? Did she believe he'd left on his own? That he was running from her? Shit. He'd have to call her and make sure she understood.

Why didn't they just kill him and get it over with? Like the last time, his wallet was still intact. He rummaged quickly through it: driver's license, credit cards, social security. Even his cash hadn't been touched.

He reached for his jacket, which had been thrown across a nearby chair. A large envelop fell to the floor. Awkwardly, he bent to pick it up. His eyes widened at its contents. There was a fist full of bills inside. Slowly, he counted the money. He hadn't seen a hundred dollar bill since his high rolling days, and there were a hundred of them. Ten thousand dollars. Ed whistled a low curse. This was serious money.

Attached to the last bill was a sticky note with a few words scrawled on it: "Take the money and stay away from Maggie Anderson. If you come back, you'll be buried in Iowa. This is your last warning."

Ed rubbed his temple and puzzled over the message. They were all in much more danger than he'd realized. He hesitated. Maybe that wasn't true. Maggie and her kids were not at risk as long as it looked like she would belly-up the farm. She was at risk if she looked successful, or if he went running back to help her.

He decided against giving her a knee-jerk phone call. He had to think. He had to consider their options. Some bastard was threatening their lives. No more scare tactics. This nutcase wasn't going to settle for anything less than Maggie's farm and destroying her future.

Ed sat across from Clint and Cassie Travers in their McHenry County farmhouse office thirty miles outside of Chicago. His brow furrowed as he studied the receipts and papers spread out on the table. A man working for Clint's detective agency had come up with incriminating evidence regarding Maggie's situation.

"So it's been Prater all along. The bastard," Ed snarled, drumming his fingers lightly on the oak table.

Nodding in agreement, Clint responded cautiously, "It looks to be the case, but that receipt for accelerant would only be circumstantial evidence in a courtroom."

"But according to this police report, it's the same type of fuel use for the barn fire."

"It's still circumstantial. It is an unusual accelerant that catches and spreads rapidly. But not everyone who buys it plans on burning down a barn."

"Right. So now what?" Ed threw the papers on the table. "Do we simply wait until Prater strikes again? Do I just disappear? I don't think anyone's going to be really safe until we have the nut behind bars."

"No need for despair," Clint observed. "My man is still following a couple leads trying to link the fellows who beat you up to Prater. We're fairly certain who the attackers are, at least the first time. The link tying them to Prater is still missing. We're very close."

The grandfather clock standing next to a floor to ceiling bookcase chimed ten evenly placed strokes. Early winter sun rays spilled through the tall windows, warming the spacious den.

Cassie snapped a lead pencil in half and then stood. Both men looked at her and remained quiet. Cassie wet her lips before directing her attention to Ed. "So things are bad. I'm still trying to understand why you think you can't call Maggie to let her know you're at least alive. That woman must be worried sick."

Slumping further in his chair, Ed shook his head. "She's in more danger if Prater finds out I'm still in the picture. She probably thinks I walked out, or that I got drunk and ran away. Maggie won't want anything to do with a drunk."

"Nonsense," Cassie protested, "she's got more faith in you than that. You're supposed to get married, for god's sake."

Ed shrugged.

Running fingers through his thick black hair, Clint said, "I expect it's time we took the initiative. You're right, Ed, we can't just sit back and wait for Prater to strike again. Each time he acts, the danger gets higher.

"I believe it's about time we set a trap for the outstanding banker of Beaverhill. That will require you going back to Iowa, Ed."

Clint laid out a plan to which Ed reluctantly agreed. His stomach knotted. He wanted to get the goods on Prater, but he wasn't so sure he was ready to deal with Maggie. Would she even believe his story? Would she take him back? Would she want him back? What the hell would he do if she'd given up on him?

As if reading his thoughts, Cassie sat down beside him and placed her hand on his trembling arm. "Harrington," she confided, "I've known you for quite a while now. I used to think you were a sexist lout. Then I began to see a gentle spirit that you tried to hide behind bravado. You've come a long ways, but you still have a few things to learn about women. We may like to be taken care of at times, but we don't want to be protected from things that matter. We may at times appear vulnerable, but never underestimate the strength of a woman."

"Thanks for your vote of confidence, I think." Grinning sheepishly, Ed continued, "I can just about hear Maggie saying the same thing."

Closing his eyes, he winced. Opening them, he looked over at Cassie. "Okay, I'm ready. Where's the phone?"

"It's over there on the desk," Cassie said softly. Both she and Clint rose. "We'll be in the kitchen." She paused. "Trust the love you two have. It's strong and has been tempered by a lot already."

- o -

Maggie answered the kitchen phone on the third ring and immediately recognized the deep gravelly voice. Her throat constricted while her heartbeat seemed suspended in weightless time. After mumbling that she was fine, tears streaming down both cheeks, she concentrated on listening. Desperately, Maggie tried to hear him out with her whole body.

With the phone cord wrapped several times around her, Maggie's senses reeled first one way and then the other. Relieved that he was safe with their Chicago friends. Horrified that someone had drugged him and thought they could buy him off. Guilty that she had initially believed he had run away from her love, and that he had climbed back into the bottle, that he had placed the lives of others at risk by getting behind the wheel of his pickup when drunk. Angry that he'd just now called—she expected Cassie had more than a little to do with that. She felt like she'd been given an overdose of Novocain. Would she ever be coherent again?

- o -

"Are you still there, Maggie?" Ed stammered. He regretted that his story had rolled off his tongue so rapidly without giving her time to react or think and without really finding out how things were with Maggie and the kids. But he'd been unable to stop the flow of words. He just hoped to God she would understand.

Choking, Maggie blurted out, "I'm here, cowboy. When are you going to stop letting people beat you over the head? Not that you don't have a hard enough head to withstand a ton of concrete."

Relief swept through his body. For a moment he felt weightless. "When they let me see them coming," he countered. "What did they tell you happened?"

"That you were driving drunk and ran off into the ditch. That you probably were too scared to come back here and simply fled. No one really looked for you because foul play wasn't suspected."

He groaned listening to the disembodied voice.

"And what did you think, Maggie?"

Maggie hesitated. "I didn't want to believe them."

"But you did," he said softly.

"Briefly," she admitted between sobs. "But Carolyn and my brother actually saw through the sham. They got me back to thinking with my heart. I'm so sorry I didn't trust you."

"Don't be," Ed said. "I don't get high grades on trust, either, or I would have called before now. You have Cassie to thank for helping me see and believe in what you and I have."

Maggie chuckled softly. "Give her a great big hug for me. So when are you coming home?"

Ed thought his heart was going to split in two at the word *home*. He went on to explain the plan for setting a trap for Prater and why it was crucial she not yet tell Johnny and Carolyn where he was. No word could leak out that he remained in contact with the Andersons. They could not even risk meeting in Des Moines or in Chicago because Prater might have someone trying to keep tabs on both of them.

And the entire family could be in dire danger if their planned trap failed. There was no telling what the deranged banker would conjure up next.

CHAPTER TWENTY

Absently, Maggie pulled at her sweater collar while sitting with one leg tucked under her. Although it was nearly mid-December, the heat in Ben Templeton's office was stifling. She glanced over at Cassie Travers sitting alertly next to her in an identical light-green cushioned chair. As planned, the Chicago woman had come along to support her friend in this moment of confrontation. Templeton sat behind his desk idly drumming his fingers, glancing frequently at the clock on the office wall.

The three of them waited for Josh Prater, who had been told that Maggie wanted to discuss the possibility of selling the farm and that she wanted Templeton to be her financial advisor in any such proceedings.

Fidgeting with the folder of papers in her lap, Maggie wondered if the banker would come. Had he been tipped off? She didn't see how that could have happened. He'd come. He'd wanted her land for as long as she could remember. He'd come.

At last, the intercom buzzed. A tinny voice announced, "Mr. Prater is here to see you, Mr. Templeton."

"Show him in," was the response.

Maggie had never seen Prater appear so cheerful. The man beamed a confident smile. Nodding, he quickly removed his coat and scarf and sat on the edge of the third chair in front of

Ben's desk. The semi-circle of chairs was now filled, with Maggie sitting in the middle.

Maggie looked at Ben Templeton. The level of anticipation in the room was palpable.

"So," Prater said, looking directly at Maggie, "you have finally come to your senses, young lady. It's never too late, I guess."

Stunned by his arrogance, Maggie merely stared at him. Maggie's muscles clinched with the effort of restraining her turbulent emotions.

Ben cleared his throat. "Before we begin, Josh, I'd like to introduce Cassie Travers to you. You may recall that Ms. Travers has been working with some of Maggie's horses in Chicago. She's a friend of Maggie's and Ed Harrington's."

"Ah, yes, the knight errant," Prater mocked, hardly acknowledging Cassie's presence. "There's a rumor about that he's disappeared. That maybe there wasn't enough here in little Beaverhill to hold him after all. My, my, Ms. Anderson, you must be disappointed on a number of counts."

Maggie couldn't keep herself from blushing, but she kept her tongue still. If she lost her composure under Prater's gloating the entire trap could spring prematurely and Prater would slither away like the rat he was.

In the ensuing silence, the only noises she could hear were the ticking of the wall clock and the pounding of her heart.

"Well, what are we waiting for?" Prater demanded. "I don't have all day. I'm a very busy man."

"So it seems. So it seems," Ben drawled, shifting his weight in his swivel chair. "Before we get down to business of considering offers, there are some other matters to clear up.

Ben peered over his glasses at Prater. "Oh, by the way," he said, "I think I neglected to say that Ms. Travers' husband operates, among other things, a detective agency out of Chicago. Seems he's had a man looking into some of the problems that have been plaguing Maggie and Mr. Harrington of late."

Prater started to speak but stopped. Beads of perspiration dotted his furrowed brow.

"Maggie, why don't you tell us about the documents you have in your lap," Ben suggested.

"I don't see what her problems have to do with selling the land," Prater interjected.

Maggie looked at Prater, who was scowling deeply.

"Patience, my friend," Ben said. "I expect it's all tied together. Do you suppose that Maggie Magee Anderson would sell her family's legacy if she weren't dealing with insurmountable problems?"

"I don't need to hear all the details to carry out a simple land transaction," the banker protested, crossing and uncrossing his legs.

"I insist, Josh. The details are quite titillating. You used to like to puzzle things out. Maybe you can be helpful this morning. Begin, Maggie."

"The first item the detective discovered is a purchase receipt for gallons of a rapid fire starter. The same kind of accelerant used to burn down my barn." Maggie glanced up from the documents. Prater's eyes were wide with surprise, if not fright. Ben gave her a satisfied smile. Maggie continued, not believing the calm in her voice. "The receipt is from a store in Ames."

"And who signed the sales slip?" Ben prompted.

"The signature is that of Joshua Prater."

"I can explain that," Prater sputtered.

"I'd like to hear that," Ben responded.

"I had some brush to burn on my property?"

"Seems like a lot of special fuel to accomplish that. What else do you have there, Maggie?"

"Copies of cash withdrawal slips for two thousand dollars and twenty-five thousand. The first occurred the day before Ed was beat up leaving Mel's Bar and Grill, and the other the day before he disappeared from Beaverhill. Oh. I forgot," she said, pointing in the banker's direction, "Mr. Prater withdrew the money from accounts he has in an Ames bank."

"So what?" Prater screamed, turning deep red. "I spend money like everyone else."

"That's a lot of cash purchases, my friend," Ben declared. Tipping back in his chair, he appeared bemused. "I wonder how many folks here in town know the president of their local bank keeps large sums of money in a competitor bank in another town. Is that all, Maggie?"

"I know what you're trying to do," Prater rasped, sitting back in his chair.

The man all of sudden looked too relaxed.

Maggie worried.

"You can't prove a damn thing, or we wouldn't be sitting here. Where's the cops?"

Determined to ignore Prater's remarks, Maggie spoke up, "There is also a handwritten signed note from a Mr. Sonny Burdette explaining that he and Mark Fellows did not kill Ed Harrington. They were paid by Prater to rough him up, drug him and deposit him in Chicago. The note says if Harrington is dead, then Prater paid someone else to do it, or he did it himself."

Pressing his hands against his chest, Prater cried out, "I didn't kill him. They weren't supposed to kill him. Oh, my God." The man sobbed. "I'm not a murderer. I'm not a murderer."

"But you did burn down the barn," Maggie said calmly, "and you could have killed Ed and me then."

Prater's eyes glazed over before he responded, "Yes, yes. It was a glorious fire. Stupendous. I was only trying to frighten you off the land."

Prater looked at Ben and his voice went flat. "Every time it looked like she might have to sell, that dumb horse trainer showed up. If we could have gotten rid of him, everything would have been fine."

"You still don't understand that by burning down my barn you were also attempting murder," Maggie said, clenching her hands in her lap. "Ed and I were in the loft when you set the fire."

"If you were a decent woman, you wouldn't have been up there. If you hadn't been whoring around in the first place, none of this would have happened."

Ignoring the shrill verbal slap, Maggie asked, "Why me, Mr. Prater? My farm isn't huge. It's worth something, but certainly more to me than to you."

Maggie retreated back in her chair in the face of the man's sneer.

"The land! That's all you can think about, is the land," he accused. "The land didn't have anything to do with it. Your mother, the bitch."

Maggie gasped, wanting to close her ears but needing to listen.

"It was all about her treachery." Prater dropped his jaw to his chest and mumbled, "She threw me over for that no-account Colt Magee."

Hearing the disbelief in his voice, Maggie realized that Prater's romantic wounds were as fresh today as they must have been decades earlier. His hysterical laugh gnawed at her soul.

"You're a spittin' image of her, and apparently just like her. Giving your body to any boy who could get it up. Married right out of high school. You should've done better than that."

The man sobbed bitterly. "You could've been my daughter."

The vacant pain in the banker's eyes chilled Maggie to the bone. Had her mother slept with the creep? She sure hoped not. She glanced quickly at Ben. He shook his head in response. They needed to hear Prater's story now that he was talking. Sorting out details would have to wait. Maggie sucked in her breath and tried to stay focused on what the banker was saying.

"No man would've been good enough for my daughter. My daughter would never have lusted like a common tramp. But not you," he yelled, pointing accusingly at Maggie, "you lusted for the land, and then for that vagabond horse trainer, and then for horses. You knew no boundaries, no decorum, no morality."

Maggie blanched under his tirade, but otherwise remained calm. How could his mind have twisted everything so? Everything she loved he tried to make dirty.

Looking furtively about the room, Prater continued, "Can't you see? I did it all for you. To save you from others and from yourself." He shivered a deep sigh, winding down like a seven day clock. "You should have been satisfied living alone. Like me."

The door to the adjoining room opened. Ed Harrington and Clint Travers entered quickly.

Looking grim, Ed moved directly to stand by Maggie. "I think we've heard enough," he said. Maggie stood. His wide open arms encircled her.

"He's not dead!" Prater gasped, pointing at Harrington. "He's not dead," he reiterated, as if trying to convince himself and forestall a dawning of his mind. He paused. The silence hung like an early morning fog.

Glaring at Ben, Prater rose and bellowed, "You tricked me! This is entrapment. None of this will hold up in court." More smugly, he added, "So much for this entire show, this charade. I've heard enough."

Clint stepped between the banker and the exit. "Oh, it will hold up all right. We're not law officers. We can hardly be accused of entrapment. But the sheriff should be coming in any moment now. Eye witness reports of what transpired here along with the tape of the meeting should go a considerable ways to getting you behind bars—a prison or a mental institution."

Letting go of Maggie, Ed stepped across to confront Prater. The banker stumbled back into his chair, where he sat cowering under Ed's steady gaze.

"You seem to have done everything in your power to destroy a lot of folks, including me," Ed said. "Looks like the only person you destroyed was yourself. Before they take you away, I have something of yours."

Reaching into his back pocket, he retrieved an envelope. "Don't quite know how you'll spend it where you're going, but I certainly have no use for it. Maybe you should learn that not everyone can be bought or frightened."

Snickering, Prater grabbed the envelope. "You're wrong. Everyone has a price. I just didn't go high enough for you. I mistook you for a cheap hustler when you were playing a higher stakes game with the pure Ms. Anderson, one worthy of a top drawer con man."

Ed grabbed the banker by his suit lapels and held him off the floor before Clint could intervene.

"Drop him," Clint demanded. "He's not worth it. A man who kills cats isn't worth your getting into trouble with the law."

"You're right," Ed responded, shoving Prater back into his chair. "Vermin is vermin whether at the track, in the city, or in a small town. If you get too close to them, you risk starting to smell like them."

Sadly, Maggie watched the sheriff lead his handcuffed brother-in-law off to jail. She wondered how Prater could carry so much hate for such a long time. What had snapped? Why had he chosen this year to come after her land in such a blatant manner? It had started before the arrival of Harrington, although the trainer had upset Prater's plans. Was the trigger simply the terribly hot summer? She doubted she'd ever really know.

Maggie moved to Ed. He hugged her tightly. Even in the excessively heated room, Maggie had been chilly ever since Prater had arrived. Now she warmed up in her lover's arms. Ed kissed the top of her head.

"You know," he said, "we may at last be free to walk around without wondering who is going to knock us over the head next."

Smiling in agreement, Ben stood to shake hands all around. "Now tell me. I'm curious. How much of what Maggie said was true, and how much of it was speculation?"

"The bank slips and sales slips were real enough," Clint offered. "Our man in the field was quite certain that Burdette and Fellows were the

397

thugs that Prater hired. While they wouldn't admit it, they were reported as bragging about making some big money in Iowa by simply transporting somebody out of town. They claimed they didn't even have to maim or kill the guy."

"So Prater confessed to more than we actually knew?"

"Yep," Ed replied. "In the note Maggie read, she indicated that Burdette and Fellows claimed not to have killed me. If I had been killed, then Prater did it himself or hired someone else to do it. I'm sure Prater was too distraught by that point to distinguish the word *if*."

"Well, it worked. Well done." Ben walked over to the coat tree and put on his coat. "Don't expect I've had so much fun in a long time. Think I'll go home for the rest of the day. This is too much excitement for an old man like me. Hope your life settles down some now, Maggie."

"Settle down sounds real fine to me," Maggie concurred, placing a hand on her friend's shoulder. "Thanks for everything, Ben. Thanks for trusting this little game without having all the facts."

Ben laughed. "I'm glad I didn't know what was coming, or what was true or not. I didn't have to worry about giving anything away to that shrewd bastard. The nerve of him, trying to take on Colt Magee's daughter."

- o -

The next afternoon, after the Travers returned to Chicago, Maggie and Ed walked through the stable reacquainting Ed with each of the horses. Each came to him like greeting an old friend. Smells of liniment, horse sweat, manure, straw and hay massaged his nostrils. Breathing deeply, Ed knew he was home.

With his arm around Maggie, Ed fought back tears. She stopped and hugged him tight. "Life is pretty good, isn't it?" she whispered.

"I don't know how it could get any better," he mumbled.

"You've been though a lot on my account," she murmured into his work shirt.

"Hah," he groaned. "Where would I be if I hadn't?"

"I think it may be time to focus on the future rather than the past," Maggie said, pulling away from him to sit on a bale of hay.

Ed joined her. "There hasn't been much time for us since I've been back. The Travers are great, but they are company, and then we had to move quickly to snare Prater before he had a chance to get wind of my return." Cupping her chin, he said, "I've missed you," then brushed his lips lightly across hers.

Her tongue wetted his lips. "Can you ever forgive me for doubting you?" she asked, holding her breath.

"There's nothing to forgive. Given the same information you had, I likely would have assumed the same thing."

"It still gnaws at me that my daughter and brother could see things more clearly than me."

"They weren't as emotionally hooked as you were." Grinning, he added, "Even teenagers and brothers can be sources of wisdom at times."

"Well, you might not want to share that thought around the kids until they turn old and gray."

"Maggie," Ed said seriously, turning to face the woman he loved, "I never had the chance to tell you why I went to Des Moines that day back in November."

Reaching into his pocket, Ed pulled out a small jewelry box. "This is yours, if you'll accept it; if you'll accept me. I love you, Maggie. I always will."

With quivering fingers, Maggie lifted the lid. Her mouth fell open. "Oh, my goodness," she squealed. "It's beautiful. The engagement ring was a simple gold band with a striking diamond at its center. Next to it was cradled a wedding ring with a row of three diamonds set off at either end by tiny sapphire stones matching the color of her eyes. "This is too much," she whimpered.

"Then you don't want it — you don't want me?"

Maggie made a croaking sound. "No, no! I love the rings. I love you. Forever, I want you. I'm just not used to wearing such gorgeous things."

"Well, you better get used to it, woman," Ed teased, "You can't walk around Keeneland or Barretts looking like a pauper. Maggie, you are the most beautiful woman I've ever met — inside and out. You are the most beautiful thing to ever happen to me. Please get used to wearing beautiful things, at least now and then. I don't want you to give up working with the horses, though."

"No need to worry about that," Maggie chuckled, moving to sit on his lap. "I want to be right next to you, mucking stalls, buying horses, training them, watching them run. And I want to look beautiful for my handsome husband. I want you to be proud of your wife."

"I couldn't be more proud. You battled and fought hard for this land, and you won."

"Yes, but I was ready to give up after the fire. If it hadn't been for you and the children, I don't know what I might have done." Maggie shuddered.

"That's the past, again. I like the idea of you being by my side and me being by yours." Ed grinned broadly. "Not only in the stable and at the track, but at the breakfast table, in the shower, and in our bed."

"Ah," Maggie moaned, kissing his chin and the corners of his mouth. "That breakfast table certainly has more possibilities than I ever imagined before you came along. I look forward to so much, I feel like I'm going to burst. Do you think the dark cloud over us has truly moved on?"

"I believe it has," Ed said, scooping her into his muscled arms. Carrying her toward the house, he wondered when the kids would be home from school.

401

EPILOGUE

Resting on her knees, Maggie watched proudly as her husband rubbed his hands all over the tiny body of the newborn filly. Her coat was as dark as coal. The animal wobbled on miniature feet and legs. Her mother, Midnight Dancer, accepted Ed's presence and had been cooperative throughout the birth. Carolyn had been inside the box stall assisting Ed during those critical birthing moments. The teenager continued beaming proudly as she now knelt beside Maggie, observing closely everything Ed was doing and how the foal responded to him.

He had told them that these first minutes and hours after birth were very critical for the foal's future. Just as it was important for the mare to bond with her offspring, it was also vital that the foal bond with human touch. That bond would make the eventual training process much more manageable. The foal would more likely become a trusting yearling and two-year-old because of the time now spent. Ed had told them that what they were watching was called imprinting.

Glancing to her left, Maggie smiled at Johnny, who had finally succumbed to sleep. It was three in the morning. Horses seldom birthed at a more suitable hour for humans, she'd been informed. With eyes bulging, Johnny had watched as Ed and his sister assisted the mare in giving birth. And then he'd giggled when the newborn attempted to stand. First, the little foal tried accomplish that task by resting on her front knees and raising her butt. Then she tried the opposite. After several false attempts, with the aid of her mother giving a push from behind, the foal stood on seemingly matchstick-sized legs. Looking around at her brand new world, her large soft brown eyes expressed curiosity and eagerness. Maggie had been glad to see that they evidenced no fear.

As her son snored softly and her daughter watched intently, Maggie hugged herself, pleased with her life and with sharing this special moment with her loved ones. A late January snowstorm howled outside the stable, but inside there was warmth and contentment.

Maggie nodded in agreement as she read the words formed and whispered on Ed's lips while he rubbed the foal's belly: "This is what it's all about."

The stable oozed awe and love. This was far better than their planned honeymoon could ever have been. Not that she still didn't look forward to it, and to a time to be completely alone with the man she loved. But there was something unparalleled about helping bring new life into the world. It was like watching a dream come to reality.

They'd been right to postpone the honeymoon. Midnight Dancer wasn't supposed to foal for another month or so, but Ed had detected signs that she would be earlier than expected. Horses, like women, weren't always predictable, he'd explained. She remembered his joshing and she smiled. He'd no more leave a horse that needed him than she would leave the land.

Prater was wrong. His obsession with the Magee farm was not simply about being jilted by a young love. It was very much wrapped up in the land, since her mom had chosen another man with whom to share her life who also had valued the land as much as she had. As much as her mom's mother and dad had. As much as her grandmother and grandfather had. Prater never understood that he could not have measured up because he failed to possess that indefinable affinity for the land and the values it embodied. Her mother would have settled for no less than that.

As Maggie watched Ed, she knew that she, too, had found a kindred spirit. Just then the little filly whinnied and stared directly at Maggie.

"Oh you're so loveable, little one," Maggie murmured, her eyes growing watery. How long before she'd know for sure? Another month? Maggie shook her head. It might be another month before she'd tell anyone, but she already knew for sure. She could feel it in her bones; she was pregnant.

It was not difficult at all for Maggie to imagine that before the year was out, her family would gather around her bed to welcome a new member into its midst. Bonding was something experienced often on the land; it never became old or routine.

Maggie winked at Midnight Dancer, envying her for the moment. The mare snorted softly, as if to acknowledge the hope and pride of mothers.

The End

About the Author

Adriana Kraft is the pen name for a husband/wife team writing sizzling romantic suspense and erotic romance. The award-winning pair has published over thirty romance novels and novellas to outstanding reviews. Long and Short Reviews: *"scorching hot...refreshing...something to read when you want straight up hotness."* Romance Junkies: *"filled with warmth, blazing hot sex, well-developed characters...not for the faint of heart."* Romantic pairings include straight m/f, lesbian, bisexual, ménage and polyamory, in both contemporary and paranormal settings.

We hope you enjoyed *Heat Wave,* and we love hearing from readers! You can find all our links at our website:

http://adrianakraft.com

:

Adriana Kraft

When It's Time to Heat Things Up

BOOK LIST

SERIES

RIDERS UP Romantic Suspense novels
Book One *Cassie's Hope*
Book Two *Heat Wave*
Book Three *Detour Ahead*
Book Four *Willow Smoke* (forthcoming, January, 2015)

SWINGING GAMES Erotic Romance novellas
Book One *Anticipation*
Book Two *Hook-Ups*
Book Three *A Tempting Taste*
Book Four *Complexities*
Book Five *The Adventure Continue*
Book Six *Who's the Coach?*
Book Seven *Dare to Adventure*
Book Eight *Pushing the Limits*
Book Nine *Too Close for Comfort*
Book Ten *Triple Play*
Book Eleven *Summer's End*
Book Twelve *Foursomes and More…*

COLORS OF THE NIGHT Erotic Romance novels
Book One *Colors of the Night*
Book Two *Aria Returns*

PURGATORY POINT Erotic Romance novels
Book One *The Mistress of Purgatory Point*
Book Two *Return to Purgatory Point*

THE DIARY Erotic Romance novels
Book One *The Diary*
Book Two *Writing Skin*

STAND ALONE NOVELS AND NOVELLAS
The Heist Romantic Suspense novel
The Unmasking Romantic Suspense novel
Cherry Tune-Up Erotic Romance novella
The Reunion Erotic Romance novel
Atlantis Woman Found Erotic Romance novella
The Best Man Erotic Romance novel
Santa's Boss Erotic Romance novella
Through the Mirror Erotic Romance novella
Sheila's Prenups Erotic Romance novella
Full Circle Erotic Romance novella

SHORT STORIES IN ANTHOLOGIES
Accidental Contact, in *Sapphic Planet*
A Taste of Ginger in *The Cougar Book*

410